Praise for #1 bestselling author Lee Child
and his Jack Reacher series

"If you're a thriller fan and you're not reading the Reacher series, you're not a thriller fan."
—*Chicago Tribune*

"The indomitable Reacher burns up the pages of every book in Child's series." —*USA Today*

"If there were such a thing as a writer-magician, Lee Child would be the face above the cloak."
—Associated Press

"Lee Child [is] the current poster-boy of American crime fiction." —*Los Angeles Times*

"Jack Reacher is a tough guy's tough guy."
—*Santa Monica Mirror*

"Reacher's just one of fiction's great mysterious strangers." —*Maxim*

"Jack Reacher is one of the best thriller characters at work today." —*Newsweek*

"Reacher is Marlowe's literary descendant, and a 21st-century knight—only tougher."
—*Minneapolis Star-Tribune*

"Child has long been one of the best contemporary thriller writers." —*The Daily Beast*

"[Lee Child is] the best thriller writer of the moment." —Janet Maslin, *The New York Times*

"No one kicks **butt** as entertainingly as Reacher."
—*Kirkus Reviews*

"[Reacher is] the stuff of myth, a great male fantasy. . . . One of this century's most original, tantalizing pop-fiction heroes."
—*The Washington Post*

"Those who haven't experienced this irresistible series should definitely start at the beginning and catch up to this book."
—*Library Journal* (starred review)

"Jack Reacher is the thinking reader's action hero."
—*Seattle Times*

LEE CHILD

Dell • New York

By Lee Child

Killing Floor
Die Trying
Tripwire
Running Blind
Echo Burning
Without Fail
Persuader
The Enemy
One Shot
The Hard Way
Bad Luck and Trouble
Nothing to Lose
Gone Tomorrow
61 Hours
Worth Dying For
The Affair
A Wanted Man
Never Go Back
Personal
Make Me
Night School
No Middle Name
The Midnight Line
Past Tense
Blue Moon

Short stories

Second Son
Deep Down
High Heat
Not a Drill
Small Wars
The Christmas Scorpion

Blue Moon

Blue Moon is a work of fiction. Names, characters, places, and incidents either are the product of the author's imagination or are used fictitiously. Any resemblance to actual persons, living or dead, events, or locales is entirely coincidental.

2020 Dell Mass Market Edition

Published in the United States by Dell, an imprint of Random House, a division of Penguin Random House LLC, New York.

DELL and the HOUSE colophon are registered trademarks of Penguin Random House LLC.

Originally published in hardcover in the United States by Delacorte Press, an imprint of Random House, a division of Penguin Random House LLC, in 2019.

This book contains an excerpt from the forthcoming book *The Sentinel* by Lee Child and Andrew Child. This excerpt has been set for this edition only and may not reflect the final content of other editions.

ISBN: 978-0-399-59356-7
Export ISBN: 978-1-9848-2022-8
Ebook ISBN: 978-0-399-59355-0

Cover design: Carlos Beltrán
Cover photograph: Shutterstock

Printed in the United States of America

randomhousebooks.com

9 8 7 6 5 4 3 2 1

Dell mass market edition: April 2020

For Jane and Ruth
My tribe

Blue Moon

Chapter 1

The city looked small on a map of America. It was just a tiny polite dot, near a red threadlike road that ran across an otherwise empty half inch of paper. But up close and on the ground it had half a million people. It covered more than a hundred square miles. It had nearly a hundred and fifty thousand households. It had more than two thousand acres of parkland. It spent half a billion dollars a year, and raised almost as much through taxes and fees and charges. It was big enough that the police department was twelve hundred strong.

And it was big enough that organized crime was split two separate ways. The west of the city was run by Ukrainians. The east was run by Albanians. The demarcation line between them was gerrymandered as tight as a congressional district. Nominally it followed Center Street, which ran north to south and divided the city in half, but it zigged and zagged and ducked in and out to include or exclude specific blocks and parts of specific neighborhoods, wherever it was felt historic precedents justified special circumstances. Negotiations had been tense. There had been minor turf wars. There had been some unpleasantness. But eventually an agreement had been reached. The arrangement seemed to work. Each side kept out of the other's way. For a long time there had been no significant contact between them.

Until one morning in May. The Ukrainian boss parked in a garage on Center Street, and walked east into Albanian territory. Alone. He was fifty years old and built like a bronze statue of an old hero, tall, hard, and solid. He called himself Gregory, which was as close as Americans could get to pronouncing his given name. He was unarmed, and he was wearing tight pants and a tight T-shirt to prove it. Nothing in his pockets. Nothing concealed. He turned left and right, burrowing deep, heading for a backstreet block, where he knew the Albanians ran their businesses out of a suite of offices in back of a lumber yard.

He was followed all the way, from his first step across the line. Calls were made ahead, so that when he arrived he was faced by six silent figures, all standing still in the half circle between the sidewalk and the lumber yard's gate. Like chess pieces in a defensive formation. He stopped and held his arms out from his sides. He turned around slowly, a full 360, his arms still held wide. Tight pants, tight T-shirt. No lumps. No bulges. No knife. No gun. Unarmed, in front of six guys who undoubtedly weren't. But he wasn't worried. To attack him unprovoked was a step the Albanians wouldn't take. He knew that. Courtesies had to be observed. Manners were manners.

One of the six silent figures stepped up. Partly a blocking maneuver, partly ready to listen.

Gregory said, "I need to speak with Dino."

Dino was the Albanian boss.

The guy said, "Why?"

"I have information."

"About what?"

"Something he needs to know."

"I could give you a phone number."

"This is a thing that needs to be said face to face."

"Does it need to be said right now?"

"Yes, it does."

The guy said nothing for a spell, and then he turned and ducked through a personnel door set low in a metal roll-up gate. The other five guys formed up tighter, to replace his missing presence. Gregory waited. The five guys watched him, part wary, part fascinated. It was a unique occasion. Once in a lifetime. Like seeing a unicorn. The other side's boss. Right there. Previous negotiations had been held on neutral ground, on a golf course way out of town, on the other side of the highway.

Gregory waited. Five long minutes later the guy came back out through the personnel door. He left it open. He gestured. Gregory walked forward and ducked and stepped inside. He smelled fresh pine and heard the whine of a saw.

The guy said, "We need to search you for a wire."

Gregory nodded and stripped off his T-shirt. His torso was thick and hard and matted with hair. No wire. The guy checked the seams in his T-shirt and handed it back. Gregory put it on and ran his fingers through his hair.

The guy said, "This way."

He led Gregory deep into the corrugated shed. The other five guys followed. They came to a plain metal door. Beyond it was a windowless space set up like a boardroom. Four laminate tables had been pushed together end to end, like a barrier. In a chair in the center on the far side was Dino. He was younger than Gregory by a year or two, and shorter by an inch or two, but wider. He had dark hair, and a knife scar on the left side of his face, shorter above the eyebrow and longer from cheekbone to chin, like an upside down exclamation point.

The guy who had done the talking pulled out a chair for Gregory opposite Dino, and then tracked around and sat down at Dino's right hand, like a faithful lieutenant. The other five split three and two and sat alongside them. Gregory was left alone on his side of the table, facing seven blank faces. At first no one spoke. Then eventually Dino asked, "To what do I owe this great pleasure?"

Manners were manners.

Gregory said, "The city is about to get a new police commissioner."

"We know this," Dino said.

"Promoted from within."

"We know this," Dino said again.

"He has promised a crackdown, against both of us."

"We know this," Dino said, for the third time.

"We have a spy in his office."

Dino said nothing. He hadn't known that.

Gregory said, "Our spy found a secret file on a standalone hard drive hidden in a drawer."

"What file?"

"His operational plan for cracking down on us."

"Which is what?"

"It's short on detail," Gregory said. "In parts it's extremely sketchy. But not to worry. Because day by day and week by week he's filling in more and more parts of the puzzle. Because he's getting a constant stream of inside information."

"From where?"

"Our spy searched long and hard and found a different file."

"What different file?"

"It was a list."

"A list of what?"

"The police department's most trusted confidential informants," Gregory said.

"And?"

"There were four names on the list."

"And?"

"Two of them were my own men," Gregory said.

No one spoke.

Eventually Dino asked, "What have you done with them?"

"I'm sure you can imagine."

Again no one spoke.

Then Dino asked, "Why are you telling me this? What has this got to do with me?"

"The other two names on the list are your men."

Silence.

Gregory said, "We share a predicament."

Dino asked, "Who are they?"

Gregory said the names.

Dino said, "Why are you telling me about them?"

"Because we have an agreement," Gregory said. "I'm a man of my word."

"You stand to benefit enormously if I go down. You would run the whole city."

"I stand to benefit only on paper," Gregory said. "Suddenly I realize I should be happy with the status quo. Where would I find enough honest men to run your operations? Apparently I can't even find enough to run my own."

"And apparently neither can I."

"So we'll fight each other tomorrow. Today we'll respect the agreement. I'm sorry to have brought you embarrassing news. But I embarrassed myself also. In front of you. I hope that counts for something. We share this predicament."

Dino nodded. Said nothing.

Gregory said, "I have a question."

"Then ask it," Dino said.

"Would you have told me, like I told you, if the spy had been yours, and not mine?"

Dino was quiet a very long time.

Then he said, "Yes, and for the same reasons. We have an agreement. And if we both have names on their list, then neither one of us should be in a hurry to get foolish."

Gregory nodded and stood up.

Dino's right-hand man stood up to show him out.

Dino asked, "Are we safe now?"

"We are from my side," Gregory said. "I can guarantee that. As of six o'clock this morning. We have a guy at the city crematorium. He owes us money. He was willing to light the fire a little early today."

Dino nodded and said nothing.

Gregory asked, "Are we safe from your side?"

"We will be," Dino said. "By tonight. We have a guy at the car crushing plant. He owes us money, too."

The right-hand man showed Gregory out, across the deep shed to the low door in the roll-up gate, and out to the bright May morning sunshine.

At that same moment Jack Reacher was seventy miles away, in a Greyhound bus, on the interstate highway. He was on the left side of the vehicle, toward the rear, in the window seat over the axle. There was no one next to him. Altogether there were twenty-nine other passengers. The usual mixture. Nothing special. Except for one particular situation, which was mildly interesting. Across the aisle and one row in front was a guy asleep with his head hanging down. He had gray hair overdue for a trim, and loose gray skin, as if he had lost a lot of weight. He could have been seventy years old. He was wearing a short blue zip jacket. Some kind of heavy cotton. Maybe waterproof. The butt end of a fat envelope was sticking out of the pocket.

It was a type of envelope Reacher recognized. He had seen similar items before. Sometimes, if their

ATM was busted, he would step inside a bank branch and get cash with his card from the teller, directly across the counter. The teller would ask how much he wanted, and he would think, well, if ATM reliability was on the decline, then maybe he should get a decent wad, to be on the safe side, and he would ask for two or three times what he normally took. A large sum. Whereupon the teller would ask if he wanted an envelope with that. Sometimes Reacher said yes, just for the sake of it, and he would get his wad in an envelope exactly like the one sticking out of the sleeping guy's pocket. Same thick paper, same size, same proportions, same bulge, same heft. A few hundred dollars, or a few thousand, depending on the mix of bills.

Reacher wasn't the only one who had seen it. The guy dead ahead had seen it, too. That was clear. He was taking a big interest. He was glancing across and down, across and down, over and over. He was a lean young guy with greasy hair and a thin goatee beard. Twenty-something, in a jeans jacket. Not much more than a kid. Glancing, thinking, planning. Licking his lips.

The bus rolled on. Reacher took turns watching out the window, and watching the envelope, and watching the guy watching the envelope.

Gregory came out of the Center Street garage and drove back into safe Ukrainian territory. His offices were in back of a taxi company, across from a pawn shop, next to a bail bond operation, all of which he owned. He parked and went inside. His top guys were waiting there. Four of them, all similar to each other, and to him. Not related in the traditional family sense, but they were from the same towns and villages and prisons back in the old country, which was probably even better.

They all looked at him. Four faces, eight wide eyes, but only one question.

Which he answered.

"Total success," he said. "Dino bought the whole story. That's one dumb donkey, let me tell you. I could have sold him the Brooklyn Bridge. The two guys I named are history. He'll take a day to reshuffle. Opportunity knocks, my friends. We have about twenty four hours. Their flank is wide open."

"That's Albanians for you," his own right-hand man said.

"Where did you send our two?"

"The Bahamas. There's a casino guy who owes us money. He has a nice hotel."

The green federal signs on the highway shoulder showed a city coming up. The first stop of the day. Reacher watched the guy with the goatee map out his play. There were two unknowns. Was the guy with the money planning to get out there? And if not, would he wake up anyway, with the slowing and the turning and the jolting?

Reacher watched. The bus took the exit. A state four-lane then carried it south, through flat land moist with recent rain. The ride was smooth. The tires hissed. The guy with the money stayed asleep. The guy with the goatee beard kept on watching him. Reacher guessed his plan was made. He wondered how good of a plan it was. The smart play would be pickpocket the envelope pretty soon, conceal it well, and then aim to get out of the bus as soon as it stopped. Even if the guy woke up short of the depot, he would be confused at first. Maybe he wouldn't even notice the envelope was gone. Not right away. And even when he did, why would he jump straight to conclusions? He would figure it had fallen out. He would spend a minute looking on the seat, and under it, and under the seat in front, because he might have kicked it in his sleep. Only after all of that would he start to look around, questioningly. By which time the bus would be stopped and people would be getting up and getting out and getting in. The aisle would be jammed. A guy could slip away, no problem. That was the smart play.

Did the guy know it?

Reacher never found out.

The guy with the money woke up too soon.

The bus slowed, and then stopped for a light with a hiss of brakes, and the guy's head jerked up, and he blinked, and patted his pocket, and shoved the envelope down deeper, where no one could see it.

Reacher sat back.

The guy with the beard sat back.

The bus rolled on. There were fields either side, dusted pale green with spring. Then came the first commercial lots, for farm equipment, and domestic automobiles, all spread over huge acreages, with hundreds of shiny machines lined up under flags and bunting. Then came office parks, and a giant out-of-town supermarket. Then came the city itself. The four-lane narrowed to two. Up ahead were taller buildings. But the bus turned off left and tracked around, keeping a polite distance behind the high-rent districts, until half a mile later it arrived at the depot. The first stop of the day. Reacher stayed in his seat. His ticket was good for the end of the line.

The guy with the money stood up.

He kind of nodded to himself, and hitched up his pants, and tugged down his jacket. All the things an old guy does, when he's about to get out of a bus.

He stepped into the aisle, and shuffled forward. No bag. Just him. Gray hair, blue jacket, one pocket fat, one pocket empty.

The guy with the goatee beard got a new plan.

It came on him all of a sudden. Reacher could practically see the gears spinning in the back of his head. Coming up cherries. A sequence of conclusions built on a chain of assumptions. Bus depots were never in the nice part of town. The exit doors would give out onto cheap streets, the backs of other buildings, maybe vacant lots, maybe self-pay parking. There would be blind corners and empty sidewalks. It would be a twenty-something against a seventy-something. A blow from behind. A simple mugging. Happened all the time. How hard could it be?

The guy with the goatee beard jumped up and hustled down the aisle, following the guy with the money six feet behind.

Reacher got up and followed them both.

Chapter 2

The guy with the money knew where he was going. That was clear. He didn't glance around to get his bearings. He just stepped through the depot door and turned east and set out walking. No hesitation. But no speed either. He trudged along slow. He looked a little unsteady. His shoulders were slumped. He looked old and tired and worn out and beaten down. He had no enthusiasm. He looked like he was en route between two points of equally zero appeal.

The guy with the goatee beard followed along about six paces behind, hanging back, staying slow, restraining himself. Which looked difficult. He was a rangy, long-legged individual, all hopped up with excitement and anticipation. He wanted to get right to it. But the terrain was wrong. Too flat and open. The sidewalks were wide. Up ahead was a four-way traffic light, with three cars waiting for a green. Three drivers, bored, gazing about. Maybe passengers. All potential witnesses. Better to wait.

The guy with the money stopped at the curb. Waiting to cross. Aiming dead ahead. Where there were older buildings, with narrower streets between. Wider than alleys, but shaded from the sun, and hemmed in by mean three- and four-story walls either side.

Better terrain.

The light changed. The guy with the money trudged across the road, obediently, as if resigned. The guy with the goatee beard followed six paces behind. Reacher closed the gap on him a little. He sensed the moment coming. The kid wasn't going to wait forever. He wasn't going to let the perfect be the enemy of the good. Two blocks in would do it.

They walked on, single file, spaced apart, oblivious. The first block felt good up ahead and side to side, but behind them it still felt open, so the guy with the beard hung back, until the guy with the money was over the cross street and into the second block. Which looked properly secretive. It was shady at both ends. There were a couple of boarded-up establishments, and a closed-down diner, and a tax preparer with dusty windows.

Perfect.

Decision time.

Reacher guessed the kid would go for it, right there, and he guessed the launch would be prefaced by a nervous glance all around, including behind, so he stayed out of sight around the cross street's corner, one second, two, three, which he figured was long enough for all the glances a person could need. Then he stepped out and saw the kid with the beard already closing the gap ahead, hustling, eating up the six-pace distance with a long and eager stride. Reacher didn't like running, but on that occasion he had to.

He got there too late. The guy with the beard shoved the guy with the money, who went down forward with a heavy ragged thump, hands, knees, head, and the guy with the beard swooped down in a seamless dexterous glide, into the still-moving pocket, and out again with the envelope. Which was when Reacher arrived, at a clumsy run, six feet five of bone and muscle and 250 pounds of moving mass, against a lean kid just then coming up out of a crouch. Reacher slammed into him with a twist and a dip of the shoulder, and the guy flailed through the air like a crash test dummy, and landed in a long sliding tangle of limbs, half on the sidewalk, half in the gutter. He came to rest and lay still.

Reacher walked over and took the envelope from him. It wasn't sealed. They never were. He took a look. The wad was about three quarters of an inch thick. A hundred dollar bill on the top, and a hundred dollar bill on the bottom. He flicked through. A hundred dollar bill in every other possible location, too. Thousands and thousands of dollars. Could be fifteen. Could be twenty grand.

He glanced back. The old guy's head was up. He was gazing about, panic stricken. He had a cut on his face. From the fall. Or maybe his nose was bleeding. Reacher held up the envelope. The old guy stared at it. He tried to get up, but couldn't.

Reacher walked back.

He said, "Anything broken?"

The guy said, "What happened?"

"Can you move?"

"I think so."

"OK, roll over."

"Here?"

"On your back," Reacher said. "Then we can sit you up."

"What happened?"

"First I need to check you out. I might need to call the ambulance. You got a phone?"

"No ambulance," the guy said. "No doctors."

He took a breath and clamped his teeth, and squirmed and thrashed until he rolled over on his back, like a guy in bed with a nightmare.

He breathed out.

Reacher said, "Where does it hurt?"

"Everywhere."

"Regular kind of thing, or worse?"

"I guess regular."

"OK, then."

Reacher got the flat of his hand under the guy's back, high up between his shoulder blades, and he folded him forward into a sitting position, and swiveled him around, and scooted him along, until he was sitting on the curb with his feet down on the road, which would be more comfortable, Reacher thought.

The guy said, "My mom always told me, don't play in the gutter."

"Mine, too," Reacher said. "But right now we ain't playing."

He handed over the envelope. The guy took it and

squeezed it all over, fingers and thumb, as if confirming it was real. Reacher sat down next to him. The guy looked inside the envelope.

"What happened?" he said again. He pointed. "Did that guy mug me?"

Twenty feet to their right the kid with the goatee beard was face down and motionless.

"He followed you off the bus," Reacher said. "He saw the envelope in your pocket."

"Were you on the bus, too?"

Reacher nodded.

He said, "I came out of the depot right behind you."

The guy put the envelope back in his pocket.

He said, "Thank you from the bottom of my heart. You have no idea. More than I can possibly say."

"You're welcome," Reacher said.

"You saved my life."

"My pleasure."

"I feel like I should offer you a reward."

"Not necessary."

"I can't anyway," the guy said. He touched his pocket. "This is a payment I have to make. It's very important. I need it all. I'm sorry. I apologize. I feel bad."

"Don't," Reacher said.

Twenty feet to their right the kid with the beard pushed himself up to his hands and knees.

The guy with the money said, "No police."

The kid glanced back. He was stunned and shaky, but he was already twenty feet ahead. Should he go for it?

Reacher said, "Why no police?"

"They ask questions when they see a lot of cash."

"Questions you don't want to answer?"

"I can't anyway," the guy said again.

The kid with the beard took off. He staggered to his feet and set out fleeing the scene, weak and bruised and floppy and uncoordinated, but still plenty fast. Reacher let him go. He had run enough for one day.

The guy with the money said, "I need to get going now."

He had scrapes on his cheek and his forehead, and blood on his upper lip, from his nose, which had taken a decent impact.

"You sure you're OK?" Reacher asked.

"I better be," the guy said. "I don't have much time."

"Let me see you stand up."

The guy couldn't. Either his core strength had drained away, or his knees were bad, or both. Hard to say. Reacher helped him to his feet. The guy stood in the gutter, facing the opposite side of the street, hunched and bent. He turned around, laboriously, shuffling in place.

He couldn't step up the curb. He got his foot in place, but the propulsive force necessary to boost himself up six inches was too much load for his knee to take. It must have been bruised and sore. There was a bad scuff on the fabric of his pants, right where his kneecap would be.

Reacher stood behind him and cupped his hands under his elbows, and lifted, and the guy stepped up weightless, like a man on the moon.

Reacher asked, "Can you walk?"

The guy tried. He managed small steps, delicate and precise, but he winced and gasped, short and sharp, every time his right leg took the weight.

"How far have you got to go?" Reacher asked.

The guy looked all around, calibrating. Making sure where he was.

"Three more blocks," he said. "On the other side of the street."

"That's a lot of curbs," Reacher said. "That's a lot of stepping up and down."

"I'll walk it off."

"Show me," Reacher said.

The guy set out, heading east as before, at a slow shuffling creep, with his hands out a little, as if for balance. The wincing and the gasping was loud and clear. Maybe getting worse.

"You need a cane," Reacher said.

"I need a lot of things," the guy said.

Reacher stepped around next to him, on the right, and cupped his elbow, and took the guy's weight in his palm. Mechanically the same thing as a stick or a cane or a crutch. An upward force, ultimately through the guy's shoulder. Newtonian physics.

"Try it now," Reacher said.

"You can't come with me."

"Why not?"

The guy said, "You've done enough for me already."

"That's not the reason. You would have said you really couldn't ask me to do that. Something vague and polite. But you were much more emphatic than that. You said I can't come with you. Why? Where are you going?"

"I can't tell you."

"You can't get there without me."

The guy breathed in and breathed out, and his lips moved, like he was rehearsing things to say. He raised his hand and touched the scrape on his forehead, then his cheek, then his nose. More wincing.

He said, "Help me to the right block, and help me across the street. Then turn around and go home. That's the biggest favor you could do for me. I mean it. I would be grateful. I'm already grateful. I hope you understand."

"I don't," Reacher said.

"I'm not allowed to bring anyone."

"Who says?"

"I can't tell you."

"Suppose I was headed in that direction anyway. You could peel off and go in the door and I could walk on."

"You would know where I went."

"I already know."

"How could you?"

Reacher had seen all kinds of cities, all across America, east, west, north, south, all kinds of sizes and ages and current conditions. He knew their rhythms and their grammars. He knew the history baked into their bricks. The block he was on was one of a hundred thousand just like it east of the Mississippi. Back offices for dry goods wholesalers, some specialist retail, some light manufacturing, some lawyers and shipping agents and land agents and travel agents. Maybe some tenement accommodations in the rear courtyards. All peaking in terms of hustle and bustle in the late nineteenth century and the early twentieth. Now crumbled and corroded and hollowed out by time. Hence the boarded-up establishments and the closed-down diner. But some places held out longer than others. Some places held out longest of all. Some habits and appetites were stubborn.

"Three blocks east of here, and across the street," Reacher said. "The bar. That's where you're headed."

The guy said nothing.

"To make a payment," Reacher said. "In a bar, before lunch. Therefore to some kind of a local loan shark. That's my guess. Fifteen or twenty grand. You're in trouble. I think you sold your car. You got the best cash price out of town. Maybe a collector. A regular guy like you, it could have been an old car. You drove out there and took the bus back. Via the buyer's bank. The teller put the cash in an envelope."

"Who are you?"

"A bar is a public place. I get thirsty, same as anyone else. Maybe they have coffee. I'll sit at a different table. You can pretend not to know me. You'll need help getting out again. That knee is going to stiffen up some."

"Who are you?" the guy said again.

"My name is Jack Reacher. I was a military cop. I was trained to detect things."

"It was a Chevy Caprice. The old style. All original. Perfect condition. Very low miles."

"I know nothing about cars."

"People like the old Caprices now."

"How much did you get for it?"

"Twenty-two five."

Reacher nodded. More than he thought. Crisp new bills, packed tight.

He said, "You owe it all?"

"Until twelve o'clock," the guy said. "After that it goes up."

"Then we better get going. This could be a relatively slow process."

"Thank you," the guy said. "My name is Aaron Shevick. I am forever in your debt."

"The kindness of strangers," Reacher said. "Makes the world go round. Some guy wrote a play about it."

"Tennessee Williams," Shevick said. "*A Streetcar Named Desire.*"

"One of which we could use right now. Three blocks for a nickel would be a bargain."

They set out walking, Reacher stepping slow and short, Shevick hopping and pecking and lurching, all lopsided because of Newtonian physics.

Chapter 3

The bar was on the ground floor of a plain old brick building in the middle of the block. It had a battered brown door in the center, with grimy windows either side. There was an Irish name in sputtering green neon above the door, and half dead neon harps and shamrocks and other dusty shapes in the windows, all of them advertising brands of beer, some of which Reacher recognized, and some of which he didn't. He helped Shevick down the far curb, and across the street, and up the opposite curb, to the door. The time in his head was twenty to twelve.

"I'll go in first," he said. "Then you come in. Works better that way around. Like we never met. OK?"

"How long?" Shevick asked.

"Couple minutes," Reacher said. "Get your breath."

"OK."

Reacher pulled the door and went in. The light

was dim and the air smelled of spilled beer and disinfectant. The place was a decent size. Not cavernous, but not just a storefront, either. There were long rows of four-top tables either side of a worn central track that led to the bar itself, which was laid out in a square shape, in the back left corner of the room. Behind the bar was a fat guy with a four-day beard and a towel slung over his shoulder, like a badge of office. There were four customers, each of them alone at a separate table, each of them hunched and vacant, looking just as old and tired and worn out and beaten down as Shevick himself. Two of them were cradling long-neck bottles, and two of them were cradling half-empty glasses, defensively, as if they expected them to be snatched away at any moment.

None of them looked like a loan shark. Maybe the barman did the business. An agent, or a go-between, or a middleman. Reacher walked up and asked him for coffee. The guy said he didn't have any, which was a disappointment, but not a surprise. The guy's tone was polite, but Reacher got the feeling it might not have been, had the guy not been talking to an unknown stranger of Reacher's size and implacable demeanor. A regular Joe might have gotten a sarcastic response.

Instead of coffee Reacher got a bottle of domestic beer, cold and slick and dewy, with a volcano of foam erupting out the top. He left a dollar of his change on the bar, and stepped over to the nearest empty four-top, which happened to be in the rear right-hand corner, which was good, because it meant he could sit with his back to the wall, and see the whole room at once.

"Not there," the barman called out.

"Why not?" Reacher called back.

"Reserved."

The other four customers looked up, and looked away.

Reacher stepped back and took his dollar off the bar. No please, no thank you, no tip. He crossed diagonally to the front table on the other side, under the grimy window. Same geometry, but in reverse. He had a corner behind him, and he could see the whole room. He took a swallow of beer, which was mostly foam, and then Shevick came in, limping. He glanced ahead at the empty table in the far right-hand corner, and stopped in surprise. He looked all around the room. At the barman, at the four lonely customers, at Reacher, and then back at the corner table again. It was still empty.

Shevick set out hobbling toward it, but he stopped halfway. He changed direction. He limped to the bar instead. He spoke to the barman. Reacher was too far away to hear what he said, but he guessed it was a question. Could have been, where's so-and-so? Certainly it involved a glance at the empty four-top in the rear corner. It seemed to get a sarcastic response. Could have been, what am I, clairvoyant? Shevick flinched away and stepped a pace into no-man's-land. Where he could think about what to do next.

The clock in Reacher's head said quarter to twelve.

Shevick limped over to the empty table, and stood for a moment, undecided. Then he sat down, opposite the corner, as if in a visitor chair in front of a desk, not in the executive chair behind it. He perched on the edge of the seat, bolt upright, half turned, watching the door, as if ready to spring up politely, as soon as the guy he was meeting walked in.

No guy walked in. The bar stayed quiet. Some grateful swallowing, some wet breathing, the squeak of the barman's towel on a glass. Shevick stared at the door. Time ticked on.

Reacher got up and walked to the bar. To the part nearest Shevick's table. He rested his elbows and looked expectant, like a guy with a new order. The barman turned his back and suddenly got busy with an urgent task all the way in the opposite corner. As in, no tip, no service. Which Reacher had predicted. And wanted. For a degree of privacy.

He whispered, "What?"

"He isn't here," Shevick whispered back.

"Is he usually?"

"Always," Shevick whispered. "He sits at this table all day long."

"How many times have you done this?"

"Three."

The barman was still busy, way far away.

Shevick whispered, "Five minutes from now I'll owe them twenty-three five, not twenty-two five."

"The late fee is a thousand dollars?"

"Every day."

"Not your fault," Reacher whispered. "Not if the guy doesn't show up."

"These are not reasonable people."

Shevick stared at the door. The barman finished

up his imaginary task, and waddled the diagonal distance from the back of the bar to the front, with his chin up, hostile, as if possibly willing to entertain a request, but very unlikely to fulfill it.

He stopped a yard from Reacher and waited.

Reacher said, "What?"

"You want something?" the guy said.

"Not anymore. I wanted to make you walk there and back. You looked like you could use the exercise. But now you've done it, so I'm all good. Thanks anyway."

The guy stared. Sizing up his situation. Which wasn't great. Maybe he had a bat or a gun under the counter, but he would never get to them. Reacher was only an arm's length away. His response was going to have to be verbal. Which was going to be a struggle. That was clear. In the end he was saved by his wall phone. It rang behind him. An old-fashioned bell. A long muted mournful peal, and then another.

The barman turned away and answered the call. The phone was a classic design, with a big plastic handset on a curly cord stretched so much it dragged on the floor. The barman listened and hung up. He jutted his chin in the direction of Shevick, all the way over at the rear corner table.

He called out, "Come back at six o'clock tonight."

"What?" Shevick said.

"You heard me."

The barman walked away, to another imaginary task.

Reacher sat down at Shevick's table.

Shevick said, "What did he mean, come back at six o'clock?"

"I guess the guy you're waiting for got delayed. He called in, so you know where you stand."

"But I don't know," Shevick said. "What about my twelve o'clock deadline?"

"Not your fault," Reacher said again. "It was the guy who missed it, not you."

"He's going to say I owe them another grand."

"Not if he didn't show up. Which everyone knows he didn't. The barman took his call. He's a witness. You were here and the other guy wasn't."

"I can't find another thousand dollars," Shevick said. "I just don't have it."

"I would say the postponement gives you a pass. It's a clear implication. Like an implied term in a contract. You were offering legal tender in the right place at the right time. They didn't show up to accept it. It's some kind of a common law principle. An attorney could explain it."

"No lawyers," Shevick said.

"Worried about them, too?"

"I can't afford one. Especially if I have to find another thousand bucks."

"You don't. They can't have it both ways. You were here on time. They weren't."

"These are not reasonable people."

The barman glared from far away.

The clock in Reacher's head hit twelve noon exactly.

He said, "We can't wait here six hours."

"My wife will be worried," Shevick said. "I should go home and see her. Then come back again."

"Where do you live?"

"About a mile from here."

"I'll walk with you, if you like."

Shevick paused a long moment.

Then he said, "No, I really couldn't ask you to do that. You've done enough for me already."

"That was vague and polite, for damn sure."

"I mean I mustn't put you out anymore. I'm sure you have things to do."

"Generally I avoid having things to do. Clearly a reaction against literal regimentation earlier in my life. The result is I have no particular place to go, and all the time in the world to get there. I'm happy to take a one-mile detour."

"No, I couldn't ask you to do that."

"The regimentation I mentioned was, as I said, in the military police, where, as I also said, we were trained to notice things. Not just physical clues, but things about how people are. How they behave and what they believe. Human nature, and so on and so forth. Most of it was bullshit, but some of it rang bells. Right now you're facing a mile walk through a backstreet neighborhood, with more than twenty grand in your pocket, which you feel weird about, because you're not really supposed to still have it, and it's a total disaster if you lose it, and you've already been mugged once today, so the truth is, all in all you're afraid of that walk, and you know I could help with that feeling, and you're also hurt from the attack, and therefore not moving well, and you know I can help with that too, so all in all you should be begging me to see you home."

Shevick said nothing.

"But you're a gentleman," Reacher said. "You wanted to give me a reward. Now if I walk you home and meet your wife, you think the very least you should do is give me lunch. But there is no lunch. You're embarrassed. But you shouldn't be. I get it. You're in trouble with a moneylender. You haven't eaten lunch in a couple of months. You look like you lost twenty pounds. Your skin is hanging loose. So we'll pick up sandwiches on the way. Uncle Sam's dime. That's where my cash comes from. Your tax dollars at work. We'll enjoy some conversation, and then I'll walk you back here. You can pay off your guy, and I'll get on my way."

"Thank you," Shevick said. "I mean it."

"You're welcome," Reacher said. "I mean it."

"Where are you headed?"

"Someplace else. Often depends on the weather. I like to be warm. Saves buying a coat."

The barman glared again, still from far away.

"Let's go," Reacher said. "A person could die of thirst in here."

Chapter 4

The man who had been due to meet Aaron Shevick at the table in the far back corner of the bar was a forty-year-old Albanian named Fisnik. He was one of the two men mentioned that morning by Gregory, the Ukrainian boss. Accordingly he had gotten a call at home from Dino, telling him to drop by the lumber yard before starting his day's work in the bar. Dino's tone of voice revealed nothing untoward. In fact if anything it sounded cheery and enthusiastic, as if praise and recognition were in store. Maybe expanded opportunities, or a bonus, or both. Maybe a promotion, or extra status in the organization.

It didn't work out that way. Fisnik ducked through the personnel door in the roll-up gate, and smelled fresh pine, and heard the whine of a saw, and headed to the offices in back, feeling pretty good about things. A minute later he was duct-taped to a wooden chair, and suddenly the pine smelled like coffins, and the saw sounded like agony. First they drilled through his knees with a cordless DeWalt sporting a quarter-inch masonry bit. Then they moved on. He told them nothing, because he had nothing to tell. His silence was taken as a stoic confession. Such was their culture. He garnered a little grudging admiration for his fortitude, but not enough to stop the drill. He died about the same time Reacher and Shevick finally left the bar.

The first half of the mile walk was through left-behind blocks just like the one that housed the bar, but then the view opened out to what might once have been a bunch of ten-acre pastures, until the GIs came home at the end of World War Two, when the pastures were plowed up and straight rows of small houses were built, all of them single story, some of them split level, depending on how the pastures had risen and fallen. Seventy years later they had all been re-roofed many times, no two exactly the same, and some had add-ons and bump-outs and new vinyl siding, and some had trimmed lawns and others had wild yards, but otherwise the ghost of mean postwar uniformity still marched through the whole development, with small lots and narrow roads and narrow sidewalks and tight right-angle turns, all scaled to the maximum steering capabilities of 1948 Fords and Chevys and Studebakers and Plymouths.

Reacher and Shevick stopped on the way at a gas station deli counter. They got three chicken salad sandwiches, and three bags of potato chips, and three cans of soda. Reacher carried the bag in his right hand and helped Shevick with his left. They limped and crept through the warren. Shevick's house turned out to be deep into it, on a cul-de-sac served by a mean turnaround barely wider than the street itself. Like the bulb on the end of an old-style thermometer. The house was on the left, behind a white picket fence that had early roses budding through it. The house was a one-story ranch, same bones and same square footage as every other house, with an asphalt roof and bright white siding. It looked well cared for, but not recently. The windows were dusty and the lawn was long.

Reacher and Shevick hobbled up a concrete path barely wide enough for the two of them side by side. Shevick took out a key, but before he could get it in the lock the door opened in front of them. A woman stood there. Mrs. Shevick, without question. There was an obvious bond between them. She was gray and stooped and newly thin like he was, also about seventy, but her head was up and her eyes were steady. The fires were still burning. She stared at her husband's face. A scrape on his forehead, a scrape on his cheek, crusted blood on his lip.

"I fell," Shevick said. "I tripped on the curb. I banged my knee. That's the worst of it. This gentleman was kind enough to help me."

The woman's gaze switched to Reacher for a second, uncomprehending, and then back to her husband.

She said, "We better get you cleaned up."

She stood back and Shevick stepped into his hallway.

His wife started to ask him, "Did you," but then she stopped, maybe embarrassed in front of a stranger. No doubt she meant to say, did you pay the guy? But some troubles were private.

Shevick said, "It's complicated."

There was silence for a moment.

Reacher held up the bag from the deli counter.

"We brought lunch," he said. "We thought it might be difficult to get out to the store, under the circumstances."

Mrs. Shevick looked at him again, still uncomprehending. And then a little wounded. Abashed. Ashamed.

"He knows, Maria," Shevick said. "He was an army detective and he saw right through me."

"You told him?"

"He figured it out. He has extensive training."

"What's complicated?" she asked. "What happened? Who hit you? Was it this man?"

"What man?"

She looked straight at Reacher.

"This man with the lunch," she said. "Is he one of them?"

"No," Shevick said. "Absolutely not. He has nothing to do with them."

"Then why is he following you? Or escorting you? He's like a prison guard."

Shevick started to say, "When I was," and then he stopped and changed it to, "When I tripped and fell, he was passing by, and he helped me up. Then I found I couldn't walk, so he helped me along. He isn't following me. Or escorting me. He's here because I'm here. You can't have one without the other. Not right now. Because I hurt my knee. Simple as that."

"You said it was complicated, not simple."

"We should go inside," Shevick said.

His wife stood still for a moment, and then turned and led the way. The house was the same on the inside as it looked from the outside. Old, well cared for, but not recently. The rooms were small and the hallways were narrow. They stopped in the living room, which had a loveseat and two armchairs, and outlets and wires but no TV.

Mrs. Shevick said, "What's complicated?"

"Fisnik didn't show," Shevick said. "Normally he's there all day. But not today. All we got was a phone message to come back at six o'clock."

"So where's the money now?"

"I still have it."

"Where?"

"In my pocket."

"Fisnik is going to say we owe them another thousand dollars."

"This gentleman thinks he can't."

The woman looked at Reacher again, and then back at her husband, and she said, "We should go get you cleaned up." Then she looked at Reacher again and pointed toward the kitchen and said, "Please put the lunch in the refrigerator."

Which was more or less empty. Reacher got there and pulled the door and found a well scrubbed space with nothing much in it, except used-up bottles of stuff that could have been six months old. He put the bag on the middle shelf and went back to the living room to wait. There were family photographs on the walls, grouped and clustered like in a magazine. Senior among them were three ornate frames holding black and white images gone coppery with age. The first showed a literal GI standing in front of the house, with what Reacher guessed was his new bride alongside him. The guy was in a crisp khaki uniform. A private soldier. Probably too young to have fought in World War Two. Probably did a three-year hitch in Germany afterward. Probably got called up again for Korea. The woman was in a flowery dress that puffed out to calf length. Both of them were smiling. The siding behind them shone in the sun. The dirt at their feet was raw.

The second photograph showed a year-old lawn at their feet, and a baby in their arms. Same smiles, same bright siding. The new father was out of uniform and in a pair of high-waisted miracle-fiber pants and a white shirt with short sleeves. The new mother had swapped out the floral dress for a thin sweater and pedal pushers. The baby was mostly wrapped up in a shawl, except for its face, which looked pale and indistinct.

The third photograph showed the three of them about eight years later. Behind them foundation plantings covered half the siding. The grass at their feet was lush and thick. The guy was eight years less bony, a little thicker in the waist, a little heavier in the shoulders. His hair was slicked back, and he was losing some of it. The woman was prettier than before, but tired, in all the ways women were, in photographs from the 1950s.

The eight-year-old girl standing in front of them was almost certainly Maria Shevick. Something about the shape of her face and the directness of her gaze. She had grown up, they had grown old, they had died, she had inherited their house. That was Reacher's guess. He was proved right by the next group of pictures. Now in faded Kodak colors, but in the same location. Same patch of lawn. Same length of wall. Some kind of a tradition. The first showed Mrs. Shevick maybe twenty years old, next to a much straighter and much leaner Mr. Shevick, also about twenty years old, their faces sharp and young and hawkish with shadows, their smiles wide and happy.

The second in the new sequence showed the same couple with a baby in their arms. It grew up in leaps and bounds, left to right across the next row down, into a toddler, then a girl about four, then six, then eight, while above her the Shevicks cycled through 1970s hairstyles, big and bushy, above tight tank tops and puffy sleeves.

The next row down showed the same girl become a teenager, then a high-school graduate, then a young woman. Then a woman who got older as the Kodak got newer. She would be nearly fifty now, Reacher figured. Whatever that generation was called. The early kids of the early boomers. Got to be called something. Everyone else was.

"There you are," Mrs. Shevick said, behind him.

"I was admiring your photographs," he said.

"Yes," she said.

"You have a daughter."

"Yes," she said again.

Then Shevick himself came in. The blood had been cleaned off his lip. His scrapes were shiny with some kind of a yellow potion. His hair was brushed.

He said, "Let's eat."

There was a small table in the kitchen, with contoured aluminum edges, and a laminate top now dulled and faded by decades of time and wiping, but once bright and sparkly and atomic. There were three matching vinyl chairs. Maybe all bought way back when Maria Shevick was a little girl. For her first grown-up dinners. Knife and fork and please and thank you. Now many years later she told Reacher and her husband to sit down, and she put the sandwiches from the deli bag on china plates, and the chips in china bowls, and the sodas in cloudy glass tumblers. She brought cloth napkins. She sat down. She looked at Reacher.

"You must think us very foolish," she said. "To have gotten ourselves in this situation."

"Not really," Reacher said. "Very unlucky, perhaps. Or very desperate. I'm sure this situation is a last resort. You sold your TV. Plus many other things, no doubt. I assume you took out a loan on the house. But it wasn't enough. You had to find alternative arrangements."

"Yes," she said.

"I'm sure there were good reasons."

"Yes," she said again.

She said nothing more. She and her husband ate slowly, one small bite at a time, one chip, one sip of soda. As if savoring the novelty. Or worrying about indigestion. The kitchen was quiet. No passing traffic, no street sounds, no commotion. There was old subway tile on the walls, and wallpaper where there wasn't, with flowers on it, like Mrs. Shevick's mother's dress, in the very first photograph, but paler and less boldly delineated. The floor was linoleum, pitted long ago by stiletto heels, now rubbed almost smooth again. The appliances had been replaced, maybe back when Nixon was president. But Reacher figured the countertops were still original. They were pale yellow laminate, with fine wavy lines that looked like heartbeats on a hospital machine.

Mrs. Shevick finished her sandwich. She drained her soda. She dabbed up the last fragments of her potato chips on a dampened fingertip. She pressed her napkin to her lips. She looked at Reacher.

She said, "Thank you."

He said, "You're welcome."

"You think Fisnik can't ask for another thousand dollars."

"In the sense of shouldn't. I guess that's different from won't."

"I think we'll have to pay."

"I'm happy to go discuss it with the guy. On your behalf. If you like. I could make a number of arguments."

"And I'm sure you would be convincing. But my husband told me you're only passing through. You won't be here tomorrow. We will. It's probably safer to pay."

Aaron Shevick said, "We don't have it."

His wife didn't answer. She twisted the rings on her finger. Maybe subconsciously. She had a slim gold wedding band, and a token diamond next to it. She was thinking about the pawn shop, Reacher figured. Probably near the bus depot, on a cheap street. But she would need more than a wedding band and a small solitaire, for a thousand bucks. Maybe she still had her mother's stuff, upstairs in a drawer. Maybe there had been random inheritances, from old aunts and uncles, pins and pendants and retirement watches.

She said, "We'll cross that bridge when we come to it. Maybe he'll be reasonable. Maybe he won't ask for it."

Her husband said, "These are not reasonable people."

Reacher asked him, "Do you have direct evidence of that?"

"Only indirect evidence," Shevick said. "Fisnik explained the various penalties to me, right back at the beginning. He had photographs on his phone, and a short video. I was made to watch it. As a consequence, we have never been late with a payment. Until now."

"Did you think about going to the police?"

"Of course we thought about it. But it was a contract voluntarily entered into. We borrowed their money. We accepted their terms. One of which was no police. I had been shown the punishment, on Fisnik's phone. Overall we thought it was too much of a risk."

"Probably wise," Reacher said, although he didn't really mean it. He figured what Fisnik needed was a punch in the throat, not contractual respect. Maybe followed by slamming him face down on the tabletop, way in the far back corner. But then, Reacher wasn't either seventy or stooped or starving. Probably wise.

Mrs. Shevick said, "We'll know where we stand at six o'clock."

They avoided the subject for the rest of the afternoon. Some kind of unspoken agreement. Instead they swapped biographies, like regular polite conversation. Mrs. Shevick had indeed inherited the house from her parents, who had bought it sight unseen through the GI Bill, all caught up in the crazy postwar land rush toward the middle class. She herself had been born a year later, like the lawn showed in the photograph, and she had grown up there, and then her parents died and she met her husband all in the same year. He was a machine tool operator, very skilled, raised nearby. An essential occupation, so he was never drafted for Vietnam. They had a daughter within a year, just the same as her parents had, and the daughter grew up there, the second generation to do so. She did well in school, and got a job. Never married, no grandchildren, but hey. Reacher noticed their tone changed the nearer the story got to the present day. It got bleaker, and strangled, as if there were things they couldn't say.

The clock in his head hit five. A mile was fifteen minutes for him, and twenty for most other people, but at Shevick's pace it was going to be close to the full hour.

"It's time," he said. "Let's go."

Chapter 5

Once again Reacher helped Shevick down the far curb, and across the street, and up the near curb, and across the sidewalk to the door. Once again he went in first. For the same reason. An unknown guy coming in immediately before a target was ten times less subconsciously connected than an unknown guy coming in immediately after. Human nature. Mostly bullshit, but sometimes it rang a bell.

The same fat guy was behind the bar. There were now nine other customers. Two pairs, and five singletons alone at separate tables. One of the singletons had been in the same spot six hours previously. Another was a woman about eighty years old. She was cradling a glass full of clear liquid. Probably not water.

There was a guy at the four-top in the far back corner.

He was a big slab of a man, maybe forty years old,

so pale he looked luminescent in the gloom. He had pale eyes, and pale eyelashes, and pale eyebrows. He had hair the color of corn silk, buzzed so short it glittered. He had thick white wrists resting on the edge of the table, and big white hands resting on a large black ledger. He wore a black suit, a white shirt, and a black silk tie. He had a tattoo coming up out of the neck of the shirt. Some kind of writing. A foreign alphabet. Not Russian. Something else.

Reacher sat down without ordering. A minute later Shevick limped in. Once again he glanced ahead at the table in the far back corner. Once again he stopped in surprise. He shuffled sideways and sat down at an empty four-top next to Reacher's.

He whispered, "That's not Fisnik."

"You sure?"

"Fisnik has dark skin and black hair."

"Have you ever seen this other guy before?"

"Never. It was always Fisnik."

"Maybe he's indisposed. Maybe that's what the phone call was about. He needed to find a replacement, which he couldn't, not before six o'clock."

"Maybe."

Reacher said nothing.

"What?" Shevick whispered.

"You sure you never saw this guy before?"

"Why?"

"Because then he never saw you before. All he has is an entry in a book."

"What are you suggesting?"

"I could be you. I could go pay this guy for you, and get all the details squared away."

"You mean if he asks for more?"

"I could attempt to persuade him. Most people do the right thing in the end. That's been my experience."

Now Shevick said nothing.

"I would need to be sure of something," Reacher said. "Otherwise I'll look stupid."

"Sure of what?"

"Is this the end of it? Twenty-two-five and you're done?"

"That's what we owe them."

"Give me the envelope," Reacher said.

"This is nuts."

"You've had a hard day. Take a load off."

"What Maria said was right. You won't be here tomorrow."

"I won't leave you with a problem. He'll either agree or he won't. If he doesn't, you won't be any worse off. But it's your call. Either way is fine with me. I'm not looking for trouble. I like a quiet life. That said, you could save yourself the walk there and back. That knee still looks pretty bad."

Shevick sat still and said nothing for a long moment. Then he gave Reacher the envelope. He took it out of his pocket and slid it across, low and furtive. Reacher took it from him. Three quarters of an inch thick. Heavy. He put it in his own pocket.

"Sit tight," he said.

He stood up and walked toward the far back corner. He considered himself a modern man, born in the twentieth century, living in the twenty-first, but he also knew he had some kind of a wide-open portal in his head, a wormhole to humanity's primitive past, where for millions of years every living thing could be a predator, or a rival, and therefore had to be assessed, and judged, instantly, and accurately. Who was the superior animal? Who would submit?

What he saw at the back table was going to be a challenge. If it came to it. If matters moved from the verbal to the physical. Not a colossal challenge. Somewhere between major and minor. The guy would be technically less skilled, almost certainly, unless he had also served in the U.S. Army, which taught the dirtiest fighting in the world, not that it would ever admit it in public. Against that the guy was big, and younger by a number of years, and he looked like he had been around the block a couple of times. He looked like he wouldn't scare easy. He looked like he was accustomed to winning. The ancient part of Reacher's brain took in all the subliminal information, and it flashed an amber warning, but it didn't stop him walking. Ahead of him the guy at the table watched him in turn, all the way, apparently making his own atavistic calculations. Who was the superior animal? The guy looked pretty confident. As if he liked his chances.

Reacher sat down where Shevick had perched six hours previously. The visitor chair. Up close the guy in the executive chair could have been a little older than he seemed at first sight. Forty-something. Maybe halfway to fifty. Fairly senior. A man of substance, chronologically, but the weighty impression was undercut by the guy's ghostlike pallor. That was the most noticeable thing about him. Plus his tattoo. It was inexpert and uneven. Prison ink. Probably not an American prison.

The guy picked up his ledger and opened it and propped it upright on his edge of the table. He peered down at it, with difficulty, like a guy playing his cards too close to his vest.

He said, "What's your name?"

"What's yours?" Reacher said.

"My name is of no importance."

"Where's Fisnik?"

"Fisnik has been replaced. Whatever business you had with him, now you have it with me."

"I need more than that," Reacher said. "This is an important transaction. This is a serious financial matter. Fisnik lent me money, and I need to pay him back."

"I just told you, whatever business you had with Fisnik, now you have it with me. Fisnik's clients are now my clients. If you owed money to Fisnik, now you owe it to me. This is not rocket science. What's your name?"

Reacher said, "Aaron Shevick."

The guy squinted down at his book.

He nodded.

He said, "Is this a final payment?"

"Do I get a receipt?" Reacher asked.

"Did Fisnik give you receipts?"

"You're not Fisnik. I don't even know your name."

"My name is of no importance."

"It is to me. I need to know who I'm paying."

The guy tapped his finger, white as a bone, against the side of his glittering head.

"Your receipt is in here," he said. "That's all you need to know."

"I could have Fisnik coming after me tomorrow."

"I told you two times already, yesterday you were Fisnik's, today you are mine. Tomorrow you will still be mine. Fisnik is history. Fisnik is gone. Things change. How much do you owe?"

"I don't know," Reacher said. "I depended on Fisnik to tell me. He had a formula."

"What formula?"

"For the fees and the penalties and the add-ons. Rounded up to the nearest hundred, plus another five hundred as an administrative charge. That was his rule. I could never work it out right. I didn't want him to think I was shortchanging him. I preferred to pay what he told me. Safer that way."

"How much do you think it should be?"

"This time?"

"As your final payment."

"I wouldn't want you to think I was shortchanging you, either. Not if you inherited Fisnik's business. I assume the same terms apply."

"Give it to me both ways," the guy said. "What you figure, and then what you think Fisnik's formula would figure. Maybe I'll cut you a break. Maybe we'll split the difference. As an introductory offer."

"I figure eight hundred dollars," Reacher said. "But Fisnik would probably figure fourteen hundred. Like I told you. Rounded up to the nearest hundred plus five as a charge."

The guy squinted down at his book.

He nodded, slowly, sagely, in complete agreement.

"But no break," he said. "I decided against. I'll take the full fourteen hundred."

He closed his book and laid it flat on the table.

Reacher put his hand in his pocket and his thumb in the envelope and peeled fourteen bills off the back of Shevick's wad. He handed them over. The pale guy recounted them with fast practiced fingers, folded them once, and put them in his own pocket.

"Are we good now?" Reacher asked.

"Paid off in full," the guy said.

"Receipt?"

The guy tapped the side of his head again.

"Now get lost," he said. "Until the next time."

"The next time what?" Reacher said.

"You need a loan."

"I hope not to."

"Losers like you always do. You know where to find me."

Reacher paused a beat.

"Yes," he said. "I do. Count on it."

He stayed where he was for a long moment, and then he got up out of the visitor chair and walked away, slowly, eyes front, all the way out the door to the sidewalk.

A minute later Shevick limped out after him.

"We need to talk," Reacher said.

Chapter 6

Shevick still had a cell phone. He said he hadn't sold it because it was an old flip worth close to nothing, and he was still using it because canceling his plan would have cost more than continuing it. Plus there were times he really needed it. Reacher told him this was one of those times. He told him to call a cab. Shevick said he couldn't afford a cab. Reacher told him yes he could, just this once.

The cab that came was an old beat-up Crown Vic, thick with orange-peel paint, with a cop-car spotlight on the driver's pillar and a taxi light strapped to the roof. Not an appealing vehicle, visually. But it worked OK. It wallowed and whined the mile to Shevick's house and pulled up outside. Reacher helped Shevick down the narrow concrete path to his door. Once again it opened before the guy could get his key in the lock. Mrs. Shevick stared out at him. There were silent questions in her face. A taxi? For your knee? Then why did the big man come back, too?

And above all: Do we owe another thousand dollars?

"It's complicated again," Shevick said.

They went back to the kitchen. The stove was cold. No dinner. They had already eaten once that day. They all sat down at the table. Shevick told his part of the story. No Fisnik. A substitute instead. A sinister pale stranger with a big black book. Then Reacher's offer to be a go-between.

Mrs. Shevick switched her gaze to Reacher.

Who said, "I'm pretty sure he was Ukrainian. He had a prison tattoo on his neck. Cyrillic alphabet, certainly."

"I don't think Fisnik was Ukrainian," Mrs. Shevick said. "Fisnik is an Albanian name. I looked it up at the library."

"He said Fisnik had been replaced. He said whatever business anyone had with Fisnik, now they had it with him. He said Fisnik's clients were now his clients. He said if you owed money to Fisnik, now you owed it to him. He made the same kind of point several times over. He said it wasn't rocket science."

"Did he want another thousand dollars?"

"He propped his book open so close to his chest it was awkward. At first I wasn't sure why. I assumed he didn't want me to see what was in it. He asked my name, and I said Aaron Shevick. He looked down at his book and nodded. Which I thought was weird."

"Why?"

"What were the odds the book happened to be

propped open at the S page? One in twenty-six. Possible, but unlikely. So then I started to think he was hiding the book not because he didn't want me to see what was in it, but because he didn't want me to see what wasn't in it. Because there was nothing in it. It was blank. That was my guess. Then he proved it. He asked me how much I owed. He didn't know. He didn't have Fisnik's previous data. It wasn't Fisnik's old ledger. It was a new blank book."

"What does all that mean?"

"It means this wasn't a routine internal reorganization. They didn't bench Fisnik and send in a pinch hitter. It was a hostile takeover from the outside. There's a whole new management now. I went back through the guy's words. His use of language. He made it clear. Someone else is muscling in."

"Wait," Mrs. Shevick said. "I heard it on the radio. Last week, I think. We're getting a new police commissioner. He says we have rival Ukrainian and Albanian gangs in town."

Reacher nodded.

"There you go," he said. "The Ukrainians are moving in on a part of the Albanians' business. You're dealing with new people now."

"Did they want the extra thousand dollars?"

"They're looking ahead, not back in the past. They're prepared to write off Fisnik's old loans. All or part. Because they have to. They have no choice. They don't know what anyone owes. They don't have the information. And why wouldn't they write it off anyway? It wasn't their money. They want his customers.

That's all. For the future. They want to service their needs for the next many years."

"Did you pay the man?"

"He asked what I owed and I took a chance and told him fourteen hundred dollars. He looked down at his blank page and nodded solemnly and agreed. So I paid him fourteen hundred dollars. At which point he said I was good to go and he confirmed I was paid off in full."

"Where's the rest of the money?"

"Right here," Reacher said. He took the envelope out of his pocket. Barely thinner than it was before. Still two hundred eleven bills in it. Twenty-one thousand one hundred dollars. He put it on the table, in the middle, equidistant. Shevick and his wife stared at it and said nothing.

Reacher said, "This is a random universe. Once in a blue moon things turn out just right. Like now. Someone started a war and you're the exact opposite of collateral damage."

Shevick said, "Not if Fisnik shows up next week wanting all this plus seven grand more."

"He won't," Reacher said. "Fisnik has been replaced. Which coming from a Ukrainian gangster with prison ink on his neck almost certainly means Fisnik is dead. Or otherwise incapacitated. He won't be showing up next week. Or any week. And you're all squared away with the new guys. They said so. You're out of the woods."

There was silence for a long moment.

Mrs. Shevick looked at Reacher.

"Thank you," she said.

Then Shevick's cell phone rang. He limped out to the hallway and took the call. Reacher heard a faint plastic quack from the earpiece. A man's voice, he thought. He couldn't make out the words. Some long stream of information. He heard Shevick reply, loud and clear, ten feet away, with a muttered assent that sounded weary and unsurprised, yet still disappointed. Then Shevick asked what was unmistakably a question.

He said, "How much?"

The faint plastic quack answered.

Shevick closed his phone. He stood still for a moment, and then he limped back into the kitchen and sat down again at the table. He folded his hands in front of him. He looked at the envelope. Not a stare, not a gaze. Some kind of a bittersweet glance. Equidistant. Equally far away from all of them.

He said, "They need another forty thousand dollars."

His wife closed her eyes and clamped her hands over her face.

Reacher said, "Who needs?"

"Not Fisnik," Shevick said. "Not the Ukrainians, either. Not any of them. This is the other end of the issue entirely. This is the reason we had to borrow money in the first place."

"Are you being blackmailed?"

"No, nothing like that. I wish it was that simple. All I can say is there are bills we have to pay. One just came due. Now we have to find another forty thousand dollars." He glanced at the envelope again. "Some of which we've already got, thanks to you." He worked it out in his head. "Technically we need to find another eighteen thousand nine hundred dollars."

"By when?"

"Tomorrow morning."

"Can you?"

"We couldn't find another eighteen cents."

"Why so quick?"

"Some things can't wait."

"What are you going to do?"

Shevick didn't answer.

His wife took her hands away from her face.

"We're going to borrow it," she said. "What else can we do?"

"Who from?"

"The man with the prison tattoo," she said. "What choice do we have? We're maxed out everywhere else."

"Can you pay it back?"

"We'll cross that bridge when we come to it."

No one spoke.

Reacher said, "I'm sorry I can't help you more."

Mrs. Shevick looked at him.

"You can," she said.

"Can I?"

"In fact you'll have to."

"Will I?"

"The man with the prison tattoo thinks you're Aaron Shevick. You have to go get our money for us."

Chapter 7

They discussed it thirty minutes more, Reacher and the Shevicks, back and forth. Certain facts were established early. The fixed points. The dealbreakers. They absolutely needed the money. No question. No debate. They absolutely needed it by morning. No leeway. No flexibility.

They absolutely would not say why.

Their life savings were gone. Their house was gone. They were newly into an old-person's mortgage arrangement, whereby they were allowed to live there the rest of their lives, but the title had already passed to the bank. The lump sum they had gotten was already spent. No more could be raised. Their credit cards were maxed out and canceled. They had borrowed against their Social Security checks. They had cashed in their life insurance and given up their landline telephone. Now that their car was gone they had sold everything of value. All they had left were personal trinkets. Between their own stuff and family heirlooms they had five nine-carat wedding bands, three small diamond rings, and a gold-plated wristwatch with a crack in the crystal. Reacher figured on the happiest day of his life the most warmhearted pawnbroker in the world might have given them two hundred bucks. No more than that. Maybe less than a hundred on a bad day. Not even a drop in the bucket.

They said they had first used Fisnik five weeks previously. They had gotten his name from a neighbor. As an item of gossip, not as a recommendation. Some kind of a scandal. Some lurid story about some other neighbor's nephew's wife's cousin borrowing money from a gangster in a bar. Name of Fisnik, imagine that. Shevick had narrowed the search radius based on detail and rumor, and he had started checking every bar within that predicted area, one by one, blushing, embarrassed, stared at, asking every barman if he knew a guy named Fisnik, until at his fourth stop a fat man with a sarcastic manner jerked his thumb at the corner table.

Reacher said, "How did it work?"

"Very easy," Shevick said. "I approached his table, and stood there, while he inspected me, and then he signaled me to sit down, so I did. I guess at first I beat about the bush a bit, but then I just came out and said, look, I need to borrow money, and I understand you lend it. He asked how much, and I told him. He explained the terms of the contract. He showed me the photographs. I watched the video. I gave him my account number. Twenty minutes later the money was in my bank. It was wired in from somewhere untrace-able via a corporation in Delaware."

"I pictured a bag of cash," Reacher said.

"We had to make our repayments in cash."

Reacher nodded.

"Two things in one," he said. "Both at the same time. Loansharking and money laundering. They wired dirty electrons and in return they got random clean cash from the streets. Plus a healthy rate of interest on top. Most money laundering involves losing a percentage, not gaining one. I guess those boys weren't dumb."

"Not in our experience."

"You think the Ukrainians will be better or worse?"

"Worse, I expect. The law of the jungle seems to be proving it already."

"So how are you going to pay them back?"

"That's tomorrow's problem."

"You have nothing left to sell."

"Something might show up."

"In your dreams."

"No, in reality. We're waiting for something. We have reason to believe it will come very soon. We have to hang tough until it does."

They absolutely would not say what they were waiting for.

Twenty minutes later Reacher stepped down the far curb unencumbered, and crossed the street in four fast strides, and stepped up the near curb, and pulled the bar door. Inside it felt brighter than before, because it was darker outside, and it was a click noisier, because there were more people, including a group of five men all squeezed around a four-top table, all reminiscing about something or other.

The pale guy was still in the far back corner.

Reacher walked toward him. The pale guy watched him all the way. Reacher dialed it back a little. There were conventions to follow. Lender and borrower. He walked what he thought of as his friendly walk, pure unselfconscious locomotion, no threat to anybody. He sat down in the same chair he had used before.

The pale guy said, "Aaron Shevick, right?"

"Yes," Reacher said.

"What brings you back so soon?"

"I need a loan."

"Already? You just paid me off."

"Something came up."

"I told you," the guy said. "Losers like you always come back."

"I remember," Reacher said.

"How much do you want?"

"Eighteen thousand nine hundred dollars," Reacher said.

The pale guy shook his head.

"Can't do it," he said.

"Why not?"

"It's a big jump up from eight hundred last time."

"Fourteen hundred."

"Six hundred of that was fees and charges. The capital sum was eight hundred only."

"That was then. This is now. It's what I need."

"You good for it?"

"I always was before," Reacher said. "Ask Fisnik."

"Fisnik is history," the pale guy said.

Nothing more.

Reacher waited.

Then the pale guy said, "Maybe there's a way I can help you. Although you got to understand, I would be taking a risk, which would have to be reflected in the price. You comfortable with that scenario?"

"I guess," Reacher said.

"And I have to tell you, I'm pretty much a round-figures guy. Can't do eighteen-nine. We would have to call it twenty. Then I would take eleven hundred off the top as an administration fee. You would get the exact amount you need. You want to hear the interest rates?"

"I guess," Reacher said again.

"Things have moved on since Fisnik's day. We're in an era of innovation now. We operate what they call dynamic pricing. We pitch the rate up or down, depending on supply and demand and things like that, but also on what we think of the borrower. Will he be reliable? Can we trust him? Questions of that nature."

"So what am I?" Reacher asked. "Up or down?"

"I'm going to start you off way up there at the very top. Where the worst risks are. Truth is, I don't like you very much, Aaron Shevick. I'm not getting a good feeling. You take twenty tonight, you bring me twenty-five, a week from today. After that, interest continues at twenty-five percent a week or part of a week, plus a late fee of a thousand dollars a day, or part of a day. After the first deadline, all sums become payable in full immediately on demand. Refusal or inability to pay on demand may expose you to unpleasant things of various different types. You have to understand that ahead of time. I need to hear you say so, in your own words. It's not the kind of thing that can be written down and signed. I have photographs for you to look at."

"Terrific," Reacher said.

The guy dabbed at his phone, menus, albums, slideshows, and he handed it over sideways, like a landscape, not a portrait, which was appropriate, because all the subjects of all the pictures were lying down. Mostly they were duct-taped to an iron bedstead, in a room with whitewashed walls gone gray with age and damp. Some had their eyeballs popped out with a spoon, and some had been grazed by an electric saw, deeper and deeper, and some had been burned with a smoothing iron, and some had been drilled with cordless power tools, which were left in the pictures as if in proof, yellow and black, top heavy and wobbling, their bits two-thirds buried in yielding flesh.

Pretty bad.

But not the worst things Reacher had ever seen.

Maybe the worst things all on one phone, though.

He handed it back. The guy dabbed through his menus again, until he got where he wanted to be. Serious business now.

He said, "Do you understand the terms of the contract?"

"Yes," Reacher said.

"Do you agree to them?"

"Yes," Reacher said.

"Bank account?"

Reacher gave him Shevick's numbers. The guy typed them in, right there on his phone, and then he dabbed a big green rectangle at the bottom of the screen. The go button.

He said, "The money will be in your bank in twenty minutes."

Then he dabbed through more menus, and suddenly raised the phone in camera mode, and snapped Reacher's picture.

He said, "Thank you, Mr. Shevick. A pleasure doing business. I'll see you again in one week exactly."

Then he tapped his bristly head with his bone-white finger, the same gesture as before. Something about remembering. Some kind of a threatening implication.

Whatever, Reacher thought.

He got up and walked away, out the door, into the dark. There was a car at the curb. A black Lincoln, with an idling engine, and an idling driver behind the wheel, leaning back in his seat, head on the cushion, elbows wide, knees wide, like limo guys everywhere, taking a break.

There was a second guy, outside the car, leaning on the rear fender. He was dressed the same as the driver. And the guy inside the bar. Black suit, white shirt, black silk tie. Like a uniform. He had his ankles crossed, and his arms crossed. He was just waiting. He looked like the guy at the corner table would look, after about a month in the sun. White, not luminescent. He had pale hair buzzed close to his scalp, and a busted nose, and scar tissue on his eyebrows. Not much of a fighter, Reacher thought. Obviously he got hit a lot.

The guy said, "You Shevick?"

Reacher said, "Who's asking?"

"The people you just borrowed money from."

"Sounds like you already know who I am."

"We're going to drive you home."

"Suppose I don't want you to?" Reacher said.

"Part of the deal," the guy said.

"What deal?"

"We need to know where you live."

"Why?"

"Reassurance."

"Look me up."

"We did."

"And?"

"You're not in the book. You don't own real estate."

Reacher nodded. The Shevicks had given up their landline telephone. The title to their house had already passed to the bank.

The guy said, "So we need to pay a personal visit."

Reacher said nothing.

The guy asked, "Is there a Mrs. Shevick?"

"Why?"

"Maybe we should visit a little with her too, while we're looking at where you live. We like to keep our customers close. We like to make a family's acquaintance. We find it helpful. Now get in the car."

Reacher shook his head.

"You misunderstand," the guy said. "This is not a

choice. It's part of the deal. You borrowed our money."

"Your milky-white friend inside explained the contract. He went through all the terms, in considerable detail. The administration fee, the dynamic pricing, the penalties. At one point he even introduced visual aids. After which he asked if I accepted the terms of the contract, and I said yes I did, so at that point the deal was done. You can't start adding extra stuff afterward, about a ride home and meeting the family. I would have to agree to that, ahead of time. A contract is a two-way street. Subject to negotiation and agreement. It can't be done unilaterally. That's a basic principle."

"You got a smart mouth."

"I can only hope," Reacher said. "Sometimes I worry I'm just pedantic."

"What?"

"You can offer me a ride, but you can't insist that I take it."

"What?"

"You heard."

"OK, I'm offering you a ride. Last chance. Get in the car."

"Say please."

The guy paused a long, long moment.

He said, "Please get in the car."

"OK," Reacher said. "Since you asked so nicely."

Chapter 8

About the safest way to transport an unwilling hostage in a passenger car was to make him drive with his seat belt off. The guys with the Lincoln didn't do that. They opted for a conventional second best instead. They put Reacher in the back, behind the empty front passenger seat, with nothing dead ahead for him to attack. The guy who had done all the talking got in next to him, on the other side, behind the driver, and he sat half sideways, watchful.

He said, "Where to?"

"Turn around," Reacher said.

The driver U-turned across the width of the street, bouncing his front right-side wheel up the far curb, and slapping it down again.

"Go straight for five blocks," Reacher said.

The driver rolled on. He was a smaller version of the first guy. Not as pale. Caucasian for sure, but not blinding. He had the same buzzed hair, golden and glittery. He had a knife scar on the back of his left hand. Probably a defensive wound. He had a spidery and fading tattoo snaking out of his right cuff. He had big pink ears, sticking straight out from the sides of his head.

Their tires pattered over broken blacktop and patches of cobblestone. After the five straight blocks they came to the four-way light. Where Shevick had waited to cross. They rolled out of the old world and into the new. Flat and open terrain. Concrete and gravel. Wide sidewalks. It all looked different in the dark. The bus depot was up ahead.

"Straight on," Reacher said.

The driver rolled through the green. They passed the depot. They tracked around, a polite distance behind the high-rent districts. Half a mile later they came to where the bus had turned off the main drag.

"Take the right," Reacher said. "Out toward the highway."

He saw the in-town two-lane was called Center Street. Then it widened to four lanes and was called a state route number. Then came the giant supermarket. The office parks were up ahead.

"Where the hell are we going?" the guy in the back said. "No one lives out here."

"Why I like it," Reacher said.

The road was smooth. Their tires hissed over it. There was no traffic up ahead. Maybe something behind them. Reacher didn't know. He couldn't risk a look.

He said, "Tell me again why you want to meet my wife."

The guy in the back said, "We find it helpful."

"How?"

"You pay back a bank loan because you're worried about your credit score and your good name and your standing in the community. But that's all gone for you. You're down in the sewer. What are you worried about now? What's going to make you pay us back?"

They passed the office parks. Still no traffic. The auto dealer was up ahead in the distance. A wire fence, ranks of dark shapes, bunting that gleamed gray in the moonlight.

"Sounds like a threat," Reacher said.

"Daughters are good, too."

Still no traffic.

Reacher hit the guy in the face. Out of nowhere. A sudden violent explosion of muscle. No warning at all. A pile driver, with all the speed and twist he could muster in the confined space available. The guy's head smashed back into the window frame behind him. A mist of blood from his nose spattered the glass.

Reacher reloaded and hit the driver. Same kind of force. Same kind of result. Leaning over the seat, a clubbing roundhouse right direct to the guy's ear, the guy's head snapping sideways, bouncing off the glass, straight into a second jabbing right to the same ear, and a third, which turned the lights out. The guy fell forward on his steering wheel.

Reacher balled himself up in the rear foot well.

A second later the car hit the auto dealer's fence at forty miles an hour. Reacher heard a colossal bang and a banshee screech and the airbags exploded and he was crushed against the seat back in front of him, which yielded and collapsed into the deflating airbag ahead of it, just as the car smashed into the first vehicle for sale, on the near end of the long line under the flags and the bunting. The Lincoln hit it hard, head on into its gleaming flank, and the Lincoln's windshield shattered and its back end came up in the air, and crashed back to earth, and the engine stalled out, and the car went still and quiet, all except for a loud and furious hiss of steam under the wrecked hood.

Reacher unfolded himself and climbed up on the seat again. He had taken all the juddering impacts on the flat of his back. He felt like Shevick had looked on the sidewalk. Shaken up. Hurting all over. *Regular kind of thing, or worse?* He guessed regular. He moved his head, his neck, his shoulders, his legs. Nothing broken. Nothing torn. Not too bad.

The same could not be said for the other two guys. The driver had been smashed in the face by the airbag, and then in the back of the head by the other guy, who had been thrown forward from the rear compartment like a spear, right out through the shattering windshield, where he still was, folded at the waist over the crumpled hood, face down. His feet were the nearest part of him. He wasn't moving. Neither was the driver.

Reacher forced open his door against the screech of distorted metal, and he crawled out, and he forced the door shut again after him. There was no traffic behind them. Nothing up ahead either, except dim twinkling headlights, maybe a mile in the distance. Coming toward them. A minute away, at sixty miles an hour. The vehicle the Lincoln had hit was a minivan. A Ford. It was all stoved in on the side. Bent like a banana. It had a banner in the windshield that said *No Accidents*. The Lincoln itself was a total mess. It was crumpled up like a concertina, all the way back to the windshield. Like a safety ad in a newspaper. Except for the guy draped on top.

The headlights up ahead were getting nearer. And now back toward town there were more. The auto dealer's fence was burst open like a cartoon drawing. Raggedy curls of wire curved neatly out the way. As if they had been blown back by the slipstream. The gap was about eight feet wide. Basically a whole section was gone. Reacher wondered if the fence had motion sensors. Connected to a silent alarm. Connected to the police department. Maybe an insurance requirement. Certainly there was plenty of stuff to steal inside.

Time to go.

Reacher stepped through the hole in the fence, stiff and sore, bruised and battered, but functioning. He stayed away from the road. Instead he stumbled along parallel to it, through fields and vacant lots, fifty feet in the dirt, out of lateral headlight range, while cars drove by in the distance, some slow, some fast. Maybe cops. Maybe not. He skirted around the blind side of the first office park, and the second, and then he changed his angle and headed for the giant supermarket's parking lot, aiming to walk through it and rejoin the main drag where it let out.

* * *

Gregory got the news more or less immediately, from a janitor cleaning up in the emergency room. Part of the Ukrainian network. The guy took a smoke break and called it right in. Two of Gregory's men, just arrived on gurneys. Lights and sirens. One bad, one worse. Both would probably die. There was talk of a car wreck out by the Ford dealer.

Gregory called his top boys together, and ten minutes later they were all assembled, around a table in the back room of the taxi company. His right-hand man said, "All we know for sure is earlier this evening two of our guys deployed to the bar to do an address check on one of the former customers from the Albanian credit operation."

"How long does an address check take?" Gregory said. "They must have finished long ago. This must be something else entirely. It's obviously separate. It can't have been the address check itself. Because who the hell lives all the way out by the Ford dealer? No one, that's who. So they let the guy out at his house and noted the address, maybe took a photograph, and then they headed over to the Ford dealer afterward. Why? Must have been a reason. And why did they crash?"

"Maybe they were chased in that direction. Or decoyed. Then bumped and run off the road. It's pretty lonely out there at night."

"You think it was Dino?"

"You got to ask, why those two in particular? Maybe they were followed from right outside the bar.

Which would be appropriate. Because maybe Dino is making a point here. We stole his business. We expected some reaction, after all."

"After he twigged."

"Maybe he has now."

"How much of a point is he going to make?"

"Maybe this is it," the guy said. "Two men for two men. We keep the loan business. It would be a surrender with honor. He's a realistic man. He doesn't have many options. He can't start a war, with the cops watching."

Gregory said nothing. The room went quiet. No sound at all, except muted chatter from the taxi radio in the front office. Through the closed door. Just background noise. No one paid any attention to it. If they had, they would have heard a driver calling in to say he had let out an old lady at the supermarket, and was going to use his waiting time while she shopped to earn an extra buck, by driving a guy home, to the old tract houses east of downtown. The guy was on foot, but he looked reasonably civilized and he had cash money. Maybe his car had broken down. It was four miles there, and four miles back. He would be done before the old lady was even out of the bakery aisle. No harm, no foul.

At that moment Dino was getting a much earlier and incomplete snapshot of part of the news. It had taken an hour to travel up the chain. It included nothing about the car wreck. Most of the day had been spent disposing of Fisnik and his named accomplice. Reorganization had been left very late. Almost an after-thought. A replacement had been sent to the bar, to pick up on Fisnik's business. The chosen guy had gotten there a little after eight o'clock in the evening. Immediately he had seen Ukrainian muscle in the street. Guarding the place. A Town Car, and two men. He had snuck around to the bar's rear fire door, and snuck a look inside. A Ukrainian guy was sitting at Fisnik's table in the far back corner, talking to a big guy, who looked disheveled and poor. Obviously a customer.

At that point the chosen replacement regrouped and retreated. He phoned it in. The guy he told called another guy. Who called another guy. And so on. Because bad news traveled slowly. An hour later Dino heard about it. He called his top boys together, in the lumber yard.

He said, "There are two possible scenarios. Either the thing about the police commissioner's list was true, and they opportunistically and treacherously used the disruption to muscle in on our moneylending business, or it wasn't true, and they planned this thing all along, and in fact tricked us into clearing the way for them."

His right-hand man said, "I suppose we must hope it was the former."

Dino was quiet for a long spell.

Then he said, "I'm afraid we must pretend it was the former. We have no choice. We can't start a war. Not now. We'll have to let them keep the moneylending business. We have no practical way to get it back. But we'll surrender it with honor. It must be two for two. We can't be seen to do less than that. Kill two of their men, and we'll call it even."

His right-hand man asked, "Which two?"

"I don't care," Dino said.

Then he changed his mind.

"No, choose them carefully," he said. "Let's try to find an advantage."

Chapter 9

Reacher got out of the taxi at the Shevick house and walked up the narrow concrete path. The door opened before he could ring the bell. Shevick stood there, with the light behind him and his phone in his hand.

"The money came through an hour ago," he said. "Thank you."

"Welcome," Reacher said.

"You're late. We thought maybe you weren't coming back."

"I had to take a minor detour."

"Where?"

"Let's go inside," Reacher said. "We need to talk."

This time they used the living room. The photographs on the wall, the amputated television. The Shevicks took the armchairs, and Reacher sat on the loveseat.

He said, "It happened pretty much like it happened with you and Fisnik. Except the guy snapped my picture. Which might be a good thing, in the end. Your name, my face. A little confusion never hurts. But if I was a real client, I wouldn't have liked it. Not one little bit. It would have felt like a bony finger on my shoulder. It would have made me feel vulnerable. Then I got outside and there was more. Two guys, who wanted to drive me home, to see where I lived, and who I lived with. My wife, if I had one. Which was another bony finger. Maybe a whole bony hand."

"What happened?"

"The three of us negotiated a different arrangement. Not linked in any way to your name or address. In fact fairly confusing as to exactly what took place. I wanted an element of mystery about it. Their bosses will suspect a message, but they won't be sure who from. They'll think the Albanians, most likely. Not you, certainly."

"What happened to the men?"

"They were part of the message. As in, this is America. Don't send an asshole who last time out was seventh on the undercard in some basement fight club in Kiev. At least take it seriously. Show some respect."

"They saw your face."

"They won't remember. They had an accident. They got all banged up. Their memories will be missing an hour or two. Retrograde amnesia, they call it. Fairly common, after physical trauma. If they don't die first, that is."

"So everything's OK?"

"Not really," Reacher said.

"What else?"

"These are not reasonable people."

"We know."

"How are you going to pay their money back?"

They didn't answer.

"You need twenty-five grand, a week from right now. You can't be late. They showed me pictures, too. Fisnik's can't have been worse. You need some kind of a plan."

Shevick said, "A week is a long time."

"Not really," Reacher said again.

Mrs. Shevick said, "Something good might happen."

Nothing more.

Reacher said, "You really need to tell me what it is you're waiting for."

It was about their daughter, inevitably. Mrs. Shevick's gaze roamed the pictures on the wall as she told the story. Their daughter's name was Margaret, shortened since childhood to Meg. She had been a bright, happy infant, full of charm and energy. She loved other children. She loved kindergarten. She loved elementary school. She loved to read and write and draw. She smiled and chattered all the time. She could persuade anyone to do anything. She could have sold ice to the Eskimos, her mother said.

She loved middle school just as much, and junior high, and high school. She was popular. Everyone liked her. She put on plays and sang in the choir and ran track and swam. She got her diploma, but she didn't go to college. Her book learning was good, but not her main strength. She was a people person. She needed to be out and about, smiling, chatting, charming folks. Bending them to her will, if truth be told. She liked a purpose.

She got an entry-level job in the spokesperson business, and she bounced around town from one PR office to another, doing whatever the local establishments had a budget for. She worked hard, and made her name, and got promoted, and by the time she was thirty she was making more than her dad ever had as a machinist. Ten years later, at forty, she was still doing well, but she felt her trajectory had slowed. Her acceleration had been blunted. She could see her ceiling above her. She would sit at her desk and think, is this it?

No, she decided. She wanted one last big score. Bigger than big. She was in the wrong place, she knew. She would have to move. San Francisco, probably, where the tech money was. Where complicated things needed explaining. Sooner or later she would have to go there. Or New York. But she dithered. Time passed. Then, amazingly, San Francisco came to her. In a manner of speaking. Later she learned there was a perpetual ongoing game, stoked up by real estate people and tech sector accountants, in which the prize was to guess correctly about where the next-but-one Silicon Valley would be. In order to get in early. For some reason her hometown checked all the secret boxes. Regenerating, the right kind of people, the right buildings, and power, and internet speed. The first advance scouts were already sniffing around.

Meg got a friend-of-a-friend introduction to a guy who knew a guy, who arranged an interview with the founder of a brand new venture. They met in a downtown coffee shop. He was a twenty-five-year-old fresh off the plane from California. Some kind of a foreign-born computer genius, with some new thing to do with medical software and apps on people's phones. Mrs. Shevick admitted she had never been exactly sure what the product was, except she knew it was the type of thing that made folks rich.

Meg was offered the job. Senior Vice President for Communications and Local Affairs. It was a fledgling ink-not-dry start-up company, so the salary wasn't great. Not much more than she was already making. But there was a whole giant package of benefits. Stock options, a huge pension plan, a gold plated health plan, a European coupe to drive. Plus weird San Francisco stuff like free pizza and candy and massages. She liked all of it. But the stock options were by far the biggest deal. One day she could be a billionaire. Literally. That was how these things happened.

At first it went pretty well. Meg did great work keeping the drums beating, and two or three times in the first year it looked like they might make it to the top of the hill. But they didn't. Not quite. The second year was the same. Still glossy and glamorous and cutting edge and the next big thing, but nothing actually happened. The third year was worse. Investors got nervous. The cash spigot was turned way down. But they hung in, lean and mean. They rented two floors of their building. No more pizza or candy. The massage tables were folded up and put away. They worked harder than ever, side by side in cramped quarters, still determined, still confident.

Then Meg got cancer.

Or, more accurately, she found out she'd had cancer for about the last six months. She had been too busy for doctor visits. She thought the weight she was losing was from working too hard. But no. It was a bad diagnosis. It was a virulent type, and it was fairly advanced. The only ray of hope was a bunch of new treatments. They were exotic and expensive, but their trials had been promising. They seemed to work. Their success rate was climbing. No other option, the doctors said. Calendars were cleared, and Meg was booked in for her first session the very next morning.

Which was when the problems started.

Mrs. Shevick said, "There was a glitch with her insurance. Her account number wouldn't run. She was prepping for chemo, and people were running in and out asking her full name and date of birth and Social Security number. It was a nightmare. They had the insurance company on the phone, and no one knew what was going on. They could see her history and they knew she was a customer. But the code wouldn't authorize. It threw up an error message. They said it was just a computer thing. No big deal. They said it would be fixed the next day. But the hospital said we couldn't wait. They had us sign a form. It said we would cover the bill if the insurance didn't come through. They said it was just a technicality. They said computer things happened all the time. They said everything would get straightened out."

"I'm guessing everything didn't," Reacher said.

"The weekend came along, which was two more sessions, and then it was Monday, and then we found out."

"Found out what?" Reacher asked, although he felt he could guess.

Mrs. Shevick shook her head and sighed and flapped her hand in front of her face, as if she couldn't form the words. As if she was all done talking. Her husband leaned forward, with his elbows on his knees, and he continued the tale.

"Their third year," he said. "When their investors got nervous. It was even worse than they knew. It was worse than anyone knew. The boss was keeping secrets. From everyone, Meg included. Behind the scenes the whole thing was falling apart. He wasn't paying the bills. Not a dime. He didn't renew the company health plan. He didn't pay the premium. He just ignored it. Meg's number wouldn't run because the policy was canceled. On her fourth day of treatment we found out she was uninsured."

"Not her fault," Reacher said. "Surely. It was some kind of fraud or breach of contract. There must be a remedy."

"There are two," Shevick said. "One is a government no-fault fund, and the other is an insurance industry no-fault fund, both of them set up for this specific reason. Naturally we ran straight to them. Right away they got to work on how to apportion responsibility between them, and as soon as that's done they're going to refund everything we've spent so far, and then take care of everything else going forward. We expect a decision any day."

"But you can't pause Meg's treatment."

"She needs so much. Two or three sessions a day. Chemo, radiation, care and feeding, all kinds of scans, all kinds of lab work. She can't get welfare. Technically she's still employed, technically with a decent salary. No one in the press is interested. Where's the story? Kid needs something, parents willing to pay. Where's the punchline? Maybe we shouldn't have signed that paper. Maybe other doors would have opened. But we did sign the paper. Too late now. Obviously the hospital wants to get paid. This is not emergency room stuff. It can't be written off. Their machines cost a million dollars. They have to buy actual physical crystals of radioactive stuff. They want the money in advance. It's what happens in cases like these. Cash on the barrelhead. Nothing happens before. Nothing we can do about it. All we can do is hang in until someone else steps up. Could be tomorrow morning. We have seven chances before the week is over."

"You need a lawyer," Reacher said.

"Can't afford one."

"There's probably an important principle in there somewhere. You could probably get one pro bono."

"We have three of that kind already," Shevick said. "They're working on the public interest aspect. Bunch of kids. They're poorer than we are."

"Seven chances before the week is over," Reacher said. "Sounds like a country song."

"It's all we got."

"I guess it almost qualifies as a plan."

"Thank you."

"Do you have a plan B?"

"Not as such."

"You could try lying low. I'll be long gone. The photograph they took will be no good to them."

"You'll be gone?"

"I can't stay anywhere a week."

"They have our name. I'm sure we can be traced. There must be old paperwork still around. One level down from the phone book."

"Tell me about the lawyers."

"They're working for free," Shevick said. "How good can they be?"

"Sounds like another country song."

Shevick didn't answer. Mrs. Shevick looked up.

"There are three of them," she said. "Three nice young men. From a public law project. Paying their dues. Good intentions, I'm sure. But the law moves slow."

Reacher said, "Plan B could be the police. A week from now, if the other thing hasn't happened yet, you could head over to the station house and tell them the story."

Shevick asked, "How well would they protect us?"

"I guess not very," Reacher said.

"And for how long?"

"Not very," Reacher said again.

"We would be burning our boats," Mrs. Shevick said. "If the other thing hasn't happened yet, then we need those people more than ever. Who else could we turn to when the next bill comes in? Going to the police would leave us with no access to anything."

"OK," Reacher said. "No police. Seven chances. I'm sorry about Meg. I really am. I really hope she makes it."

He stood up, and felt large in the small boxy space.

Shevick said, "Are you going?"

Reacher nodded.

"I'll get a hotel in town," he said. "Maybe I'll swing by in the morning. To say so long, before I hit the road. If I don't, it was a pleasure meeting you. I wish you the best of luck with your troubles."

He left them there, sitting quiet in the half empty room. He let himself out the front door, and he walked down the narrow concrete path to the street, and onward past parked cars and dark silent houses, and when he hit the main drag he turned toward town.

Chapter 10

There was a particular block on the west side of Center Street that had two restaurants side by side fronting on the sidewalk, and a third on the north side of the block, and a fourth on the south side, and a fifth in back, fronting on the next street over. All five were doing well. They were always busy. Always buzzing. Always talked about. They were the city's gourmet quarter, right there, packed tight. The produce trucks and the linen services loved it. One stop, five customers. Deliveries were easy.

So were collections. It was a Ukrainian block, being west of Center. They came by for their protection money regular as clockwork. One stop, five customers. They loved it. They came late in the evening, when the registers were full. Before anyone else got paid. They would walk in, always two guys, always together, dark suits and black silk ties and pale blank faces. Nothing was ever said. Technically it would have been difficult to prove illegality. In fact nothing had been said, even back at the beginning, many years before, except a subjective aesthetic opinion, and then a concerned and sympathetic murmur. *Nice place you've got here. Be a shame if anything happened to it.* Polite conversation. After which a hundred dollar bill was offered, but was greeted with a shake of the head, until a second hundred was added, which was greeted with a nod. After the first encounter the cash was usually left in an envelope, usually at the maître d' station. Usually it was handed over without a word. Technically a voluntary activity. No overt demands had been made. No offers had been solicited. A thousand dollars for a stroll around the block. Almost legal. Nice work if you could get it. Naturally there was competition for the gig. Naturally it was won by the big dogs. The senior lieutenants, looking for a quiet life.

That particular evening, they didn't get one.

They had parked their car on the curb on Center Street, and they had started with the two establishments right there, fronting on the sidewalk, and then they had worked the block counterclockwise, making their third stop on the north side, and their fourth on the back street, and their fifth on the south side. After which they kept on going, intending to turn the last corner, and thereby complete the square, and arrive back at their car.

All of which they did. Without noticing a couple of important things. Up ahead on the next block was a tow truck, facing away, parked, but idling with its reversing lights showing. And about level with it, on the opposite sidewalk, was a man in a black raincoat, walking fast toward them. What did that mean? They didn't ask. They were senior lieutenants, looking for a quiet life.

They split up around the hood of their car, the passenger going one way, and the driver going the other. They pulled their doors, not exactly synchronized, but close. They glanced around, still standing, one last time, chins up, in case anyone was in doubt who owned the block.

They missed the tow truck start to move, slowly, backward, straight toward them. They missed the man in the raincoat step off the far sidewalk, at an angle, straight toward them.

They slid into their seats, butts, knees, feet, but before they could get their doors closed a shape had peeled out of the shadows on one side, and the man in the raincoat had arrived on the other, both with small semiautomatic .22-caliber pistols in their hands, both pistols with long fat suppressors screwed to their muzzles, which went *blat blat blat* as multiple rounds were fired close range into the seated heads, which were right there at waist level. Both guys in the car fell forward and inward, away from the guns. Their shattered heads bumped together, near the clock on the dash, as if they were fighting for space.

Then their doors were slammed shut. The tow truck backed up. The shape from the shadows and the man in the raincoat ran to meet it. The driver jumped out. Together they got the car craned up. All three jumped back in the tow truck. They drove off, slow and sedate. A common sight. A disabled vehicle, undignified, being dragged backward through the streets on its front wheels, with its ass way up in the air. Nothing was visible above the window line. Gravity was making sure of that. By then both guys would be piled in the foot wells. Limp and floppy. Rigor was still some hours away.

They drove direct to the crushing plant. They unhooked the car and left it on a patch of oil-soaked dirt. A huge backhoe drove over. Instead of a bucket it had giant forklift spears on the front. It lifted the car and drove it to the crusher. It set it down on a steel floor in a three-sided box not much bigger than the car itself. It backed away. The box's fourth side folded up into place. Its top folded down.

Engines roared and hydraulics clanked and the box's sides crushed inward, relentlessly, grating, groaning, scraping, tearing, a hundred and fifty tons of force behind each one. Then they stopped, and wheezed back to where they had started, and a piston pushed out a cube of crushed metal about a yard on a side. It rested for a moment on a heavy iron grille. For leaking fluids to drain away. Gasoline and oil and brake fluid and whatever it was in the air conditioner. Plus other fluids, on this occasion. Then a brother to the first backhoe came along. Instead of forklift spears it had a claw. It picked up the cube and drove it away and stacked it in a wall of a hundred other cubes.

Only then did the man in the raincoat call Dino. Total success. Two for two. Honor even. They had effectively traded the moneylending for the gourmet quarter. Which was a short term loss, but maybe a long term gain. It was a foot in the door. It was a landing zone that could be first defended, and then expanded. Above all it was proof the map could be redrawn.

Dino went to bed happy.

Reacher had been glad of the lucky taxi in the supermarket parking lot. Partly for the time it had saved. He had figured the Shevicks would be worried. And partly for the effort it had saved, especially right then, all bruised and battered. But it had done him no favors. It had let him stiffen up. His walk back to town was painful.

His sense of direction told him the best route was the one he already knew. Back past the bar, past the bus depot, and onward to Center Street, where the chain hotels would be clustered, maybe a little ways south, all within a block or two. He knew cities. He walked faster than he wanted to, and paid attention to his posture, head up, shoulders back, arms loose, back straight, finding all the aches and pains, fighting them, chasing them out, yielding nothing.

There was no one in the street outside the bar. No parked car, no insolent muscle. Reacher backed up and looked in the grimy window. Past the dusty harps and shamrocks. The pale guy was still at the table in the far corner. Still luminescent. There was no one with him. No hapless customer, down in the sewer.

Reacher moved on, getting looser, walking better. He came out of the old blocks at the four-way light, and walked on past the bus depot, watching the sky ahead for the glow of neon. For skyline buildings with lit-up names. Which could be banks or insurance companies or local TV. Or hotels. Or all of the above. There were six of them in total. Six towers, standing proud. The downtown cluster. A brave statement.

Most of the glow was to his half left, which was south of west. He decided to cut the corner and head straight there. He made a left and crossed Center Street, into a thoroughfare that in its bones was no better than the street with the bar, but a lot of money had been spent on it, and it was all gussied up. The street lights were working. The brick was clean. No establishments were boarded up. Most of them were offices of one kind or another. Not necessarily commercial ventures. Mostly worthy causes. Municipal services, and so on. A family counsellor. The local HQ of a political party. All were dark, except for one. Across the street, at the far end of the block. It was lit up bright. It had been rebuilt like a traditional old storefront. It had a sign in the window. Printed on the glass, in big letters, in an old-fashioned style, like the Marine Corps typewriters of Reacher's youth. The sign said: The Public Law Project.

There are three of them, Mrs. Shevick had said.

From a public law project.

Three nice young men.

Behind the window was a modern blond-wood workspace, crammed with old-fashioned khaki-and-white paperwork. There were three guys sitting at desks. Young, certainly. Reacher couldn't tell if they were nice. He wasn't prepared to venture an opinion.

They were all dressed the same, in tan chino pants and blue button-down shirts.

Reacher crossed the street. Up close he saw what were presumably their names, printed on the glass of the door. Same typewriter style, but smaller. The names were Julian Harvey Wood, Gino Vettoretto, and Isaac Mehay-Byford. Which Reacher thought was a whole lot of names, for just three guys. They all had a lot of letters after their names. All kinds of doctoral degrees. One from Stanford Law, one from Harvard, one from Yale.

He pulled the door and stepped inside.

Chapter 11

All three guys looked up, surprised. One was dark, one was fair, and one was in the middle. They all looked to be in their late twenties. They all looked tired. Hard work, late nights, pizza and coffee. Like law school all over again.

The dark one said, "Can we help you?"

"Which one are you?" Reacher said. "Julian, Gino, or Isaac?"

"I'm Gino."

"Pleased to meet you, Gino," Reacher said. "Any chance you know an old couple named Shevick?"

"Why?"

"I just spent a little time with them. I became familiar with their troubles. They told me they had three lawyers from a public law project. I'm wondering if that's you. In fact I'm assuming it is. I'm asking myself how many public law projects a city this size could support."

The fair one said, "If they're our clients, then obviously we can't discuss their case."

"Which one are you?"

"I'm Julian."

The neither dark nor fair one said, "And I'm Isaac."

"I'm Reacher. Pleased to meet you all. Are the Shevicks your clients?"

"Yes, they are," Gino said. "So we can't talk about them."

"Make it like a hypothetical example. In a case like theirs, is either one of the no-fault funds likely to pay out within the next seven days?"

Isaac said, "We really shouldn't discuss it."

"Just theoretically," Reacher said. "As an abstract illustration."

"It's complicated," Julian said.

"By what?"

"I mean, theoretically speaking, such a case would start out simple, but then it would get very complicated if family members stepped in to act as guarantors. Such a move would downgrade the urgency. I mean that literally. It would mark it down a grade. The no-fault funds are dealing with tens of thousands of cases. Maybe hundreds of thousands. If they know for sure a patient is currently receiving care anyway, they assign a different code. Like a lower grade. Not exactly bottom of the pile, but more like back burner. While more urgent stuff is handled first."

"So the Shevicks made a mistake by signing the paper."

"We can't discuss the Shevicks," Gino said. "There are confidentiality issues."

"Theoretically," Reacher said. "Hypothetically. Would it be a mistake for hypothetical parents to sign the paper?"

"Of course it would," Isaac said. "Think about it from a bureaucrat's point of view. The patient is getting treatment. The bureaucrat doesn't care how. All he knows is there's no negative PR liability for him. So he can take his sweet time. The hypothetical parents should have stood firm and said no. They should have refused to sign."

"I guess they couldn't bring themselves to do that."

"I agree, it would have been tough, under the circumstances. But it would have worked. The bureaucrat would have been obliged to get his checkbook out. Right there and then. No choice."

"It's an education thing," Gino said. "People need to know their rights ahead of time. It can't be done in the moment. It's your kid, lying on a gurney. There's too much emotion."

Reacher asked, "Is anything going to happen in the next seven days?"

No one answered.

Which Reacher figured was an answer in itself.

Eventually Julian said, "The problem is, now they have time to argue. The government fund is taxpayer money. The legislation is unpopular. Therefore the government will want the insurance fund to pay. The insurance fund is shareholder money. Bonuses depend on it. Therefore the insurance fund will bounce it back to the government, over and over again, as long as it takes."

"For what?"

"For the patient to die," Isaac said. "That's the big prize for the insurance fund. Because then we're into a whole other argument. The surrogate contractual relationship was between the no-fault fund and the deceased. What is there to reimburse? The deceased spent no money. Her care was funded by the generosity of relatives. Which happens all the time. Medical donations between family members are so common the IRS has a whole separate category. But it's not like buying stock in a corporation. You don't benefit from an eventual upside. There's a clue in the name. It's a donation. It's a gift, freely given. It doesn't get reimbursed. Especially not by and to parties who weren't even in the original voided agreement. It's a matter of legal principle. Precedents are unclear. It could go all the way to the Supreme Court."

"So nothing in the next seven days?"

"We'd be happy with the next seven years."

"They're deep into loan sharks."

"The bureaucrat doesn't care how."

"Do you?"

Julian said, "Our clients won't let us anywhere near their financial business."

Reacher nodded.

He said, "They don't want you to burn their boats."

"Their words exactly," Gino said. "They feel busting the loan sharks would leave them with no access to money in the future, should they need it, which experience tells them they probably will."

Reacher asked, "Do they have other legal remedies anywhere?"

"Hypothetically," Julian said. "The obvious strategy would be a civil suit against the delinquent employer. Absolutely couldn't fail. But obviously never pursued in a case like this, because the cause of action itself will have already exposed the defendant as a fraud, thereby ruining him, thereby giving the successful plaintiff no assets to collect against."

"Nothing else they can do?"

"We petition the court on their behalf," Gino said. "But they stop reading where it says she's getting treatment anyway."

"OK," Reacher said. "Let's hope for the best. Someone just told me a week is a long time. Thanks for your help. Much appreciated."

He backed away and pushed the door and stepped out to the street. He stopped on the corner to fine tune his direction. A right and a left, he thought. That should do it.

Behind him he heard the door open again. He heard footsteps on the sidewalk. He turned and saw Isaac walking toward him. The one who was neither dark nor fair. He was five-nine, maybe, and solid as a bull seal. His pants were cuffed.

He said, "I'm Isaac, remember?"

"Isaac Mehay-Byford," Reacher said. "J.D. from Stanford Law. Tough school. Congratulations. But I'm guessing you're from the other coast originally."

"Boston," he said. "My dad was a cop there. You remind me of him, a little bit. He noticed things, too."

"Now you're making me feel old."

"Are you a cop?"

"I was," Reacher said. "Once upon a time. In the army. Does that count?"

"It might," Isaac said. "You could give me some advice."

"About what?"

"How did you come to know the Shevicks?"

"I helped him out of a jam this morning. He hurt his knee. I walked him home. They told me the story."

"His wife calls me now and then. They don't have many friends. I know what they're doing for money. Sooner or later they're going to run out of room."

"I think they already have," Reacher said. "Or they will, in seven days."

"I have a crazy personal theory," Isaac said.

"About what?"

"Or maybe I'm just deluding myself."

"About what?" Reacher asked again.

"The last thing Julian said. About the civil suit, against the employer. No point pursuing it because the assets are worthless. Usually good advice. Good advice in this case, too, I'm sure. Except actually I'm not sure."

"Why not?"

"The guy was famous here for a spell. Everyone was talking about him. Ironically Meg Shevick did a great job with the PR. Lots of tech sector mythology, lots of young entrepreneur stuff, lots of positive immigration spin, about how he came to this country with nothing, and made such a success. But I heard negative things, too. Here and there, fragments, gossip, bits and pieces, all unconnected. All hearsay and uncorroborated, too, but from people who should know. I became weirdly obsessed with figuring out how all those random pieces fit together, behind the public image. There seemed to be three main themes. He was all about himself, he was ethically challenged, and he seemed to have way more money than he should. My crazy personal theory was that if you joined the dots the one and only way they could be joined, then logically you were forced to conclude he was skimming off the top. Which would have been easy for an ethically challenged person. There was a tsunami of cash back then. It was insane. I think it was irresistible. I think he shoveled millions of dollars of investor money under his own personal mattress."

"Which would explain how the company went down so fast," Reacher said. "It had no reserves. They had been stolen. The balance sheet was all messed up."

"The point is that money might still be there," Isaac said. "Or most of it. Or some of it. Still under his mattress. In which case the civil suit would be worth it. Against him personally. Not against the company."

Reacher said nothing.

Isaac said, "The lawyer in me tells me it's a hundred to one. But I would hate to see the Shevicks go down without checking it out. But I don't know how to do it. That's what I need advice about. A real law firm would hire a private investigator. They would locate the guy and dig through his records. Two days later we would know for sure. But the project doesn't have the budget. And we don't get paid enough to chip in ourselves."

"Why would they need to locate the guy? Has he disappeared?"

"We know he's still in town. But he's laying low. I doubt if I could find him by myself. He's very smart, and if I'm right, he's also very rich. Not a good combination. It lengthens the odds."

"What's his name?"

"Maxim Trulenko," Isaac said. "He's Ukrainian."

Chapter 12

Gregory heard the first whispers out of the gourmet quarter an hour after the events there took place. His bookkeeper called to say his nightly report would be delayed because he was still waiting on two particular bagmen who hadn't checked in yet. Gregory asked which two, and the bookkeeper told him the guys who did the five restaurants. At first Gregory thought nothing of it. They were grown-ups.

Then his right-hand man called to say the same two bagmen hadn't been answering their phones for some time, and their car wasn't where it should be, so accordingly word had gone out to the taxi fleet, with a description of the car, which for once had gotten an instant response. Two separate drivers said the exact same thing. Some time ago they had seen a car just like that getting a tow. Rear wheels off the ground, behind a medium-sized tow truck. Three silhouettes in the tow truck's cab. At first Gregory thought nothing of it. Cars broke down.

Then he asked, "But why would that stop them answering their phones?"

In his head he heard Dino's voice. *We have a guy at the car crushing plant. He owes us money, too.* Out loud he said, "He's making it four for two. Not two for two. He must have lost his mind."

His guy said, "The restaurant block is worth less than the moneylending. Perhaps that's the message."

"What is he now, a CPA?"

"He can't afford to look weak."

"Neither can I. Four for two is bullshit. Put the word out. I want two more of his by morning. Make it decorative this time."

Reacher made the right and the left and came up on a sturdy triangle of three high-rise hotels, all national mid-market chains, two of them east of Center Street, and one of them west. He picked one out at random, and spent five whole minutes of his life at its front desk, using his passport as his photo ID, and his ATM card as his preferred method of payment, and then signing his name two times, in two different places, on two different lines, for two different reasons. He had gotten into the Pentagon easier, back in the day.

He took a city map from the lobby and rode up to his room, which was a plain bland space with nothing to commend it, but it had a bed and a bathroom, which were all he needed. He sat on the bed to look at the map. The city was shaped like a pear, gridded out with streets and avenues, pulling upward at the top toward the distant highway. The Ford dealer and the agricultural machinery would be right at the tip, where the stalk would be. The hotels were plumb in the middle of the fat part. The business district. There was an art gallery and a museum. The development with the Shevick house was halfway to the eastern limit. On the map it looked like a tiny squared-up thumbprint.

Where would a very smart and very rich guy choose to lie low?

Nowhere. That was Reacher's conclusion. The city was big, but not big enough. The guy had been famous. He had employed a Senior Vice President for Communications. Everyone was talking about him. Presumably his picture had been in the paper all the time. Could such a person become an instant overnight hermit? Not possible. The guy had to eat, at least. He had to go out and get food, or have it brought to him. Either way people would see him. They would recognize him. They would talk. A week later there would be bus tours to his house.

Unless the guys who brought him food didn't talk.

The population of Ukraine was about forty-five million. Some of them had come to America. No reason to believe they all knew each other. No reason to assume a connection. But a connection was the only way for a person to hide, in a city that size. The only guarantee of success was to be concealed and protected and catered to by a loyal and vigilant force. Like a secret agent in a safe house. Staring longingly out a window, while discreet couriers came and went.

Seven chances before the week is over, he thought.

He folded the map and jammed it in his back pocket. He rode down to the lobby and stepped out to the street. He was hungry. He hadn't eaten since lunch with the Shevicks. A chicken salad sandwich, a bag of potato chips, and a can of soda. Not much, and a long time ago. He turned and walked on Center Street, and within a block and a half he realized that in terms of food service, most places were already closed. It was already too late in the evening.

Which was OK. He didn't want most places.

He walked north on Center, to where in his mind's eye the fat part of the pear began to thin, and then he turned back south and sat on a bus bench and watched the ebb and flow in front of him. It was a slow motion exercise. Mostly the place was empty. There were long quiet gaps between vehicles. Pedestrians came and went, often in groups of four or five, which based on age and appearance were sometimes the last restaurant parties letting out and heading home, and sometimes the first fashionably late arrivals at whichever establishments were newly cool. Which seemed to be split about fifty-fifty east and west of Center, judging by the general drift. Which was actually more than a drift. There was some energy in it. Some attraction.

Also heading in one direction or the other was the occasional loner. A man, every time, some of them looking down at the sidewalk, some of them staring rigidly ahead, as if embarrassed to be seen. All of them anxious to get where they were going.

Reacher got up off the bus bench and followed the

drift to the east. Up ahead he saw a glamorous quartet pass through a door on the right. When he got there he saw a bar dressed up to look like a federal prison. The bartenders were wearing orange jumpsuits. The only staff member not in costume was a big guy on a stool inside the door. He was wearing black pants and a black shirt. He had black hair. Albanian, almost certainly. Reacher knew that part of the world. He had spent time there. The guy looked like a recent transplant. He had a smug look on his face. He had power, and he enjoyed it.

Reacher drifted onward. He followed a furtive but determined man around a corner and saw him go in an unmarked door, just as another man came out, all red in the face and happy. Gambling, Reacher thought. Not prostitution. He knew the difference. He had been an MP thirteen years. He guessed the guy going in thought he was about to win back what he lost yesterday, and the guy coming out had just won enough to pay his debts, with enough left over for a bouquet of flowers and dinner for two. Unless fate would be better served by continuing the winning streak. It was a tough decision. Almost a moral choice. What was a guy to do?

Reacher watched.

The guy opted for flowers and dinner.

Reacher drifted onward.

Albanian collections tended to be made later in the evening, because their scene tended to start later, which meant registers filled later. Their method was completely different than on the other side of Center Street. They didn't go inside. No menacing presence. No dark suits. No black silk ties. They stayed in the car. They had been asked not to upset the various clienteles of the various establishments they serviced. They could be mistaken for cops or agents of some other kind. Bad for business. In no one's interest. Instead a runner would bring out the envelope, hand it through the car window, and duck back inside. Thousands of dollars, for a ride around the block. Nice work if you could get it.

Two blocks east and one block north of the gambling club Reacher had seen was a trio of side-by-side establishments all owned by the same family. First a bar, then an open-all-night convenience store, and in third place a liquor store. Their contributions were collected by a veteran pair, both retired leg-breakers, both much respected. They had a practiced rhythm for driving from door to door. It was about thirty feet from one to the next. One guy drove, and the other guy sat behind him. Their preferred method. The far back window was down two inches. The envelope was passed into a void. No contact. Nothing too close. Then the pedal was blipped, and a sluggish surge through the transmission propelled the car thirty feet, to the next door, where an envelope was passed into a void. And so on, except that night at the third stop outside the liquor store it wasn't an envelope. It was a fat black suppressor on the end of a gun.

Chapter 13

The gun was a Heckler & Koch MP5 submachine gun, and evidently it was set to fire threes, because that was what the guy in the back of the car received, aimed blind but smart, slightly back, stitching low to medium, hoping for legs and arms and maybe his chest. Meanwhile the driver was getting much the same thing from the other side, but mostly to his head, through the shattering glass, from another H&K, dancing in from the opposite sidewalk.

After which the car's doors were wrenched open, almost symmetrically, the guy from the far sidewalk shoving the driver into the empty seat alongside him and taking his place, while the guy from the liquor store crowded in the back. They slammed their doors and the car took off, all its seats filled, its occupants arranged diagonally, two guys feeling pretty good about things, plus one guy dead and one guy dying.

* * *

By that time Reacher was two blocks the other side of Center Street. He had figured out the demarcation line between Albanian and Ukrainian territory. He had found exactly what he was looking for. He was in a bar with small round cabaret tables and a stage in back. On the stage was a guitar-bass-drums trio, and on the tables were late-night small-bite menus. There was an espresso machine on the bar back. There was a guy on a stool inside the door. Black suit, white shirt, black tie, white skin, fair hair. Ukrainian for sure.

All good, Reacher thought. Everything he needed, and nothing he didn't.

He chose a table on the far side of the room, about halfway in, and he sat with his back to the wall. In the left corner of his eye was the guy on the stool, and in the right corner was the band. They were pretty good. They were playing blues covers in a 1950s jazz style. Soft round tones from the guitar, not too loud, woody thumps from the bass, brushes skittering over the snare drum. No vocals. Most of the crowd was drinking wine. Some had pizzas about the size of a teacup saucer. Reacher checked the menu. They were called personal size. Plain or pepperoni. Nine dollars.

A waitress came by. She fit the 1950s music. She was petite and gamine, maybe in her late twenties, neat and slender and dressed all in black, with short dark hair and lively eyes and a shy but contagious smile. She could have been in an old-time black and white movie, with jazz on the soundtrack. Probably someone's sassy little sister. Dangerously advanced. Probably wanted to wear pants to the office.

Reacher liked her.

She said, "May I bring you something?"

Reacher ordered two glasses of tap water, two double espressos, and two pepperoni pizzas.

She asked, "Is someone joining you?"

"I'm worried about malnutrition," he said.

She smiled and left and the band kicked into a mournful rendition of Howlin' Wolf's old song "Killing Floor." The guitar took the vocal line, with a tumble of pearl-like notes explaining how he should have quit her, since his second time, and went on to Mexico. At the door people kept on coming in, always two or more together, never alone. They all paused a second, like Reacher had before, obediently, for the doorman's scrutiny. He looked at them one by one, up and down and in the eye, and he moved them inside with a millimetric jerk of his head, toward the fun beyond his shoulder. They walked past him, and he crossed his arms and slumped back on his stool.

Two songs later the waitress brought his food. She set it all out. He said thank you. She said he was welcome. He said, "Does the guy at the door ever stop anyone coming in?"

"Depends who they are," she said.

"Who does he stop?"

"Cops. Although we haven't seen cops in here for years."

"Why cops?"

"Never a good idea. Whatever happens, if the wind changes, suddenly it's bribery or corruption or entrapment or some other big thing. That's why cops have their own bars."

"Therefore he hasn't stopped anyone coming in for years. Now I'm wondering what he's for, exactly."

"Why are you asking?"

"I'm curious," Reacher said.

"Are you a cop?"

"Next you're going to tell me I look like your dad."

She smiled.

"He's much smaller," she said.

She turned away with a last look, which was not a wink, but it was close. Then she was gone. The band played on. The guy at the door was counting, Reacher figured. He was a cuckoo in the nest. Most likely the protection money was on a percentage basis. The guy counted the crowd so the owners couldn't fudge the numbers. Plus maybe he offered a nominal security presence. To sweeten the deal. So everyone felt better.

The waitress came back before Reacher was finished. She had his check in a black vinyl wallet. She was about to go off duty. He rounded it up and added ten for a tip and paid in cash. She left. He finished his meal but stayed at his table a moment, watching the guy at the door. Then he got up and walked toward him. No other way to leave the restaurant. In the door, out the door.

He stopped level with the stool.

He said, "I have an urgent message for Maxim Trulenko. I need you to figure out a way to get it to him. I'll be here tomorrow, same time."

Then he moved onward, out the door, to the street. Twenty feet away on his right the waitress came out the staff-only door. At the exact same moment. Which he hadn't expected.

She stopped on the sidewalk.

Petite, gamine, going off duty.

She said, "Hi."

He said, "Thanks again for looking after me, and I hope you enjoy the rest of your evening."

He was counting time in his head.

She said, "You too, and thank you for the very nice tip."

She stayed about seven feet away, a little tense, a little up on her toes. All kinds of body language going on.

He said, "I try to think what kind of tip I would like, if I was a waitress."

"That's an image I'll never unsee."

He was counting time in his head because one of two things was about to happen. Either nothing or something. Maybe nothing, because maybe Maxim Trulenko's name meant nothing to them. Or maybe something, because maybe Trulenko's name was top of the list of their VIP clients.

Time would tell.

The waitress asked, "So what are you, if you're not a cop?"

"I'm between jobs right now."

If Trulenko's name was on a list, the likely protocol would be for the guy at the door to call it in or text it in, immediately, and then, either because of an instruction in an immediate response, or because it was part of the protocol anyway, he would come out to detain and delay, any way he could, at least long enough to snap a picture with his phone, hopefully long enough for a roving surveillance team to show up. Or a roving snatch squad. No doubt they had plenty of vehicles. And not a huge patch to patrol. Half of a pear-shaped city.

"I'm sorry about your situation," the waitress said. "I hope you find something soon."

"Thank you," Reacher said.

It would take the guy inside maybe forty seconds to make the call, or to text back and forth, and then get set, and take a breath, and step out the door behind them. In which case he was due right about then.

If it was something.

Maybe it was nothing.

The waitress asked, "What kind of work do you like to do?"

The guy stepped out the door behind them.

Reacher moved to the curb and turned around, to make a shallow triangle, with the waitress now on his left, and the guy on his right, and empty space at his back.

The guy looked at Reacher, but spoke to the waitress.

He said, "Run along now, kid."

Reacher glanced at her.

She mouthed something at him. Could have been, *Watch where I go*. Then she ran along. Not literally. She turned and crossed the street at a brisk walk, and Reacher glanced over his shoulder twice, just briefly, not long between, like frames from a video, the first of which showed her already half a block away, striding north on the far sidewalk, and the second of which showed her gone completely. Through a doorway, therefore. Toward the end of the block.

The guy on his right said, "I would need your name, before I could put you in touch with Max Trulenko. And maybe first we should talk it through, you and me, about how you came to know him, just to put his mind at rest."

"When could we do that?" Reacher asked.

"We could do that right now," the guy said. "Come inside. I'll buy you a cup of coffee."

Detain and delay, Reacher thought. Until the snatch squad showed up. He looked left and right along the street. No headlights. Nothing coming. Not yet.

He said, "Thanks, but I just had dinner. I'm all set. I'll come back tomorrow. About the same time."

The guy took out his phone.

"I could text him your photo," he said. "As a first step. That would be quicker."

"No thanks," Reacher said.

"I need you to tell me how you know Max."

"Everyone knows Max. He was famous here for a spell."

"Tell me the message you have for him."

"His ears only," Reacher said.

The guy didn't answer. Reacher checked the street. Both ends. Nothing coming. Not yet.

The guy said, "We shouldn't get off on the wrong foot. Any friend of Max's is a friend of mine. But if you know Max, obviously you know we have to check you out. You wouldn't want anything less for him."

Reacher checked the street. Now there was something coming. There was a pair of bucking, bouncing headlight beams coming around the southwest corner of the block, faster than the front suspension could comfortably handle. They swept and dipped and settled straight and then rose up high, as the rear end of the car squatted down under heavy acceleration.

Straight at them.

"I'll see you again," Reacher said. "I hope."

He turned and crossed the street and went north, away from the car. And saw a second car coming around the northwest corner of the block. Same bouncing headlight beams. From the other direction. Heavy acceleration. Straight at him. Probably two guys in each car. Decent numbers, and their response time was quick. They were on Defcon One. Therefore Trulenko was important. Therefore their rules of engagement would be pretty much whatever they wanted them to be.

Right then Reacher was the meat in a bright light sandwich.

Watch where I go.

A doorway, toward the end of the block.

He turned around, hunching away from the light, and he saw one doorway after another, looming up out of the jagged moving shadows. Most of the doors belonged to retail operations, with nothing but dusty gray dimness inside, like closed stores everywhere, and some of the doors were plainer and stoutly made of wood, presumably for private quarters above, but none of them were open, not even a tempting inch, and none of them had a rim of light around the frame.

He moved north, because the waitress had been going north, and the shadows gave up more doors, one by one, but they were all the same as before, mute and gray and stubbornly closed.

The cars came closer. Their lights got brighter. Reacher gave up on doorways. He figured he had misheard. Or misread her lips. At that point his brain started cycling through scenarios involving two guys from the south and two from the north, no doubt all four of them armed, although probably not with shotguns, so close to downtown, therefore handguns only, possibly suppressed, depending on their de facto arrangement with the local police department. As in, don't frighten the voters. But against any instinct toward caution would be extreme reluctance to disappoint their bosses.

The cars slowed to a stop.

Reacher was pinned right in the middle.

Rule one, set in stone since he was a tiny kid, back when he first realized he could be either frightened or frightening, was to run toward danger, not away from it. Which right then gave him his pick of forward or backward. He chose forward. North, the way he was already going. No break in his stride. No reversal of momentum. Faster and harder. Glare ahead of him and glare behind him. He kept on going. Instinctive, but also sound tactics. As sound as they could be, under the dismal circumstances. In the sense of making the best of a very bad hand. He was distorting the picture, at least. What the pointy-heads would call altering the battle space. The guys ahead would feel mounting pressure the closer he got. The guys behind would have longer shots. Both conditions would impair efficiency. Ultimately below fifty percent, with a bit of luck. Because the guys behind would worry about friendly fire. Their buddies up ahead were right next to the target.

The guys behind might take themselves out of the fight voluntarily.

Making the best of a very bad hand.

Reacher hustled onward.

He heard car doors open.

On his left, as he hustled, he saw retail store doorways jumping in and out of the headlight shadows, one by one, all of them mean and closed tight. Until one of them wasn't. Because it wasn't a doorway. It was an alley. On his right the traffic curb was unbroken, but on his left there was a gloomy eight-foot gap between buildings, paved the same way as the municipal sidewalk. A pedestrian thoroughfare of some kind. Public. Leading where? He didn't care. It was dark. It was guaranteed to let out somewhere a whole lot better than an empty street lit up bright by four headlight beams from two face to face automobiles.

He ducked into the alley.

He heard footsteps start behind him.

He hustled on. The depth of a building later, the alley widened out to a narrow street. Still dark. The footsteps behind him kept on coming. He stayed close to the buildings, where the shadows were deepest.

A door opened in the darkness ahead.

A hand grabbed his arm and pulled him inside.

Chapter 14

The door closed again softly and three seconds later the footsteps clattered by outside, at a slow and wary jog. Then silence came back. The hand on Reacher's arm pulled him deeper into darkness. Small fingers, but strong. They passed into a different space. A different acoustic. A different smell. A different room. He heard the scrabble of fingertips, searching for a light switch on a wall.

The light came on.

He blinked.

The waitress.

Watch where I go.

An alley, not a doorway. Or an alley leading to a doorway. An alley leading to a doorway with a door left open a tempting inch.

"You live here?" he asked.

"Yes," she said.

She was still dressed for work. Black denim pants,

black button-up shirt. Petite, gamine, short dark hair, eyes full of concern.

"Thank you," Reacher said. "For inviting me in."

"I tried to think what kind of tip I would like," she said. "If I was a stranger the doorman was looking at sideways."

"Was he?"

"You must have stirred something up."

He didn't answer. The room they were in was a cozy space with muted colors, full of worn and comfortable items, some of them maybe from the pawn shop, cleaned and fixed up, and some of them bolted together from the remains of old industrial components. The frame from some kind of an old machine held up the coffee table. Same kind of thing with a bookshelf. And so on. Repurposing, it was called. He had read about it in a magazine. He liked the style. He liked the result. It was a nice room. Then he heard a voice in his head: *Be a shame if anything happened to it.*

"You work for them," he said. "You shouldn't be offering me refuge."

"I don't work for them," she said. "I work for the couple who own the bar. The guy on the door is the cost of doing business. It would be the same wherever I worked."

"He seemed to think he could boss you around."

"They all do. Part of inviting you in is paying them back."

"Thank you," he said again.

"You're welcome."

"I'm Jack Reacher," he said. "I'm very pleased to meet you."

"Abigail Gibson," she said. "People call me Abby."

"People call me Reacher."

She said, "I'm very pleased to meet you, Reacher."

They shook hands, quite formally. Small fingers, but strong.

He said, "I stirred it up on purpose. I wanted to see if and how fast and how hard they would react to something."

"What something?"

"The name Maxim Trulenko. You ever heard of him?"

"Sure," Abby said. "He just went bankrupt. Some kind of dot-com bust. He was famous here for a spell."

"I want to find him."

"Why?"

"He owes people money."

"Are you a debt collector? You told me you were out of work."

"Pro bono," Reacher said. "Temporary. For an old couple I met. So far exploratory only. Just a toe in the water."

"Doesn't matter if he owes people money. He hasn't got any. He's bankrupt."

"There's a theory he hid some private cash under his mattress."

"There's always a theory like that."

"I think in this case it might be right. Purely as a logical proposition. If he was broke, he would have been found by now. But he hasn't been found by now, therefore he can't be broke. Because the only way not to be found by now is to pay the Ukrainians to hide him. Which requires money. Therefore he still has some. If I find him soon, there might be some left."

"For your old couple."

"Hopefully enough to cover their needs."

"The only way not to be found is not to be broke," she said. "Sounds like something out of a fortune cookie. But I guess they proved it was true tonight."

Reacher nodded.

"Two cars," he said. "Four guys. He's getting good value."

"You shouldn't mess with these people," Abby said. "I've seen them up close."

"You're messing with them. You opened your door."

"That's different. They'll never know. There are a hundred doors."

He said, "Why did you open your door?"

"You know why," she said.

"Maybe they just wanted a cozy chat."

"I don't think so."

"Maybe all I would have gotten was a stern talking to."

She didn't answer.

"You knew they wanted worse than that," he said. "That's why you opened your door."

"I've seen them up close," she said again.

"What would they have done?"

"They don't like people getting in their business,"

she said. "I think they would have messed you up bad."

"Have you seen that kind of thing happen before?"

She didn't answer.

"Anyway," Reacher said. "Thanks again."

"You need anything?"

"I should get going. You've done enough for me already. I have a hotel room."

"Where?"

He told her. She shook her head.

"That's west of Center," she said. "They have eyes in there. The texts will have already gone out, with your description."

"They seem to be taking it very seriously."

"I told you," she said. "They don't like people in their business."

"How many of them are there?"

"Enough," she said. "I was going to make coffee. You want some?"

"Sure," Reacher said.

She led the way to her kitchen, which was small and mismatched but clean and tidy. It felt like home. She knocked old grounds out of a filter basket, and rinsed a pot, and set the whole thing going. It burped and slurped and filled the room with a rich aroma.

"I guess it doesn't keep you awake," Reacher said.

"This is my evening time," she said. "I go to bed when the sun comes up. Then I sleep all day."

"Makes sense."

She opened a wall cupboard and took down two white china mugs.

"I'm going to take a shower," she said. "Help yourself if it's ready before I am."

A minute later he heard running water, and after that the gentle whine of a hairdryer. The coffee machine tinkled and sputtered. Abby got back just as it finished. She looked pink and damp and she smelled of soap. She was wearing a knee-length dress that looked like a man's button-down shirt, but longer and slimmer. Probably not a whole lot underneath it. Certainly her feet were bare. After-work attire. A cozy evening at home. They poured their coffee and took their mugs back to the living room.

"You didn't answer my question," she said. "I guess you didn't get a chance."

"What question?" he said

"What kind of work do you like to do?"

In response he gave her his capsule bio. Easy to understand at first, then harder later. Son of a Marine, childhood in fifty different places, then West Point, then the military police in a hundred different places, then the reductions in force when the Cold War ended, leading directly to his sudden head-first introduction to civilian life. A straightforward story. Followed by the wandering, which was not so straightforward. No job, no home, always restless. Always moving. Just the clothes on his back. No particular place to go, and all the time in the world to get there. Some people found it hard to understand. But Abby seemed to get it. She asked none of the usual dumb questions.

Her own story was shorter, because she was younger. Born in a suburb in Michigan, raised in a suburb in California, loved books and philosophy and theater and music and dance and experiment and performance art. Came to town as an undergraduate student, and never left. A temporary gig waiting tables for a month turned into ten years. She was thirty-two. Older than she looked. She said she was happy.

They went back and forth to the kitchen for refills of coffee and ended up facing each other at opposite ends of the sofa, Reacher sprawling comfortably, Abby sitting cross-legged, with the tails of her shirt dress tucked down demurely between her bare knees. Reacher didn't know much about philosophy or theater or dance or experiment or performance art, but he read books when he could, and he heard music when he could, so he was able to keep up. A couple of times they found they had read the same stuff. Same with music. She called it her retro phase. He said it felt like yesterday. They laughed about it.

It got to two o'clock in the morning. He figured he could get a room at an Albanian hotel. One block further east. Just as good. He could afford to waste what he had already laid out. He was more annoyed about the five minutes of his life. At the desk. He would never get that back.

Abby said, "You can stay here, if you like."

He was pretty certain there was one more button undone than before, on the front of her shirt dress. He felt he could trust his judgment on the matter. He was an observant man. He had previously inspected the original gap many times. It had been very appealing. But the new gap was better.

He said, "I didn't see a guest room."

She said, "I don't have one."

"Would this be a lifestyle experiment?"

"As opposed to what?"

"Normal reasons."

"I guess a mixture."

"Works for me," Reacher said.

Chapter 15

Dino's two guys were simply missing all night. From the liquor store onward, not a trace. Their phones were dead. No one had seen their car. They had disappeared into thin air. Which of course was impossible. But still, no one woke Dino. A small-scale search was mounted instead. All the likely neighborhoods. No results. The two guys stayed missing. Until seven o'clock in the morning, right there on their own property, when a guy stacking lumber with a forklift in a side yard backed up and found them, behind the last of the ten-by-two cedar.

Then they woke Dino.

The side yard was separated from direct contractor access by a wire fence eight feet high. The two guys had been hung upside down from the top of the fence. They had been slit open. Gravity had tumbled their guts out, on their chests, on their faces, on the ground beneath them. After death, happily. They both had crusted gunshot wounds. One had his head mostly gone.

No sign of their car. No tracks, no nothing.

Dino called a meeting in the back office boardroom. Just fifty yards from the gruesome discovery. Like a battlefield general, on hand to examine the terrain up close.

He said, "Gregory must be out of his mind. We were the original victims here, we got the short end of every stick, and now he wants to rub it in by making it four for two as well? That's bullshit. How lopsided does he want it to get? What the hell is he thinking?"

"But why so nasty?" his right-hand man said. "Why all the drama with their intestines hanging out? Surely that's the key to this thing."

"Is it?"

"Got to be. It was already gratuitous. This was unnecessary. Like they were mad at us. Like revenge for something. As if we had gotten the better of them somehow."

"Well, we didn't."

"Maybe there's something we don't know. Maybe we actually did get the better of them somehow, but we haven't caught on to it yet."

"Caught on to what?"

"We don't know yet. That's the point."

"All we got is the restaurant block."

"So maybe it's special in some way. Maybe it's a good producer. Maybe we get better access to people. All the bigwigs must eat there. With their wives and so on. Where else would they go?"

Dino didn't answer.

His guy said, "Why else would they get so angry?"

Still Dino didn't answer.

Then he said, "Maybe you're right. Maybe the restaurant block is worth more than the moneylending. I sincerely hope so. We got lucky, they got resentful. But whatever, four for two is bullshit. We can't live with that. Put the word out. Level the score by sunset."

Reacher woke at eight in the morning, warm, relaxed, peaceful, partially entwined with Abby, who slept on undisturbed. She was tiny beside him. She was more than a foot shorter, and less than half his weight. In repose she was soft and boneless. In motion she had been hard and lithe and strong. And certainly experimental. Her performance had been an art. That was for damn sure. He was a lucky man. He breathed deep and gazed up at the unfamiliar ceiling. It had cracks in the plaster, like a river system, painted over many times, like healed scars.

He disentangled himself gently and slid out of bed and padded naked to the bathroom, and then to the kitchen, where he set the coffee going. He went back to the bathroom and took a shower, and then he collected his clothes from all over the living room, and he got dressed. He took a third white china mug from the wall cabinet, and poured his first cup of the day. He sat at a tiny table in the window. The sky was blue and the sun was up. It was a beautiful morning. Faint sounds came in. Traffic and voices. People hustling and bustling, going to work, starting their day.

He got up and got a refill and sat back down again. A minute later Abby came in, naked, yawning, stretching, smiling. She took coffee and padded across the kitchen and sat in his lap. Naked, soft, warm and fragrant. What was a guy to do? A minute later they were back in bed. Even better than the first time. Experimental all around. Twenty whole minutes, soup to nuts. Afterward they fell back, gasping and panting. He thought, not bad for an old guy. She snuggled against his chest, spent, breathing hard. He sensed the physical release in her. Some kind of bone-deep animal satisfaction. But something else also. Something more. She felt safe. She felt safe, and warm, and protected. She was luxuriating in it. She was celebrating the fact she was feeling it.

"Last night," he said. "In the bar. When I asked you about the guy on the door, you asked me if I was a cop."

"You are a cop," she murmured.

"Was a cop," he said.

"Close enough for a first impression. I'm sure it's a look you never lose."

"Did you want me to be a cop? Were you hoping I was?"

"Why would I be?"

"Because of the guy on the door. Maybe you thought I could do something about him."

"No," she said. "Hoping would have been a waste of time. The cops don't do anything about those guys. Never. Too much hassle. Too much money changing hands. Those guys are pretty much safe from the cops, believe me."

Old disappointments in her voice.

As an experiment he asked, "Would you have liked it if I could have done something about him?"

She snuggled tighter. Unconsciously, he thought. Which he figured had to mean something.

She said, "That particular guy?"

"He was the one in front of me."

She paused a beat.

"Yes," she said. "I would have liked it."

"What would you have liked me to do to him?"

He felt her stiffen against him.

She said, "I guess I would have liked you to mess him up."

"Bad?"

"Real bad."

"What have you got against him?"

She wouldn't answer.

After a minute he said, "There was something else you mentioned last night. You said texts would have gone out, with my description."

"As soon as they realized they lost you."

"To hotels and such."

"To everybody. That's how they do it now. They have automated systems. They're very good at technology. They're very advanced with computers. They're always trying new scams. Sending out an automatic all-points bulletin is easy in comparison."

"And literally everyone gets the same alert?"

"Who are you thinking of in particular?"

"Potentially, a guy in a different division. In the moneylending section."

"Would that be a problem?"

"He has a photograph of me. A close-up of my face. He'll recognize the description, and he'll text the picture in response."

She snuggled closer. Relaxed again.

"Doesn't really matter," she said. "They're all out looking for you anyway. Your description is more than enough. A photograph of your face doesn't add much. Not from a distance."

"That's not the problem."

"What is?"

"The moneylending guy thinks my name is Aaron Shevick."

"Why?"

"The Shevicks are my old couple. I did some business on their behalf. It seemed like a good idea at the time. But now the wrong name is out there. They could dig for an address. I wouldn't want them showing up at the Shevick house, looking for me. That could lead to all kinds of unpleasantness. The Shevicks have enough on their plates already."

"Where do they live?"

"Halfway to the eastern city limit, in an old postwar development."

"That's Albanian territory. It would be a very big deal for the Ukrainians to go there."

"They already took over their moneylending bar," Reacher said. "That was way east of Center. The battle lines seem relatively fluid right now."

Abby nodded sleepily against his chest.

"I know," she said. "They all agree they can't have

a war, because of the new police commissioner, but all kinds of things seem to be happening."

Then she took a deep breath and held it and sat up and shook herself awake and said, "We should go now."

"Where?" Reacher asked.

"We should go make sure your old couple is OK."

Abby had a car. It was parked in a garage a block away. It was a small white Toyota sedan, with a stick shift and no hubcaps. Plus electrical ties holding on one of the fenders. Plus a crack in the windshield that made the view out front look like two overlapping halves. But the engine started and the wheels steered and the brakes worked. The glass in the windows was plain, not tinted, and Reacher felt his face was close to it, clearly visible to those outside, crammed as he was in a cramped interior. He watched for Town Cars, like he had crashed at the Ford dealer, and seen the night before, coming at him north and south on the street, but he saw none at all, and no pale men in dark suits either, loitering on corners, watching.

They drove the same way he had walked, past the bus depot, through the light, into the narrower streets, past the bar, and out again to the wider spaces. The gas station with the deli counter was up ahead.

"Pull in there," Reacher said. "We should take them some food."

"Are they OK with that?"

"Does it matter? They got to eat."

She pulled in. The menu was the same. Chicken

salad or tuna salad. He got two of each, plus chips, plus soda. Plus a can of coffee. Quitting eating was one thing. Coffee was a whole different thing entirely.

They drove into the development and worked their way around the tight right-angle turns to the cul-de-sac near its center. They parked by the picket fence, with its nudging rosebuds.

"This is it?" Abby said.

"Owned by the bank now," Reacher said.

"Because of Max Trulenko?"

"And some well meaning mistakes."

"Will they be able to get it back from the bank?"

"I don't know much about that kind of stuff. But I don't see why not. It's all money and assets moving back and forth. Buying and selling. I don't see why a bank would want to get in the way of a thing like that. I'm sure somehow it could find a way to turn a profit on the deal."

They walked up the narrow concrete path. The door opened before they got to it. Aaron Shevick stood there. He had a worried look on his face.

"Maria has disappeared," he said. "I can't find her anywhere."

Chapter 16

Aaron Shevick might have been a hotshot machinist in the distant past, but he was no kind of a useful witness in the present day. He said he had heard no traffic outside. He had seen no cars on the street. They had gotten up at seven o'clock in the morning and had eaten a small breakfast at eight. Then he had walked to the convenience store to buy a quart of milk, for future small breakfasts. When he got home Maria was nowhere to be seen.

"How long were you gone?" Reacher asked.

"Twenty minutes," Shevick said. "Maybe more. I'm still walking slow."

"And you looked all through the house?"

"I thought maybe she had fallen. But she hadn't. Not in the yard, either. So she went out somewhere. Or someone took her."

"Let's start with she went out somewhere. Did she take her coat?"

"She didn't need her coat," Abby said. "It's warm enough without. A better question would be, did she take her purse?"

Shevick looked in what he called all the usual places. There were four of them. A particular spot on the kitchen countertop, a particular spot on an entryway bench in the hallway area opposite the front door, a particular peg in the coat closet where they also hung their umbrellas, and lastly, a spot on the living room floor next to her armchair.

No purse.

"OK," Reacher said. "That's a good sign. Very persuasive. It means most likely she went out voluntarily, under her own steam, in an orderly fashion, not in any kind of panic, and not under any kind of duress."

Shevick said, "She might have left her purse somewhere else." He glanced all around, helpless. It was a small house, but even so it hid a hundred hiding places.

"Let's look on the bright side," Reacher said. "She picked up her purse, she hooked it on her elbow, and she walked away down the path."

"Or they threw her in a car. Maybe they forced her to bring her purse. Maybe they knew how it would look to us. They're trying to throw us off the trail."

"I think she went to the pawn shop," Reacher said.

Shevick was quiet a long moment. Then he raised a finger in a be-right-back kind of a way, and he limped down the corridor to the bedroom. A minute later he limped back carrying an ancient shoebox. It had faded pastel pink and white candystripes on it, and a faded black and white label pasted to the short end, with a manufacturer's name, and a line drawing of a shoe, which was a proudly chunky woman's lace-up, and a size, which was four, and a price, which was a penny shy of four bucks. Maybe the shoes Maria Shevick was married in.

"The family jewelry," Shevick said.

He lifted the lid. The box was empty. No nine-carat wedding bands, no diamond engagement rings, no gold-plated watch with a crack in the crystal.

"We should go pick her up," Abby said. "It will be a sad walk home otherwise."

Organized crime's traditional staples were usury, narcotics, prostitution, gambling, and protection rackets. Throughout their half of the city the Ukrainians ran them all with great skill and aplomb. Narcotics were doing better than ever. Weed had largely gone away, because of creeping legalization all over the place, but exploding demand for meth and oxy more than made up the difference. Profit was sky high. Pushed even higher by a percentage royalty on all the Mexican heroin sold in the city itself, from the western limit to Center Street. Every single gram. Gregory's greatest success. He had negotiated the deal himself. The Mexican gangs were notorious barbarians, and it took a lot to impress them. But Gregory had persisted. Two of their street corner guys upside down with their guts out had finally done the trick. Before death, unhappily. At that point the Mexicans had started to fear for future recruitment. Street corner guys didn't make much. Enough to risk getting shot, maybe, but not enough to risk getting hung up-side down and slit wide open from throat to groin. While still alive. Hence the royalty. It kept everyone happy.

Prostitution was doing fine, too, mostly because of what Gregory thought of as a built-in advantage. Ukrainian girls were very beautiful. Many of them were tall and slender and very blonde. None of them had any chance of advancement at home. In the old country they had nothing ahead of them except a life-time of mud and drudgery. No fine clothes, no high-rise apartments, no Mercedes-Benzes. They knew that. So they were happy to come to America. They understood the paperwork was complicated and the process expensive. They knew they would have to re-imburse their helpers, for the upfront outlay, just as quickly as they could. And definitely before they moved on, to whatever it was that came next, which would hopefully involve fine clothes and high-rise apartments and Mercedes-Benzes. They were told all of that was coming soon. But first there would be a brief period of employment. Only afterward would they get access to all those glittering opportunities. But not to worry. There was a system already in place. It was well organized. It was pleasant work, and very social. Mostly just mixing with people. Like public relations. They would enjoy it. They might even get a jump on meeting the right kind of guy.

They were graded on arrival. Not that any of them was ugly. Gregory had a wide choice. There were al-ways a hundred thousand ready to jump on a plane. They were all fresh and flawless and fragrant. Surprisingly the most valued were not the youngest. Not at the top end of the market. Certainly there were plenty of guys willing to pay to get blown by kids younger than their granddaughters, but experience showed the guys with the really big bucks found that kind of extreme a little creepy. Experience showed such a guy preferred a slightly older woman, maybe even twenty-seven or twenty-eight, with a faint air of sophistication and worldliness about her, with a hint of approaching maturity, maybe a smile line or two, so he wouldn't feel like a molester. So he would feel like he had a junior colleague in his room, maybe a rising executive, seeking advice or a raise or a promotion, any or all of which she might get, if she played her cards right.

Such a woman usually stayed about five years in that role. Somehow she never made it to the fine clothes and the high-rise apartments and the Mercedes-Benzes. Somehow she never quite paid off her debt. No one had thought about interest rates. Sometimes such a woman would do another five years, if she was wearing well, on the mature page of the website, and if she wasn't wearing well, then her price would be dropped a couple hundred bucks an hour, and she would soldier on as well as she could, for as long as she could. After that, she would be taken off the website altogether, and sent to one of their many backstreet massage parlors, where the shortest appointment was twenty minutes, and where she would be dressed in an abbreviated version of a nurse's uniform, and rubber gloves, and put to work sixteen hours a day.

Each such parlor was managed by a parlor boss, who was assisted by a deputy parlor boss. Like the women who worked under them, they were generally not the pick of the litter. But on the plus side their job was very straightforward. They had only three tasks. They had to deliver a set number of dollars every week. They had to maintain enthusiasm among their staff. They had to maintain order among their customers. That was it. Such a specification attracted a particular type of candidate. Nasty enough to get the dollars, tough enough to subdue the customers, bent enough to enjoy the staff.

At one particular parlor two blocks west of Center their names were Bohdan and Artem. Bohdan was the boss. Artem was the deputy. So far their day was going well. They had gotten a text about a guy to be on the lookout for. With a brief verbal description, mostly about his size and weight, both of which seemed impressive. They had scrutinized their stream of customers. No such guy. But plenty of other guys. So far all well behaved. All satisfied. No issues with staff, either, beyond a small thing in the morning, when one of the older ones was late, and then not sufficiently apologetic about it. She was offered a choice of forfeits. She chose the leather paddle, as soon as she came off duty. Bohdan would administer the punishment, and Artem would video it. It would be on their porn sites an hour later. It might have earned a few bucks by the morning. A win-win. All good. So far their day was going well.

Then two customers came in who looked different. Darkish hair, darkish skin, sunglasses. Short dark raincoats. Black jeans. Almost like a uniform. Which happened. Mostly because of the university. There were all kinds of folks in town. Mostly they dressed like where they came from. Hence these two. Maybe they were scholars, visiting from overseas. Maybe they were sampling the illicit charms of their host nation, purely for research. Purely to achieve a better mutual understanding.

Or not.

They pulled matching guns out from under their matching coats. Two H&K MP5 submachine guns, with integral suppressors. By coincidence the same brand and the same model the Ukrainians themselves had used the night before, outside the liquor store. Small world. The two guys gestured Bohdan and Artem to stand together, side by side, shoulder to shoulder. They each fired a round into the floor, to show their guns were silenced. Two spitting bangs. Loud, but not enough to bring someone running.

They said in bad Ukrainian, with heavy Albanian accents, that they were offering a choice. There was a car outside, and Bohdan and Artem could go get in it, or they could get gut shot right there, right then, with the guns just proved quiet enough to bring no one running. They could bleed to death on the floor, twenty minutes of agony, and then they could get dragged out by the heels, and put in the car anyway.

Their choice.

Bohdan didn't answer. Not right away. Neither did Artem. They were genuinely uncertain. They had heard about Albanian torments. Maybe getting gut shot was better. They said nothing. The building was silent. Not a sound. The massage cubicles were all in a line, on a long corridor, the other side of a closed inner door. The front of house area could have been a lawyer's waiting room. Some kind of under the table compromise with the city. Out of sight, out of mind. Don't frighten the voters. Gregory had done the deal.

Then the silence was broken. There was a sound. The faint click of heels in the inner corridor. *Tap, tap, tap.* Five-inch spikes, like they all had to wear. Clear plastic, sometimes. Stripper shoes. The Americans had a word for everything. *Tap, tap, tap.* One of them was moving, maybe from the restroom back to her cubicle. Or from one cubicle to another. From one client to the next. Some girls were popular. Some got requests.

The heels kept on coming. *Tap, tap, tap.* Maybe she was headed for a cubicle all the way up front.

Tap, tap, tap.

The inner door opened. A woman stepped through. Bohdan saw it was one of the older ones. In fact the one due to get the paddle when she came off duty. Like all of them she was half-wearing a half-size shiny white latex version of a nurse's uniform, complete with a little white cap pinned up top. The hem of her skirt rode six inches higher than the tops of her stockings. She raised her hand, one finger vaguely ahead of the others, like people do, simultaneously as an apology for an interruption and the introduction of a question.

She never got there. Whatever mundane issue was on her mind remained unexpressed. More towels, more lotion, new rubber gloves. Whatever it was. The door swinging open was in the left corner of the left-hand guy's eye, and he fired instantly, a neat quiet stitch of three into her center mass. No reason for it. Some kind of hyper state. Some kind of fever pitch. A twitch of the muzzle, a twitch of the trigger finger. There was no echo. Just a long, ragged, plastic, fleshy thump as the woman went down.

Bohdan said, "Jesus Christ."

It changed the argument. Getting gut shot was no longer a theory. Visual aids had been introduced. Ancient human instinct took over. Stay alive a minute longer. See what happens next. They got in the car voluntarily. By chance they crossed Center Street and entered Albanian territory at the exact same moment the woman in the nurse costume died. She was alone on the floor of the parlor, half in and half out of the back corridor. All the clients had fled. They had jumped over her and run. Likewise her co-workers. They had all done the same thing. They were all gone. She died alone, in pain, uncomforted and unconsoled. Her name was Anna Ulyana Dorozhkin. She was forty-one years old. She had first come to the city fifteen years earlier, at the age of twenty-six, all excited about a career in PR.

Chapter 17

Aaron Shevick didn't know exactly where the city's pawn shops were. Reacher's guess was they would be somewhere on the same radius as the bus depot. At a discreet distance from the fancy neighborhoods. He knew cities. There would be low-rent enterprises packed tight throughout the outlying blocks. There would be window tinting and laundromats and dusty old mom-and-pop hardware stores and off-brand auto parts. And pawn shops. The problem was planning a route. They wanted to be able to pick Mrs. Shevick up if she had already done her business and was already walking home. Not knowing her destination made that difficult. In response they drove wide loops, finding a pawn shop, checking inside through the window, not seeing her, setting out home until they were sure she couldn't still be ahead of them, and then driving back and starting over with the next place they saw.

In the end they found her all the way west of Center, stepping out of a grimy pawn shop across a narrow street from a taxi dispatcher and a bail bond office. Mrs. Shevick, right there, large as life, head up, her purse hooked on her elbow. Abby pulled over next to her and Aaron wound down his window and called out to her. She was very surprised to see him, but she got over it fast. She got right in the car. Less than ten seconds, beginning to end. Like it had been arranged in advance.

She was embarrassed at first, in front of Abby. A stranger. *You must think us very foolish.* Aaron asked her how much she had gotten for the rings and the watch, and she just shook her head and wouldn't answer.

Then eventually she said, "Eighty dollars."

No one spoke. They drove back east, past the depot, through the four-way light.

At that moment, in his office, Gregory was getting the news about his massage parlor. By chance another of his guys had been passing by on unrelated business. He had sensed something wrong. Too quiet. He had gone inside. The place was completely deserted. Nothing but an old hooker, shot dead on the floor, in a big pool of blood. No one else. No clients. Apparently all the other hookers had run away. There was no trace of Bohdan or Artem. Artem's phone was lying on his desk, and Bohdan's jacket was still on the back of his chair. Not good signs. They meant they had not left the premises voluntarily. They meant they had left under some kind of duress.

Gregory called his top boys together. He told them the facts. Then he told them to think hard for sixty seconds, and come up with first an analysis of what the hell was going on, and second what the hell to do about it.

His right-hand man spoke first.

"This is Dino's doing," he said. "I think we all know that. He's a man on a mission. We took two of his guys, with the trick about the spy in the police station, so he took two of ours, up at the Ford dealer. Which was fair. Can't dispute it. What goes around comes around. Except evidently he didn't like losing the loan business, so he decided to punish us by taking two more of our guys, on the restaurant block. So we took two more of his, outside the liquor store last night. Which was then four for four. A fair exchange. End of story. Except apparently Dino doesn't agree. Apparently he feels he has a point to make. Perhaps an ego thing. He wants to be two guys ahead at all times. Perhaps it makes him feel better. So now he's made it six for four."

"What should we do about it?" Gregory asked.

His guy was quiet for a very long time.

Then he said, "We didn't get where we are by being stupid. If we make it six for six, he'll make it eight for six. And so on, forever. It will be a slow-motion war. We can't get into a war right now."

"So what should we do?"

"We should suck it up. We're down two guys and

the restaurant block, but we got the loan business instead. Overall we came out ahead."

Gregory said, "Makes us look weak."

"No," his guy said. "It makes us look like the grown-ups, playing the long game, with our eyes on the prize."

"We're down two men. It's humiliating."

"If a week ago Dino had offered to trade all of his loan business for two of our men and the restaurant block, we would have bitten his hand off. We came out way ahead. Dino is humiliated, not us."

"It feels weird, just to leave it."

"No," his guy said again. "It feels smart. We're playing chess here. And right now we're winning."

"What will they do to our guys?"

"Nothing pleasant, I'm sure."

No one spoke for a minute.

Then Gregory said, "We need to find the hookers. Can't let them run away. Bad for discipline."

"We're on it," someone said.

Silence again.

Then Gregory's phone rang. He answered and listened and hung up.

He looked straight at his right-hand man.

He smiled.

"Maybe you're right," he said. "Maybe having the loan business puts us ahead."

"How so?" his guy asked.

"Now we have a name," Gregory said. "And a photograph. The guy who asked about Max Trulenko last night is called Aaron Shevick. He's a customer. Currently he owes us twenty-five thousand dollars. We're working on getting his address. Apparently he's a big ugly son of a bitch."

Abby parked on the curb next to the picket fence, and they all got out and walked up the narrow concrete path. Maria Shevick took her keys from the purse on her elbow and unlocked the door. They went inside. Maria saw the can of coffee on the kitchen counter.

"Thank you," she said.

"Pure self-interest," Reacher said back.

"You want some?"

"I thought you'd never ask."

Maria opened the can and set the machine going. She joined Abby in the living room. Abby was looking at the photographs on the wall.

She asked, quietly, gently, "What's the latest news on Meg?"

"It's a brutal treatment," Maria said. "She's in a special isolation unit, either out of her mind on pain-killers, or fast asleep, because they sedate her. We can't visit. We can't even talk on the phone."

"That's awful."

"But the doctors are optimistic," Maria said. "So far, anyway. We'll know more soon. They'll do another scan before long."

"If we pay for it first," her husband said.

Six chances before the week is over, Reacher thought.

He said, "We think Meg's old boss is still in town. We think he still has money. Your lawyers reckon the best strategy is to sue him direct. Absolutely can't fail, they said."

"Where is he?" Shevick asked.

"We don't know yet."

"Can you find him?"

"Probably," Reacher said. "That kind of thing used to be part of my job."

"The law moves slow," Maria said, like she had once before.

They ate the lunch from the gas station deli. In the living room, because the kitchen had only three chairs. Abby sat cross-legged on the floor where the TV used to be, and ate off her lap. Maria Shevick asked her what she did for a living. Abby told her. Aaron talked about the good old days before computer controlled machine tools. When everything was cut by eye and feel, to a thousandth of an inch. They could make anything. American workers. Once the greatest natural resource in the world. Now look what happened. A crying shame.

Reacher heard a car in the street. The soft hiss and squelch of a big sedan. He got up and stepped into the hallway and looked out the window. A black Lincoln Town Car. Two guys in it. Pale faces, fair hair, white necks. They were trying to turn the car around. Back and forth, back and forth, across the narrow width. They wanted to be facing in the right direction. For a fast getaway, perhaps. Abby's Toyota didn't help. It was in the way.

Reacher went back to the living room.

He said, "They figured out Aaron Shevick's address."

Abby stood up.

Maria said, "They're here?"

"Because someone sent them," Reacher said. "That's the thing we have to remember. We've got about thirty seconds to figure this out. Whoever sent them knows where they are. If anything happens to them, this house becomes ground zero for retribution. We should try to avoid that if possible. If we were somewhere else, no problem. But not here."

Shevick said, "So what do we do?"

"Get rid of them."

"Me?"

"Any of you. Just not me. I'm the one they think is Aaron Shevick."

There was a knock at the door.

Chapter 18

There was a second knock at the door. No one moved. Then Abby took a step, but Maria put a hand on her arm, and Aaron went instead. Reacher ducked into the kitchen, and sat there, listening. He heard the door open, and then a missed beat from the step, just silence, as if the two guys were momentarily set back by the fact that the man who had opened the door was not the man they were looking for.

One of them said, "We need to speak with Mr. Aaron Shevick."

Mr. Aaron Shevick said, "Who?"

"Aaron Shevick."

"I think he was the last tenant."

"You rent here?"

"I'm retired. Too expensive to buy."

"Who's your landlord?"

"A bank."

"What's your name?"

"I'm not sure I want to tell you that, until you state your business."

"Our business is private, with Mr. Shevick alone. It's a very sensitive matter."

"Wait a minute," Shevick said. "Are you from the government?"

No answer.

"Or the insurance fund?"

One of the two guys said, "What's your name, old man?"

Menace in his voice.

Shevick said, "Jack Reacher."

"How do we know you're not Aaron Shevick's dad?"

"We would have the same name."

"Father-in-law, then. How do we know he's not in the house right now? Maybe you took over the lease and he squats in a room. We know he's not exactly swimming in cash right now."

Shevick said nothing.

The same voice said, "We're coming in to take a look."

There was the sound of Shevick getting shoved aside, and then footsteps in the hallway. Reacher stood up and moved behind the kitchen door. He opened a drawer, and another, and another, until he found a cooking knife. Better than nothing. He heard Abby and Maria move out of the living room and into the hallway.

The footsteps kept on coming.

He heard Abby say, "Who are you?"

"We're looking for Mr. Aaron Shevick," one of the guys said.

"Who?"

"What's your name?"

"Abigail," Abby said.

"Abigail what?"

"Reacher," she said. "These are my grandparents, Jack and Joanna."

"Where's Shevick?"

"He was the last tenant. He moved out."

"Where did he go?"

"He didn't leave a forwarding address. He gave the impression he was having serious financial problems. I think basically he skipped in the night. He ran away."

"You sure?"

"I know who lives here, mister. This is a two-bedroom house. One for my grandparents, and one for me, when I'm here. For guests, when I'm not. There are no squatters. I think I would have noticed."

"Did you ever meet him?"

"Who?"

"Mr. Aaron Shevick."

"No."

"I met him," Maria Shevick said. "When we first saw the house."

"What did he look like?"

"I remember him as being tall and powerfully built."

"That's the guy," the voice said. "How long has he been gone?"

"About a year."

No response. The footsteps moved on, to the living room door. The voice said, "You've been here a year and you don't have a TV yet?"

"We're retired," Maria said. "These things are expensive."

The voice said, "Huh."

Reacher heard a quiet, scratchy click. Then the footsteps retreated. Back down the hallway. To the front door. To the front step. To the narrow concrete path. Reacher heard the car start up, and then he heard it drive away. The soft hiss and squelch of a big sedan.

Silence came back.

He put the knife in its place in the drawer, and he stepped out of the kitchen.

"Nice work, everyone," he said.

Aaron looked shaky. Maria looked pale.

"They took a photograph," Abby said. "Like a parting shot."

Reacher nodded. The quiet, scratchy click. A cell phone, imitating a camera.

"A photograph of what?" he said.

"The three of us. Partly for their report. Partly for their just-in-case database. But mostly to intimidate. It's what they do. People feel vulnerable."

Reacher nodded again. He remembered the luminous guy in the bar. Raising his phone. The little *snitch* of a sound. *If I was a real client, I wouldn't have liked it.*

The Shevicks stepped into the kitchen, to make more coffee. Reacher and Abby went to the living room, to wait for it.

Abby said, "Intimidation is not the only issue with that photograph."

"What else?" Reacher said.

"They'll text the picture. Among themselves. That's what they do. In case someone can fill in another part of the puzzle. Sooner or later everyone will get the text. The guy on the door at work will get it. He knows I'm not Abigail Reacher. He knows I'm Abby Gibson. So do a lot of other guys on a lot of other doors, because I've worked a lot of other places. They'll start asking questions. They already don't like me."

"Do they know where you live?"

"I'm sure they could make my boss tell them."

"When will they send the text?"

"I'm sure they already have."

"Is there someplace else you could stay?"

She nodded.

"I have a friend," she said. "East of Center Street. Albanian territory, happily."

"Can you work there?"

"I have before."

Reacher said, "I sincerely apologize for the disruption."

"I'm thinking of it as an experiment," she said. "Someone once told me that every day a woman should do something that scared her."

"She could join the army."

"You need to be based east of Center anyway. We can stick together. At least tonight."

"Will that be OK with your friend?"

"I hope so," she said. "Will the Shevicks be OK tonight?"

Reacher nodded.

"People believe their own eyes," he said. "In this case their own eyes were the luminous guy's in the bar. He met me. His phone took my picture. I am Aaron Shevick. It's set in stone. In their minds Shevick is a big tall guy from a younger generation. You could tell by the things they said. They accused him of being Shevick's dad, or his father-in-law, but they never accused him of being Shevick himself. So they'll be OK. As far as those guys are concerned, they're just an old couple named Reacher."

Then Maria called through to say the coffee was ready.

The manager of the grimy pawn shop across the narrow street from the taxi dispatcher and the bail bond office came out the door and dodged a truck and ducked into the taxi place. He ignored the weary guy on the radio and pushed on through to the back. To Gregory's outer office. Gregory's right-hand man looked up and asked him what he wanted. He said something had happened. Quicker to walk it across the street than put it in a text.

"Put what in a text?" the right-hand man asked.

"This morning I got an alert and a photograph about a man named Shevick. A big ugly son of a bitch."

"Have you seen him?"

"Is Shevick a common name in America?"

"Why?"

"I had a client named Shevick this morning. But a small old woman."

"Possibly related. Possibly an elderly aunt or cousin."

The guy nodded.

"That's what I thought," he said. "But then I got another alert, and another photograph. The same old woman is in it. But her name is different. In the new alert they're calling her Joanna Reacher. But this morning for me she signed Maria Shevick."

Chapter 19

Reacher and Abby left the Shevicks in their kitchen and headed out to the Toyota. Reacher was already packed. His toothbrush was in his pocket. But Abby wanted to drop by her place to pick up some stuff. Which was reasonable. In turn Reacher decided he wanted to drop by the public law project to get an answer to a question. Both destinations were in Ukrainian territory. But it would be safe enough, he thought. Possibly. On the downside, there were two photographs out there, plus potentially the Toyota's description and license plate. On the upside, it was broad daylight, and they would be in and out real fast.

Safe enough, he thought. Possibly.

They drove in through the still-shabby blocks and he found the law project again, near the hotels, just west of Center, at the end of its gentrified street. Which had a different feel by day than night. All the other offices were open. People were going in and out. There were cars parked both sides on the curb. But no black Lincolns and no unexplained pale men in suits.

Safe enough. Possibly.

Abby backed into a space and parked. She and Reacher got out and walked to the door. Only two guys were at their desks. No sign of Isaac Mehay-Byford. Just Julian Harvey Wood and Gino Vettoretto. Harvard and Yale. Good enough. They greeted Reacher and shook Abby's hand and said they were pleased to meet her.

Reacher said, "What if Max Trulenko has hidden money stashed away?"

"That's Isaac's theory," Gino said.

"There's always a rumor like that," Julian said.

"I think this time it's true," Reacher said. "Last night I dropped Trulenko's name to the doorman where Abby works. About three minutes later four guys showed up in two cars. Which was a pretty impressive response. It was platinum-level protection. These guys don't do anything except for cash. Therefore Trulenko is paying them. Top dollar, to get four guys in two cars inside three minutes. Therefore he still has money of his own."

"What happened with the four guys?" Gino asked.

"They lost me," Reacher said. "But along the way I think they might have proved Isaac's point."

"Do you know where Trulenko is?" Julian asked.

"Not precisely."

"We would need an address, to serve the papers.

And to get his bank accounts frozen. How much money do you suppose he has?"

"I have no idea," Reacher said. "More than me, I'm sure. More than the Shevicks, I'm damn sure."

"I guess we would sue him for a hundred million dollars, and settle for whatever he has left. With a bit of luck it will be enough."

Reacher nodded. Then he asked what he had come to ask. He said, "How long would all that take?"

Gino said, "They would never go to court. They couldn't afford to. They know they would lose. They would settle ahead of a trial. They would beg us to let them. It would be lawyer to lawyer, back and forth, mostly by e-mail. The only issue would be letting Trulenko keep a couple cents on the dollar, so he doesn't have to live under a bridge the rest of his life."

"How long would all that take?" Reacher asked again.

"Six months," Julian said. "Certainly no more than that."

The law moves slow, Maria Shevick had said, many times.

"No way of hurrying it along?"

"That is hurrying it along."

"OK," Reacher said. "Say hey to Isaac for me."

They hustled back to the Toyota. It was still there. Unnoticed, unwatched, unsurrounded, and unticketed. They got in. Abby said, "It's like one movie is playing in slow motion, and the other one is running all speeded up."

Reacher said nothing.

Abby's place was close by in terms of physical distance, but it was three sides of a square away in terms of one-way streets. They came on it from the north.

There was a car outside the door.

Parked on the curb. A black Lincoln, facing away. It had dark glass in the rear compartment. From a distance it was impossible to tell who was inside.

"Pull over," Reacher said.

Abby stopped thirty yards north of the Lincoln.

Reacher said, "Worst case there are two guys in it and I bet their doors are locked."

"What would the army tell you to do?"

"Fire armor-piercing rounds in sufficient quantity to subdue resistance. And then fire tracer at the gas tank in sufficient quantity to subdue evidence."

"We can't do that."

"Sadly. But we better do something. That's your house. They're poking their noses where they don't belong."

"Safer to ignore them, surely."

"Only in the short term," Reacher said. "We can't let them have it all their own way. We need to send a message. They're out of line. They squeezed your address out of an innocent couple with enough taste to hire you and book that band. They need to know there are certain things they shouldn't do. And they need to know they're messing with the wrong people. We need to scare them a little bit."

Abby was quiet a beat.

"You're nuts," she said. "You're one guy. You can't take them on."

"Someone has to. I'm used to it. I was a military policeman. I got all the lousy jobs."

She was quiet another beat.

"Your concern is their doors are locked," she said. "Because if they are, you can't get to them."

"Correct," Reacher said.

"I could walk around the block and go in the back door. I could turn on all the lights inside. That might get them out of the car for you."

"No," Reacher said.

"OK, I could leave the lights off and at least get my stuff."

"No," Reacher said again. "For the same reason. They might be waiting inside the house. The car could be empty. Or one and one."

"That's creepy."

"I told you. There are certain things they shouldn't do."

"I could live without my stuff. I mean, you do. It's clearly possible. It could be part of the experiment."

"No," Reacher said again. "It's a free country. If you want your stuff, you should have it. And if they need a message, they should get one."

"OK, works for me. But how do we do it?"

"That depends on how experimental you want to be."

"What do you want me to do?"

"I'm pretty sure it will work out fine."

"What will?"

"But you'll probably worry about it ahead of time."

"Try me."

"Ideally I would like you to drive up behind the Lincoln and nudge it in the back bumper at about walking pace."

"Why?"

"The doors will unlock. For the first responders. The car will think it's in a minor accident. There's a little doo-dad in there somewhere. A safety mechanism."

"So then you can open the doors from the outside."

"That would be the first tactical objective. All else would follow."

"They might have guns."

"For a limited period only. After which I would have them."

"What if the guys are in the house?"

"I suppose we could set the car on fire. That would send a message."

"That's crazy."

"Let's take it one step at a time."

"Will my car get wrecked?"

"It has federal bumpers. Should be good up to five miles an hour. Conceivable you could need another electrical tie."

"OK," she said.

"Remember to keep your foot on the clutch pedal. You don't want to stall out. You want to be ready to reverse away."

"Then what?"

"You park and go get your stuff, while I tell the guys in the car what they need to do."

"Which is what?"

"Follow you to some dubious place east of Center. After that it's up to them."

She was quiet another long beat.

Then she nodded. A bob of her short dark hair. A gleam in her eye. A smile on her lips, half grim, half excited.

"OK," she said again. "Let's do it."

At that moment Gregory's right-hand man was laying out what little he knew. He was in the inner office, across the desk from his boss. Which was an intimidating place to be. The desk was massive, ornately carved from toffee-colored wood. The desk chair was huge, made of tufted green leather. Behind the chair was a tall heavy bookcase that matched the desk. Altogether imposing. Not a comfortable place to be, when telling a confusing story.

He said, "At six o'clock last night Aaron Shevick was a big ugly sadsack nobody paying back a loan. At eight he was a big ugly sadsack nobody taking out a new loan. But at ten he was different. He was a man about town, enjoying the band, flirting with the waitress, eating bite-size pizzas and drinking six-dollar cups of coffee. Then on the way out of the bar he was different again. He was a tough guy talking about Max Trulenko. He's like three people in one. We have no idea who he really is."

Gregory asked, "Who do you think he is?"

His guy didn't answer. Instead he said, "Meanwhile we dug up his last known address. But he wasn't there. He moved out a year ago. The new tenants are an old retired couple named Jack and Joanna Reacher. Their granddaughter was visiting. Her name is Abigail Reacher. Except it isn't. Her name is Abigail Gibson. She's the waitress Shevick was flirting with last night. We know all about her. She's a troublemaker."

"How so?"

"A year or so ago she told the police about something she saw. We straightened it out. We showed her the error of her ways. She promised to reform, which is why we let her keep working."

Gregory bent his neck to the left, and held it, and to the right, and held it. As if it was hurting.

He said, "But now she's flirting with Shevick, and showing up at his last known address under a phony name."

"It gets worse," his guy said. "Grandma Reacher was in our pawn shop this morning, but she signed her name Shevick."

"Really?"

"Maria Shevick."

"And then she showed up at Aaron Shevick's last known address."

"We have no idea who these people really are."

"Who do you think they are?" Gregory asked again.

"We didn't get where we are by being stupid," his guy said. "We should consider every possibility. Start with Abigail Gibson. We're getting a new police commissioner. Maybe he's getting a jump on reading the files. Her name is in there. Maybe he reached out. Maybe he put the big guy in the field to work with her."

"He's not commissioner yet."

"All the more reason. We think we're still safe."

Gregory said, "You think Shevick is a cop?"

"No," his guy said. "We know the cops. We would have heard. Someone would have talked to us."

"Then who is he?"

"Maybe he's FBI. Maybe the police department asked for outside help."

"No," Gregory said. "A new commissioner wouldn't do that. He would want his own people on the job. He would want all the glory for himself."

"Then maybe he's an ex-cop or ex-FBI and Dino hired him to mess with us."

"No," Gregory said again. "Same as the new commissioner. Dino wouldn't hire outside help. He doesn't trust anyone enough. Like we don't."

"Then who is he?"

"He's a guy who borrowed money and then asked about Max. Which I agree is an odd combination."

"What do you want to do about him?"

"Watch the house you found," Gregory said. "If he lives there, he'll show up sooner or later."

Abby kept her seat belt on. Reacher took his off. He braced his palm against the dash. She put the gear stick in first.

"Ready?" she said.

"Walking speed," he said. "It's going to seem awful fast when you get there. But don't slow down. Maybe better to close your eyes for the last bit."

She pulled away from the curb and rolled down the street.

Chapter 20

Walking speed was customarily reckoned to be about three miles an hour, which was about two hundred seventy feet a minute, so it took the battered white Toyota twenty whole agonizing seconds to close the gap on the parked Lincoln. Abby lined it up and took a nervous breath and held it and closed her eyes. The Toyota rolled on unchecked and smacked hard into the Lincoln's back bumper. Walking speed, but still a big noisy impact. Abby was thrown forward against her belt. Reacher used both hands on the dash. The Lincoln bucked forward a foot. The Toyota bounced backward a foot. Reacher stumbled out, one fast pace, two, three, straight ahead to the Lincoln's rear right-hand door. He grabbed the handle.

The safety doo-dad had done its work.

The door opened. There were two guys inside. Elbow to elbow in the front, belts off, reclined, recently comfortable, now a little shaken up and bounced around. Their heads had come to rest on their seat backs, which made them waist-high to Reacher as he slid in behind them, which made them easy to grab, one in each palm, which made them easy to crash together like the guy in back of the orchestra with the cymbals. And again, after a little more bouncing around, and then ramrod straight forward, the left-hand guy into the rim of the steering wheel, and the right-hand guy into the dashboard roll above the glove box.

Then it was both hands inside their suit coats, leaning over their shoulders from the rear compartment, searching, finding leather straps, and shoulder holsters, and pistols, which he took. He found nothing more in their waistbands, and, leaning all the way forward, he found nothing more strapped around their ankles.

He sat back. The pistols were H&K P7s. German police issue. Beautifully engineered. Almost delicate. But also steely and hard edged. Therefore manly.

Reacher said, "Wake up now, guys."

He waited. Through the window he saw Abby step through her door, into her house.

"Wake up, guys," he said again.

And they did, soon enough. They came back groggy and blinking, looking around, trying to piece it together.

Reacher said, "Here's the deal. There's an incentive attached. You're going to drive me east. Along the way I'm going to ask you questions. If you lie to me, I'll feed you to the Albanians when we get there. If you tell me the truth, I'll get out and walk away and let you turn around and drive home again unharmed. That's the incentive. Take it or leave it. Are we clear?"

He saw Abby come out of her house, with a bulging bag. She heaved it across the sidewalk to her car. She dumped it in the back. She got in the front.

Inside the Lincoln the guy behind the wheel clutched his head and said, "Are you crazy? I can't even see straight. I can't drive you anywhere now."

"No such word," Reacher said. "My advice is try very hard."

He buzzed down his window and stuck his arm out and signaled Abby to go ahead and pull around and lead the way. He watched her hesitant maneuver. The Toyota's front fender was no longer horizontal. It was hanging down diagonally, way lower than it should have been. The passenger-side corner was about an inch away from scraping on the blacktop. Maybe two electrical ties would be required. Possibly three.

"Follow that car," he said.

The guy behind the Lincoln's wheel took off as clumsy as a first-timer. Beside him his partner craned around as far as a cricked neck would let him, and he looked out the corner of his eye, straight at Reacher.

Who said nothing. Up ahead the battered white Toyota was making good progress. Heading east on the cross streets. The Lincoln followed behind it. The guy at the wheel got better at driving. Much smoother.

Reacher said, "Where is Max Trulenko?"

At first neither one of them spoke. Then the guy with the bad neck said, "You're a lousy cheat."

"How so?" Reacher said.

"What our own people would do to us if we told you Trulenko's location is worse than anything the Albanians could do to us. Which makes it a phony choice. It's not an incentive. Plus we're guys who sit in cars and watch doors. You think they would tell folks like us where Trulenko is? So the truthful answer is, we don't know. Which you will say is a lie. Which makes it another phony choice, not an incentive. So do what you got to do. Just spare us the pious bullshit along the way."

"But you know who Trulenko is."

"Of course we do."

"And you know someone is hiding him somewhere."

"No comment."

"But you don't know where."

"No comment."

"If your life depended on it, where would you look?"

The guy with the neck didn't answer. Then the driver's cell phone rang. In his pocket. A jaunty little marimba tune, plinking away, over and over, muffled. Reacher thought about coded warnings and secret SOS alerts, and he said, "Don't answer it."

The driver said, "They'll come looking for us."

"Who will?"

"They'll send a couple of guys."

"Like you two? Now I'm really scared."

No answer. The phone stopped.

Reacher asked, "What's your boss's name?"

"Our boss?"

"Not the boss of sitting in cars watching doors. The top boy. The *capo di tutti capi*."

"What does that mean?"

"Italian," Reacher said. "The boss of all bosses."

No response. Not at first. They glanced at each other, as if trying to share a mute decision. How far could they go? On the one hand, *omerta*. Also Italian. A code of absolute silence. A code to live by, and to die for. On the other hand, they were currently in deep trouble. Personally and individually. In the real world, in the here and now. Dying for a code was all well and good in theory. In practice things were different. Right then number one on their to-do list was not honorable or glorious sacrifice, but living long enough to drive home afterward.

The guy with the neck said, "Gregory."

"That's his name?"

"In English."

Then they glanced at each other again. Different looks. Some new discussion.

"How long have you been over here?" Reacher asked. Because he wanted them back on track. Because answering questions eventually became a habit. Start with the easy ones, and work up to the hard ones. A basic interrogation technique. Again the two guys shared a glance, seeking each other's permission. On the one hand, and on the other hand.

"Eight years we have been here," the driver said.

"Your English is pretty good."

"Thank you."

Then the other guy's phone rang. The guy with the neck. Also in his pocket. Equally muffled, but a different tone. A digital reproduction of an old-fashioned electric telephone bell, like in the moneylending bar, on the wall behind the fat guy, a long muted mournful peal, and then another.

"Don't answer it," Reacher said.

"They can track us with them," the guy said.

"Doesn't matter. They can't react quickly enough. My guess is two minutes from now all this will be over. You'll be heading home anyway."

A third muffled peal, and a fourth.

"Or not," Reacher said. "Maybe two minutes from now the Albanians will have you. Either way it's going to happen fast."

Up ahead the Toyota slowed and pulled in at the curb. The Lincoln stopped behind it. On a block with old brick buildings and old brick sidewalks and old bricks showing under pocked blacktop on the street. Two-thirds of the buildings were closed down and boarded up, and the open third seemed to be conducting no kind of reputable business. *Some dubious place east of Center*. Abby had chosen well.

The phone stopped ringing.

Reacher leaned way over and turned the motor off and pulled the key. He sat back. They turned to look at him. A P7 in his left hand, and the car key in his right.

He said, "If your life depended on it, where would you look for Max Trulenko?"

No response. More glances. Both kinds. At first apprehensive and rock-and-a-hard-place frustrated, like before, and then different. The new discussion.

The guy with the neck said, "They'll be suspicious

of us. They'll want to know how come we were brought all the way out here and then let go again."

"I agree, it's a matter of perception."

"That's the problem. They'll assume we traded something."

"Tell them the truth."

"That would be suicide."

"A version of the truth," Reacher said. "Carefully selected and curated. Some parts redacted. But all of it still absolutely true in itself. Tell them a woman came out the door you were watching, with a bag of stuff, and she got in a car, and you followed her here. Give them any address on this block. Tell them you figured if Gregory thought the house was worth watching, he would certainly like to know where the missing occupant was currently hiding out. Be a little aw-shucks about it. You'll get a pat on the head and a gold star for initiative."

The driver said, "Not mention you at all?"

"Always safer that way."

More glances at each other. Looking for holes in the cover story. Not finding any. Then turning back and looking at Reacher again. The gun rock steady in his left hand, the car key tiny in his right.

He said, "Where would a sensible fellow start the search?"

The two guys turned to the front and glanced at each other again, still apprehensive, but then a little bolder, and bolder still, as they talked themselves into it. They weren't being asked for facts, after all. They hadn't been trusted with facts. Not lowly people like them. They were being asked for an opinion. That was all. Where would a sensible fellow look? Pure hypothetical speculation. Third-party commentary. Just polite conversation, really. And of course flattering, to a lowly person, that his opinion was sought at all.

Reacher watched the process. He saw the boldness build. He saw the firming of jaws, and the drawing of breaths, and the filling of lungs. Ready to talk, both physically and figuratively. But ready for something else, too. Something bad. The new discussion. Some crazy idea. It was coming off them like a smell. The fault was his own. Completely. Because of the phony choice. The guy was right. And because of the question about the capo. No doubt a scary figure, capable of terrible retributions. And because of the happy conclusion to the cover story. The pat on the head and the gold star. The wrong thing to say to frustrated, ambitious people. It got them thinking. Pats on the head and gold stars were great, but better still was promotion and status, and after eight long years best of all would be finally getting out of sitting in cars watching doors. They wanted to move up the ladder. Which they knew would take more than following a girl to an address. They would need a greater achievement.

Capturing Aaron Shevick would qualify. Which was who they thought he was, obviously. They had gotten texts, the same as everyone. The description and the photograph. They hadn't asked who he was. Most people would. They would say, who the hell are you? What do you want? But these guys had shown no curiosity at all. Because they already knew. He was a guy they got texts about. Therefore important. Therefore a prize. Therefore crazy ideas.

His own fault.

Don't do it, he thought.

Out loud he said, "Don't do it."

The driver said, "Do what?"

"Anything stupid."

They paused a beat. He guessed they would start by telling him something true. Too hard to coordinate a lie with silent glances. It would be like a teaser. It would be something that required a couple seconds of thought, and then the careful formulation of a follow-up question. All to make him momentarily preoccupied. To give them time to jump him. The guy with the neck would corkscrew over from the front and land with his chest on Reacher's left arm, and his hips on Reacher's right arm, whereupon the driver would come over the top and attack his undefended head. With his cell phone, edge on, if he had any sense, and no inhibitions about smashing up a precision piece of electronics. Which most people were willing to do, in Reacher's experience, when their lives depended on it.

Don't do it, he thought.

Out loud he said, "Where would you look for Max Trulenko?"

The driver said, "Where he works, of course."

Reacher put a momentarily blank look on his face, but inside he was thinking of nothing, and formulating no follow-up questions. He was just waiting. Time passed in quarter-second beats, like a racing heart, at first nothing, then still nothing, then the guy with the neck launching, hard and clumsy, his arms spearing out ahead of him, his feet thrusting, his back arching, aiming to get most of his bulk beyond the point of no return, so that even if he landed on the seat back gravity would do the rest of his work for him, dumping him into Reacher's lap, in an undignified but equally effective manner.

He didn't get to the point of no return.

Reacher jammed the gun against the seat back and shot the guy through the upholstery. Then he repelled the falling corpse with his elbow. Like a double tap. One, two, gunshot, elbow. The shot was loud, but not terrible. The interior of the thick Lincoln seat squab had acted like a huge suppressor. All kinds of wool and horsehair in there. All kinds of cotton batting. Natural absorption. One minor problem. Some of it had caught on fire. Plus the driver was leaning forward, leaning down, feeling under the dashboard near his shins. Then coming back up and twisting around. In his hand was a tiny pocket gun. Maybe Russian. Secured out of sight with hook and loop tape. Reacher shot him through his own seat back. It caught on fire, too. A nine-millimeter round. The muzzle hard against the padding, a massive explosion of superheated gases. Maybe never taken into account, during Lincoln's design process.

Reacher opened the door and slid out to the sidewalk. He put the guns in his pocket. Fresh air blew inside the car and the tiny fires perked up. Not just smoldering. There were actual flames. Small, like a lady's fingernail, dancing inside the seats.

Abby said, "What happened?"

She was standing near her own car, very still, on the sidewalk, looking in through the Lincoln's windshield.

Reacher said, "They showed extraordinary loyalty to an organization that doesn't seem to treat them very well."

"You shot them?"

"Self-defense."

"How?"

"They blinked first."

"Are they dead?"

"We might need to give them another minute. Depends how fast they're bleeding."

She said, "This has never happened to me before."

He said, "I'm sorry it had to."

"You killed two people."

"I warned them. I told them not to. All my cards were on the table. It was more like assisted suicide. Think of it that way."

"Did you do it for me?" she asked. "I told you I wanted them messed up."

"I didn't want to do it at all," he said. "I wanted to send them home, safe and sound. But no. They tried their best. I guess they did what I would have done. Although I hope I would have done it better."

"What should we do about it?"

The flames were licking higher. The vinyl on the seat backs was bubbling and splitting and peeling, like skin.

Reacher said, "We should get in your car and drive away."

"Just like that?"

"For me it's all about the shoe on the other foot. What would they do for me? That's what sets the bar."

She was quiet a beat.

Then she said, "OK, get in the car."

She drove. He sat in the passenger seat. His extra weight on that side dipped the suspension down just enough that the old Toyota's newly falling-off fender banged against the blacktop now and then, unpredictable and irregular, like spaced-out Morse code played on a bass drum, all the way along their route.

Chapter 21

No one would dream of calling the cops about a burning car on a two-thirds abandoned block on the east side of the city. Such a thing was obviously someone else's private business, and obviously best kept that way. But plenty of people dreamed about calling Dino's people. Always. About anything that might be useful. But especially about news like this. It might get them ahead. It might make their names. Some of them made dangerous up-close inspections, flinching away from the heat. They saw burning bodies inside. They wrote down the license plate, before the flames consumed it.

They called Dino's people and told them it was a Ukrainian car on fire. It was the type of Lincoln they used west of Center. As far as anyone could tell the two bodies in it were dressed in suits and ties. Which was standard practice over there. Looked like they had been shot in the back. Which was standard practice everywhere. Case closed. They were the enemy.

At which point Dino himself took over.

"Let it burn," he said.

While it did, he called his inner council together. In back of the lumber yard. Which a few of them didn't like, because lumber was combustible, and something somewhere was currently on fire. Maybe throwing sparks. But they all came. His right-hand man, and his other top boys. No choice.

"Did we do this?" Dino asked them.

"No," his right-hand man said. "This is not ours."

"Are you sure?"

"By now everyone knows about the massage parlor. Everyone knows we're four for four, honors even, game over. We have no rogues, or mavericks, or private business. I guarantee that. I would have heard."

"Then explain this to me."

No one could.

"At least the practical details," Dino said. "If not the actual meaning."

One of his guys said, "Maybe they drove in to have a meeting. Their contact was waiting on the sidewalk. He got in the back seat to chat. But he shot them instead. Maybe threw in a burning rag."

"What contact waiting on the sidewalk?"

"I don't know."

"A local person?"

"Probably."

"One of our guys?"

"Could be."

"Like an anonymous snitch?"

"It's possible."

"So anonymous we never noticed him before? So furtive he escaped our attention all these years? I don't think so. I think such a master of tradecraft would be waiting in a coffee shop on Center Street. He would be talking to some random kid in a hoodie. He wouldn't let two men in suits in a Town Car anywhere near him. Not within a million miles. Especially not all the way out in this part of town. He might as well publish a confession in the newspaper. So it wasn't a meeting."

"OK."

"And why would he shoot them?"

"I don't know."

Another guy said, "Then the shooter must have been in the back seat all along. They drove out here as a threesome."

"Therefore the shooter is one of them."

"Has to be. You don't let an armed man ride behind you unless you know him."

"Where is he now?"

"He got out and maybe a second car picked him up. Something anonymous. Not another Town Car. Someone would have seen it leaving."

"How many people in the second car?"

"Two, I'm sure. They always work in pairs."

"Therefore overall not a small operation," Dino said. "It must have required a certain amount of resources, and planning, and coordination. And secrecy. Five guys drove out here. I assume two of them didn't know what was about to happen."

"I guess not."

"But why did it happen? What was the strategic objective?"

"I don't know."

"Why did he set the car on fire?"

"I don't know," the guy said again.

Dino looked around the table.

He asked, "Do we all agree the shooter was in the back seat all along, and therefore was one of them?"

Everyone nodded, most of them gravely, as if coming to a weighty conclusion made inevitable by many hours of deliberation.

"And then after he shot the guys in the front seats, we know he set the car on fire."

More nods, this time faster and brisker, because some things were self-evident.

"Why all that?" Dino asked.

No one answered.

No one could.

"It feels like myth and legend," Dino said. "It feels highly symbolic. Like the Vikings burning their warriors in their boats. Like a ceremonial funeral pyre. Like a ritual sacrifice. It feels like Gregory is making an offering to us."

"Of two of his men?" his right-hand man asked.

"The number is significant."

"How?"

"We're getting a new police commissioner. Gregory can't afford to fight a war. He knows he went too far. Now he's apologizing. He's making peace. He knows he was in the wrong. Now he's trying to make it right. He's making it six for four, in our favor. As a gesture. So we don't have to do it ourselves. He's showing that he agrees with us. He agrees we should be ahead in the count."

No one responded.

No one could.

Dino got up and walked out. The others heard his footsteps click through the outer office, and through the big corrugated shed. They heard his driver start his car. They heard it drive away. The yard went quiet.

At first no one spoke.

Then someone said, "An offering?"

Silence for a moment.

"You see it different?" the right-hand man asked.

"We would never do a thing like that. Therefore neither would Gregory. Why would he?"

"You think Dino is wrong?"

A huge, dangerous question.

The guy looked all around.

"I think Dino is losing it," he said. "A Viking funeral pyre? That's crazy talk."

"Those are bold words."

"Do you disagree with them?"

Silence again.

Then the right-hand man shook his head.

"No," he said. "I don't disagree. I don't think it was a sacrifice or an offering."

"Then what was it?"

"I think it was outside interference."

"Who?"

"I think someone killed those guys here so Gregory would blame us for it. He'll attack us, we'll attack him back. We'll end up destroying each other. For someone else's benefit. So someone else can move in on both our turf. I think that might be the intention."

"Who?" the guy asked again.

"I don't know. But we're going to find out. Then we're going to kill them all. They're completely out of line."

"Dino wouldn't sign off on that. He thinks it's an offering. He thinks everything is sweetness and light now."

"We can't wait."

"Are we not going to tell him?" the guy asked.

The right-hand man was quiet a beat.

Then he said, "No, not yet. He would only slow us down. This is too important."

"Are you the new boss now?"

"Maybe. If Dino has really lost it. Which you said first, by the way. Everyone heard you."

"I meant no disrespect. But this is a very big step. We better be sure we know what we're doing. Otherwise it's a betrayal. The worst kind. He'll kill us all."

"Time to choose up sides," the right-hand man said. "Time for us all to place our bets. It's either Viking rituals or it's some out-of-towner's takeover bid. Which will kill us all faster than Dino could anyway."

The guy didn't speak for ten long seconds.

Then he said, "What should we do first?"

"Put the fire out. Haul the wreck to the crusher. Then start asking around. Two cars drove in. One was a big shiny Lincoln. Someone will remember the other one. We'll find it, and we'll find the guy who was in it, and we'll make him tell us who he's working for."

* * *

At that moment Reacher was four streets away, in the front parlor of a battered row house owned by a musician named Frank Barton. Barton was Abby's friend in the east of the city. Also present in the house was Barton's lodger, a man named Joe Hogan, once a U.S. Marine, now also a musician. A drummer, to be exact. His kit took up half the room. Barton played the bass guitar. His stuff took up the other half. Four instruments on stands, amplifiers, giant loudspeaker cabinets. Here and there among the clutter were narrow armchairs, thinly upholstered with stained and threadbare fabrics. Reacher had one, Abby had one, and Barton had the third and last. Hogan sat on his drum stool. The white Toyota was parked outside the window.

Barton said, "This is crazy, man. I know those guys. I play the clubs over there. They never forget. Abby can't go back there, ever again."

"Unless I find Trulenko," Reacher said.

"How will that help?"

"I think a defeat of that magnitude would change things a little."

"How?"

Reacher didn't answer.

Hogan said, "He means the only route to a high-value target like Trulenko will be straight through the top levels of the organization. Therefore afterward the remaining survivors will be no better than low-level drones running around like chickens with their heads cut off. The Albanians will eat them for breakfast. They'll own the whole city. What the Ukrainians were once upon a time worried about won't matter a damn anymore. Because the Ukrainians will all be dead."

Once a U.S. Marine. A sound grasp of strategy.

"This is crazy," Barton said again.

Six chances before the week is over, Reacher thought.

Chapter 22

Gregory's right-hand man knocked on the inner office door and entered and took a seat in front of the massive desk. He ran through what he knew. Two guys had been deployed outside Abigail Gibson's house. They were now missing. They were not answering their phones. Their car was no longer where it should be.

Gregory said, "Dino?"

"Maybe not."

"Why?"

"Maybe this was never Dino. Not at first, anyway. We made certain assumptions. Now we need to take a fresh look at the facts. Think about the first two, who got in the wreck up at the Ford dealer. Who was their last known contact?"

"They were doing an address check."

"On Aaron Shevick. And who was observed flirting with the waitress outside of whose house two more guys just disappeared?"

"Aaron Shevick."

"No such thing as a coincidence."

"Who is he?"

"Someone is paying him. To set you and Dino at each other's throat. So that we destroy each other. So the someone can take over."

"Who?"

"Shevick will tell us. When we find him."

The Albanians hauled the smoking wreck to the crusher, and then they started asking around. The inner council. The top boys. Unused to legwork. Their question was fairly simple. Did you see a two-vehicle convoy, one of which was a Lincoln Town Car? No one lied to them. They were pretty sure about that. Folks had seen what happened to people who lied to them. Instead everyone racked their brains. But results were disappointing. Partly because the concept of the convoy was sometimes hard to grasp. During rush hour, for instance, there were no two-car convoys. There were hundred-and-two-car convoys. Anywhere downtown, at the best of times, maybe twenty-two-car. Who knew which two were the convoy in question? People didn't want to give the wrong answer. Not when the top boys were asking.

So a different way was found, to ask the same question. It was quickly agreed that among the traffic there had been a handful of black Lincolns. Probably six in total. Three of them had been the fat-ass kind the Ukrainians drove. The top boys encouraged detailed descriptions of what had been in front of each of them, and what had been behind. There was a two-car convoy in there somewhere.

Three separate witnesses remembered a small white sedan with a hanging-off front fender. In each report it was ahead of one particular Lincoln, which seemed attentive to its lane changes and such, definitely as if following it. Coming out of the west of the city, heading east.

The two-car convoy.

The small white sedan was maybe a Honda. Or the other H. Hyundai. Or maybe Kia. Was there another new brand? Or maybe it wasn't a new brand at all, because it was a pretty old car. Could have been a Toyota. Yes, that was it. A Toyota Corolla. Poverty spec. That was the final conclusion. All three witnesses agreed.

No one had seen it leave.

The top boys put the word out. All eyes open. An old white Toyota Corolla sedan, with a hanging-off front fender. Report back immediately.

By that point it was late in the afternoon, which was a respectable time for musicians to start their day. Hogan warmed up with a steady 4/4 beat, hi-hat working, ride cymbal ticking. Barton plugged in a battered Fender and turned on his amp, buzzing and humming. He laid down a line, looping and sinuous, staying firmly in the pocket with the kick drum, coming home on the two and the four, launching again on the one of the new measure. Reacher and Abby listened for a spell, and then went to find the guest room.

It was upstairs at the front of the house, a small space over the street door, with a round window made of wavy glass that could have been a hundred years old. The Toyota was directly below. The bed was a queen. The night table was an old guitar amplifier tipped up on its end. There was no closet. There was a row of brass hooks instead, screwed to the wall. The thump of the drums and the bass roared up through the floor.

"Not as nice as your place," Reacher said. "I'm sorry."

Abby didn't answer.

Reacher said, "I asked the guys in the Lincoln where Trulenko was. They didn't know. So then I asked their opinion about a smart first place to look. They said where he works."

"Does he work?"

"Got to admit, I hadn't thought of it that way."

"Maybe in exchange for hiding him. Maybe there's no money left after all. Maybe he's working his passage."

"That would be a drag," Reacher said.

"Why else would he work?"

"Maybe he was getting bored."

"Possible."

"What kind of work would he do?"

"Nothing physical," Abby said. "He looked like a pretty small guy. His picture was in the paper all the time. He was young but his hair was going and he wore eyeglasses. He won't be breaking rocks in a quarry. He'll be in an office somewhere. Organizing data systems or something. That's what he was good at. His new product was an app on your phone that linked your vital signs direct to your doctor. In real time, just in case. Or something like that. Or maybe your watch linked to your phone, and then to the doctor. No one really understood it. But anyway, Trulenko is a desk guy. A thinker."

"So he's in an office somewhere on the west side of the city. With accommodations either very close by, or integrated. With security. Maybe an underground bunker. With a single bottleneck entrance, heavily defended. No one gets in or out except for known and trusted faces."

"Therefore you can't get near him."

"I agree there will be an element of challenge."

"More like impossible."

"No such word."

"How big of a place would it be?"

"I don't know," Reacher said. "A couple dozen people, maybe. Or more. Or less. Some kind of nerve center. Where they send all the texts. You said they were good with technology."

"There can't be many suitable locations."

"See?" Reacher said. "We're making progress already."

"No point, if the money is gone."

"His employers will have some. I never met a poor gangster."

"The Shevicks can't sue Trulenko's new-found employers. They had nothing to do with it. It's not their fault."

"By that point the spirit of the law might feel more important than the letter."

"You would steal it?"

Reacher moved to the window and looked down.

"The capo over there is a guy named Gregory," he said. "I would ask him to consider it a charitable donation. For a hard-luck story I heard about. I could deploy a number of arguments. I'm sure he would agree. And if he's profiting from Trulenko's labor in some way, then it's almost the same thing as taking Trulenko's own money anyway."

Abby got a faraway look in her eyes, and she put her hand up to her cheek, as if automatically.

"I heard of Gregory," she said. "Never met him. Never even saw him."

"How did you hear about him?"

She didn't answer. Just shook her head.

He said, "What happened to you?"

"Who says anything did?"

"You just saw two dead bodies. Now I'm talking about threatening people and stealing their money. I'm that kind of guy. We're standing by a queen bed. Most women would be edging out the door by now. You're not. You really, really don't like these people. Must be a reason."

"Maybe I really like you."

"I live in hope," Reacher said. "But I'm realistic."

"I'll tell you later," she said. "Maybe."

"OK."

"What now?"

"We should go get your bag. And we should go move your car. I don't want it parked right outside. They already saw it at the Shevick house. Someone else might have seen it driving in today. We should go put it somewhere random. Always safer that way."

"How long will we have to live like this?"

"I live like this all the time. I would have been pushing up daisies long ago if I didn't."

"Frank said I can't ever go home again."

"And Hogan saw how you could."

"If you get Trulenko."

"Six chances before the week is over."

They went downstairs again into the deep bass groove, and onward out to the car. Abby wrestled her bag off the rear seat and hauled it back to the hallway. They closed the door on it and got in the car. It started the second time and dragged its fender on the tight turn out of its boxed-in slot. They drove a random zigzag route, through different parts of the neighborhood, some of them shabbily residential, some of them commercial, including two full blocks dedicated to the construction trade, including an electrical warehouse, and a plumbing warehouse, and a lumber yard. Then came progressive stages of decay, all the way to abandoned blocks just like the place where the Lincoln had burned.

"Here?" Abby asked.

Reacher looked all around. Desolation everywhere. No owners, no occupants, no residents. No innocent doors to get busted down, if the car was spotted nearby. No risk of collateral damage.

"Works for me," he said.

She parked and they got out and she locked up and they walked away. They went back more or less the same way they had come, cutting the corners off some of the widest zigs and zags of their earlier random route, but always keeping track of it. Their surroundings grew cleaner and better maintained. They came to the blocks dedicated to the construction trade. First up in the reverse direction came the lumber yard. There was a guy standing in the scoop between the sidewalk and the gate. Somewhat sentry-like. Maybe there to check loads in and out. Presumably lumber got scammed and stolen like anything else.

They passed the guy by and walked on, to the plumbing warehouse, the electrical warehouse, and onward, through a tangle of streets. They heard the bass and drums a hundred yards away.

The reports came in fast, but not fast enough. One after the other the members of the inner council got hurried calls on their cell phones. An old white Toyota Corolla with a half-off front fender had been seen driving one block, then another, then another. No rhyme or reason in terms of direction. No obvious destination. Generally it seemed to be headed toward the tumbledown neighborhoods where not even homeless people lived.

Then came the paydirt call. A reliable guy a hundred yards away saw the car slow, stop, and park. Two people got out. The driver was a small woman with short dark hair. In her twenties or thirties, and dressed all in black. Her passenger was a huge guy, about twice her size. He was older, easily six-five and two-fifty, built like a brick outhouse, and dressed like a refugee. They locked the car and walked away together, and were lost to sight very quickly, after the first corner they turned.

All that information was shared immediately, by calls and voicemails and texts. Fast, but not fast enough. The message got to the guy at the lumber yard gate about ninety seconds after a small dark-haired woman and a huge ugly guy had walked right past. Close enough to touch. More minutes were spent getting cars together, and then they streamed away in the direction the couple had been walking.

No result. The small woman and the big man were long gone. They had disappeared somewhere in a crowded residential neighborhood, maybe ten blocks by ten of shabby row houses packed tightly together. Maybe four hundred separate addresses. Plus basements and sublets. Full of deadbeats and weirdoes, who either came and went at all hours, or never went out at all. Hopeless.

The top boys put a new word out. All eyes open. A small dark-haired woman, younger, and a big ugly guy, older. Report back immediately.

Chapter 23

Neither Barton nor Hogan had a gig that night, so they closed down their jam when Reacher and Abby got back, and proposed a chill evening in, maybe with Chinese delivery, maybe a bottle of wine, maybe a little weed, some conversation, some stories, some catch-up. Maybe put some records on. All good, until Abby's cell phone rang.

It was Maria Shevick, calling from Aaron Shevick's phone. She and Abby had exchanged numbers. Just in case. And this felt like a just-in-case situation. Maria said a black Lincoln Town Car was parked outside her house. Two guys in it, watching. They had been there all afternoon. They looked like they were set to stay.

Abby passed her phone to Reacher.

He said, "They're looking for me. Because I mentioned Trulenko. They got worried. Just ignore them."

Maria asked, "Suppose they knock on the door?"

Seventy, stooped, and starving.

He said, "Let them search the house. Show them whatever they want to look at. They'll see I'm not there, and they'll go back to their car, and after that all they'll need to do is watch the sidewalk. Should be relatively painless."

"Very well."

"Any news on Meg?"

"Good and bad," Maria said.

"Start with the good," Reacher said.

"I think for the first time the doctors truly believe she's improving. I can hear it in their voices. Not what they say, but the way they say it. Their words are always circumspect. But now they're excited. They think they're winning. I can tell."

"What's the bad news?"

"They'll want to confirm it with tests and scans. Which we'll have to pay for first."

"How much?"

"We don't know yet. A lot, I'm sure. They have amazing machines now. There have been dramatic advances in soft tissue analysis. It's all very expensive."

"When will they need it?"

"Obviously half of me wants it to be as soon as possible. And obviously the other half doesn't."

"You should do what is right medically. We'll figure out the rest as we go along."

"We can't borrow it," Maria said. "You would have to do it for us, because they think you're Aaron Shevick. But now, for you, that would be a trap. Because you asked about Trulenko."

"Aaron could borrow it under my name. Or any name. They're new at this game. They have no system for checking. Not yet, anyway. It's an option. If you need it fast."

"You said you could find Trulenko. You said it used to be part of your job."

"The question is when," Reacher said. "I figured I had six chances before the week is over. Now maybe not so many. I need to work on a faster plan."

"I apologize for my tone."

"No need," Reacher said.

"This is all very stressful."

"I can only imagine," Reacher said.

They hung up and Reacher passed the phone back to Abby.

Barton said, "This is crazy, man. I'm going to keep on saying it, because it's going to keep on being true. I know those people. I play their clubs. I've seen what they do. One time, there was a piano player they didn't like. They smashed his fingers with a hammer. The guy never played again. You can't take them on."

Reacher looked at Hogan and asked, "Do you play their clubs?"

"I'm a drummer," Hogan said. "I play anywhere they pay me."

"Have you seen what they do?"

"I agree with Frank. These are not pleasant people."

"What would the Marine Corps do about them?"

"Nothing. The pointy-heads would hand them off to the SEALs. Much more glamorous. The Corps wouldn't get a sniff."

"What would the SEALs do?"

"A lot of planning first. With maps and blueprints. If we're assuming a hardened bunker of some kind, they would look for emergency exits, or delivery bays, or incursions by ventilation shafts or water pipes or sewers, and places where they could gain access by demolition of walls between adjacent structures. Then they would plan simultaneous assaults from everywhere they could, at least three or four places, with three- or four-man teams in each location. Which would probably get the job done, except it might be hard to keep any single person of interest alive. There would be a lot of crossfire. It would depend on dimensions and visibility."

Reacher asked, "What were you, in the Corps?"

"Infantry," Hogan said. "Just a plain old jarhead."

"Not a bandsman?"

"That would have been too logical for the Corps."

"Were you always a drummer?"

"I was as a kid. Then I stopped. Then I took it up again in Iraq. Every big base had a kit lying around somewhere. I was advised I would enjoy creating patterns I alone controlled. I was advised I would find it helpful, since I could already play a bit anyway. Also I was advised it would get rid of aggression."

"Who advised you?"

"Some old sawbones. I laughed it off at first. But then I found I was really enjoying it again. I realized I should have been doing it all my life. I've been playing catch-up ever since. Trying to learn. I missed a few years."

"You sounded pretty good to me."

"Now you're blowing smoke. And trying to change the subject. You're one guy. You're not a SEAL team."

"I'll figure it out. By definition there must be a dozen better plans than what the navy would come up with. All I need to do is find the guy."

"There can't be many suitable locations," Abby said again.

Reacher nodded and went quiet. The conversation bounced around him. The other three seemed to be good friends. They had worked together now and then, in the fluid world of clubs, and music, and dance, and men in suits on the door. They all had stories, some of them funny, and some of them not. They seemed to draw no distinction between the Ukrainians and the Albanians. They seemed to think that working east and west of Center was equally good and bad.

A kid in a car brought Chinese food. Reacher shared hot and sour soup with Abby and sweet and sour chicken with Barton. They drank wine. He drank coffee. When he finished, he said, "I'm going for a walk."

Abby said, "Alone?"

"Nothing personal."

"Where?"

"West of Center. I need to hurry this up. The Shevicks are about to get hit by another big bill. They can't wait."

"Crazy, man," Barton said.

Hogan didn't speak.

Reacher got up and stepped out the front door.

Chapter 24

Reacher walked west, toward the nighttime glow of the tall downtown buildings. The banks and the insurance companies and the local TV. And the chain hotels. All clustered astride Center Street, all penetrated by one faction or the other, all probably unaware of the fact, at management level, unless the manager was also the mole. Along the way he passed bars and clubs and storefront restaurants. Here and there he saw men in suits on the door. He ignored them. Wrong faction. He was still east of Center. He walked on.

If he had eyes in the back of his head, he would have seen one of the men in suits think hard for a second, and then send a text.

He walked on. He crossed Center Street three blocks north of the first tall building, into a neighborhood no different, with bars and clubs and storefront restaurants, some of them with men in suits on the door, just the same, except the suits were different, and the ties were silk, and the faces were paler. This time he watched them all carefully, from the shadows when he could, looking for the kind of guy he wanted. Which was alert, but not too alert, and tough, but not too tough. There were several candidates. In particular three looked good. Two were in wine bars, and one was in some kind of a lounge. Maybe a comedy club.

Reacher chose the one sitting nearest the street door. A tactical advantage. It was the lounge. The guy was right inside the glass. Reacher walked toward him, three-quarters in his field of vision. The guy noticed the movement. Turned his head. Reacher stopped walking. The guy stared. Reacher moved on again. Straight toward him. The guy remembered. Texts, descriptions, photographs, names. Aaron Shevick. Be on the lookout.

Reacher stopped again.

The guy pulled out his phone, and jabbed at it.

Reacher pulled out his gun, and aimed it. One of the two H&K P7s taken from the guys in the Lincoln. Before it burned up. German police issue. Beautifully engineered. Steely and hard edged. The guy froze. Reacher was three steps away. Just enough time. Tempting. The guy dropped his phone and put his hand up under his armpit to get his own gun.

Not enough time.

The guy was right inside the door. Right inside the glass. Reacher got to him before his gun was halfway out, and he pressed the H&K's muzzle against his right eye, hard enough not to get shaken loose, hard enough to get the guy's attention, which it did right away, because the guy went immediately quiet and still. With his left hand Reacher picked up his phone, and then took his gun, which was another H&K P7, just like the two he had already. Maybe standard issue west of Center. Maybe a bulk order, at a good price, from some bent German copper.

With his left hand he put the phone and the gun in his pockets. With his right hand he pressed his own H&K harder on the guy's eyeball.

"Let's take a walk," he said.

The guy got up off his stool, awkward, all bent backward against the pressure, and he shuffled around and backed out the door, to the sidewalk, where Reacher turned him right, and pushed him six more backward paces, and turned him right again, backward into an alley that smelled like a garbage receptacle and a kitchen door.

Reacher backed the guy against the wall.

He said, "How many people saw?"

The guy said, "Saw what?"

"You with a gun to your head."

"A few, I guess."

"How many came to help you out?"

The guy didn't answer.

"Yeah, none of them," Reacher said. "No one likes you. No one would piss on you if you were on fire. So it's just you and me now. No one is going to ride to the rescue. Are we clear on that?"

"What do you want?"

"Where is Max Trulenko?"

"No one knows."

"Someone must."

"Not me," the guy said. "I promise. I swear on my sister's life."

"Where is your sister right now?"

"Kiev."

"Which makes your promise kind of theoretical. Don't you think? Try again."

"On my life," the guy said.

"Which is not so theoretical," Reacher said. He pressed harder with the H&K. Through the steel he felt the guy's eyeball squash. He felt the jelly.

The guy gasped and said, "I swear I don't know where Trulenko is."

"But you heard of him."

"Of course."

"Does he work for Gregory now?"

"That's what I heard."

"Where?"

"No one knows," the guy said. "It's a big secret."

"You sure?"

"On my mother's grave."

"Which is where?"

"You got to believe me. Maybe six people know where Trulenko is. I ain't one of them. Please, sir. I'm just a doorman."

Reacher took the gun away. He stepped back. The guy blinked and rubbed his eye and stared through the gloom. Reacher kicked him hard in the nuts, and left him there, doubled over, making all kinds of retching and puking sounds.

* * *

Reacher got back to Center Street with no trouble anywhere. His problems started immediately after that. When he was east of Center, which he didn't understand at all. Wrong faction, surely. But right away he felt eyes on him. He felt people watching him. No benevolence in their gaze. He knew that absolutely. He got a chill on his neck. Some kind of an ancient instinct. A sixth sense. A survival mechanism, baked deep in the back of his brain by evolution. How not to get eaten. Millions of years of practice. His hundred-thousand-times-great-great-grandmother, stiffening, changing course, looking for the trees and the shadows. Living to fight another day. Living to have a kid, who a hundred thousand generations later had a descendant also looking for the shadows, not on the verdant savannah but on the gray nighttime streets, as he slid by lit-up clubs and bars and storefront restaurants.

It was the men in suits who were watching him. Organized guys. Made men, and the soon-to-be. Why? He didn't know. Had he upset the Albanians too? He didn't see how. Mostly he had done them a favor, surely, according to their own crude calculus. They should be giving him a parade.

He moved on.

He heard a footstep far behind him.

He kept on walking. The glow of Center Street was long gone, both literally and figuratively. The streets ahead were narrow and dark, and got shabbier with every step. There were parked cars and alleys and deep doorways. Two out of three street lights were busted. There were no pedestrians.

His kind of place.

He stopped walking.

More than one way not to get eaten. Grandma's instinct worked for today. A hundred thousand generations later her descendant's instinct worked for tomorrow, too. And forever. More efficient. Natural selection, right there. He stood in the half gloom for a minute, and then backed away into deep shadow, and listened.

He heard the diamond scrape of a leather sole on the sidewalk. Maybe forty feet back. Some kind of hastily arranged surveillance. Some guy, suddenly ordered off his stool and out into the night. To follow. But for how long? That was the critical question. All the way home, or only as far as a hastily arranged up-ahead ambush?

Reacher waited. He heard the leather sole again. Or its opposite number, on the other foot, taking a cautious step, moving forward. He pressed deeper into the shadows. Into a doorway. He leaned up against ribs of carved stone. A fancy entrance. Some long-forgotten enterprise. No doubt rewarding while it lasted.

He heard the scrape of the shoe again. Now maybe twenty feet back. Making progress. He heard nothing from the other direction. Just city quiet, and old air, and the faint smell of soot and bricks.

He heard the shoe again. Now ten feet back. Still making progress. He waited. The guy was already within range. But another couple of steps would make the whole thing more comfortable. He sketched out the geometry in his head. He put his hand in his pocket and found the H&K he had used before. Because he knew for sure it worked. Always an advantage.

Another step. The guy was maybe seven feet away. Not small. The sound of his shoe was a faint, heavy, grinding, spreading crunch. The sound of a big guy, creeping slow.

Now four feet away.

Show time.

Reacher stepped out and turned to face the guy. The H&K gleamed in the dark. He aimed it at the guy's face. The guy went cross-eyed, trying to stare at it in the poor illumination.

Reacher said, "Don't make a sound."

The guy didn't. Reacher listened beyond his shoulder. Did the guy have back-up behind him? Apparently not. Nothing to hear. Same as up ahead. City quiet, and old air.

Reacher said, "Do we have a problem?"

The guy was six feet and maybe two-twenty, maybe forty years old, lean and hard, all bone and muscle and dark suspicious eyes. His lips were clamped tight and pulled back in a rictus grin that could have been worried, or quizzical, or contemptuous.

"Do we have a problem?" Reacher asked again.

"You're a dead man," the guy said.

"Not so far," Reacher said. "In fact right now you're closer to that unhappy state than I am. Don't you think?"

"Mess with me, and you're messing with a lot of people."

"Am I messing with you? Or are you messing with me?"

"We want to know who you are."

"Why? What did I do to you?"

"Above my pay grade," the guy said. "All I got to do is bring you in."

"Well, good luck with that," Reacher said.

"Easy to say, with a gun in my face."

Reacher shook his head in the gloom.

"Easy to say anytime," he said.

He stepped back a pace, and put the gun back in his pocket. He stood there, empty-handed, palms out, with his arms held away from his sides.

"There you go," he said. "Now you can bring me in."

The guy didn't move. He was five inches down in height, maybe thirty pounds in weight, maybe a whole foot in reach. Evidently unarmed, because otherwise his weapon would have been out and in his hand already. Evidently unsettled, too, by Reacher's gaze, which was steady, and calm, and slightly amused, but also undeniably predatory, and even a little unhinged.

Not a good situation for the guy to be in.

Reacher said, "Maybe we could get to the same place a different way."

The guy said, "How?"

"Give me your phone. Tell your boss to call me. I'll tell him who I am. The personal touch is always better."

"I can't give you my phone."

"I'm going to take it anyway. Your choice when."

The gaze. Steady, calm, amused, predatory, unhinged.

The guy said, "OK."

Reacher said, "Take it out and set it down on the sidewalk."

The guy did.

"Now turn around."

The guy did.

"Now run away as far and as fast as you can."

The guy did. He took off at a musclebound sprint and was immediately swallowed up by the urban darkness. His footsteps rang out long after he had disappeared from sight. This time he made no attempt at stealth. Reacher listened to the rapid slapping and crunching and sliding until the sound quieted down and faded away to nothing. Then he picked up the phone and walked on.

Three blocks from Barton's house, Reacher took off his jacket, and folded it into a square, and rolled the square into a tube, and stuffed the tube inside a rusted mailbox outside a one-story office building with boarded-up windows and fire damage on the siding. He walked the rest of the way in his T-shirt only. The nighttime air was cool. It was still springtime. The full weight of summer was yet to come.

Hogan was waiting for him in Barton's hallway. The drummer. Once a U.S. Marine. Now enjoying patterns he alone controlled.

"You OK?" he asked.

"Were you worried about me?" Reacher said.

"Professionally curious."

"I wasn't playing a gig with the Rolling Stones."

"My previous profession."

"Objective achieved," Reacher said.

"Which was what exactly?"

"I wanted a Ukrainian phone. Apparently they text each other a lot. I figured I could look back and see where they're up to with this. Maybe they mention Trulenko. Maybe I could make them panic, and make them move him. That would be the time of maximum opportunity."

Abby came down the stairs. Still dressed.

She said, "Hey."

Reacher said, "Hey back."

"I heard all that. Good plan. Except won't they just kill the phone remotely? You won't hear from them, and they won't hear from you."

"I chose the guy I took it from pretty carefully. He was relatively competent. Therefore relatively trusted. Maybe relatively senior. Therefore relatively reluctant to fess up that I took his lunch money. I left him a little embarrassed. He won't report anything in a hurry. It's a pride thing. I think I have a few hours, at least."

"OK, good plan, except nothing."

"Except I'm not great with phones. There might be menus. All kinds of buttons to press. I might delete something by mistake."

"OK, show me."

"And even if I don't delete them by mistake, the texts are probably in Ukrainian. Which I can't read without the internet. And I'm really not great with computers."

"That would be the second step. We would need to start with the phone. Show me."

"I didn't bring it here," Reacher said. "The guy in the Lincoln claimed they could be traced. I don't want someone knocking on the door five minutes from now."

"So where is it?"

"I hid it three blocks from here. I figured that was safe enough. Pi times the radius squared. They would have to search nearly a thirty-block circle. They wouldn't even try."

Abby said, "OK, let's go take a look."

"I also got an Albanian phone. Kind of accidentally. But in the end the same kind of deal. I want to read it. Maybe I can figure out what they're mad with me about."

"Are they mad with you?"

"They sent a guy after me. They want to know who I am."

"That could be normal. You're a new face in town. They like to know things."

"Maybe."

Hogan said, "There's a guy you should talk to."

Reacher said, "What guy?"

"He comes to gigs sometimes. A dogface, just like you."

"Army?"

"Stands for, aren't really Marines yet."

"Like *Marine* stands for muscles are requested, intelligence not expected."

"This guy I'm talking about speaks a bunch of old Commie languages. He was a company commander late on in the Cold War. Also he knows what's going on here in town. He could be helpful. Or at least useful. With the languages especially. You can't rely on a computer translation. Not for a thing like this. I could call him, if you like."

"You know him well?"

"He's solid. Good taste in music."

"Do you trust him?"

"As much as I trust any dogface who doesn't play the drums."

"OK," Reacher said. "Call him. Can't hurt."

He and Abby stepped out to the nighttime stillness, and Hogan stayed behind, in the half-lit hallway, dialing his phone.

Chapter 25

Reacher and Abby covered the three block distance via a roundabout route. Obviously if the phones were truly traceable, they might have already been discovered, in what was clearly a temporary stash, in which case surveillance might have been set up against their eventual retrieval. Better to play it safe. Or as safe as possible, which wasn't very. There were shadows and alleys and deep doorways and two out of every three street lights were busted. There was plenty of habitat for hidden nighttime watchers.

Reacher saw the rusty mailbox up ahead. The middle of the next block. He said, "Pretend we're having some kind of a deep conversation, and when we get level with the mailbox we stop to make an especially big point."

"OK," Abby said. "Then what?"

"Then we ignore the mailbox completely and we

move on. But at that point very quietly. We glide away."

"An actual pretend conversation? Or just moving our lips, like a silent movie?"

"Maybe whispered. Like we're dealing with secret information."

"Starting when?"

"Now," Reacher said. "Keep on walking. Don't slow down."

"What do you want to whisper about?"

"I guess whatever is on your mind."

"Are you serious? We could be walking into a dangerous situation here. That's what's on my mind."

"You said you want to do one thing every day that scares you."

"I'm already way over quota."

"And you survived every time."

"We could be walking into a hail of gunfire."

"They won't shoot me. They want to ask me questions."

"You absolutely sure?"

"It's a psychological dynamic. Like in the theater. It's not necessarily the kind of thing that has a yes or no answer."

The mailbox was coming up.

"Get ready to stop," Reacher whispered.

"And give them a stationary target?"

"Only as long as it takes to make a big imaginary statement. Then we move on again. But very quietly, OK?"

Reacher stopped.

Abby stopped.

She said, "What kind of big imaginary statement?"

"Whatever is on your mind."

She was quiet a beat.

Then she said, "No. What's on my mind is I don't want to make a statement about what's on my mind. Not yet. That's my statement."

"Go," he said.

They moved on. As quiet as they could. Three paces. Four.

"OK," Reacher said.

Abby said, "OK what?"

"No one here."

"And we know this how?"

"You tell me."

She was quiet another beat, and then she said, "We were quiet because we were listening."

"And what did we hear?"

"Nothing."

"Exactly. We paused right by the target, and we heard no one stepping out or tensing up, and then we moved on, and we heard no one stepping back and relaxing, or scuffling around, waiting for word on plan B. Therefore there's no one here."

"That's great."

"So far," Reacher said. "But who knows how long these things take? Not my area of expertise. They could be here any minute."

"So what should we do?"

"I guess we should take the phones someplace else. We should make them start the search all over again."

Two blocks south they saw headlight beams coming out of a cross street. Like a distant early warning. Seconds later a car made the left and drove up toward them. Slowly. Maybe searching. Or maybe just a regular nighttime driver worried about a ticket or a DUI. Hard to tell. The headlights were low and wide spaced. A big sedan. It kept on coming.

"Stand by," Reacher said.

Nothing. The car drove past, same steady speed, same decided direction. An old Cadillac. The driver looked neither left nor right. An old lady, peering out from underneath the rim of the steering wheel.

Abby said, "Whatever, we better be quick about this. Because like you said, we don't know how long these things take."

They walked back, four fast paces, and Reacher pulled his rolled-up jacket out of the rusty mailbox.

Abby carried the phones. She insisted. They walked another three blocks on another roundabout route and found a bodega open late. No man in a suit on the door. No suits anywhere, as a matter of fact. The clerk at the register was wearing a white T-shirt. There were no other customers. The space was crowded with humming chiller cabinets and bright with fluorescent light. There was a two-top table in back, unoccupied.

Reacher got two cardboard cups of coffee and carried them back to the table. Abby had the phones laid out side by side. She was looking at them, conflicted, as if half eager to get started on them, and half worried about them, as if they were pulsing secret SOS signals out into the ether. *Find me, find me.*

Which they were.

She said, "Can you remember which was which?"

"No," he said. "They all look the same to me."

She clicked one to life. No password required. For speed, and arrogance, and easy internal review. She dabbed and swiped through a bunch of screens. Reacher saw a vertical array of green message bubbles. Texts. Unreadable foreign words, but mostly regular letters, the same as English. Some were doubled up. Some had strange accents above or below. Umlauts and cedillas.

"Albanian," Reacher said.

Out on the street a car drove by. Slowly. Its headlight wash scoured a thin blue blade of light across the room. All the way along the back wall, and then all the way along the end wall, and then it was gone. Abby clicked the second phone to life. No password. She found another long sequence of text messages, to and from. Green bubbles, one after the other. All in the Cyrillic alphabet. Named for Saint Cyril, who worked on alphabets in the ninth century.

"Ukrainian," Reacher said.

"There are hundreds of texts here," Abby said. "Literally hundreds. Maybe thousands."

Another car drove by outside, faster.

Reacher said, "Can you make out the dates?"

Abby scrolled and said, "There are at least fifty since yesterday. Your picture is in some of them."

Another car drove by outside. This time slowly.

Lights on bright. Searching for something, or worried about a ticket. A glimpse of the driver. A man in dark clothing, his face lit up spooky by the lights on his dash.

"There are at least fifty Albanian texts too," Abby said. "Maybe more."

"So how do we do this?" Reacher asked. "We can't take the phones home. We can't copy out all this crap onto napkins. We would make mistakes. And it would take forever. We don't have time."

"Watch me," Abby said.

She took out her own phone. She squared the Ukrainian phone on the tabletop. She hovered her own phone above it, parallel, moving in, moving out, until satisfied.

"Taking a picture?" Reacher asked.

"Video," she said. "Watch."

She held her own phone in her left hand, and with her right forefinger she scrolled through a long and complex chain of Ukrainian texts on the captured phone, at a moderate speed, on and on, consistent, five seconds, ten, fifteen, twenty. Then the end of the chain bounced to a halt and she shut off the recording.

She said, "We can play it and pause it as much as we want. We can freeze it anywhere. Just as good as having the phones themselves."

She did the same thing with the Albanian phone. Five seconds, ten, fifteen, twenty.

"Nice work," Reacher said. "Now we should move these phones again. Can't leave them here. This place doesn't deserve a visit from the goon squad."

"So where?"

"I vote back in the mailbox."

"But that's ground zero for their search. If they're behind the curve a little, they could be getting there right about now."

"Actually I'm hoping being in a small metal box will cut off the transmissions. They won't be able to search at all."

"Then they never could."

"Probably not."

"Then there never was any danger."

"Until we took them out."

"How long does it take, for a thing like that?"

"We already agreed, neither one of us knows."

"Does it have to be that mailbox? How about the nearest mailbox?"

"No collateral damage," Reacher said. "Just in case."

"You don't really know, do you?"

"It's not necessarily the kind of thing that has a yes or no answer."

"Are the transmissions cut off or not?"

"I'm guessing probably. Not my area of expertise. But I listen to people talk. They're forever bitching and moaning about their calls cutting out. For all kinds of reasons, all of which sound much less serious than getting shut in a small metal box."

"But right now they're right here on the table, so there is currently a degree of danger."

Reacher nodded.

"Getting larger every minute," he said.

* * *

This time Reacher carried the phones, for no reason other than normal squad rotation. There were plenty of cars around. Plenty of bouncing, blinding head-light beams. All kinds of makes and models. But no Lincoln Town Cars. No sudden changes in speed or direction. Apparently no interest at all.

They put the phones in the mailbox and squealed it shut. This time Reacher kept his jacket. Not just for the warmth. For the guns in the pockets. They set out to walk back to Barton's house. They got less than a block and a half.

Chapter 26

Nothing to do with complex triangulations of cell phone signals, or GPS pinpoint telltales accurate to half a yard. Much later Reacher figured it had happened the old-school way. A random guy in a random car had remembered his pre-watch briefing. That was all. Be on the lookout. A man and a woman.

Reacher and Abby made a right, intending to make the next left, which involved walking the length of a cobblestone block, on a narrow sidewalk, defined on the right-hand side by an unbroken sequence of iron-bound loading docks in back of the next street's buildings, and on the left-hand side by a sporadic line of cars parked on the curb. Not every space was filled. Maybe fifty-fifty. One of the cars was parked the wrong way around. Head on. It had no nighttime dew on it. In the split second it took the back of Reacher's brain to spark the front, the car's door opened, and the driver's gun came out, followed by the driver's hand, and then the driver himself, in a smooth athletic crouch, concealed behind the open door, aiming level through the open window.

At Reacher, at first. Then at Abby. Then back again. And again. Back and forth. Like on a TV show. The guy was making it clear he was covering both of them at once. He was wearing a blue suit. And a red tie, tied tight.

They won't shoot me. They want to ask me questions.

It's a psychological dynamic. Like in the theater.

It's not necessarily the kind of thing that has a yes or no answer.

The gun was a Glock 17, a little scratched and worn. The guy was using a two-handed grip. Both wrists were resting on the window rubber. His trigger finger was in position. The gun was steady. Its left-right arc was controlled and horizontal only. Competent, except that a crouch was an inherently unstable position, and also a pointless one, because a car door offered no kind of meaningful protection against a bullet. Better than aluminum foil, but not much. A smart guy would stand straight and rest his wrists on top of the door. More commanding. Easier to transition to whatever came next, like walking or running or fighting.

The guy with the gun called out, "Keep your hands where I can see them."

Reacher called back, "Do we have a problem?"

The guy called out, "I don't have a problem."

"OK," Reacher said. "Good to know." He turned to Abby and said, quieter, "You could head back to the corner, if you like. I could join you there in a minute. This guy wants to ask me questions, is all."

But the guy called out, "No, she stays, too. Both of you."

A man and a woman.

Reacher turned to face front again, and used the maneuver to conceal half a step of forward progress.

He said, "We stay for what?"

"Questions."

"Ask away."

"My boss will ask the questions."

"Where is he?"

"Coming."

"What's on his mind?"

"Many things, I'm sure."

"OK," Reacher said. "Put the gun away and come out from there and we'll all wait together. Right here on the sidewalk. Until he shows up."

The guy stayed crouched behind his door.

The gun didn't move.

"You can't use it anyway," Reacher said. "Your boss wouldn't like it if he showed up and found us dead or wounded or in shock or in a coma. Or quivering with some kind of traumatic stress disorder. He wants to ask us questions. He wants coherent answers that make sense. Plus the cops wouldn't stand for it. I don't care what kind of accommodations you think you got with them. A gunshot on a city street at night is going to get a reaction."

"You think you're a smart guy?"

"No, but I'm hoping you are."

The gun didn't move.

Which was OK. The trigger was the important part. Specifically the finger. Which was connected to the guy's central nervous system. Which could get all frozen up, even if just temporarily, with doubts and thoughts and second guesses.

Or at least slowed down a beat.

Reacher took another step. He raised his left hand halfway, palm out, patting the air, a conciliatory gesture, but also urgent, as if there was an immediate problem to solve. The guy's gaze followed the moving object, and appeared to miss Reacher's right hand, which was also moving, but slower and lower. It slipped unobtrusively into his right-hand pockct, where the H&K was that he knew for sure worked.

The guy said, "We wait in the car. Not on the sidewalk."

"OK," Reacher said.

"Doors closed."

"Sure."

"You in the back, me in the front."

"Until your boss shows up," Reacher said. "Then he can get in the front with you. He can ask his questions. Is that the plan?"

"Until then you keep quiet."

"Sure," Reacher said again. "You win. You're the man with the gun, after all. We'll get in the car."

The guy nodded, satisfied.

After which it was easy. The guy dropped the outer fingers out of his two-handed grip, and pressed them hard on the window rubber, tented, like a pianist playing an emphatic chord, which could have been a semaphore signal that a conclusive agreement had been reached, but was more likely simple physics, as the guy prepared to boost and balance and bounce his way up out of his crouch. Which by then had been going on a long time, to bad effect, in terms of numbness and tingle. Either way the gun came under reduced control, and its butt tipped back and its barrel tipped up, which again could have been seen as a gesture, that the immediate threat was thereby formally withdrawn, in favor of newfound cooperation, but was more likely weight and balance and a natural backward rotation around the trigger guard.

Reacher left the H&K in his pocket.

He took a long pace forward and kicked the car door gently. It clanged back and whacked the guy in the knees, and that small pulse of force rolled him backward over the balls of his feet, agonizingly slow, but irresistible, until finally he rolled over on his back, helpless, like a turtle. His hands whipped up to break his fall and the clenched Glock hit the sidewalk with a plastic smack and bounced loose and skittered away. But then the guy jerked sideways and rolled once and sprang up, from the horizontal to the vertical almost instantly, and without apparent effort. Athletic, like he had been minutes before, getting out of the car. All of which meant Reacher got there half a step late.

The guy danced sideways, out of range of the swing of the still-open driver's door, and then he came up with another instant change of direction, suddenly leaning in and launching a clubbing right at Reacher's face, which Reacher saw coming, so he ducked and twisted and took it high on the shoulder, all sharp knuckles, not much of a blow, but even so the action and reaction opened up a fractional gap between them, just a split second, which given the guy's speed meant he could dance away again, scuffing his feet across the ground, glancing down, searching for his gun.

Physically Reacher could have been called athletic in his own right, but it was a heavyweight kind of athleticism, a kind of weightlifter savagery, not nimbleness. He was fast, but not real fast. He was not capable of an instant reversal of momentum. Which meant he spent a certain half second of time locked in a neutral position, neither stop nor go, during which interval the other guy threw another punch, which Reacher ducked and dodged again, and like before the guy danced away to safety and searched on another radius, scuffing his feet, glancing down in the dark. Reacher kept on coming, a half step at a time, dodging and weaving, on the one hand slow in comparison, but on the other hand hard to stop, especially with the kind of weak blows so far attempted, and furthermore the guy was tiring all the time, hopping about and breathing hard.

The guy danced away.

Reacher kept on coming.

The guy found his gun.

The side of the guy's shoe tapped against it and sent it skittering an extra inch, with a brief plastic scraping sound, unmistakable. The guy froze for an imperceptible period, just a blink of time, thinking as fast as he was about to act, and then he swooped down, twisting, his right hand whipping through a long arc, aiming to snatch up the gun and grab it tight and whirl it away to safety. An instinctive calculation, based on space and time and speed, all four dimensions, with his own generous capabilities no doubt accurately accounted for, and his opponent's capabilities no doubt cautiously estimated, based on worst-case averages, plus a safety margin, for the purposes of the arithmetic, which still showed plenty of time for a guy as quick as he was. Reacher's own instinctive calculation came to the same conclusion. He agreed. No way could he get there first.

Except that some of his disadvantages carried their own compensation. His limbs were slow because they were heavy, and they were heavy because they were not only thick but also long. In the case of his legs, very long. He drove hard off his left foot and kicked out with his right, stretching low, a huge vicious wingspan, aiming at anything, any part of the guy, any part of the swoop, any window of time, whatever came along.

What came along was the guy's head. A freak result. Four dimensional geometry gone wrong. His slight hesitation, Reacher's primeval thrust, triggered by instinct, soaked in ancient all-or-nothing aggression. The guy chose to keep his head up and his arm long, all the better to scoop up the gun and wheel away, but Reacher was already there, like a batter early on a fastball, a foul ball for sure, and the guy hit the first inch of his follow-through, his temple solidly against the welt of Reacher's shoe, not a perfect connection, but close to it. The guy's neck snapped back and he scraped and clattered cheek-down on the side-walk.

Reacher watched him.

He said, "Do you see his gun somewhere?"

The guy wasn't moving.

Abby said, "I see it."

"Pick it up. Finger and thumb, butt or barrel."

"I know how."

"Just checking. Always safer that way."

She darted in, knelt, picked up the Glock, and darted back.

The guy still wasn't moving.

She said, "What should we do about him?"

Reacher said, "We should leave him right where he is."

"And then what?"

"We should steal his car."

"Why?"

"His boss is coming. We need to leave the right kind of message."

"You can't declare war on them."

"They already did. On me. For no apparent reason. So now I'm offering a robust initial response. I'm saying their policy should be reconsidered. It's a standard diplomatic move. Like playing chess. It gives them a chance to parley, no harm, no foul. I hope they see that."

Abby said, "This is the Albanian mob we're talking about. You're one guy. Frank is right. This is crazy."

"But it's happening," Reacher said. "We can't roll the clock back. We can't wish it away. We just have to deal with it the best we can. So we can't leave the car here. Too meek and mild. Like we're saying, oops, sorry. Like we didn't really mean it. We got to make a point. We got to say, don't mess with us, or you get a kick in the head and your car stolen. That way they'll take it seriously. They'll act with an element of tactical caution. They'll assemble larger forces."

"That's a bad thing."

"Only if they find us. Assuming they don't, all they're doing by bunching up is leaving bigger gaps elsewhere, for us to walk through."

"Walk through where?"

"I guess the ultimate goal would be a face to face meeting with the big boss. Gregory's equivalent."

"Dino," Abby said. "That's crazy."

"He's one guy. Same as me. We could have an exchange of views. I'm sure it's just a misunderstanding."

"I have to work in this town. One side of Center or the other."

"I apologize," Reacher said.

"You should."

"But that's why we need to do this right. We need to play to win."

"OK, we'll steal the car."

"Or we could set it on fire."

"Stealing is better," she said. "I want to get out of here as fast as I can."

They drove the car four blocks into a tangle of blank urban streets, and they left it on a corner, keys in, all four doors standing open, plus the hood, plus the trunk. Somehow symbolic. Then they walked back to Barton's place, via a long circuitous route, and they checked all four sides of his block before they stepped to his door. He was up, waiting, with Hogan.

Plus a third guy, who Reacher had never seen before.

Chapter 27

The third guy in Barton's hallway had the kind of hair and skin that made a person look ten years younger than he really was, which therefore in reality made him about Reacher's own generation. He was smaller and neater. He had sharp watchful eyes set deep either side of a blade of a nose. He had a long unruly lock of hair that fell across his forehead. He was dressed with a modicum of style, in good shoes and corduroy pants and a shirt and a jacket.

Joe Hogan said, "This is who I was telling you about. The dogface who knows all the old Commie languages. His name is Guy Vantresca."

Reacher stuck out his hand.

"Pleased to meet you," he said.

"Likewise," Vantresca said, and he shook hands, and then he did so all over again, with Abby.

Reacher said, "You got here fast."

"I was still awake," Vantresca said. "I live close by."

"Thanks for helping out."

"Actually that's not why I'm here. I came to warn you off. You can't mess with these people. Too many, too nasty, too protected. That would be my assessment."

"Were you Military Intelligence?"

Vantresca shook his head.

"Armor," he said.

A company commander late on in the Cold War, Hogan had called him.

"Tanks?" Reacher asked.

"Fourteen of them," Vantresca said. "All mine. All facing east. Happy days."

"Why did you learn the languages?"

"I thought we were going to win. I thought I might be ruling a civilian district. Or at least ordering a bottle of wine in a restaurant. Or meeting girls. It was a long time ago. Plus Uncle Sam paid for it. Back then the army liked education. Everyone was getting postgraduate degrees."

Reacher said, "Too many and too nasty are subjective judgments. We can talk about that kind of stuff later. But too protected is different. What do you know about that?"

"I do some corporate consulting. Mostly physical security of buildings. But I hear things, and I get asked things. Last year a federal project ran a set of integrated numbers from all across the nation, and it turned out the two most law-abiding populations in America were the Ukrainian and Albanian communities right here in town. They don't even get parking tickets. That suggests a very close relationship with all levels of law enforcement."

"But there must be a red line somewhere. I suggested to one of them that gunfire on the city streets at night would get a reaction, and the guy didn't argue. In fact I guess he agreed with me, because he didn't pull the trigger."

"Plus we're getting a new police commissioner. They're nervous. But there's still plenty of boring invisible stuff their side of the line. Generally speaking this type of thing isn't about bullets in the street. It's about someone having a cozy chat with a potential witness, out of sight, out of earshot, probably in the witness's own home, probably in a meaningful location, like an infant daughter's bedroom, about what a weird thing memory is, how it comes and goes, how it fades in and out, how it plays tricks, and about how it's no shame at all to say, look, man, I just can't recall. People I know say that kind of case is very hard to investigate and very easy to bury."

"How many of them are there?"

"Too many. Like I said. Too many, too nasty, too protected. You should forget it."

"Where was your company in the order of battle?"

"Pretty near the tip of the spear," Vantresca said.

"In other words hopelessly outnumbered, from day one and possibly forever."

"I get the point you're trying to make. But I had fourteen Abrams tanks. They were the finest fighting vehicles in the world. They were like something out of a science fiction book. I wasn't walking through the Fulda Gap in a pair of pants and a jacket."

"As always with armored people, you over-fetishize the machine. That said, clearly you felt you were more lethal than them. Outnumbered, but nastier. But in turn they were certainly protected, by a whole giant nation. One out of three in your favor. Two out of three against. But even so, you would have started your engines, if they had told you to."

"I get the point," Vantresca said again.

"And you expected to win," Reacher said. "Which is why you learned the languages. Which are all I really need right now. I'm taking this one step at a time. First I need to understand what they're saying in the texts, and then I need to use what I learn, in order to figure out what to do next. No combat readiness yet. No warnings necessary."

"Suppose what you learn is that it's hopeless?"

"Not an acceptable outcome. Can only be a failure of planning. Surely they taught you that in Germany."

"OK," Vantresca said. "One step at a time."

They worked in the kitchen and started with the Ukrainian language. Vantresca admired Abby's video capture. Smart, to the point, and efficient. He tapped his finger on the screen, in a slow, syncopated rhythm, play, pause, play, pause, and he read aloud from the freeze-framed screen, at first slow and halting, and then sometimes stopping altogether.

Because linguistically he was in trouble from the start. These were text messages, full of unknown slang, and single-letter abbreviations, and in-group acronyms, and also full of what could only be misspellings, unless in fact they were deliberate simplifications, perhaps following a convention developed especially for the medium. No one knew. Vantresca said the task could take him some time. He said it would be like translating a difficult foreign language while simultaneously breaking an espionage code. Or maybe two codes, given the oblique allusions and elisions any self-respecting gangster could be expected to use.

Abby got her laptop and worked with him side by side, tackling individual words with on-line dictionaries, or searching the single-letter abbreviations, or the acronyms, on language blogs, and word-nerd sites. She made notes on scraps of paper. A couple of things fell into place, but even so the work was slow. Never had so much come from so little. She had made the video as fast as she dared, five, ten, twenty seconds, scrolling at speed, pumping on and on. Now that vivid blur was giving up thousands and thousands of words, each one a challenge and a puzzle, most of them with two or three plausible solutions.

Reacher let them work. He hung out in the front parlor, with Barton and Hogan, in the spaces between the drums and the speaker cabinets. One cabinet was gray and about the size of a refrigerator. It had eight dirty circles on its grill. Reacher sat on the floor and leaned his back against it and it didn't move at all. Barton hauled his battered Fender up into his lap, and played it unplugged, barely audible, with up and down runs of soft buzzy notes.

Hogan said, "Do you think we would have won? Do you think Vantresca would have wound up using his languages?"

"On balance I think we would have prevailed," Reacher said. "As a technical matter I think we would have shut them down before they shut us down. Hard to call it winning, given the mess it would have made. But whatever, the tip of the spear would have been vaporized long ago. I'm afraid your friend wasted his time in school."

Barton played a descending arpeggio, some kind of diminished minor chord, and ended with a bang on the open bottom string. Plugged in, it would have demolished the house. Unplugged, the string rattled and clattered against the frets, and gave out no fundamental at all. Barton looked at Reacher and said, "Now you're the tip of the spear."

"I'm not looking to start a war," Reacher said. "All I want is the Shevicks' money. If I can get it some kind of easy way, I absolutely will, believe me. I don't feel the need to meet any of them face to face on the field of battle. In fact I would be happier not to."

"You won't get the option. They must have Trulenko buttoned up pretty tight. Layers and layers. I've seen them do it, when a name comes to one of their clubs. They have a man on the corner, and a man on the door, and a man on the next door along, plus a couple of extra guys just roaming around."

"What do you remember about Trulenko?"

"He was a nerd, like all those guys. I remember thinking it shouldn't turn out that way. I was cool in high school. Now the nerds are billionaires and I'm scraping a living. I guess I should have learned software, not music."

"If he was working, what would he be doing?"

"Is he working?"

"Someone used that word."

"Then computers, I'm sure. That's what he was good at. He was one of the top boys. His app was something to do with doctors, but basically all that stuff is computer software, isn't it?"

Abby stuck her head in the door.

"We figured it out," she said. "We're ready to go with the Ukrainian. They mention Trulenko twice."

Chapter 28

Vantresca reset the video so it would play from the beginning, but before he ran it he said, "Overall there's some weird shit going down. Apart from anything else they're in an uproar because they're losing people. Two guys got in a wreck up at the Ford dealer. Then two bagmen got taken off a block in the gourmet quarter. Then two more guys got taken out of a massage parlor. Then two more guys went missing outside of Abby's house. Total of eight so far."

"It's carnage out there," Reacher said.

"What's interesting is they blamed the Albanians for the first six. But the language changed for the last two. Now they're blaming you. They think you're on some secret New York or Chicago payroll, covertly employed to stir things up down here. There's an all-points bulletin out on you. Under the name of Shevick. Which in the end could prove to be a bigger problem."

Vantresca clicked Abby's phone and started the video. At first he let it spool at the same speed she had recorded it. On the screen the shadow of her fingertip was visible on the right side of the image, scooting up, up, up. Then Vantresca paused and restarted and paused again, until he found the bubble he wanted. It contained a photograph above the text. Aaron and Maria Shevick, and Abigail Gibson, in the hallway of the Shevicks' home, looking startled and a little uneasy. Reacher remembered the sound he heard from behind the kitchen door. The quiet, scratchy click. The cell phone, imitating a camera.

Vantresca said, "The text below the image says the people in the picture are Jack, Joanna, and Abigail Reacher."

He played and paused, played and paused, through four more bubbles. He stopped on a fifth. He said, "Right here they've already figured out it's Abby Gibson, not Abigail Reacher. Next message down, they're sending a guy to her place of work, to get her home address."

He moved the video on.

"And here they have her home address, and now they're sending a car to her house, with orders to bring her in if they find her."

"All's well that ends well," Reacher said.

"It gets worse," Vantresca said. He moved the video on again, to a fat green bubble from later in the day, which had the same photograph in it again, above a dense block of Cyrillic writing. Vantresca read out loud, "It has been reported that the old woman named

Joanna Reacher in the picture above was in our pawn shop where she signed her name Maria Shevick."

"Shit," Reacher said. "That was their shop?"

"She should have expected it. Most everything is theirs, on the west side. Problem is, she gave them her real name. Which makes it at least somewhat likely she gave them her real address and her real Social Security number, too. Which puts them one step away from finding out she's Aaron Shevick's legal wife. From that point on it's not going to be rocket science to figure out who's really who. Whereupon they can act as fast as they like. They're already waiting outside the house."

"They'll be plunged into an existential crisis. Do they want Aaron Shevick the name, or Aaron Shevick the physical human being who borrowed their money and is apparently covertly stirring them up? What, after all, is the nature of identity? It's a question they'll have to wrestle with."

"Are you a West Pointer?"

"How could you tell?"

"The level of bullshit. This could get very serious. Obviously they want the right physical human being, but however they set about getting him, you got to figure a little china will get broken along the way. Starting right inside that house."

Reacher nodded.

"I know," he said. "Believe me. It's already very serious. They're seventy years old. But I don't see what I can do about their physical safety. Not around the clock. The only rational response would be evacuate them to a safe location. But where? I don't have the resources." He paused a beat. Then he said, "Normally with this kind of thing, I would say, go stay with your daughter. I'm sure they would love to."

Vantresca moved the video to a fat bubble from late the night before. He said, "This is where you say the name Trulenko to the doorman where Abby worked. From here the conversation spins off in two different directions. First, about you. They can't understand why a downmarket applicant for credit would ask that question. Two different worlds. From there they develop the theory you're a provocateur paid by an outside organization."

"And the second direction is about Trulenko himself," Abby said. "There are two separate mentions. First a status check and a threat assessment. Which comes back negative. All secure. But an hour later, they start to worry."

"Because I got away," Reacher said. "When you hauled me in your door. They knew I was still on the loose."

Vantresca said, "They pulled four crews off their regular assignments and told them to report for extra guard duty. They told the existing guards to fall back and form up again as Trulenko's personal detail. They call it Situation B, which we think is a kind of Defcon level. It's clearly pre-planned, probably rehearsed, maybe even used before."

"OK," Reacher said. "A crew is what, two guys in a car?"

"You would know."

"Therefore eight guys in total. Reinforcing how many to start with? How many do they deploy on an

everyday zero-threat basis? Not more than four, probably, if they can also seamlessly change into a personal detail afterward. So four fall back and eight
take over the perimeter."

"You against twelve guys."

"Not if I pick the right spot on the perimeter. I
could sneak in a gap."

"Best case, four guys."

"Moot point, unless the phone tells the eight guys
exactly where to report, for their extra guard duty. A
street address would be helpful."

Vantresca didn't answer.

Reacher looked at Abby.

She said, "It does say exactly where."

"But?"

"It's an incredibly difficult word. I looked it up all
over the place. Originally it seemed to mean either a
hive or a nest or a burrow. Or all three. Or somewhere in between. For something that might have
hummed or buzzed or thrashed around. Like a lot of
ancient words it was biologically inexact. Now it
seems to be used exclusively as a metaphor. Like in
the movies, when you see the mad scientist in his lab,
full of lit-up machines and crackling energy. That's
how the word is used now."

"Like a nerve center."

"Exactly."

"So all the phone says is, report to the nerve center."

"Obviously they know where it is."

"The guys I spoke to didn't," Reacher said. "I
asked them, and I believed them. It's classified infor-

mation. Which means the crews they just hauled off their regular duties were senior people. In the know."

"Makes sense," Vantresca said. "The pick of the litter. Only the best for Situation B."

"Told you so," Hogan said. "The only route is straight through the top levels."

Barton said, "Crazy."

Vantresca and Abby started work on the Albanian messages, using the same system as before, side by side at the kitchen table. Vantresca was less familiar with the language, but the texts themselves were more formal and grammatical than their Ukrainian counterparts, so altogether the work went faster. And there was much less to do. All the relevant stuff came during the last few hours. Some of it was familiar. Reacher was once again taken to be a provocateur paid by outside forces. Some of it was new. The white Toyota had been seen driving in. Reacher and Abby had been seen getting out together, after parking way out in the wastelands. A small, slender woman with short dark hair, and a big ugly man with short fair hair. Be on the lookout.

"Technically I think it means plain-featured," Abby said. "Or handsome in a rugged kind of way. Not ugly as such."

Reacher said, "Sticks and stones may break my bones, but words will never hurt me."

"These might," Vantresca said. He was at the end of the video. The last Albanian text. He said, "They're actively looking for you. They're giving an estimate of your current position. They're guessing you're somewhere inside a particular twelve-block rectangle."

"And are we?"

"Not far from its exact geographic center."

"That's not good," Reacher said. "They seem to have plenty of information."

"They have a lot of local knowledge. They have a lot of fingers in a lot of pies, and a lot of eyes behind a lot of windows, and a lot of cars on a lot of streets."

"Sounds like you've been studying up on them."

"Like I said, I hear things. Everyone has a story. Because everyone comes up against them, sooner or later. Whatever you're into, it's the cost of doing business, east of Center Street. People get used to it. Ultimately they see it as reasonable. Ten percent, like the church used to take, back in the olden days. Like taxes. Nothing to be done about it. That part becomes quite civilized. As long as you pay. Which everyone does, by the way. These are scary people."

"Sounds like personal experience."

"A couple of months ago I helped a journalist from Washington, D.C., with her local arrangements. I have a private security license. My number is listed in all the national directories. I don't know what her story was going to be about. She wouldn't tell me. Organized crime, I supposed, because that was what she seemed to be interested in. The Albanians and the Ukrainians both. More the Ukrainians, to be honest. That was my impression. But somehow she said the wrong thing east of Center and her first encounter was with the Albanians. They had a face to face discussion. A handful of them, and just her, on her own, in the back room of a restaurant. She came out and had me drive her straight to the airport. Not even her hotel first. She didn't want to stop and get her stuff. She was terrified. Deep down scared. She was acting like an automaton. She took the first flight out and never came back. If they could make that happen just by talking to her, you better believe they can make a whole bunch of people keep their eyes peeled for a pair of strangers. Sheer intimidation. That's how they get their information."

"That's not good either," Reacher said. "I don't want to bring bad luck to this household."

Neither Barton nor Hogan had a comment, one way or the other.

"We can't use hotels," Abby said.

"Maybe we can," Reacher said. "Maybe we should. It might be a way of accelerating the process."

"You're not ready," Hogan said.

Barton said, "Stay the night. You're already here. The neighbors don't have X-ray vision. We have a lunchtime gig tomorrow. If you need to get going, you can ride along in the van. No one will see."

"Where is the gig?"

"At a lounge west of Center. Closer to Trulenko than you are now."

"Does the lounge have a guy on the door?"

"Always. Probably best to get out around the corner."

"Or not, if we wanted to accelerate the process."

"We have to work there, man. It's a good gig for us. Do us a favor and accelerate the process someplace else. If you need to. Which I hope you don't. Because it's crazy."

"Deal," Reacher said. "We'll ride with you tomorrow. Thank you very much. And for your hospitality tonight."

Vantresca left ten minutes later. Barton locked the doors. Hogan put headphones on and lit a blunt the size of Reacher's thumb. Reacher and Abby went upstairs, to the room with the tipped-up guitar amplifier for a nightstand. Three blocks away a brand new text message failed to reach the Albanian phone in the abandoned metal mailbox. A minute later the same thing happened with the Ukrainian phone.

Chapter 29

Dino's right-hand man had the given name Shkumbin, which was a beautiful river deep in the heart of his beautiful homeland. But it was not an easy name to use in English. At first most people said it Scum Bin, some of them tauntingly, but those only once. When they could speak again, after months of dental procedures, they seemed very willing to try very hard with the sound of his name's initial syllable. Although that could have been less than perfect reconstructive work. But eventually Shkumbin got tired of hurting his knuckles, and he took his dead brother's name, partly as a convenience, and partly as a tribute. Not his elder dead brother's name, which had been Fatbardh, which meant may he be the fortunate one, which was another beautiful name, but again, hard to use in English. Instead Shkumbin now went by his younger dead brother's name, which was Jetmir, one who will live a good life, another warm sentiment, and this time easy to say in English, and memorable, quite flashy and futuristic, even if really a traditional blessing, and even if a bit communist-sounding, like a Red Army test pilot in a Soviet comic book, or a hero cosmonaut on a propaganda billboard. Not that Americans seemed to care about that stuff anymore. Ancient history.

Jetmir got to the conference room in back of the lumber yard office and found the rest of the inner council already assembled. Apart from Dino himself, of course. Dino had not been informed. Not yet. It was their second meeting without him. A big step. One meeting might be explained away. To explain two was exponentially harder.

To explain three would be impossible.

Jetmir said, "The missing phone came back on line for almost twenty minutes. It sent nothing and received nothing. Then it went dark again. Like they're hiding out deep in a basement or something, or an underground cellar, but then they came up to the street, just for a short time, maybe to walk to the corner store and back."

"Did we get a location?" someone asked.

"We got a pretty good triangulation, but it's a densely populated area. Every corner has a store. But it's right where we thought they would be. Close to the center of the shape we marked out."

"How close?"

"I say we forget the twelve blocks we figured before. We can squeeze it down to the middle four. Maybe the middle six, to be certain."

"In a basement?"

"Or somewhere there's no signal."

"Maybe they took the battery out. And then put it back in."

"To do what? I told you, they didn't make or receive a call."

"OK, a basement."

"Or a building with a thick iron frame. Somewhere like that. Keep an open mind. Tell everyone to squeeze in tight. Really flood the area. Look for lights behind drapes. Look for cars and pedestrians. Knock on doors and ask questions if necessary."

At that same moment Jetmir's opposite number on the other side of Center Street was also in a meeting, also of his inner council, in the room in back of the taxi company, across from the pawn shop, next to the bail bond operation. But in his case his boss was present. Gregory was right there, as always, at the head of the table, presiding. He had called the meeting himself, right after he heard about one of his downtown guys getting stuck up by Aaron Shevick.

He said, "This latest incident feels completely different to me. There was no attempt at deception. He wasn't expecting us to blame the Albanians for it. It was completely blatant, face to face. Apparently he has been instructed to abandon his earlier tactics. In favor of a new phase. I think a mistake. They have revealed more about themselves than they will discover about us."

"The phone," his right-hand man said.

"Precisely," Gregory said. "Taking the gun was to

be expected. Anyone would. But why the instruction to take the phone?"

"It's a necessary component of their new strategy. They're going to attempt to inflict electronic damage. To weaken us further. They're going to try to get inside our operating system through our phones."

"Who in the whole wide world would have the skills and the experience and the sheer confidence and the deluded arrogance to even hope to succeed with that?"

"Only the Russians," his right-hand man said.

"Precisely," Gregory said again. "Their new tactic has revealed their identity. Now we know. The Russians are moving in on us."

"Not good."

"I wonder if they took an Albanian phone, too."

"Probably. The Russians don't like sharing territory. I'm sure they plan to replace us both. This is going to be very tough. There are a lot of them."

There was silence for a long moment.

Then Gregory asked, "Can we beat them?"

His right-hand man said, "They won't get inside our operating system."

"Not what I asked."

"Well, whatever we bring to the fight, they bring twice the men, twice the money, and twice the material."

"These are desperate times," Gregory said.

"Truly."

"They call for desperate measures."

"Like what?"

"If the Russians are going to bring twice as much

as we can, then we need to rebalance the scale. Simple as that. Just temporarily. Just for the time being. Until the present crisis has passed."

"How?"

"We need to form a short-term defensive alliance."

"Who with?"

"Our friends east of Center."

"With the Albanians?"

"They're in the same boat."

"Would they do it?"

"Against the Russians, they're going to need it just as much as we do. If we join forces, we might just match them. If we don't, we can't. United we stand, divided we fall."

Silence again.

"It's a big step to take," someone said.

"I agree," Gregory said. "Even weird and crazy. But necessary."

No one spoke after that.

"OK," Gregory said. "I'll go talk to Dino again, first thing in the morning."

Reacher woke up in the gray gloom of night, with the clock in his head showing ten minutes to four. He had heard a sound. A car, on the street, outside and below the round window. The bite and grind of brakes, the compression of springs, the stress of tires. A car, slowing to a stop.

He waited. Abby slept on beside him, warm, and soft, and comfortable. The old house creaked and ticked. There was a stripe of light under the door out to the hallway. The bulb over the stairs was still on. Maybe another fixture too, in a downstairs room. The kitchen or the parlor. Maybe Barton or Hogan was still up. Or both of them, shooting the shit. Ten to four in the morning. Musicians' hours.

Out on the street the car's engine idled quietly. The faint thrash of belts, the whir of a fan, the rustle of pistons slapping up and down, uselessly. Then a faint muted thump from under the hood, and a sensation of new permanence.

The transmission had been shoved forward into park.

The engine turned off.

Silence again.

A door opened.

A leather sole clapped down on the sidewalk. A seat spring clicked as weight was lifted off. A second shoe joined the first. Someone stood up straight, with a tiny huff of effort.

The door closed.

Reacher slid out of bed. He found his pants. He found his shirt. He found his socks. He laced his shoes. He slipped his jacket on. Reassuring weight in the pockets.

One floor below there was a loud knock at the street door. A booming, wooden sound. Ten to four in the morning. Reacher listened. Heard nothing. In fact less than nothing. Certainly less than before. Like a hole in the air. It was the negative sound of two guys previously shooting the shit, now dumbstruck and craning around and thinking what the hell? Barton and Hogan, still up. Musicians' hours.

Reacher waited. *Deal with it,* he thought. *Don't make me come downstairs.* He heard one of them get to his feet. A sideways shuffle. Looking out the window, probably, through a crack in the drapes, sideways, obliquely.

He heard a low voice say, "Albanian."

It was Hogan's voice.

Barton's voice whispered back, "How many?"

"Just one."

"What does he want?"

"I was out sick the day they taught predicting the future."

"What should we do?"

The knock came again, *boom, boom, boom,* heavy and wooden.

Reacher waited. Behind him Abby stirred and said, "What's happening?"

"There's an Albanian footsoldier at the door. Almost certainly looking for us."

"What time is it?"

"Eight minutes to four."

"What are we going to do?"

"Barton and Hogan are downstairs. They haven't gone to bed yet. Hopefully they can deal with it."

"I should put some clothes on."

"Sad, but true."

She dressed like he had, fast, pants, shirt, shoes. Then they waited. The knock came for a third time. *Bang, boom, bang.* The kind of knock you didn't ignore. They heard Hogan offer to get it. They heard Barton accept. They heard Hogan's footsteps across the hallway floor, solid, determined, implacable. The

U.S. Marine. The drummer. Reacher wasn't sure which counted for more.

They heard the door open.

They heard Hogan say, "What?"

Then a new voice. Quieter, because it was outside the structure, not inside, and because of its pitch, which was instantly two things in one, both conversational and mocking. Friendly, but not really.

The voice said, "Everything OK in there?"

Hogan said, "Why wouldn't it be?"

"I saw the light inside," the voice said. "I was worried you had been woken up in the night by a misfortune or a calamity."

It was talking low, but even so it was a big voice, full of physical power, from a big chest and a thick neck, and also full of command and arrogance and entitlement. The guy was accustomed to getting his own way. He had the kind of voice that never said please and never heard no.

Deal with it, Reacher thought. *Don't make me come downstairs.*

Hogan said, "We're good in here. Nothing to worry about. No misfortunes. No calamities."

"You sure? You know we like to help out when we can."

"No help required," Hogan said. "The light was on because not everyone sleeps at the same time. Not a hard concept to grasp."

"Hey, I know all about that," the Albanian guy said. "Here I am, working all night long, keeping the neighborhood safe. Actually, you could help me with that, if you like."

250 | LEE CHILD

Hogan didn't answer.

The guy said, "Don't you want to help me with that?"

Still no reply.

"What goes around comes around," the guy said. "It's that kind of thing. You help us now, we'll help you, down the road. Could be important. Could be just what you need. Could solve a big problem. On the other hand, if you get in our way now, we could make things tough for you later. In the future, I mean. All kinds of different ways. For instance, what do you do for a living?"

"What help?" Hogan said.

"We're looking for a man and a woman. He's older, she's younger. She's petite and dark-haired, he's big and ugly."

Deal with it, Reacher thought. *Don't make me come downstairs.*

"Why are you looking for them?" Hogan asked.

The guy at the door said, "We think they're in terrible danger. We need to warn them. For their own sake. We're trying to help. It's what we do."

"We haven't seen them."

"You sure?"

"Hundred percent."

"One more thing you could do," the guy said.

"What?"

"Call us if you see them. Would you do that for us?"

No answer from Hogan.

"It's not much to ask," the guy said. "Either you feel like helping us out with a ten-second phone call, or you don't, I guess. Either way is fine. It's a free country. We'll make a note and move right along."

"OK," Hogan said. "We'll call."

"Thanks. Any time, night or day. Don't delay."

"OK," Hogan said again.

"One last thing."

"What?"

"Another way you could help me out."

"How?"

"Obviously I'm going to report this address as what we call in our business a place of zero concern. Targets clearly not there, just regular folks going about their regular business, and so on and so forth."

"Good," Hogan said.

"But in our business we take process very seriously. We like numbers. At some point I'm sure to be asked, with what exact degree of confidence do I make that assessment?"

"Hundred percent," Hogan said again.

"I hear you, but at the end of the day, that's just a verbal report by an interested party."

"All you got."

"My point exactly," the guy said. "It would really help me out if I could take a walk through your property and see for myself. Then we got a foundation of solid evidence to go on. Case closed. We wouldn't need to bother you again. Maybe you would get an invitation to the July Fourth picnic. One of the family now. A solid guy who helps out."

"It's not my property," Hogan said. "I rent a room. I don't think I have the authority."

"Maybe the other gentleman, in the living room."

"You need to take our word for it, and you need to leave now."

"Don't worry about the weed," the guy said. "Is that it? I could smell it down the street. I don't care about weed. I'm not a cop. I'm not here to bust you. I'm a representative from the local mutual aid society. We work hard in the community. We achieve impressive results."

"Take our word for it," Hogan said again.

"Who else is in the house?"

"No one."

"Been alone all night?"

"We had people over for the evening."

"What people?"

"Friends," Hogan said. "We had Chinese food and a little wine."

"Did they stay over?"

"No."

"How many friends?"

"Two."

"A man and a woman, by any chance?"

"Not the man and woman you're looking for."

"How do you know?"

"Because they can't be. They're just regular folks. Like you said."

"You sure they didn't stay over?"

"I saw them leave."

"OK," the guy said. "Then you have nothing to worry about. I'll just take a quick glance around. I'll know right away anyway. I have some experience in these matters. I was a police detective back in Tirana. Usually I found it impossible for a person to be in a house without leaving visible clues somewhere, including about who they were, and why they were there."

Hogan had no answer.

Reacher and Abby heard footsteps in the hallway directly below them. The guy had stepped inside.

Abby whispered, "I can't believe Hogan let him in. Obviously this guy will look everywhere. It won't be a quick glance around. Hogan fell for it."

"Hogan is doing fine," Reacher said. "He's a U.S. Marine. He has a sound grasp of strategy. He gave us plenty of time to get dressed and make the bed and get the window open, so that right about now, as the guy steps inside, we climb outside, and we hide on the roof or in the yard, and the guy doesn't find us, and he goes away happy, all without a single moment of confrontation. The best fights are the ones you don't have. Even Marines understand that."

"But we're not climbing out the window. We're just standing here. We're not following the plan."

"There might be an alternative approach."

"Like what?"

"Maybe something more army than Marine Corps."

"Like what?" she said again.

"Let's wait and see what happens," he said.

Below them they heard the guy tramp his way into the parlor.

They heard him say, "You're musicians?"

"Yes."

"You play our clubs?"

"Yes."

"Not anymore, unless your attitude improves."

No reply. Silence for a second. Then from above they heard the guy move out to the hallway again, and onward into the kitchen.

"Chinese food," they heard him say. "Lots of containers. You were telling the truth."

"Plus wine," Hogan said. "Like I told you."

They heard a clink. Two empty bottles, picked up or knocked together or otherwise examined or inspected or disturbed.

Then silence.

Then they heard the guy say, "What's this?"

They heard the air suck out of the room.

No sound at all.

Until they heard the guy answer his own question.

They heard him say, "It's a scrap of paper with the Albanian word for ugly written on it."

Chapter 30

Reacher and Abby stepped out the bedroom door, to the upstairs hallway. Below them in the kitchen there was no sound. Just some kind of silent tension, hissing and crackling off the tile. Reacher pictured worried glances, Barton to Hogan, Hogan to Barton.

Abby whispered, "We should go down there and help them out."

"We can't," Reacher said. "If that guy sees us here, we can't let him leave."

"Why not?"

"He would report back. This address would be blown forever. Barton could get all kinds of problems in the future. They would stop him playing their clubs, for sure. Hogan, too. Same boat. They got to eat."

Then he paused.

Abby said, "What do you mean, can't let him leave?"

"There are a number of options."

"You mean take him prisoner?"

"Maybe this house has a cellar."

"What are the other options?"

"There's a range. I'm pretty much a whatever works kind of guy."

Abby said, "I guess this is my fault. I shouldn't have left the paper."

"You were defending me. It was nice of you."

"Still a mistake."

"Spilled milk," Reacher said. "Move on. Don't waste mental energy."

Below them the conversation started up again.

They heard the guy ask, "Are you learning a new language?"

No answer.

"Probably better not to start with Albanian. And probably better not to start with this particular word. It's kind of subtle. It has a bunch of meanings. Country people use it. I guess originally it's an old folk word, from long ago. It's quite rare now. Not used often."

No response.

"Why did you write it on a scrap of paper?"

No reply.

"Actually I don't think you did. I think this is a woman's handwriting. I told you, I have experience in these matters. I was a police detective in Tirana. I like to keep abreast of relevant data. Especially concerning my new country. The woman who wrote this word is too young to have learned formal cursive penmanship in school. She's less than forty."

No answer.

"Perhaps she's your friend, who came to dinner. Because the paper was left on the table among the cartons of food. In what they call the same archaeological layer. Which means they were deposited at the same time."

Hogan said nothing.

The guy asked, "Is your friend who came to dinner less than forty?"

Hogan said, "She's about thirty, I guess."

"And she came over for Chinese food and a little wine."

No answer.

"And maybe some weed, and some gossip about people you both know, and then some serious conversation, about your lives, and the state of the world."

"I suppose," Hogan said.

"In the middle of which she suddenly jumped up and found a scrap of paper and wrote a single rare and subtle word in a foreign language completely unknown to most Americans. Can you explain that to me?"

"She's a smart person. Maybe she was talking about something. Maybe it was the exact right word, if it's so rare and subtle. Smart people do that. They use foreign words. Maybe she wrote it down for me. So I could look it up later."

"Possible," the guy said. "Some other time, I might have shrugged my shoulders and let it go at that. Stranger things have happened. Except I don't like coincidences. Especially not four all at once. First coincidence is she wasn't here alone. She had a male partner. Second coincidence is, I've seen that rare word a lot in the last twelve hours. In text messages on my phone. Contained in descriptions of our male fugitive. Like I said at the beginning, a man and a woman. I said she's small and dark, and he's big and ugly."

Upstairs in the hallway Abby whispered, "This is going to turn bad."

Like a waitress smelling a bar fight coming.

"Probably," Reacher said.

Below them they heard the guy say, "The third coincidence is that a phone with copies of those same messages on it was stolen last night. At one point recently it was switched on for twenty minutes. No calls were made or received. But twenty minutes is long enough to read plenty of texts. Long enough to note down the hard words to work on later."

Hogan said, "Lighten up, man. No one had a stolen phone."

"The fourth coincidence is that the stolen phone was stolen by the big ugly guy in the description. We know that for sure. We got a full report. The guy was acting alone at the time, but he is known to associate with a small dark-haired woman. Who was undoubtedly your dinner guest, because she wrote the word on the paper. Undoubtedly she copied it from the stolen phone. Because how else would she know that word? Why else would she be interested in that word right now?"

"I don't know, man," Hogan said. "Maybe we're talking about different people."

"He went out and stole the phone and brought it

back to her. Did she instruct him to, ahead of time? Is she his boss? Did she send him on a mission?"

"I have no clue what you're talking about, man."

"Then you better get a clue," the guy said. "You have been caught harboring enemies of the community. Doesn't reflect well on you."

"Whatever," Hogan said.

"You want to move out of state?"

"I would prefer you to."

Silence for a long moment.

Then the guy spoke again. Some new menace in his voice. Some new thought. He said, "Did they walk or drive?"

"Who?"

"The man and the woman you were harboring."

"We weren't harboring diddly squat. We had friends over for dinner."

"Walk or drive?"

"When?"

"When they left your house at the end of the evening. When they didn't stay over."

"They walked."

"Do they live close by?"

"Not very," Hogan said, cautiously.

"So a walk of some length. We're watching these blocks very carefully. We didn't see a man and a woman walking home."

"Maybe they had a car parked around the corner."

"We didn't see a man and a woman driving home, either."

"Maybe you missed them."

"I don't think we would have."

"Then I can't help you, man."

The guy said, "I know they were here. I saw the food they ate. I have the note they transcribed from the stolen phone. Tonight these are the most heavily watched blocks in the city. They were not seen leaving. Therefore they're still here. I think they're upstairs, right now."

Silence for another long moment.

Then Hogan said, "You're a pain in the ass, man. Go ahead up and take a look. Three rooms, all of them empty. Then get out of the house and don't come back. Don't send an invitation to the picnic."

In the hallway upstairs Abby whispered, "We could still climb out the window."

"We didn't make the bed," Reacher whispered back. "And I decided we need this guy's car. We can't let him leave anyway."

"Why do we need his car?"

"Something I just realized we need to do."

Below them the guy's footsteps crossed the hallway. Toward the bottom of the stairs. A heavy tread. The old floor creaked and yielded under it. Reacher left his gun in his pocket. He didn't want to use it. *A gunshot on a city street at night is going to get a reaction.* Too many complications. Evidently the Albanian guy thought the same way. His right hand snaked into view and gripped the stair rail. No gun. His left hand followed. No gun. But they were big hands. Smooth and hard, broad and discolored, thick blunt fingers, with what looked like a manicure done by a steak mallet.

The guy stepped up on the bottom stair. Big shoe.

Large size. Wide fitting. Thick heavy legs. Bulky shoulders, a too-tight suit jacket. Maybe six-two, maybe two-twenty. Not a scrappy little Adriatic guy. A big side of beef. Once upon a time a police detective in Tirana. Maybe size was a requirement. Maybe it got better results.

The guy kept on climbing. Reacher backed away, out of sight. He figured he would step up and say hello just as the guy got to the top. From where he had the furthest to fall. All the way back down again. Maximum distance. Better than just falling on the floor. More efficient. The footsteps kept on coming. Every board squeaked. Reacher waited.

The guy got to the top.

Reacher stepped out.

The guy stared at him.

Reacher said, "Tell me about the rare and subtle word."

In the hallway below, he heard Hogan say, "Oh, shit."

The guy at the top of the stairs didn't answer.

Reacher said, "Tell me about the bunch of meanings. Repulsive to the eye, no doubt, unpleasant to look at, hideous, offensive, unsightly, base, degraded, vile, repellent. All that good modern-day stuff. But if it's originally an old folk word from years ago, then it's mostly about fear. In most languages the words share a root. Things you feared, you called ugly. The creature who lived in the forest was never handsome."

The guy didn't answer.

Reacher said, "Are you guys scared of me?"

No reply.

Reacher said, "Take out your phone and place it on the floor at your feet."

The guy said, "No."

"And your car keys."

"No."

"I'm going to take them anyway," Reacher said. "Up to you when and how."

The same gaze. Steady, calm, amused, predatory, unhinged.

At that point the guy had two basic choices. He could think of something clever to say back, or he could skip the whole talk-fest altogether, and move straight to the action. Reacher was genuinely uncertain which way he would jump. Downstairs he had seemed to like the sound of his own voice. That was for sure. Once upon a time a police detective. He liked holding court. He liked revealing how the crime was solved. On the other hand, banter alone wasn't going to win the day. He knew that. Sooner or later something of substance would have to be thrown in the mix. Why not start at the end?

The guy launched off the head of the stairs, off powerful legs, shoulders up, head down, aiming to charge, aiming to plant a shoulder in Reacher's chest, aiming to knock him backward off balance. But Reacher was at least fifty percent ready, and he twitched forward toward the guy and threw a vicious right uppercut, except not vertically, more out at a forty-five degree angle, so that the guy's charging, ducking face met it exactly square on, his own on-rushing two-twenty meeting Reacher's opposite-direction two-fifty in a colossal rupture of kinetic energy, face against fist, enough to lift the guy up off his heels, and dump him down on his butt, except the floor wasn't there, so the guy somersaulted backward down the stairs, one complete flailing rotation, wide and high, and then he crashed against the bottom wall in a spatter of limbs.

Like a train wreck.

From which he got up. More or less immediately. He blinked twice and staggered once and then stood up straight. Like in an afternoon movie. Like a monster taking an artillery shell to the chest, and swiping absentmindedly at a scorched patch of fur with a battered paw, all the while staring forward implacably.

Reacher started down the stairs. The hallway at the bottom was narrow. Barton and Hogan were backing away into the front parlor. Through the open door. The Albanian guy was standing still. Tall and proud and hard as a rock. Apparently resentful at his recent treatment. His nose was bleeding. Hard to tell if it was broken. Hard to tell if there was anything left to break. The guy was no spring chicken. He had lived a hard life. A police detective in Tirana.

The guy took a step forward.

Reacher matched it. They both knew. Sooner or later all you could do was slug it out. The guy feinted left and threw a snap right, low, aimed for Reacher's center mass, the straightest path to the target, but Reacher saw it coming and twisted away and took it on a slab of muscle high on his side, which hurt, but not as much as it would have, where it was headed before. The twist away was a pure reflex action, a jammed-wide-open panic response from his automatic nervous system, a sudden breathtaking gasp of adrenaline, no finesse at all, no modulation, no precision, just maximum available torque, instantly applied, which was a lot, which meant there was a lot of stored energy just hanging there for a split second, like a giant spring tightly wound, ready to suddenly unwind in the opposite direction, with exactly the same violent speed and force, a perfect equal and opposite reaction, but this time controlled, and timed, and aimed, and crafted. This time with the returning elbow setting out on an arc of its own, like a guided missile, coming up, riding the background rotation of his center mass, adding extra relative velocity of its own, then chopping down hard against the side of the guy's head, a fraction above and in front of his ear, a colossal blow, like getting hit with a baseball bat or an iron bar. It would have busted most skulls it met. It would have killed most guys. All it did to the Albanian was bounce him off the parlor doorframe and drop him to his knees.

From which he got up immediately. He rose vertically on straightening legs, hands out wide and moving, as if seeking extra leverage, or balance, as if swimming through a thick and viscous fluid. Reacher stepped in and hit him again, the same elbow, but from the other direction, on the forehand not the backhand, above the left eye, bone against bone, jarring, the guy falling back, eyes blank, but inevitably recovering, and blinking, and stepping up once more, this time not stopping, this time swinging straight into a snapping roundhouse right, aimed at the left side of Reacher's face, but not getting there, because Reacher hunched into it and let it glance off his shoulder. And this time Reacher didn't stop either. He spun out of the hunch, this time with his left elbow leading, unexpected, scything around, clubbing down, hitting the guy in the face, below the eye, to the side of the nose, where the roots of the front teeth run. Whatever that part was called.

The guy staggered back and clutched at the parlor doorframe, and then kind of fell around it into the room, like tripping over it, but vertically, whirling backward, helpless. Reacher followed, and saw the guy go down. He bounced off the immense eight-speaker cabinet and thumped on his back on the floor.

He put his hand under his suit coat.

Reacher stopped.

Don't do it, he thought. Reaction. Complications. *I don't care what kind of accommodations you think you got.* The law moved slow, as Mrs. Shevick knew. She had no time for slow.

Out loud he said, "Don't do it."

The guy paid no attention.

Chapter 31

The big blunt hand slid higher under the coat, the palm flattening, opening, the fingertips seeking ahead for the butt of the gun. Probably a Glock, like the other guy. Point and shoot. Or not, preferably. Reacher scoped out the time and the space and the relative distance. The guy's hand still had inches to travel, a grip still to organize, a draw, an aim, all while lying on his back, and maybe groggy from blows to the head. In other words slow, but still faster than Reacher could beat, under the circumstances, because whatever else, the guy's hand was already way up high under his coat, slow as it was, whereas both of Reacher's hands were still down below his waist, held low and away from his sides, wrists bent back, in a *whoa calm down don't do it* kind of gesture.

Far from his jacket pockets.

Not that he wanted to use a gun.

Not that he needed to.

He saw a better alternative. Somewhat improvised. By no means perfect. On the upside, it would get the job done. No question about that. With an extremely rapid deployment time, followed by speed and efficiency thereafter. That was the good news. On the downside, it was almost certainly a gross breach of etiquette. Almost certainly professionally offensive. Also no doubt personally offensive. Like guys out west with their hats. Some things you just didn't touch.

Some things you had to.

Reacher snatched Barton's Fender bass out of its stand and gripped it vertically by the neck and instantly smashed it straight down, end-on into the Albanian guy's throat. Like thrusting a post hole shovel deep into hard-packed dirt. Same kind of action, same kind of aim, same kind of violent stabbing downward force.

The Albanian guy went still.

Reacher put the guitar back in its stand.

"I apologize," he said. "I hope I didn't damage it."

"Don't worry," Barton said. "It's a Fender Precision. It's a ten-pound plank of wood. I got it from a pawn shop in Memphis, Tennessee, for thirty-four dollars. I'm sure worse things have happened in its life."

The clock in Reacher's head showed ten past four in the morning. The guy on the floor was still breathing. But in a shallow, desperate kind of a way, with a reedy plastic wheeze, in and out, in and out, as fast as he could. Like panting. But without getting anywhere.

Probably the fault of the strap button on the bottom of the guitar, punching a half-inch ahead of the mass of the body itself. Probably clipped a vital component. Larynx, or pharynx, or some other kind of essential structure, made of cartilage and spelled with letters from late in the alphabet. The guy's eyes were rolled up in his head. His fingers were scrabbling gently against the floor, as if trying to get a grip or a purchase on something. Reacher squatted down and went through his pockets, and took his gun, and his phone, and his wallet, and his car keys. The gun was another Glock 17, not recent vintage, worn, but well maintained. The phone was a flat black thing with a glass screen, the same as every other phone. The wallet was a black leather item molded by time into the shape of a potato. It was stuffed with hundreds of dollars in cash, and a raft of cards, and a local in-state driver's license, with the guy's picture on it, and the name Gezim Hoxha. He was forty-seven years old. He drove a Chrysler, according to the logo on his car keys.

Hogan asked, "What are we going to do with him?"

Abby said, "We can't let him go."

"We can't keep him here."

Barton said, "He needs medical attention."

"No," Reacher said. "He waived that right when he knocked on the door."

"That's harsh, man."

"Would he take me to the hospital? Or you? The shoe on the other foot. That's what sets the bar. Anyway, we can't. Hospitals ask too many questions."

"We can answer their questions. We were in the right. He pushed his way in. He was a home invader."

"Try telling that to a cop getting a grand a week under the table. Could go either way. Could take years. We don't have time."

"He might die."

"You say that like it's a bad thing."

"Well, isn't it?"

"I would trade him for the Shevicks' daughter. If you asked me to put a value on things. Anyway, he hasn't died so far. Maybe not in the peak of condition, but he's hanging in there."

"So what are we going to do with him?"

"We need to stash him somewhere. Just temporarily. Out of sight, out of mind. Out of harm's way. Until we know for sure, one way or the other."

"Know what?"

"What his long-term fate is likely to be."

Silence for a beat.

Then Barton asked, "Where could we stash him?"

"In the trunk of his car," Reacher said. "He'll be safe and secure. Maybe not very comfortable, but a crick in the neck is the least of his problems right now."

"He could get out," Hogan said. "They have a safety device now. A plastic handle that glows in the dark. It pops the trunk from the inside."

"Not in a gangster car," Reacher said. "I'm sure they removed it."

He lifted the guy under the arms, and Hogan lifted him by the feet, and they carried him out to the hallway, where Abby scooted ahead and opened the street door. She craned out in the dark and checked left and right. She waved an all-clear, and Reacher and Hogan lurched out with the guy, across the sidewalk. The car on the curb was a black sedan, with a low roof and a high waistline, which made the windows look shallow from top to bottom, like slots. They reminded Reacher of the vision ports in the side of an armored vehicle. Abby put her hand in Reacher's pocket and found the guy's key. She blipped it and the trunk lid raised up. Reacher dumped the guy's shoulders in first, and then Hogan shuffled around and folded the guy's legs in afterward. Reacher checked all around the inside of the lock. No glow-in-the-dark handle. Removed.

Hogan stepped away. Reacher looked down at the guy. Gezim Hoxha. Forty-seven years old. Once a police detective in Tirana. He closed the trunk lid on him, and stepped away to join the others. Once a police detective in the United States Army.

Hogan said, "We can't leave the car here. Not right outside the house. Especially not with their boy in the trunk. Sooner or later they'll cruise by and spot it and check it."

Reacher nodded.

"Abby and I need to use it," he said. "We'll park it someplace else when we're done."

"You're going to drive around with him in the trunk?"

"Keep your enemies close."

"Where are we going?" Abby asked.

"When the guy in the trunk talked about people getting banned from playing in their clubs, I thought, yeah, that's obviously a problem, because they got to eat. Then I remembered saying the same words to you once before. When we stopped at the gas station deli counter, on the way to visit with the Shevicks. You asked were they OK with that. I said they got to eat. Their cupboards are always bare. Especially now. I bet they haven't left the house since the Ukrainians arrived out front. I know how people are. They would be shy and embarrassed and scared to walk past the car, and certainly neither one would let the other do it alone, and they wouldn't do it together, either, because then the house would be empty behind them, and they would be suspicious the Ukrainians would sneak in and rummage through their underwear drawers. So all things considered, I bet they didn't eat anything yesterday, and won't eat anything today. We need to take them some food."

"What about the car out front of their house?"

"We'll go in the back. Probably through someone else's yard. We'll do the last part on foot."

First they drove to the giant supermarket on the road out of town. Like most such places it was open all night, cold, empty, vast, cavernous, flooded with bright hard light. They rolled a cart the size of a bathtub through the aisles, and they filled it up with four of everything they could think of. Reacher paid at the check-out register, all in cash, all from Gezim Hoxha's potato-shaped wallet. It seemed like the least the guy could do, under the circumstances. They packed the groceries carefully, into six balanced bags. Doing the last part on foot meant carrying them, maybe a decent distance, maybe over gates and fences.

They unlocked the Chrysler and lined up the bags on the rear seat. There was no sound from the trunk. No commotion. Nothing at all. Abby wanted to check if the guy was OK.

"What if he isn't?" Reacher said. "What are you going to do about it?"

"Nothing, I guess."

"No point checking, then."

"How long are we going to leave him in there?"

"As long as it takes. He should have thought about all this before. I don't see how his welfare suddenly becomes my responsibility, just because he chose to attack my welfare first. I'm not clear how that works exactly. They started it. They can't expect me to provide a health plan."

"We should be magnanimous in victory. Someone said that."

"Full disclosure," Reacher said. "I told you before. I'm a certain kind of person. Is the guy in the trunk still breathing?"

"I don't know," Abby said.

"But there's a possibility."

"Yes, there's a possibility."

"That's me being magnanimous in victory. Normally I kill them, kill their families, and piss on their ancestors' graves."

"I never know when you're kidding me."

"I guess that's true."

"Are you saying you're not kidding me now?"

"I'm saying in my case magnanimity is in short supply."

"You're taking food to an old couple in the middle of the night."

"That's a different word than *magnanimous*."

"Still a nice gesture."

"Because one day I could be them. But I'll never be the guy in the trunk."

"So it's purely tribal," Abby said. "Your kind of people, or the other kind."

"My kind of people, or the wrong kind."

"Who's in your tribe?"

"Almost nobody," Reacher said. "I live a lonely life."

They drove the Chrysler back toward town, and took the left that led them into the east side hinterland, through the original city blocks, and out toward where the Shevicks lived. The old postwar development lay up ahead. By that point Reacher felt he knew it well enough. He figured they could get to a parallel street without the Ukrainians ever seeing them pass by, even at a distance. They could sneak around to the rear of the block and park outside the Shevicks' back-to-back neighbor's house. The Chrysler would be lined up with the Lincoln, more or less exactly, nose to nose and tail to tail, but about two hundred feet apart. The depth of two small residential lots. Two buildings in the way.

They cut the lights and idled through the narrow streets, slowly, in the dark. They took a right, ahead of their usual turn, and a left, and they eased to a stop in what they were sure was the right spot. Outside the Shevicks' back-to-back neighbor. A ranch house with pale siding and an asphalt roof. The same but different. The front half of the structure butted out into an open front yard. The rear half of the structure was included in a large rectangle of head-high fence that ran all around the back yard. To get a mower from front to back, there was a fold-back section of fence, like a gate.

The house had five windows facing the street. One had drapes closed tight behind it. Probably a bedroom. People sleeping.

Abby said, "Suppose they see us?"

Reacher said, "They're asleep."

"Suppose they wake up?"

"Doesn't matter."

"They'll call the cops."

"Probably not. They'll look out the window and see a gangster car. They'll close their eyes and hope it goes away again. By morning, if anyone were to ask them, they'll have decided the safest approach is to have forgotten all about it. They'll say, what car?"

Reacher turned the motor off.

He said, "A dog would be a bigger problem. It might start barking. There might be others around. They could set up a big commotion. The Ukrainians might get out to check. Out of sheer boredom, if nothing else."

"We bought steaks," Abby said. "We have raw meat in those bags."

"Is a dog's sense of smell better than its hearing, or is it the other way around?"

"They're both pretty good."

"About a third of U.S. households own a dog. Just over thirty-six percent, to be precise. Which gives us a little worse than a two in three chance of being OK. Plus maybe it won't bark anyway. Maybe the neighborhood dogs are calm. Maybe the Ukrainians are too lazy to get out to check. Too warm, too comfortable. Maybe they're fast asleep. I think it's safe enough."

"What time is it?" Abby asked.

"Just past twenty after five."

"I was thinking about that line I told you, about doing something that scares you, every day. Except it's only twenty past five in the morning, and I'm already on my second thing."

"This one doesn't count," Reacher said. "This one is a walk in the park. Maybe literally. Maybe their landscaping is nice."

"Also on the subject of twenty past five in the morning, surely the Shevicks won't be up yet."

"They might be. I can't imagine they're sleeping well at the moment. If I'm wrong and they are sleeping well, you can wake them up. You can call them on your phone when we get there. You can tell them we're right outside their kitchen window. Tell them not to turn on any lights at the front of the house. An undisturbed visit is what we want."

They got out of the car and stood for a second in the silence. The night was gray and the air was damp with mist. Still no noise from the trunk. No kicking, no banging, no yelling. Nothing. They hauled the grocery bags off the rear bench and divided them up. Two and two for Reacher, one and one for Abby. Neither one of them overburdened or lopsided. Good to go.

They stepped into the neighbor's front yard.

Chapter 32

It was too dark to tell whether the landscaping was nice, but by smell and feel and inadvertent physical contact they could tell it was conventionally planted, with the normal kind of stuff in the normal kind of places. At first underfoot was a lawn of tough, springy grass, maybe some new hybrid strain, slick and cold with nighttime damp. Then came a crunchy area, some kind of broken slate or shale, maybe a path, maybe a mulch, and beyond it came spiky and coniferous foundation plantings, that scratched loudly at the grocery bags as they brushed by.

Then came the fold-back section of fence, which judging by the state of the lawn got hauled open and shut at least once every couple of weeks, all season long. Even so, it was stiff and noisy. At one point early in its travel it let out a wood-on-wood sound somewhere between a yelp and a bark and a shriek and a groan. Brief, but loud.

They waited.

No reaction.

No dog.

They squeezed through the gap they had opened, shuffling sideways, groceries leading, groceries following. They walked through the back yard. Up ahead in the gloom was the back fence. Which was also the Shevicks' back fence. In reverse. A mirror image. Theoretically. If they were in the right place.

"We're good," Abby whispered. "This is it. Has to be. Can't go wrong. Like counting squares on a chessboard."

Reacher stood up tall on tiptoe and looked over the fence. He saw a gray nighttime view of the back of a ranch house with pale siding and an asphalt roof. The same but different. But the right place. He recognized it by the way part of the lawn met the back wall of the house. It was the spot where the family photographs had been taken. The GI and the girl in the hoop skirt, with raw dirt at their feet, the same couple on a year-old lawn with a baby, the same couple eight years later with eight-year-old Maria Shevick, on grass by then lush and thick. Same patch of lawn. Same length of wall.

The kitchen light was on.

"They're up," Reacher said.

Climbing the fence was difficult, because it was in poor condition. The rational approach would have been to bust through it, or kick it down. Which they ruled out on ethical grounds. Instead they spent more than half their climbing energy fighting for equilibrium, trying to keep their weight vertical, not out to the side. They wobbled back and forth like a circus act. They sensed a point beyond which the whole thing would collapse, like a long rotten rippling curtain, maybe the whole width of the yard. Abby went first, and made it, and Reacher passed her the six grocery bags, one at a time, laboriously, hoisting each one high over the fence, and then letting it down as low as he could, the top of the cedar board digging into the crook of his elbow, until it was low enough for her to reach up and safely take.

Then came his turn to climb. He was twice as heavy and three times as clumsy. The fence swayed and yawed a yard one way, then a yard the other. But he got it stabilized and held it steady, and then kind of rolled off, in an inelegant maneuver that left him on his back in a flowerbed, but also left the fence still standing.

They carried the groceries to the kitchen door, and tapped on the glass. Heart attack time, potentially, for the Shevicks, but they survived. There was a little gasping and fluttering of fingers and fanning for breath, and a little embarrassment about bathrobes, but they got over it fast enough. They stared at the grocery sacks with a mixture of emotions on their faces. Shame and lost pride and empty stomachs. Reacher got them to make coffee. Abby packed their refrigerator and stacked their shelves.

Maria Shevick said, "We're up because we got a call from the hospital. It's an around-the-clock operation, obviously. We told them they should call anytime, night or day. It's in our notes, I expect. They called to say they want to do another scan, first thing tomorrow morning. They're still excited."

"If we pay," Aaron Shevick said.

"How much this time?" Reacher asked.

"Eleven thousand."

"When?"

"We need it by close of business today."

"I guess you already looked under the sofa cushions."

"I found a button. From a pair of my pants. It was missing eight years. Maria sewed it back on."

"It's still early in the day," Reacher said. "There are still a lot of hours to go, before the close of business."

"We were going to skip it this time around," Aaron said. "After all, what will it tell us? If it's good news, it will make us happy, of course, but that's self-indulgent, not medicine. If it's bad news, we don't want to know anyway. So we weren't sure exactly what we would be getting, for our eleven thousand dollars. But then the doctors said they need to know the extent of the progress. They said they need to calibrate a new dosage based on what they find. Either up or down. With a certain amount of timing and precision. They said anything else would be perilous."

"How do you normally pay them?"

"With a bank wire."

"Do they take cash?"

"Why?"

"Cash is usually the quickest thing to rustle up, when time is running short."

"From where?"

"Every day presents different opportunities. Worst case scenario, we could sell their car. Maybe up at the Ford dealer. I heard their used lot needs inventory."

"Yes, they take cash," Shevick said. "Like a casino. They have a line of tellers behind bulletproof glass."

"OK," Reacher said. "Good to know."

He stepped out to the darkened hallway, and lined up at a distance with a front window. He looked out to the street. The Lincoln was still there. The same one. Big and black, now dewed over and inert. Two vague shapes in it. Heads and shoulders, slumped down in the gloom. Guns under their arms, no doubt. Wallets in their pockets, almost certainly. Probably stuffed with cash, if they were anything like their opposite number from Tirana. Probably hundreds of dollars. But probably not eleven thousand.

He stepped back to the kitchen. Maria Shevick gave him a cup of coffee. His first of the day. She asked them to stay for breakfast. She would fix it. They could all eat together, like a party. Reacher wanted to say no. The food was for the old folks themselves, not random guests. Plus he wanted to get out of there before the sun came up. While it was still dark. It was likely to be a busy day. There was a lot to do. But the breakfast idea seemed to mean something to the Shevicks, and Abby was OK with it, so he said yes. Much later he wondered exactly how much different the day would have turned out, if he hadn't. But he didn't think about it for long. Spilled milk. Wasted energy. Move on.

* * *

Maria Shevick grilled bacon and fried eggs and made toast and brewed a second pot of coffee. Aaron tottered in with the stool from their bedroom dressing table, to make a fourth seat. Maria was right. In the end the meal turned into a party. Like a secret in the dark. Abby told a joke about a guy with cancer. For a beat it could have gone either way. But her performer's instinct was sure and true. After a second of silence Aaron and Maria burst out laughing, hard, their shoulders heaving, on and on, some kind of pent-up relief coming out, some kind of catharsis. Maria slapped her hand on the table, so hard her coffee spilled, and Aaron drummed his feet on the floor, so hard he hurt his knee again.

Reacher watched the sun come up. The sky went gray, then gold. The yard out the window took shape. Vague forms loomed out of the dark. The fence. The distant hump of the back-to-back neighbor's asphalt roof.

"Who lives there?" he asked. "Whose yard did we walk through?"

"Actually it's the woman who told us about Fisnik," Aaron said. "She told us the story about the other neighbor's nephew's wife's cousin borrowing money from a gangster in a bar. I have a feeling she went to see him herself, a little later. She got her car fixed all of a sudden. No other visible means of support."

Maria made a third pot of coffee. Reacher thought, what the hell. The sun was already over the horizon. He stayed in his seat and drank his share. Then somehow the conversation came back to money, and suddenly everyone seemed to hear the same clock ticking. The close of business, getting nearer.

"Except cash is good all night long," Reacher said. "Right? The close of business thing is about the bank wires only. As long as they have a teller open, we're good until the moment they put her on the gurney."

"From where?" Aaron said again. "Eleven thousand is a lot of sofa cushions."

"Hope for the best," Reacher said.

He and Abby left the way they had come, this time with empty hands, and in the late dawn light, therefore faster, but not much easier. The fence was still difficult. The fold-back section was still stiff and noisy.

Their car was gone.

Chapter 33

The black Chrysler, with its low roof, and its high waistline, and its shallow windows, and its closed trunk lid. No longer there. The space at the curb was empty.

Abby said, "The guy got out."

"I don't see how he could," Reacher said.

"Then what happened?"

"My fault," Reacher said. "I got it ass backward. About the public response. The woman looked out the window and saw a gangster car and didn't get nervous. She called gangster HQ instead. Maybe she's obliged to. Maybe it was part of her deal with Fisnik. When she got her car fixed. They claim to have eyes everywhere. Maybe that's how. So she called them and they came right over, and they checked it out."

"Did they open the trunk?"

"Operationally we have to assume they did. Equally we have to assume the guy is still functioning.

Which puts Barton and Hogan in immediate danger. They're probably fast asleep right now. You better call them."

"If they're asleep their phones will be off."

"Try anyway."

She did.

Their phones were off.

"That language guy," Reacher said. "The tanker. Did you get his number?"

"Vantresca?"

"Yes."

"No."

"OK," Reacher said. "We're leaving here on foot. No choice. The small slender woman, and the big ugly man. Broad daylight. Eyes everywhere. Probably not a walk in the park anymore. Probably your second thing of the day."

"Back to Frank Barton's house?"

"We need to warn them somehow."

"I'll keep trying the phone. But they'll sleep till ten. You know how it is. Their gig starts at twelve."

"Wait," Reacher said. "You can find Vantresca on your phone. He said he had a private security license, and his number was listed in the national directories."

Abby searched. She typed and swiped and tapped and scrolled.

She said, "Got him."

Then she said, "It looks like it's just an office landline. He won't be in yet."

"Try anyway."

She did. She put the phone on speaker and held it

balanced on her palm. They heard a series of clicks, as if the call was being bounced from one place to another.

She said, "Maybe out of hours it forwards to his house."

It did exactly that. Vantresca answered. He sounded all squared away. He sounded crisp, and alert, and cheerful. And corporate. He said, "Vantresca Security, how may I help you?"

Reacher said, "Guy, this is Reacher. The MP. Abby and I got your number from a directory. On that thing everyone talks about."

"The internet?"

"That's it. But this is not official, OK? Not for the after-action report."

"OK."

"Also it's a shoot-first kind of thing. Just do it, right now, and ask questions later."

"Do what right now?"

"Go check your pal Joe Hogan is OK. And Frank Barton."

"Why wouldn't they be?"

"I said questions later."

"That one now."

"The Albanians may be close to confirming where we were last night. May already have confirmed. Hogan and Barton aren't answering their phones. We hope because they're asleep."

"OK, on my way."

"Get them out of there, even if they're OK so far. Could go south anytime."

"Where will they go?"

"They can go crash at my house," Abby said. "No one is watching it anymore."

"How long do they need to be gone?"

"A day," Reacher said. "That seems to be the way the wind is blowing. No need to pack a big suitcase."

Vantresca clicked off. Abby put her phone away. Reacher redistributed the things in his pockets, to balance his load. Abby buttoned her coat. They set out walking. A small woman and a big man. Broad daylight. Eyes everywhere.

Gregory had said he would go talk to Dino again, first thing in the morning, and what Gregory said, Gregory meant. He got up early, and dressed the same way he had before, on his previous visit. Tight pants, tight shirt. Nothing to hide. No gun, no knife, no wire, no bomb. Necessary, but not comfortable. The dawn air was too cold for single layers. He waited for a little warmth, and until there were shadows. He wanted daylight hours to be visibly underway. It was a matter of presentation. He was a man of energy and vigor, as fresh as the new day, taking charge, taking action, bright and early. Not a mistimed nightcrawler coming in out of the gloom.

Once again he drove to the garage on Center Street. Then he walked. Once again he was followed all the way. Once again calls were made ahead. When he got where he was going he found the same six figures, in the same half circle between the sidewalk and the lumber yard's gate. Like chess pieces. The same defensive formation.

Once again one of the six figures stepped up. It was Jetmir. Once again partly a blocking maneuver, and partly ready to listen.

Gregory told him, "I need to speak with Dino."

Jetmir asked, "Why?"

"I have a proposal."

"What kind?"

"At this point it's for his ears only."

"On what general subject?"

"A matter of urgent mutual interest."

"Mutual," Jetmir said. "A concept in short supply recently."

An impertinence, given their disparity in rank. Only one step apart, but it was the biggest step of all.

But Gregory didn't react.

He said, "I believe we were both deceived."

Jetmir paused a beat.

"In what way?" he said.

"The fox got the blame, but really it was the dog who did it. You probably have a folk tale in your culture. Or a similar saying."

"Who is the dog?" Jetmir asked.

Gregory didn't answer directly.

Instead he said, "That's for Dino's ears only."

"No," Jetmir said. "Given the history of recent days, you'll understand that Dino will not feel well disposed toward taking a meeting with you at this time. Not without an extensive preview of the issue at hand, and a good word, both from me. I'm sure you would operate in the same manner, under the same circumstances. You have a staff for a reason. So does Dino."

Gregory said, "Tell him we didn't start killing your guys, and I don't believe you started killing our guys. Ask him if he could get on board with that theory."

"And if he can?"

"Ask him what it means."

"What does it mean?"

"That's enough of a preview. Now I'm requesting the courtesy of a meeting."

"Then who killed our guys? And yours? You're saying someone was running a false-flag operation against both of us at once."

Gregory said nothing.

"Yes or no answer," Jetmir said. "Do you believe there was outside interference?"

"Yes," Gregory said.

"Then we should talk. Dino delegated the matter to me."

"This is above your pay grade. With respect. There's a reason staffs have bosses."

"Dino isn't here," Jetmir said.

"When will he get in?"

"He was in early. He already left again."

"I'm serious," Gregory said. "This is very urgent."

"Then talk to me. Dino will tell you to anyway. Right now you're wasting time."

Gregory said, "Did they take phones from you?"

Jetmir paused a long moment.

He said, "You ask because clearly they took phones from you, which would indicate an imminent data attack, which narrows the field, when it comes to potential opponents."

"We think narrows it all the way down to the only one who would dare."

"Dino will say you Ukrainians are always obsessed with the Russians. It's a well known fact. You would accuse them of anything."

"Suppose this time it's true?"

"Neither one of us can beat the Russians."

"Not separately."

"Is that your proposal? I'll make sure Dino gets it."

"I'm serious," Gregory said again. "This is very urgent."

"I'm taking it seriously. Dino will get back to you as soon as he can. Maybe he'll walk over to see you himself. To the taxi office."

"Where he will be treated with the same courtesy I have enjoyed here."

"Perhaps we'll become accustomed to trusting each other," Jetmir said.

"Time alone will tell," Gregory said.

"Perhaps we'll become friends."

Gregory had no answer to that. He walked away. Out of the scoop, onto the sidewalk, and west, toward Center. Jetmir stood and watched him go. Then he turned away and ducked back inside, through the judas gate, to the low corrugated shed, with the smell of pine and the whine of saws.

Where his cell phone rang. With bad news. A made man from the night watch by the name of Gezim Hoxha had been found half dead in the trunk of his own car, abandoned way out on the edge of a ticky-tack old housing development. A tip had been called in by one of their old moneylending customers, hoping for points off her next loan. At that time no suspects had yet been identified. But a careful search of the area was already underway. There were extra cars on the streets. There were plenty of eyes wide open.

Reacher and Abby threaded their way out of the Shevicks' development by following their inward route in reverse, keeping well out of sight of the parked Ukrainian car, staying on side streets wherever possible, until the very last moment, when they had to make a right and join the main drag, that led past the gas station with the deli counter, and on toward downtown. Up until then they felt pretty good. But from that point onward the exposure was pitiless. The sun was bright. The air was clear. There was no possibility of concealment. It was a standard urban streetscape. On the left, a three-story brick façade, with dusty windows and mean doors. Then a brick sidewalk, and a stone curb, and a blacktop street, and a stone curb, and a brick sidewalk. On the right, a three-story brick façade, with dusty windows and mean doors. No cover anywhere taller than a hydrant, or wider than a light pole.

Only a matter of time.

Abby's phone rang. She answered. Vantresca. She put him on speaker. She walked with her phone out in front of her, carried flat on her hand. She looked like a carving from an old Egyptian tomb.

Vantresca said, "I got Barton and Hogan. They're

OK. They're right here in the car with me. They told me what happened last night. No one has been to their house since then."

Reacher asked, "Where are you now?"

"We're setting out over to Abby's, like she said. Barton knows where it is."

"No, come pick us up first."

"They told me you had a car."

"Unfortunately it just got repossessed. With the guy still in the trunk. Which is why I was worried about Barton's address."

"No one has been to the house," Vantresca said again. "Not so far. Clearly the guy isn't talking yet. Maybe he can't. Barton told me about the Precision Bass."

"A blunt instrument," Reacher said. "But the point is right now we're walking. Right now our asses are hanging out in the breeze. We need a rendezvous for an emergency evacuation."

"Where are you exactly?"

Which was a difficult question. There were no legible street signs. They were either faded or rusted out or missing altogether. Maybe hit by a streetcar, the year the *Titanic* went down. The year Fenway Park opened for business. Abby did something with her phone. She kept Vantresca on the line, and came up with a map. There were pointers and arrows and pulsing blue spheres. She read out the street and the cross street.

"Five minutes," Vantresca said. "Maybe ten. Morning rush hour is coming. What is the exact location for the pick-up?"

Another good question. They couldn't stand on the corner like they were hailing a taxi. Not if exposure was their main concern. Reacher looked all around. Unpromising. Small commercial enterprises, not yet open. All faintly seedy. The kind of places where gray-faced individuals weaseled in about ten o'clock, after a last furtive backward glance. Reacher knew cities. On the next block he could see a waist-high double-sided chalkboard tented on the sidewalk, which probably meant a coffee shop, which would be open at that hour, but maybe hostile. No man on the door, in such a place on such a street, but maybe a sympathizer at the espresso machine, hoping for points off his loan.

"There," he said.

He pointed to a narrow building across the street, about ten yards farther on. At the front it was propped up with steeply angled balks of wood. As if it was in danger of falling down. The wood supports were shrouded in a tough black net. Maybe a local regulation. Maybe the city worried about stressed chips of brick randomly flinging themselves outward from the faulty wall, to the detriment of passersby, or those lingering beneath. Whatever the reason, the result in practical terms could be used as an improvised semi-hideaway, because a person could squeeze in behind the net, and then just stand there, semi-obscured from view.

Maybe sixty percent obscured. It was a thick net.

Maybe forty percent. It was a sunny morning.

Better than nothing.

Abby relayed the information.

"Five minutes," Vantresca said again. "Maybe ten."

"What kind of car?" Reacher asked him. "We don't want to squeeze out again for the wrong people."

"It's an '05 S-Type R in anthracite over charcoal."

"Remember what I said about armor people?"

"We glamorize the machine."

"I didn't understand what any of those words meant."

"It's a moderately old Jaguar," Vantresca said. "The hardcore sports version of the first refresh of the retro model they designed at the end of the nineties. With the upgraded cam followers and the bored-out motor. And the supercharger, obviously."

"Not helping," Reacher said.

Vantresca said, "It's a black sedan."

He clicked off. Abby put her phone away. They started across the street, on a shallow diagonal, heading for the propped-up building.

A car came around the corner.

Fast.

A black sedan.

Too soon. Five seconds, not five minutes.

And not an old Jaguar.

A new Chrysler. With a low roof, and a high waistline, and shallow windows. Like slots. Like the vision ports in the side of an armored vehicle.

Chapter 34

The black Chrysler came on toward them, then slowed a step, then picked up again. Like a stumble. Like the automotive equivalent of a double take. As if the car itself couldn't believe what it was seeing. A small slender woman and a big ugly man. Suddenly right there on the street. Front and center in the windshield. Large as life. Be on the lookout.

The car jammed to a stop and the front doors opened. Both of them. Twenty feet away. Two guys. Two guns. The guns were Glock 17s. The guys were right-handed. Smaller than Gezim Hoxha, but bigger than the average. Not scrappy little Adriatic guys. That was for sure. Both wore black pants and black T-shirts. And sunglasses. Neither one had shaved. No doubt they had been dragged out of bed and sent on patrol immediately after Hoxha's car had been found.

They took a step forward. Reacher glanced left, glanced right. No cover taller than a hydrant or wider than a light pole. He put his hand in his pocket. The H&K that he knew for sure worked. That he also knew for sure he didn't want to use. A gunshot on a city street at night would get a reaction. Ten times worse in the innocent morning sunshine. There would be more officers on the day watch than the night watch. They would all deploy. There would be dozens of cars, lights flashing, sirens going. There would be news helicopters and cell phone video. There would be paperwork. There would be hundreds of hours in a room with a cop and a table screwed to the floor. Abby's phone log would implicate Barton and Hogan and Vantresca. The mess would spread far and wide. Could take weeks to resolve. Which Reacher didn't want, and the Shevicks didn't have.

The guys with the Glocks took another step. They were coming in from wide, around their thrown-open doors, guns first, shuffling steps, rigid two-handed grips, concentrated squints over their front sights.

Another step. And another. Then the guy on Reacher's right, who had been the driver, kept on coming, but the other guy stopped. The passenger. A wheel play. Like sheepdogs. They wanted to get one of them around and behind, to press Reacher and Abby toward the other one, toward the far sidewalk, toward the three-story wall, where they would finally run out of room. An obvious, instinctive tactic.

Which depended on Reacher and Abby first staying where they were, and then rotating meekly in place, and then stumbling backward.

Not going to happen.

"Abby, take a step back," Reacher said. "With me."

He stepped back. She stepped back. The driver's geometry was distorted. His envelope was enlarged. Now he had further to go.

"Again," Reacher said.

He stepped back. She stepped back.

"Stand still," the driver said. "Or I'll shoot."

Reacher thought, will you? It was one of life's great questions. The guy had all the same structural inhibitions as Reacher himself. The dozens of squad cars, with their lights flashing and their sirens going. The news helicopters and the cell phone video. The paperwork. The hours in the room with the cop. Which would produce an uncertain outcome for the guy. Inevitable. Could go either way. There were no guarantees. *Don't frighten the voters.* There was a new police commissioner on the way. Plus the guy had professional obligations to consider. There were questions to be answered. They thought Reacher was an outside agitator. *We want to know who you are.* There would be bonus points for his capture still able to talk. There would be punishments for his delivery dead or comatose or mortally wounded. Because the dead and the comatose couldn't talk, and the mortally wounded didn't last long enough to talk, when they brought out the spoons, and the electric saws, and the smoothing irons, and the cordless power tools, or whatever other grotesque procedures were favored east of Center. So would the guy shoot? Unlikely, Reacher thought. Probably not. But always possible.

Was he prepared to bet his life on it? Probably yes. He had before. He had gambled and won. Ten thousand generations later his instincts were still working. He had walked away, and lived to tell the tale. In any case he was fundamentally indifferent. No one lived forever.

But was he prepared to bet Abby's life on it?

The driver said, "Show me your hands."

Which would be game over. The point of no return, right there. Which was getting close anyway. The geometry had gone bad. The driver and the passenger had gotten about sixty degrees apart. They were well positioned for enfilade fire. The likely sequence of events was easy to predict. Reacher would shoot through his pocket and hit the driver. One down. No problem. But then the sixty-degree turn toward the passenger would be slow and clumsy, because his hand would be still all snagged up inside his pocket, which would give the passenger time to fire, maybe two or three rounds, which would either hit Abby, or Reacher himself, or both, or miss altogether. Almost certainly the lattermost, he thought, in the real world. The guy was already jumpy. By then he would be startled and panicked. Most handgun rounds missed their target under the best of circumstances.

But would he bet Abby's life on that?

"Show me your hands," the driver said again.

Abby said, "Reacher?"

Ten thousand generations said stay alive and see what the next minute brings.

Reacher took his hands out of his pockets.

"Take your jacket off," the driver said. "I can see the weight from here."

Reacher took his jacket off. He dropped it on the blacktop. The guns in the pockets bumped and clanked. The Ukrainian H&Ks, the Albanian Glocks. His entire arsenal.

Almost.

The driver said, "Now get in the car."

The passenger backed up to the Chrysler. Reacher thought he was going to open the rear door for them, like a guy outside a fancy hotel. But he didn't. He opened the trunk instead.

"Good enough for Gezim Hoxha," the driver said.

Abby said, "Reacher?"

"We'll be OK," he said.

"How?"

He didn't answer. He got in first, crossways, on his side in a U shape, and then Abby got in the space he was leaving in front of him, curled on her side in a fetal position, like they were spooning in bed. Except they weren't. The passenger closed the lid with a cheap metal clang. The world went dark. No luminous handle. Removed.

At that moment Dino was on the phone to Jetmir. A summons, to a meeting in Dino's office, right then, immediately. Clearly there was something on Dino's mind. Jetmir got there inside three minutes and sat down in front of the desk. Dino was looking at his phone. At the long sequence of texts about Gezim

Hoxha, found half dead in the trunk of his car, next to an old housing development.

"Hoxha and I go back a long way," Dino said. "I knew him when he was a cop in Tirana. He busted me once. He was the meanest bastard in Albania. I liked him. He was a solid guy. Why I gave him a job here."

"He's a good man," Jetmir said.

"He can't talk," Dino said. "He may never. He has a serious injury to his throat."

"We must hope for the best."

"Who did this?"

"We don't know."

"Where did it happen?"

"We don't know."

"When exactly did it happen?"

"He was found at dawn," Jetmir said. "Obviously the attack was prior to that, by an hour or two, possibly."

"Here's what I don't understand," Dino said. "Gezim Hoxha is a man with valuable experience, having been a policeman in Tirana, and therefore he's a man of great substance in our organization, and I gave him his job myself, and he has been with us a very long time, and he has served us well, and therefore all in all he's considered a very senior figure here. Am I right?"

"Yes."

"Then why was he running errands in the middle of the night?"

Jetmir didn't answer.

Dino said, "Did I ask him to do something? Have I forgotten?"

"No," Jetmir said. "I don't think so."

"Did you ask him to do something?"

Look for lights behind drapes. Knock on doors and ask questions if necessary.

"No," Jetmir said.

"I don't understand it," Dino said. "I don't run around in the middle of the night. I have people for that. Hoxha should have been tucked up in bed. Why wasn't he?"

"I don't know."

"Who else was running around in the middle of the night?"

"I don't know."

"You should know. You're my chief of staff."

"I could ask around."

"I already did," Dino said. His tone changed. "Turns out a lot of guys were running around in the middle of the night. Clearly connected to something serious enough to leave a mean old bastard like Hoxha with a stoved-in throat. Given the stakes involved and the numbers involved, that sounds like a big deal to me. Sounds like something I should have been involved with. At the discussion stages at least. Sounds like something that should have gotten my personal approval. That's the way we do business here."

Jetmir didn't reply.

Dino was quiet a long time.

Then finally he said, "Also I hear Gregory came by this morning. He paid us another state visit. Naturally I'm wondering why I wasn't informed."

Jetmir didn't speak. Instead the inevitable remaining paragraphs of the conversation played out inside his head, fast, abbreviated, like speed chess. Back and forth. Dino would chip away relentlessly, remorselessly, until the betrayal was fully revealed, in all its damning detail. Perhaps he already knew. *I could ask around. I already did.* He knew some, at least. Jetmir went cold. Suddenly he thought perhaps it was already too late. Then he recovered and thought perhaps it was not. He simply didn't know. In which case, better safe than sorry. An ancient instinct. Ten thousand generations of his own slipped his hand under his coat, one, and came back with his gun, two, and shot Dino in the face, three. From a yard away, across the desk. Dino's head kicked back an inch and blood and brain slop and bone fragments slapped the wall behind him. The nine-mil round was loud in the small wood room. Colossally loud. Like a bomb. After it there was hissing silence for a long second, and then people burst in. All kinds of people. Made men from nearby offices, guys from the inner council, lumber yard workers covered in dust, doormen, bagmen, legbreakers, all of them shouting and running and pulling guns, like in a movie, when the president goes down. Confusion, madness, mayhem, panic.

At that moment the black Chrysler pulled in at the lumber yard gate, with Reacher and Abby in the trunk.

Chapter 35

The driver paused with his foot on the brake. The gate was open but there was no one watching it. Which was unusual. But the guy was keen to get in and display his prize, so he didn't think too much about it. He just drove in and swooped around and reversed toward the roll-up door. The passenger climbed out and smacked a green mushroom button with his palm. The door moved up slowly, with the rattle of chains and the clatter of metal slats. The driver backed in under it. He shut down the motor and got out and joined the passenger at the rear of the car. They pulled their guns and stood well back.

The driver blipped the button on the key fob.

The trunk lid raised up, slow, damped, majestic.

They waited.

Nothing.

The smell of pine, but no whine of saws. The low corrugated shed was quiet. There was no one in it.

Then from somewhere deep in the back they heard voices, dulled by walls and doors, but nevertheless loud and panicked and confused. And footsteps too, urgent, agitated, but going nowhere. Just milling around in place. As if something weird was going down in one of the inner offices.

They listened.

Maybe Dino's office itself.

About the first eight guys into the room saw the exact same thing. Dino, behind his desk, collapsed in his chair, slack and puddled, with his head blown apart. And Jetmir, in a chair in front of the desk, with a Glock in his hand. Literally a smoking gun. They could see the haze and smell the burned powder. Three of the first eight were inner council guys, who had at least a partial clue as to what might have happened. The other five were low level men. They had no idea. They were locked in a mental loop that made no sense at all. Did not compute. Jetmir was the second-most important man in the world. His word was law. He was unimpeachable. He was obeyed and admired and revered. Stories were told. He was top of the heap. He was a legend. But he had killed Dino. And Dino was the boss. The first-most important man in the world. All a guy's loyalty and fealty was owed to him alone. Such was their code. Like a blood oath. Like a medieval kingdom. A matter of absolute duty.

One of the five with no idea was a legbreaker from a town called Pogradec, on the shores of Lake Ohrid, whose sister had once been molested by a party official. Dino had restored the family's honor. The legbreaker was a simple man. He was as faithful as a dog. He loved Dino like a father. He loved that he loved him. He loved the structure, and the hierarchy, and the rules, and the codes, and the iron certainty they gave his life. He loved it all, and he lived by it all. He pulled out his gun and shot Jetmir in the chest, three times, deafening in the crowded space, and then instantly he himself was shot down by two other guys simultaneously, one of them a bagman who seemed to be acting on pure autopilot alone, defending the new boss, even though the new boss had just shot the old boss, and the other shooter a member of the inner council, who had some inkling of what it was all about, and some hope of salvaging something from the wreckage. But a vain hope, because his second round was a through-and-through, which killed a bagman standing behind the legbreaker, and the doorman crowding in behind the bagman fired back in a panic, pure reflex, and he hit the inner council guy in the head, so a second inner council guy shot the doorman in retaliation, and a foreman from the yard who had a beef with the council fired back at him, and missed, but hit the third council guy with a ricochet, pure accident, high on the arm, who howled and blasted back, multiple rounds, the muzzle of his Glock dancing and jerking uncontrolled, the rounds going everywhere, into the mass of more men crowding in, falling, slipping, sliding on the blood-slick floor, going down, until the councilman's Glock clicked on empty, and a hissing, roaring version of silence came back, thrumming and buzzing in the air, but not complete, because right then and far away some other loud sound started up to pierce it.

The new sound was more gunshots. Just two rounds. Deliberate. Carefully spaced. A nine-millimeter handgun. Muffled by distance. Maybe all the way over at the front of the shed. Maybe near the roll-up door.

The driver and the passenger stood well back from the Chrysler's trunk, with their guns still aimed right at it, in the same solid two-handed feet-apart stances they had used before, but with their necks twisted around, comically, almost as far as they would go. They were peering behind their left shoulders, at the far back corner of the shed, way in the distance, where a corridor led away to the administrative quarters. Where the commotion was.

Then the shooting started back there. Far away, muffled, thumping, contained. First came three solo rounds, a fast triple, *thud thud thud,* and then a hail of more all at once, and more, and more, and then finally the repeated thumping of a handgun being fired unaimed and in anger, until it ran out.

Then there was a second of silence.

The driver and the passenger turned back to the Chrysler.

Still nothing. The trunk lid, raised. No sign of the occupants.

They turned back to the corner.

Another second of silence.

Back to the Chrysler. Still nothing. No raised heads, no glances out. No signs of life at all. The driver and the passenger glanced at each other. Suddenly worried. Maybe there was exhaust gas in the trunk. Maybe there was a leak. A cracked pipe. Maybe the man and the woman had suffocated.

The driver and the passenger took a cautious step forward.

And another.

Still nothing.

They checked the far back corner again. Still silence. They took another step. To where they could see in the trunk. They glanced in, nervous. What they saw was all different. The man and the woman had changed positions. Originally he had gotten in at the back, and she had curled up in the space he left in front of him. Now he was in front, and she was behind him. Shielded by him. Originally he had gotten in with his head on the left, and now his head was on the right. Which meant he was lying on his left shoulder. Which meant his right arm was free to move. And he was moving it. Real fast. In his hand was a small steel automatic. It came to rest aimed at the driver's head.

Reacher shot the driver through the forehead, and re-aimed right and shot the passenger through the left eye. With the Ukrainian H&K from his boot. From when he rebalanced the load in his pockets, before they walked out of the Shevicks' development. Two on the left, two on the right, and one in his sock. Always a good idea.

He raised up an inch and peered out cautiously. He saw a long low corrugated shed, full of the smell of raw softwood, but empty of people. No one there at all. Presumably an HQ of some kind. Maybe the lumber yard they had seen before. Once while driving, once on foot. A cover operation. The dull metal looked the same. Like the electrical warehouse and the plumbing depot.

He sat up and took a better look. Still no people. Still no one there. He rolled out and got to his feet. He helped Abby out after him. She looked at the dead guys sprawled on the floor. Not pretty. One had one eye, and the other had three.

She looked around the empty shed.

"Where are we?" she said.

But he didn't get a chance to tell her what he figured, because right then two new things happened. A bunch of guys ran in from somewhere and swarmed toward the far back corner of the shed, where there was some kind of an archway, that seemed to lead through to other rooms beyond. And simultaneously a bunch of guys ran out in the other direction, through the archway from the other rooms, to the main floor of the shed. They were wild looking characters. Guns out, white in the face, all hopped up and trembling from some kind of mad adrenaline. The two groups collided. There was crazy shouting and there were yelled questions and blurted incoherent answers, all in a foreign language Reacher assumed was Albanian. Then one guy pushed another guy in the chest, and the other guy pushed back, and someone fired his gun, and the first guy went down, and someone else touched the muzzle of his gun to the shooter's temple and pulled the trigger, point blank, like a punishment, like an execution, and the shooter's head blew up, whereupon the whole situation looked like it was turning into chaos fast, except someone shouted loud and pointed urgently, all the way down the long diagonal distance, and everyone else shut up and turned to look.

A small slender woman and a big ugly man.

Once Reacher had read a paperback book he found on a bus, about how people like to second guess themselves for hours or days, whereas really they know the truth in the blink of an eye. He liked the book because it agreed with him. He had learned to trust his first flash of instinct. Therefore he knew at that point all bets were off. No questions would be asked. *We want to know who you are.* Not anymore. Now they were in the grip of some kind of crazy turmoil and bloodlust. There would be no more bonus points for still able to talk. That offer was way past its best-by date.

So even before the pointing guy's shout died to an echo Reacher fired three rounds into the mass of distant figures. Three down for sure. Couldn't miss. The rest scattered like roaches. Reacher ducked back and caught Abby by the elbow and pulled her behind the car. Behind the rear flank. He glanced sideways, out the roll-up door. He recognized the gate, and the scooped-out curb, and the street. He knew where he was.

The gate was open.

He whispered, "Scoot along and get in the passenger door. Then scoot over and drive us out of here. It's a straight shot. Put your foot down and don't even look. Keep crouched down in your seat."

Abby said, "What time of day is it?"

"This doesn't count. People pay money for this kind of thing."

"Where they get spattered with paint, not bullets."

"So this is more authentic. They would pay more."

Abby crouched her way along the flank of the car, and reached up to the handle from below, and slipped her fingers in the bottom seam, and eased the door open, just wide enough to get in, twisting, slithering low, her belly pressed to the seat.

"The key's not in," she whispered.

One of the distant figures fired a single round. It passed a foot over the trunk lid, two feet over Reacher's head. The crack of the shot slurred to a boom, as the metal roof vibrated like a giant drum skin.

Abby whispered, "They took the key with them. Think about it. They must have opened the trunk remotely."

"Fabulous," Reacher said. "I guess I'll have to go get it."

He dropped his cheek to the concrete and looked down the length of the shed from under the car. He saw five guys on the ground. Two from the initial internal dispute, and three from his first three rounds. Two of those were still, and one was moving. But only a little. No great vigor or enthusiasm. He would have nothing much to contribute for a day or two. There were nine guys still vertical, crouched behind whatever cover they had been able to find. Which wasn't much. There was a pyramid of chemical drums. Preservative, maybe. There were low stacks of lumber, but not many. Inventory was sparse. It was a cover operation. No serious business intent.

Reacher rolled on his back and smacked the magazine out of the H&K and counted the rounds remaining. Two left, plus one in the chamber, for a total of three. Not encouraging. He put the mag back in the gun and rolled on his side and squirmed along the flank of the car until he was back at the trunk. The driver and the passenger lay about five feet away. One eye and three eyes. Their heads lay in pools of blood. The driver was closer, which was good, because he had seemed to be the take-charge guy. The senior figure. He would have the key. In his suit coat pocket, probably. On the left. Because he was right-handed. He would have held his gun in his right and blipped the fob with his left.

Another round came in and smacked the end wall, a foot high. The crack of the shot, the boom of the roof, the metallic echo, then silence again. Then footsteps. Scuffed, hasty, tentative. Someone was moving up. Moving closer. Reacher checked the view again, under the car. The nine live guys were gesturing and waving and pointing. Hand signals. They were coordinating an advance. They were aiming to leapfrog forward, one at a time, two at a time, from one spot to the next. In the lead was a wide guy who looked a little like Gezim Hoxha. Same kind of age, same kind of build. He was tensing up ready, aiming to spin off the chemical drums and make it to a stack of boards wrapped in plastic, maybe fifteen feet further on. The others would fill in behind him. Their likely rate of advance was rapid. They faced no structural impediments.

Time to slow them down.

Only one sure way.

Reacher straightened his arm under the car and aimed very carefully. Like a classic one-handed shooting position, except rotated ninety degrees, because he was lying on his side on the floor. He waited until the guy's back leg braced for action, and then he fired, leading the target by an inch or two, and the guy stepped right into the bullet. It caught him high in the chest, left side. Which was fine. All kinds of vital stuff in that area. Arteries, nerves, veins. The guy went down and the advance stalled. The back eight hunkered down like turtles. Only one sure way, which was to make an example of the point man, right in front of their eyes.

Two rounds left. Not encouraging.

Reacher squirmed around and rolled over on his front and elbowed-and-toed to where his head was level with the back bumper. The nearest part of the driver was his right foot. Reacher lay flat and stretched out his arm. He was about a yard short. But his plan was made. Better to drag the guy behind the car first, and go through his pockets second. Safer that way. Reacher took a breath and slid out fast and grabbed the driver's ankle and hauled on it hard. He was back behind cover in a second. The driver's head left a snail trail of blood on the concrete. Reacher's brief display of himself triggered a furious volley of four fast rounds from the hunkered-down positions, but they were all late and they all missed.

Reacher stayed in a crouch and dragged the driver another yard. He rolled him over. Then two simultaneous processes unspooled in parallel. Reacher started searching for the car key, and the eight live Albanians started thinking about what he was doing and why he was doing it. And evidently they weren't dumb. They figured it out pretty fast. About the same time Reacher got his hand in the driver's left-hand coat pocket, the Albanians started firing at the car. It was a big target. Sixteen feet long, five feet high. They shredded it. First all the driver's side windows shattered, and rounds punched and clanged through the sheet metal, and then the whole car slumped down on the left as the tires were shot out, and green oily fluid dripped down underneath. Reacher crawled back to where Abby was half in and half out of the passenger seat. He dragged her out and closed her door and pushed her along to where the front wheel was, behind the engine block, which was the safest spot. Relatively speaking. Under the circumstances. The noise was deafening. Rounds came through the busted far side windows and shattered the near side windows. Pebbles of glass rained down. Rounds clanked and smacked into the bodywork. From closer and closer. They were advancing again.

Reacher had two rounds left.

Not encouraging.

He glanced out the roll-up door. Bright morning sunshine. The gate, open. The street, empty. Maybe thirty yards to the scooped-out curb. Maybe seventy more to the first corner. Ten seconds for an athlete. At least twenty for him. Maybe more. With eight guys chasing right behind him. Not good. Except maybe less than twenty seconds for Abby. She might be faster. She might be a small target receding into the distance ahead of a much slower and larger target. She might be OK. If she would agree to run on ahead. Which he knew she wouldn't. There would be an argument. They would miss what would likely be a one-time opportunity. Inevitable. Human nature. Mostly bullshit, but sometimes it rang a bell.

The gate was open.

Human nature. The driver had pulled in during what had obviously been an uproar. Yet he had gone right ahead and popped the trunk. Because he was eager. He couldn't wait. He wanted the praise and the plaudits. He wanted to be man of the hour. In other words he had sacrificed appropriate tactical caution in favor of his ego. He had been rushed and careless. Reacher remembered peeling off his jacket. He remembered dropping it on the street. He remembered the guns in the pockets bumping and clanking on the blacktop. The two Ukrainian H&Ks, and the two Albanian Glocks. All loaded. Probably more than forty rounds between them.

What would a rushed and careless guy do with a jacket dropped on the street?

Reacher crawled back to the rear passenger door and opened it the same way Abby had opened the front, craning up to the handle, pulling on the bottom edge, easing it wide. A waterfall of glass pebbles fell out. Tufts of upholstery stuffing drifted in the air.

His jacket was dumped on the back seat.

He pulled it toward him. It felt heavy. Partly from window fragments all over it, weighing it down, but mostly because of the metal in the pockets. It was all still there. Two H&Ks, two Glocks. He leaned his back on the rear wheel and checked them over. The H&K that he knew for sure worked had a round chambered and six more in the magazine. The other H&K had a round chambered and a full magazine. Likewise both Glocks. A total of fifty-two rounds, all of them fat little nine-millimeter Parabellums, winking in the smoky light. Against eight opponents, all of which would be low on ammunition by that point, after disabling the Chrysler with such reckless enthusiasm.

More encouraging.

He hooked a finger through all four trigger guards and crawled back to Abby.

Chapter 36

Abby sat with her back against the front tire, hugging her knees, her head ducked between them as low as it would go. Directly behind her was the big V-8 engine block, which was hundreds of pounds of iron, almost three feet long and about a foot and a half high. No doubt a tanker like Vantresca would have ridiculed it as defensive armor, but under the circumstances it was the best they could get. Against handgun rounds it would do its job.

Reacher took up position eight feet back, in a posture the army called modified sitting. His butt was on the concrete. His left leg was bent, like an upside down V, and so was his right, but it was folded down flat on the floor, like a triangle pointing outward, in a different direction, with the heel of his boot wedged up against the cheek of his butt. His left elbow was propped on his left knee, and his left hand was supporting his right forearm, which was straight out from the shoulder. Altogether he was a human geodesic dome, braced and rigid in every separate vector. Which was why the army liked the position enough to give it a name. His eight-feet-back location was textbook, too. It meant he could keep very low. From the far side of the car all that would show above the line of the hood would be the muzzle of his gun, his eyes, and the top of his head. He could skim his rounds exactly nine millimeters over the sheet metal and keep his trajectories flat and level. All good. Except it meant he was firing directly over Abby's head. She would feel the slipstream in her hair.

He started with a Glock. It seemed appropriate. It was an Albanian weapon. And it was full. Total of eighteen rounds. He figured it might get the job done all by itself. But still he laid out the others, in a fan shape by his right knee. Hope for the best, plan for the worst. Partly to test the gun and partly to get the party started he put a round into the pyramid of chemical drums. Second level up, which would be center mass on a standing man. There was a crack and a boom and a clang, and thick brown liquid gurgled out of the hole in the drum, which appeared more or less where he intended it to. The Glock worked OK.

A guy on the right craned up and fired a round from behind a stack of boards, then ducked back down again. The round hit the car. Maybe the driver's door. Poor shooting. Snatched and panicky. A guy on the left tried to do better. He leaned out and aimed. He was static and exposed for half a second. Mistake. Reacher hit him in the chest, and again in the head, after he was down, just to be sure. Three rounds gone. Seven guys left. They had all backed off a yard. Maybe rethinking their whole approach. There was a certain amount of low conversation. Plenty of whispered to and fro. Some kind of plan being made. Reacher wondered how good it would be. Probably not very. The obvious play was to split up, into two squads, and send one out a back entrance, and around the building, and back in through the roll-up door. Which would give Reacher a two-front problem. It was what he would have done. But the remaining seven guys seemed to have no leader. Their command structure seemed to have collapsed. Maybe some kind of a coup. Or a failed coup. A palace revolution. He had heard the muffled shooting when they arrived. First doubly muffled by the trunk lid, then more distinct after it was raised. It was clear a whole bunch of people were getting it in the head. Far away in the back offices, where the bigwigs lived.

The plan turned out to be a conventional infantry assault based on fire and movement. In other words some would shoot and some would run, and then those who had run would drop down and shoot, and those who had shot would jump up and run. Like leapfrog, with bullets. But not many. They were low on ammunition. Which took the sting out. Covering fire was supposed to be heavy enough to distract or suppress or intimidate or bewilder. Or at least to pre-occupy. But Reacher was able to more or less ignore it. Ten thousand generations were screaming at him to take cover, but the front part of his brain was fighting back with the new stuff, math and geometry and probabilities, calculating how likely it was that seven random guys could hit a target as small as a man's eyes and the top of his head, at range, with handguns, while agitated, and the covering fire was weak enough that the ancient reflexes lost the argument, and were boxed up and put away, leaving the modern man to do his lethal work undisturbed. It was like shooting ducks in a carnival sideshow. The guys on the right laid down the fire, and two guys from the left stood up and charged.

Reacher hit the first.

He hit the second.

They thumped on the concrete, which seemed to spark some kind of over-literal obedience to the part of the plan about getting up when the other side dropped down, because immediately two guys on the right jumped up and ran, completely premature and uncovered.

Reacher hit the first.

He hit the second.

They went down, sliding, sprawling, coming to rest.

Three guys left.

Like a carnival sideshow.

Then it wasn't. Then it was something Reacher had never seen before. It was something he never wanted to see again. Afterward he was grateful Abby had her head ducked down and her eyes screwed shut. There was a long, long moment of ominous silence, and then all three remaining guys jumped up simultaneously, firing wild, roaring, screaming, heads thrown back, eyes bulging, insane, primitive, like berserkers from an ancient legend, like dervishes from an ancient myth. They charged the car, still roaring, still screaming, still firing wild, like a mad epic gesture, like cavalry charging tanks, three crazy men heading for certain death, knowing it, wanting it, needing it, seeking it, demanding it.

Reacher hit the first.

He hit the second.

He hit the third.

The long low shed went quiet.

Reacher unwound his contorted position and got to his feet. He saw a total of twelve sprawled bodies, in a ragged line stretching back fifty feet. He saw blood on the concrete. He saw a wide pool of brown preservative. It was still dripping out of the drum.

Plink, plink, plink.

He said, "All good now."

Abby looked up at him.

She didn't speak.

He shook pebbles of glass out of his jacket and put it on. He put the guns back in the pockets. He made a mental note: forty-four rounds remaining.

He said, "We should go check the back offices."

She said, "Why?"

"They might have money."

Reacher and Abby stepped and minced around the bodies and the blood and the chemical spill, all the way to the far back corner. Ahead of them through the archway was a long narrow corridor. Doors to the left, doors to the right. First on the left was a windowless room with four laminate tables pushed together end to end. Like a boardroom. First on the right was a plain office with a desk and a chair and file cabinets. No clue about its function. No cash in the cabinets. Nothing in the desk either, except normal office crap and a dozen cigars and a box of kitchen matches. They moved on. They found nothing of interest, until the last door on the left.

There was an outer office, and an inner office. Like a suite. Some kind of a CEO set-up. Like a commanding officer and an executive officer. The doorway between the two was piled high with bodies. There were more in the room beyond. Twelve in total. Including a guy behind a big desk, shot once in the face, and a guy in a chair, shot three times in the chest. A bizarre, static tableau. Infinitely still. Absolutely silent. It was impossible to reconstruct what had happened. It looked like everyone had shot everyone else. Some kind of unexplained rampage.

Abby stayed out of the inner office. Reacher went in. He put his hands high on the door jambs and clambered over the piled bodies. He trod on backs and necks and heads. Once inside he picked his way around behind the desk. The guy who had been shot in the face was slumped in a leather chair with wheels. Reacher moved it out the way. He checked the desk drawers. Right away in the bottom left he found a metal cash box, about the size of a family bible, painted stern metallic colors, like something from an old-time country savings and loan. It was locked. He pulled the chair closer again and patted the dead guy's pockets. Felt keys in the pants, right side. A decent bunch. He pulled them out, finger and thumb. Some were big, some were small. The third small key he tried opened the box.

In it was a lift-out tray at the top, with a handful of greasy ones and fives, and a scattering of nickels and dimes. Not good. But it got better. Under the tray was a banded brick of hundred dollar bills. Brand new. Unbroken. Fresh from the bank. A hundred notes. Ten thousand dollars. Close to what the Shevicks needed. Short by a grand, but better than a poke in the eye.

Reacher put the money in his pocket. He threaded his way back to the door. He climbed over the bodies again.

Abby said, "I want to go."

"Me, too," Reacher said. "Just one more thing."

He led her back to the first office they had seen. On the right, opposite the boardroom. The cigar smoker. Newly dead, Reacher assumed. But not from smoking. He took the box of kitchen matches from his desk. And paper, from everywhere he could find it. He struck a match and lit a sheet. He held it until it flamed up high. Then he dropped it in a trash basket.

Abby asked him, "Why?"

"It's never enough just to win," he said. "The other guy has got to know for sure he lost. Plus it's safer this way. We were here. We probably left traces. Best to avoid any kind of confusion later on."

They struck match after match and lit sheet after sheet of paper. They dropped them in every room. Gray smoke was drifting when they left the corridor.

They lit the shrink wrap around the piles of boards. Reacher dropped a match in the pool of preservative, but it sputtered out immediately. Not flammable. Which made sense, in a lumber yard. But gasoline was flammable. That was for damn sure. Reacher took the gas cap off the shattered car and dropped the last sheet of burning paper down the filler neck.

Then they hustled. Thirty yards to the scooped-out curb, seventy more to the first corner, and then they were gone.

Abby's phone was full of missed calls from Vantresca. He said he was waiting across the street from the propped-up building with the heavy black net. He said he had been waiting there a long time. He said he didn't know what to do next. Abby called him back. Between them they worked out a new rendezvous. He would drive in one direction, and they would walk in the other direction, and they would spot each other somewhere along the way. Before they set out again Reacher looked back the way they had come. Half a mile away there was a thread of smoke in the sky. The next time he checked it was a pillar of smoke, a mile away. Then it was a distant boiling black mass with flames dancing at the base. They heard fire truck sirens, booming and barking, more and more of them, until the faraway sound was a continuous bass wail. They heard police car sirens echoing through the east side streets.

Then Vantresca showed up in a black car. It was wide and squat and muscular. It had a chrome hood ornament, in the shape of a big cat leaping. A jaguar, presumably, for a Jaguar. It was small inside. Vantresca was driving. Hogan was next to him in the front. Barton was in the back. Only one place left. Abby had to sit in Reacher's lap. Which was OK with him.

Hogan said, "Something is on fire over there."

"Your fault," Reacher said.

"How?"

"You pointed out that if the Ukrainians go down, the Albanians would take over the city. I didn't want that to happen. It felt like it would be a win-lose."

"So what's on fire?"

"The Albanian HQ. It's in the back of a lumber yard. It should burn for days."

Hogan said nothing.

Barton said, "Someone else will take over."

"Maybe not," Reacher said. "The new commissioner will have a clean slate. Maybe it's easier to stop new people coming in than it is to get old people out."

Vantresca said, "What next?"

"We need to find the Ukrainian nerve center."

"Sure, but how?"

"I guess we need to know exactly what it does. That might tell us what to look for. To some extent form follows function. For instance, if it was a drug lab, it would need exhaust fans, and gas and water, and so on and so forth."

"I don't know what it does," Vantresca said.

"Call the journalist," Reacher said. "The woman you helped. She might know. At least she might know what they're into. If necessary we could work it out backward, about what kind of place they would need."

"She won't talk to me. She was terrified."

"Give me her number," Reacher said. "I'll call her."

"Why would she talk to you?"

"I have a nicer personality. People talk to me all the time. Sometimes I can't stop them."

"I would have to go to my office."

"Go to the Shevicks' first," Reacher said. "I have something for them. Right now they need reassurance."

Chapter 37

Gregory pieced the story together from early word he got three separate ways, from a cop on his payroll, and a guy in the fire department who owed him money, and a secret snitch he had behind a bar on the east side. Right away he called a meeting of his inner council. They gathered together, in the office in back of the taxi dispatcher.

"Dino is dead," Gregory said. "Jetmir is dead. Their entire inner council is dead. Their top twenty are gone, just like that. Maybe more. They are no longer an effective force. Nor will they ever be, ever again. They have no leadership prospects. Their most senior survivor is an old bruiser named Hoxha. And he was spared only because he was in the hospital. Because he can't talk. Some leader he would make."

Someone asked, "How did it happen?"

"The Russians, obviously," Gregory said. "Shock

and awe east of Center, clearing half the field, pre-empting a possible defensive alliance, before turning their full might on us alone."

"Good strategy."

"But badly executed," Gregory said. "They were clumsy at the lumber yard. Every cop and every fire-fighter in the city is over there. The east side will be no use to anyone for months to come. Too much scrutiny. Bribes only go so far. Some things can't be ignored. I bet the whole thing is already on the television. In the spotlight, literally. Where no one wants to be. Which makes the west side the whole enchilada now. Now they'll want it more than ever."

"When will they come for us?"

"I don't know," Gregory said. "But we'll be ready. Starting right now, we'll go to Situation C. Tighten the guard. Take up defensive positions. Let no one through."

"We can't sustain Situation C indefinitely. We need to know when they're coming."

Gregory nodded.

"Aaron Shevick must know," he said. "We should ask him."

"We can't find him."

"Do we still have people at the old woman's house?"

"Yes, but Shevick never shows up there anymore. Probably the old woman tipped him off. Obviously she's his mother or his aunt or something."

Gregory nodded again.

"OK," he said. "There's your answer. Call our boys

and tell them to bring her in. She can get him on the phone, while we're working on her. He'll come running, the first time he hears her scream."

Vantresca had picked them up a mile from the lumber yard, which meant the Shevicks' house was another mile further on, to the southwest, like two sides of a triangle. The black Jaguar rumbled through the streets. By then it was mid-morning. The sun was high. The neighborhood was harsh with light and shadows. Reacher asked Vantresca to pull over at the gas station with the deli counter. They parked in the back, next to the car wash tunnel. A white sedan was inching its way through, under the thrashing brushes. There was blue foam and white bubbles everywhere.

Reacher said, "I guess now we can put the Shevicks in an east side hotel. No need to hide anymore. There's no one left to care if we're seen walking in with them."

"They can't afford it," Abby said.

Reacher checked Gezim Hoxha's potato-shaped wallet.

He said, "They don't need to."

"I'm sure they would prefer it all spent on Meg."

"It's a drop in the ocean. And this ain't a democracy. They can't stay in their house anymore."

"Why not?"

"We need to get this thing rolling. I want their capo unsettled. Gregory, right? I want him to hear us knocking at the door. Might as well start right here, with the guys outside the house. They've been cluttering up the place long enough. But there might be a response. So the Shevicks need to move out. Just for the time being."

"There's no room in the car," Barton said.

"We'll take their Lincoln," Reacher said. "We'll drive the Shevicks to a fancy hotel in the back of a Town Car. They might like that."

"They live on a cul-de-sac," Vantresca said. "We'll be approaching head on. No element of surprise."

"For you, maybe," Reacher said. "I'll go in the back again, and come out through the house. Behind them. While they're trying to figure out who the hell you guys are. That should be a surprise."

The Jaguar rolled back out to the main drag, and took the early right, and the left, and stopped in the same spot Reacher and Abby had parked the Chrysler, before dawn, outside the Shevicks' back-to-back neighbor. Outside the informer's house, whose calls would henceforth go unanswered, because the instrument on the other end of the line had long ago melted. Like the Chrysler had been, the Jaguar was lined up exactly parallel with the Lincoln, nose to nose and tail to tail, about two hundred feet apart, the depth of two small residential lots, with two buildings in the way. But only for a moment. Reacher got out, and it rolled onward.

Reacher walked through the neighbor's front yard and wrenched open the fold-back section of fence. He walked through the neighbor's back yard. To the rickety back fence. Which was either the neighbor's, or the Shevicks', or shared. He had no great desire to climb it again. So he kicked it down. If it was the Shevicks', then Trulenko could buy them a new one.

If it was the neighbor's, then tough shit, for being an informer. If it was shared, then fifty-fifty on each of the above.

He walked through the Shevicks' back yard, past the spot where the photographs had been taken, to their kitchen door. He knocked gently on the glass. No response. He knocked again, a little louder. Still no response.

He tried the handle. Locked, from the inside. He looked in through the window. Nothing to see. No people. Just the heart-monitor countertops and the atomic table and the vinyl chairs. He tracked along, past the photography spot, to the next window in line. Their bedroom. No one in it. Just a made bed and a closed closet door.

But an open room door. Beyond which he saw a moving shadow out in the hallway. A complicated two-headed, four-legged shape. One half tall, the other half short. Slight movement, like a halfhearted struggle and an easy restraint.

Reacher put his hand in his pocket. Chose a fresh Glock. Seventeen rounds, plus one in the chamber. He hustled back to the kitchen door. He took a breath, and another, and backhanded his elbow through the glass, and snaked his hand in and turned the lock, one smooth movement, and he stepped inside. Noisy, obviously, which meant right on time a head stuck in, around the door to the hallway, to find out what the hell was going on. A pale face, pale eyes, fair hair. Black suit coat, white shirt, black silk necktie. Reacher aimed an inch below the knot of the tie, but he was a fair man, so he didn't fire until he saw a hand with a gun swing into clear air, on a fast arc a yard below the face, whereupon he pulled the trigger and blew a hole in the guy big enough to stick his thumb in. The round went through and through and punched into the far wall beyond. The guy went down vertically, like a cut puppet.

The roar of the shot died away.

Silence from the hallway.

Then a faint muffled whimper, like a weak old person trying to scream, with a strong man's hand clamped over his mouth. Or her mouth. Then the scrape of a shoe, hopeless, going nowhere. Token resistance. The dead guy was leaking blood on the parquet. It was soaking into the seams. A mess. Reacher found himself figuring a couple of yards would need to be replaced. Trulenko could pay for it. Plus spackle, for the bullet hole in the wall. And paint. Plus new glass for the kitchen door. All good.

Silence from the hallway. Reacher backed away to the outside door. *The obvious play was to split up, into two squads, and send one out a back entrance, and around the building.* He stepped over the broken glass and out to the yard. He turned right, and right, and right again. He paused a beat at the front of the house. He saw the Lincoln, parked on the street, with no one in it. No sign of the Jaguar. Not yet. He traced its route in his head. North to the next major cross street, west to the main drag, south to their usual turn, and then into the development, with its narrow streets and its tight right-angle corners. Five minutes, maybe. Six maximum. They wouldn't get lost. Abby knew the way.

He moved along the front of the house, on the grass a yard from the wall, because of the foundation plantings. He looked in the hallway window at a shallow angle. Saw a second guy with a pale face and a black suit. He had his meaty left palm clamped over Maria Shevick's mouth. In his right hand he held a gun, with its muzzle jammed hard against the side of her head. Another H&K P7, steely and delicate. His finger was tight on the trigger. Aaron Shevick was standing a yard away, rigid, wide eyed, plainly terrified. His lips were clamped. Clearly he had been told to keep quiet. Clearly he wasn't about to risk disobedience. Not with a gun to his wife's head.

Reacher checked the end of the cul-de-sac again. Still no Jaguar. The guy holding Maria was staring inward at the kitchen door. Waiting for whoever was in there to come on out. Directly into a classic standoff. *Drop the gun or I'll shoot the old lady.* Except the guy couldn't shoot the old lady, because a split second after he pulled the trigger he would get his own head blown off. A classic standoff. A permanent triangle. The threat vectors would go around and around forever, like a feedback loop, howling and screaming.

Reacher worked out the angles. The guy was a head taller than Maria Shevick. In a literal sense. He was holding her against him, her back to his front, with the clamped left hand, and the top of her head fit neatly under his chin. Then came his own head. At that point Reacher was looking at it from the side. A slabby white cheek, a small pink ear, buzzed fair hair glittering over ridges of bone. He was over thirty, but maybe not yet forty. Was he senior enough to know where their nerve center was? That was Reacher's main question.

And the answer was no, he thought. Like before. *We're guys who sit in cars and watch doors. You think they would tell folks like us where Trulenko is?* The guy was no use.

Unfortunate.

Especially for him.

Reacher dropped to the ground and elbowed-and-toed his way to the narrow concrete path, and over it, and beyond it. The front door was standing open. The guy was still staring at the kitchen. Still waiting. Reacher squirmed around until his angle of view through the open door was a quarter circle different than his oblique glance in through the window. Now he was looking at the back of the guy's head. A wide white neck, tight rolls of hard flesh, the glittering buzz cut over lumps of bone. He was looking at it all from a very low angle. He was prone on the ground, outside at grade level, below the step, below the threshold, below the hallway floor. He was aiming the Glock at a steep upward angle. At a point where the guy's spine met his skull. Which was as high as he dared to go. He wanted the round to dig in, not crease off. Which happened, sometimes, with shallow angles. Some people had skulls like concrete.

He counted to three, and breathed out, long and slow.

He pulled the trigger. The guy's head cracked open like a dropped watermelon and the bullet came out the top of his skull and lodged in the ceiling directly above him. The air was instantly full of pink and purple mist. Instant brain death. Messy, but necessary, with a finger hard on a trigger. The only safe way. Medically proven.

The guy fell away from behind Maria Shevick like she was shucking off a big winter coat and letting it float to the floor. She was left standing alone, a yard from her husband, both of them mute and rigid. The crash of the shot died away to silence. The pink mist drifted down, infinitely slow.

Then the Jaguar showed up.

Reacher's plan had been to present the hotel idea as a fun adventure, and then to top it off by handing over the ten grand in hundreds, all crisp and new and sweet smelling. It didn't work out that way. Maria Shevick had blood and bone fragments in her hair. Aaron was shaky. He was an inch away from losing it. Vantresca took them out and sat them in the back of his Jaguar. Abby packed a bag for them. She went from room to room, grabbing up what she thought they would need. Reacher and Hogan carried the bodies out and put them in the Lincoln's trunk, less their money, their guns, and their phones. Familiar work, by that point. Reacher gave Vantresca cash from Gezim Hoxha's potato-shaped wallet, to pay for the Shevicks' hotel room. Vantresca said he would drive them there and check them in. He would ride upstairs with them and settle them down. Reacher said the other four would stay behind and deal with the Lincoln.

"What do we do with it?" Barton asked.

"Drive it," Reacher said.

"Where?"

"You have a gig. We need to go get your van and load up your stuff."

"With them in the trunk?"

"You ever been on a plane?"

"Sure."

"There was probably a coffin in the baggage hold. Dead people are forever getting repatriated."

"You know the gig is west of Center."

Reacher nodded.

"In a lounge," he said. "With a guy on the door."

Chapter 38

Barton's van was stored on a vacant lot behind a razor wire fence with a chained gate. He and Hogan got it out and Reacher and Abby followed them back to the house in the Lincoln. The van was a beat-up third-hand soccer mom vehicle, with the rear seats taken out and the windows covered over with black plastic. Reacher helped them load it. He had done many odd jobs since leaving the army, but he had never been a rock'n'roll roadie before. He carried Barton's lethal Precision in a hard-shell case, plus a back-up instrument, plus an amplifier head the size of a rich man's suitcase, and then finally the huge eight-speaker cabinet. He carried Hogan's disassembled drum kit. He packed it all in.

Then he and Abby followed the van again, in the Lincoln, heading west toward Ukrainian territory. Noon was coming. The day was close to halfway over. Reacher drove. Abby counted the money they had taken from the guys in the trunk. Not much. A total of two hundred ten dollars. *We're guys who sit in cars.* Clearly on a lower per diem than an old horse like Gezim Hoxha got. Their phones showed the same barrage of texts they had seen before, plus a whole string of new ones. All in Ukrainian. Abby recognized the shapes of some of the words, from her crash course the night before, with Vantresca.

"They're changing the situation again," she said.

"To what?" Reacher asked.

"I can't read it. I don't know which letter it is. Presumably either up to C, or back down to A."

"Probably not back down," Reacher said. "Under the circumstances."

"I think they're blaming the Russians. I think they're calling Aaron Shevick a Russian."

"Where are the texts coming from?"

"All the same number. Probably an automated distribution system."

"Probably in a computer in the nerve center."

"Probably."

"Check the phone log."

"What am I looking for?"

"The call that told them to go get Maria Shevick."

Abby dabbed and scrolled her way to a list of recent calls.

"The last one incoming was about an hour ago," she said. "Fifty-seven minutes, to be precise."

Reacher timed his way through what had happened, but in reverse, like a stopwatch running backward. Following the van west, loading the van, getting the van, leaving the house, about four minutes and thirty seconds spent at the house, walking through the Shevicks' yard, walking through the neighbor's yard, getting out of the car. Out of the Jaguar, which was lined up parallel to the Lincoln, nose to nose and tail to tail, but about two hundred feet apart. Fifty-seven minutes. The two guys could have been getting out of their own car at the exact same moment.

He said, "Where did the call come from?"

She checked.

"A weird cell number," she said. "Probably a disposable drugstore phone."

"Probably a senior figure. Maybe even Gregory himself. It was a major strategic decision. They want to know when the Russians are coming. They think I can tell them. They wanted Maria as leverage. They must think we're related."

"What kind of leverage?"

"The wrong kind. Call the number back."

"Really?"

"There are things that need to be said."

Abby put the phone on speaker and chose an option from the call log menu. Dial tone filled the car. Then a voice answered, with a foreign word that could have been hello, or yes, or what, or shoot, or whatever else people say when they answer the phone.

Reacher said, "Speak English."

The voice said, "Who are you?"

"You first," Reacher said. "Tell me your name."

"Are you Shevick?"

"No," Reacher said. "You're confused about that. You're confused about a lot of things."

"Then who are you?"

"You first," Reacher said again.

"What do you want?"

"I have a message for Gregory."

"Who are you?"

"You first," Reacher said, for the third time.

"My name is Danilo," the guy said.

Abby stiffened in her seat.

"I am Gregory's chief of staff," the guy said. "What is your message?"

"It's for Gregory," Reacher said. "Transfer the call."

"Not until I know who you are. Where are you from?"

"I was born in Berlin," Reacher said,

"You're East German? Not Russian?"

"My dad was a U.S. Marine. He was deployed to our embassy. I was born there. A month later I was somewhere else. Now I'm here. With a message for Gregory."

"What's your name?"

"Jack Reacher."

"That's the old man."

"I told you, you're confused about that. I'm not as young as I was, but I'm not old yet. Overall I'm doing OK. Now transfer the call."

The guy named Danilo went quiet for a long moment. The chief of staff. A big decision. Like an executive officer. You didn't bug the CO with the small stuff, but you made damn sure you knew which small stuff was really big stuff in disguise. And then, the biggest bureaucratic rule of all: if in doubt, play it safe.

Danilo played it safe. There was a click, and a long moment of dead air, and another click, and then a new voice came on, with a foreign word that could have been hello, or yes, or what, or shoot, or whatever.

Reacher said, "Speak English."

Gregory said, "What do you want?"

"You got caller ID?"

"Why?"

"So you can tell who's calling you."

"You told Danilo your name is Reacher."

"But whose phone am I on?"

No answer.

"They're dead," Reacher said. "They were useless. Like all your guys have been useless. They're going down like flies. Pretty soon you'll have no one left."

"What do you want?"

"I'm coming for you, Gregory. You were going to hurt Maria Shevick. I don't like people like you. I'm going to find you, and I'm going to make you cry like a little girl. Then I'm going to rip your leg off at the hip and beat you to death with it."

Gregory paused a beat, and said, "You think you can do that?"

"I'm pretty sure."

"Not if I see you first."

"You won't," Reacher said. "You haven't yet. You never will. You can't find me. You're not good enough. You're an amateur, Gregory. I'm a professional. You won't see me coming. You could go all the way to Situation Z and it wouldn't help you. My advice right now is say your goodbyes and make your will."

He clicked off and threw the phone out the window.

Abby said, "Danilo."

A small voice. Hesitant.

Reacher said, "What about him?"

"He was the guy," she said.

"What guy?"

"Who did the thing to me."

Chapter 39

Abby started her story at a red light and continued it through three more. She spoke in a small, quiet voice. Diffident, uncertain, full of pain and embarrassment. Reacher listened, mostly saying nothing in response. It seemed like the best thing to do.

She said thirteen months previously, she had been waiting tables in a bar west of Center. It was new and hip and it made a lot of money. A flagship enterprise. As such it always had a man on the door. Mostly he was there to collect Gregory's percentage, but sometimes he took on a security role. Like a bouncer. Which was Gregory's way. He liked to offer the illusion of something in exchange. Abby said she was OK with all of that, fundamentally. She had worked in bars all her adult life, and she knew protection money was an inescapable reality, and she knew a bouncer had occasional value, when drunk guys were grabbing her ass and making lewd suggestions. Most of the time she was content to make a deal with the devil. She went along to get along, and sometimes she looked away, and other times she benefited from a little intervention.

But one night a young guy was in, twenty-something, for a birthday celebration. He was a geeky guy, thin, hyped up, always in motion, laughing out loud at random things. But totally harmless. She said truth to tell, she wondered if he had a mental dysfunction. Some kind of screw loose, that made him overexcited. Which he was, undeniably. Even so, no one really objected. Except a guy in a thousand-dollar suit, who had maybe been expecting a different kind of ambience. Maybe more sophisticated. He was with a woman in a thousand-dollar dress, and between them they acted out all kinds of dissatisfied body language, telegraphing it, semaphoring it, huffing and puffing, getting more and more exaggerated, until even the doorman noticed.

Whereupon the doorman did what he was supposed to, which was to eyeball the interested parties, and assess them carefully, in terms of which of them was likely to be of greater future value, in terms of cold hard future revenue. Which was obviously the couple in the thousand-dollar clothes. They were drinking fancy cocktails. Their tab was going to be a couple hundred bucks. The geeky twenty-something was drinking domestic beer, very slowly. His tab was going to be about twelve dollars. So the doorman asked the geeky guy to leave.

Abby said, "Which I was still OK with, at that point. I mean, yeah, it was sad, and it sucked, but this is the real world. Everyone is trying to stay in business. But when they got face to face, I could see the doorman really hated the kid. I think it was the mental thing. Definitely the kid was a little off. The doorman reacted to it. It was primitive. Like the kid was the other, and had to be rooted out. Or maybe the doorman was deep down scared. Some people are, by mental illness. But whichever, he dragged the kid out the back, not the front, and beat him nearly to death. I mean, really, really badly. Broken skull, arm, ribs, pelvis, leg. Which was not OK with me."

Reacher said, "What did you do about it?"

"I went to the cops. Obviously I knew Gregory was paying off the whole department, but I imagined there must be a line somewhere, that they wouldn't let him cross."

"Don't frighten the voters."

"But clearly this didn't. Because nothing ever happened. The cops ignored me completely. No doubt Gregory straightened it all out behind the scenes. Probably with one phone call. Meanwhile I was left hanging out in the breeze. All alone and exposed."

"What happened?"

"Nothing, the first day. Then I was called to a disciplinary tribunal. They love all that stuff. Organized crime is more bureaucratic than the post office. There were four men at a table. Danilo chaired the meeting. He never spoke. Just watched. At first I wouldn't speak either. I mean, it was bullshit. I don't work for them. They don't make rules for me. As far as I was concerned, they could take their tribunal and stick it where the sun don't shine. Then they explained the realities to me. If I didn't cooperate, I would never work again, west of Center. Which is half the jobs I get, obviously. I really couldn't afford to lose them. I would have starved. I would have had to leave town and start over somewhere else. So in the end I said OK, whatever."

"How was it?"

She shrugged and shook her head and didn't answer the question directly. Not with a one-word description. Instead she said, "I had to confess to my crime, in detail. I had to explain my motivation, and show where I later realized I had been misguided. I had to apologize most sincerely, over and over again, for going to the police, for criticizing the doorman, for thinking I knew better. I had to promise them I was a reformed character. I had to assure them it was safe to let me keep on working. I had to make a formal application. I had to say, please sir, let me work in your half of town. In a nice voice. Like a good little girl."

Reacher said nothing.

Abby said, "Then we moved to the punishment phase. They explained there had to be a forfeit. Something that would demonstrate my sincerity. They brought in a video camera with a tripod. I had to stand up straight, chin out, shoulders back. They said they were going to slap my face. That was the forfeit. Forty times. Twenty on the left, twenty on the right. They were going to film it. I was told to look brave and try not to cry. I was told not to cringe away, but to offer myself proudly and willingly, because I deserved it."

Reacher said nothing.

Abby said, "They started the camera. It was Danilo who hit me. It was awful. Open hand, but really hard. He knocked me down half a dozen times. I had to get up and smile and say, sorry, sir. I had to get back in position, willing and eager. I had to count. One, sir, two, sir. I don't know what was worse, the pain or the humiliation. He stopped halfway through. He said I could quit if I wanted. But I would lose the deal. I would have to leave town. So I said no. He made me ask out loud. I had to say, please sir, I want you to keep on slapping my face. When he was done I was all red and swollen and my head was ringing and I was bleeding in my mouth. But it's the camera I think about now. It was for the internet, I'm sure. Had to be. Some porn site. The abuse and humiliation sub-genre. Now my face will be out there forever, getting slapped."

Up ahead, Barton's van started to slow.

"OK," Reacher said. "Danilo. Good to know."

Chapter 40

The lounge was in the basement of a wide brick building on a decent street three blocks from the first of the downtown high-rises. There were coffee shops and boutiques on the ground floor, and other enterprises above. Maybe twelve in total. They all shared a freight entrance in back, where Barton parked. Reacher slotted the Lincoln next to him. Between them they hauled the stuff to the elevator. Then Vantresca showed up, in his Jaguar. He parked on the other side of the van and got out and said, "I'm with the band."

Barton and Hogan rode down with their gear. Reacher and Abby stayed on the street. Abby asked Vantresca about the Shevicks.

"They're hanging in there," Vantresca said. "They're on a high floor. It feels safe and remote. They're taking showers and taking naps. I showed them how room service works. They'll be OK. They seem pretty resilient. They're too old to be snow-flakes. At least they can watch TV now. They were happy about that. Tried not to show it."

Abby gave him the second Ukrainian phone. The one Reacher didn't throw out the car window. Van-tresca read through the string of new texts. He said, "They know the Albanians are wiped out. They think they're both being attacked by Russian organized crime. They've gone to Situation C. They're tighten-ing the guard. They're taking up defensive positions. They're saying, let no one pass. With an exclamation point. Very dramatic. Sounds like a slogan on an old Eastern Bloc billboard."

"Any mention of Trulenko?" Reacher asked.

"Nothing. Presumably he's part of tightening the guard."

"But they're not shutting him down."

"Doesn't say so."

"Therefore what he does can't be interrupted. Even for a war with Russian organized crime. That should tell us something."

"What?"

"I don't know," Reacher said. "Did you stop by your office?"

Vantresca nodded. He pulled a slip of paper out of his back pants pocket. He handed it over. A name, and a number. Barbara Buckley. *The Washington Post*. A D.C. area code.

"Waste of time," Vantresca said. "She won't talk to you."

Reacher took the captured phone from him. He

dialed the number. The phone rang. The call was answered.

He said, "Ms. Buckley?"

"Not here," a voice said. "Try later."

The phone went down again. Almost noon. The day half over. They rode the empty freight elevator down to the basement, where they found Barton and Hogan setting up. They had two friends on stage with them. A guy who played guitar, and a woman who sang. A regular lunchtime date for all of them, once a week.

Reacher hung back in the shadows. The room was large, but low. No windows, because it was a basement. There was a bar all the way across the right-hand wall, and a rectangle of parquet dance floor, and some chairs and tables, and some standing room only. There were maybe sixty people already inside. With more filing in. Past a guy in a suit on a stool. He was in the far left corner of the room. Not exactly a doorman. More like a bottom-of-the-stairs man. But his role was identical. Counting heads, and looking tough. He was a big individual. Broad shoulders, wide neck. Black suit, white shirt, black silk necktie. In the near left corner of the room was a double-wide corridor, that led to the restrooms, and a fire exit, and the freight elevator. It was the way they had come in. There were wide hoops of colored spotlights fixed to the ceiling, all trained inward on the stage. Not much else in the way of illumination. A dim fire exit sign at the head of the corridor, and another behind the man on the stool.

All good.

Reacher drifted back to the stage. The gear was all set up. It was humming and buzzing gently. Barton's Precision Bass was leaning against his monster cabinet. Ready for action. His back-up instrument was on a stand next to it. Ready for emergencies. Barton himself was at a table close by. Eating lunch. A hamburger. He said the band got free food. Whatever they wanted off the menu, to a max of twenty bucks.

Reacher asked him, "What kind of stuff are you going to play?"

"Covers, mostly," he said. "Maybe a couple of our own songs."

"Are you loud?"

"If we want to be."

"Do people dance?"

"If we want them to."

"Make them dance the third number," Reacher said. "Make it loud. Every eye on you."

"That part usually comes at the end."

"We don't have time."

"We have a rock and roll medley. Everyone dances to that. I guess we could bring it in early."

"Works for me," Reacher said. "Thank you."

All good.

Plan made.

The house lights went down and the stage lights came up and the band kicked into its opening number, which was a mid-tempo rocker with a sad verse and an exuberant chorus. Reacher and Abby drifted away to the near right corner of the room, diagonally opposite the man on the stool. They drifted through the crowd at the bar, following the right-hand wall, aiming for the far right corner. They got there just as the band started its second number, which was faster and hotter than the first. They were warming up the crowd. Getting them ready for the rock and roll medley coming next. They were pretty good at it. They were hitting the spot. Absurdly Reacher wanted to stop and dance. Something about the pulse of the beat. He could see Abby felt the same way. She was walking ahead of him. He could see it in her hips. She wanted to dance.

So, absurdly, they did. In the dark, beyond the rim of the crowd, close to the wall, bopping away, maintaining some element of linear progress, in a two steps forward, one step back kind of a way, but basically just having fun. Some kind of release, Reacher figured, or relief, or diversion, or consolation. Or normality. What two people who just met should be doing.

All around them other people were doing it, too. More and more. So that when the third number started the place went wild, with people crushing in on the parquet floor, hopping around, plus a wide halo of more on the carpet, bumping tables, spilling drinks, going crazy. *Make them dance. Make it loud. Every eye on you.* Barton had delivered big time.

Reacher and Abby stopped dancing.

They ghosted the rest of the way along the back wall, behind the mass of dancers, toward the far left corner, where they arrived directly behind the man on the stool. They waited in the gloom six feet away,

until a gaggle of latecomers started down the stairs.
The man on the stool looked up at them. Reacher
stepped behind him and clapped a hand down on his
shoulder. Like a friendly greeting. Or a pretend surprise, just horsing around, like some guys do. Reacher
figured that was all the latecomers saw. What they
didn't see was his fingers curling under the guy's shirt
collar, twisting it, tightening it. What they also didn't
see was his other hand, low down behind, jamming
the muzzle of a gun hard against the base of the guy's
spine. Really hard. Hard enough to cause a puncture
wound all by itself, even without pulling the trigger.

Reacher leaned forward and spoke in the guy's ear.

He said, "Let's go take a walk."

He pulled with his left and pushed with his right
and maneuvered the guy backward off the stool. He
stood him upright and got him balanced. He twisted
his collar harder. Abby stepped up and patted his
pockets and took his phone and his gun. Another
steel P7. The band fell straight into the second song
in the medley. Faster and louder. Reacher leaned forward again.

He yelled, "Hear that backbeat? I could shoot you
four to the bar and no one in here would notice a
damn thing. So do exactly what I tell you."

He pushed the guy along the left-hand wall, stiff,
awkward, four-legged, like the shadow he had seen in
the Shevicks' hallway. Abby kept pace a yard away,
like a wingman. She roved back and forth. She ducked
in and out. The band went straight into the third part
of the medley. Faster and louder still. Reacher hustled
the guy harder. Ran him all the way to the mouth of

the corridor. To the freight elevator. Up to the street. Out to the dock. Out to the daylight. He hauled him around to the rear of the Lincoln. He stood him up straight and made him watch.

Abby pressed the button on the key fob.

The trunk lid raised up.

Two dead guys. Same suits, same ties. Limp, bloody, stinking.

The guy looked away.

Reacher said to him, "That's you, a minute from now. Unless you answer my questions."

The guy said nothing. He couldn't speak. His collar was twisted too tight.

Reacher asked, "Where does Maxim Trulenko work?"

He slackened his grip half an inch. The guy panted a couple of breaths. He glanced left, glanced right, glanced up to the sky, as if he was considering his options. As if he had options to consider. Then he looked down. At the dead guys in the trunk.

Then he stared.

He said, "That's my cousin."

"Which one?" Reacher asked. "The one I shot in the head, or the one I shot in the throat?"

"We came here together. From Odessa. We arrived in New Jersey."

"You must be confusing me with someone who gives a shit. I asked you a question. Where does Maxim Trulenko work?"

The guy said the word they had seen in the text message. Biologically inexact. Either a hive or a nest or a burrow. For something that hummed or buzzed or thrashed around.

"Where is it?" Reacher said.

"I don't know," the guy said. "It's a secret operation."

"How big is it?"

"I don't know."

"Who else works there?"

"I don't know."

"Do Danilo and Gregory work there?"

"No."

"Where do they work?"

"In the office."

"Is that separate?"

"From what?"

"The word you used. The hive."

"Of course it is."

"Where is the office?"

The guy named a street, and a cross street. He said, "Behind the taxi company, across from the pawn shop, next to the bail bonds."

"We were right there," Abby said.

Reacher nodded. He slid his hand around under the guy's collar, from the back, to the side. He dug down with his fingers until he felt the inside face of the guy's necktie centered in the meat of his palm. He felt it through the cotton of the collar. A silk necktie, at that point about an inch and a half wide. More tensile strength than steel. Silk shimmered because its fibers were triangular, like elongated prisms, which did nice things with light, but which also locked together so tight it was virtually impossible to pull them apart end to end. A steel cable would give way sooner.

Reacher bunched his fist. Took up what slack there was. At first his hand was square on. All his knuckles were lined up parallel with the crushed rim of the collar. Like he was hanging one-handed from a rung on a ladder. Then he rotated his thumb toward him, and his pinkie knuckle away from him. As if he was trying to spin the ladder, like an airplane propeller. Or like a tweak on a rein, turning a horse. All of which drove his pinkie knuckle into the side of the guy's neck. Which in turn tightened the stronger-than-steel strap against the other side of his neck. Reacher held it like that for a spell, and then he turned his hand another small angle. And then another. The doorman was calm. The pressure was all side to side, not front to back. He wasn't choking for lack of air. Not thrashing around in desperate panic. Instead the arteries in his neck were closed off and no blood was reaching his brain. Relaxed. Peaceful. Like a narcotic. Warm and comfortable.

Sleepy.

Almost there.

Almost done.

Reacher held it a whole extra minute, just to be sure, and then he tipped the guy in the trunk with his cousin, and he slammed the lid. Abby looked at him. As if to ask, are we going to kill them all? But not disapproving. Not accusatory. Merely a request for information. He thought to himself, I hope so.

Out loud he said, "I should try *The Washington Post* again."

She passed him the dead guy's phone. There was a brand new text on the screen. As yet unread. It had Reacher's own picture in a fat green bubble. The surprise portrait from the moneylending bar. The pale guy, raising his phone. Below the photo was a block of Cyrillic writing. Some long screed about something or other.

"What the hell is their problem now?" he said.

"Vantresca will tell us," she said.

He dialed *The Washington Post* from memory, having done it not long before. Once again the phone rang. Once again the call was answered.

Once again he said, "Ms. Buckley?"

"Yes?" a voice said.

"Barbara Buckley?"

"What do you want?"

"I have two things for you," Reacher said. "Some good news, and a story."

Chapter 41

In the background on the line Reacher heard all kinds of hustle and bustle. A big open space. Maybe a low hard ceiling. The clatter of keyboards. A dozen conversations. He said, "I'm guessing you're at a desk in a newsroom."

Barbara Buckley said, "No shit, Sherlock."

"I'm guessing you've got tickers and cable news on screens all around you."

"Hundreds of them."

"Maybe right now one of them is showing regional coverage of a fire in a lumber yard in a city you know."

No answer.

Reacher said, "The good news is the lumber yard was the Albanian gang's HQ. It's burning to the ground. Most of them are dead inside. The rest have fled. They're history. The things they said to you don't apply anymore. From when you had that meeting, a couple months ago. In the back room of the restaurant. Those threats are now gone forever. As of today. We believe it was important you should know as soon as possible. It's a part of our victims' rights protocol."

"Is this the police department?"

"Strictly speaking, no."

"But you are law enforcement?"

"Which has many levels."

"Which level are you?"

"Ma'am, with the greatest possible respect, you're a journalist. There are some things better not said out loud."

"You mean, you could tell me, but then you would have to kill me?"

"Ma'am, we don't really say that."

"Are you speaking from there?"

"I would prefer not to discuss specific locations. But I will say it's very warm here."

"Wait," she said. "How did you even find me? I didn't report the threats to anyone."

Reacher took a breath, ready to launch into the second part of his script, but she beat him to it, like the investigative reporter he guessed she was, with a rapid-fire chain of fast connections and assumptions and wild-ass guesses, all of which ended up pretty much where he would have wanted to anyway. She said, "Wait, the only person who could have known anything about this was the guy who drove me to the airport afterward, who was the local help I hired, who was ex-military, a fairly senior rank, which I know for sure because obviously I checked him out, so it must have been him who reported it, presumably to a friend or an associate with a particular interest, possibly in the Pentagon, which is probably where you come from. Some secret three-letter agency no one has ever heard of."

Reacher said, "Ma'am, I would very much prefer not to confirm or deny."

"Whatever," she said. Then she took a breath and her voice changed a little. She said, "I appreciate the call. Thank you. Your protocol works well."

"Feel better?"

"You said you had a story for me. Is that it? The Albanians are gone?"

"No," Reacher said. "Something different. Involving you."

"I won't go public. I dropped the story. Not what a fearless reporter is supposed to do."

"This is the other side of the coin," Reacher said. "This is where the fearless reporter breaks the case wide open. Because of the research you did. You came here for a reason. Which wasn't the Albanians. You gave the impression you were much more interested in the Ukrainians. It would help us to know the basis for that interest."

"I don't understand."

"What did you think the Ukrainians were doing?"

"I understood the question. What I didn't understand was why you were asking it. You're a secret three-letter agency. Surely you know why you're there. Or is this what you do now? You outsource the actual investigative part of the investigation to newspapers?"

Reacher took a breath, and launched the third part of his script. He said, "Clearly you derived information from somewhere. As did we, of course. But your somewhere was not the same place as our somewhere. I can pretty much guarantee that. Therefore if we make you the star of the show, we keep ourselves in the shadows. We throw suspicion in the wrong direction. We protect our sources. They live to fight another day. Which might be important. But the rules of engagement require that we hear a credible accusation from a credible person before we can proceed. We can't just make it up. It's subject to review."

"Are you recording this?"

"I would need your permission."

"You would admit I broke the case?"

"I think we would be obliged to spin it that way. Best all around. No one would look at our guys. Plus we don't care anyway. I don't want to go on TV."

"I'm a journalist," Buckley said. "No one would call me credible."

"These are just boxes to check. We would take a tarot card reader."

"It started with a rumor I heard from a friend of a friend. The story was, whatever was claimed politically, the intelligence professionals had in fact traced the fake news on the internet all the way back to the Russian government in Moscow, and they had also gotten pretty good at blocking it, except suddenly they had a sudden setback. The rumor was somehow the Russians had gotten inside. They were operating inside the United States, and the blocking didn't work anymore."

"OK," Reacher said.

"But I got to thinking. Obviously there was nothing coming out of their embassy, because we would have known. We're all over that place, electronically. And they didn't move the whole project here, because it's not just us they're messing with. They're hacking the world. So obviously they outsourced the American part of the project to someone who was already here. Like a straightforward business deal. Like a franchise. But who? The Russian mob in the U.S. isn't good enough, and anyway, no way would the Russian government want to be in business with them. I tried to figure it out. I had some information. The geeks at the paper follow this stuff. They have league tables, like the NFL. All those old Soviet states are pretty good at technology. Estonia, for instance. And Ukraine, they figured. But Moscow and Kiev can't talk. They're at permanent loggerheads. But Moscow can talk to the Ukrainian mob in the U.S. Same people, same talent, but a different place. And it would be perfect cover. It's a very unlikely link. And the geeks said the Ukrainians were just about good enough to do it, in a technology sense. So I figured that was what had happened. An annual contract, between the Russian government and Ukrainian organized crime in America, probably worth at least tens of millions of dollars. I have no proof, but I bet I'm right. Call it a journalist's guess."

"OK," Reacher said again.

"But then a couple months ago they suddenly got much better at doing it. They went way beyond just good enough. It happened more or less overnight. Suddenly they were doing really smart stuff. The geeks said they must have brought in new talent. No other way of doing it. Maybe a consultant from Moscow. So I went there to check. Naively I thought I might see a Russian walking around town, looking lost."

"So you already aimed to break the story."

"But I didn't."

"Where would you have looked?"

"I had no idea. That was going to be my next step. But I never got that far."

"OK," Reacher said. "Thank you."

"Is that enough?"

"Credible person, credible reason. The boxes are checked."

"Thank you again, for the first part of the call. I do feel better."

"It's a great feeling," Reacher said. "Isn't it? You're alive, and they ain't."

At the end of their hour Barton and Hogan came up to the street, damp with exertion, loaded with gear. Vantresca was helping them. He read the new text. The photograph, in the fat green bubble. He said, "This is absurd."

Reacher said, "He took me by surprise."

"Not the photograph. The message is from Gregory himself. He says you're the vanguard of an attack from a direction he can no longer reliably discern. It is even possible you are an agent of the Kiev government. You must therefore be captured at all costs. You must be brought to him alive."

"Better than the alternative, I suppose."

"Did the doorman tell you anything?"

"Plenty," Reacher said. "But the journalist told me more."

"She talked to you?"

"It's about fake news on the internet. It was coming in from Russia. Now it's inside the United States. We can't block it anymore. She figured Moscow hired the Ukrainians as a proxy. Then about two months ago the standard went way up. She said the geeks at the paper figured the Ukrainians must have brought in new talent. No other way to explain it."

"Trulenko went into hiding about two months ago."

"Exactly," Reacher said. "He's smart with computers. He's managing the contract. The Russian government is paying Gregory, and Gregory is paying Trulenko. After taking a healthy percentage for himself, I'm sure. Must feel like Christmas morning. The journalist said the contract could be worth tens of millions of dollars."

"What did the doorman tell you?"

"It's a secret satellite operation physically separate from the main office. He didn't know where it is, or how big it is, or who works there, or how many."

"You call that telling you plenty?"

"If we put the two things together, we can start to work out what they need. Security, accommodations, reliable power, reliable internet speed, isolated, but close enough for easy supply and resupply."

"Could be any basement in town. They could have run new wires and put in a couple of cots."

"More than cots," Reacher said. "This is an annual

contract. No doubt renewable. Could be a long-term project."

"OK, as well as the wires, they also brought in wallboard and paint and put carpet on the floor. Maybe king-size beds."

"We better start looking," Abby said.

"Something else first," Reacher said. "That awful photograph reminded me. I want to go pay that guy a visit. It's after twelve o'clock. I bet he's holding a bunch of repayments. The Shevicks need money today. We're still a grand short."

This time Abby drove. Reacher could feel the weight in the back. The rear end of the car squatted and dragged. There were more than six hundred pounds in the trunk. Maybe never taken into account, during Lincoln's design process.

They stopped short of the bar, in a side street. Did Situation C call for extra guards everywhere? Reacher guessed not everywhere. Insufficient manpower. They would consolidate their resources only where they mattered most. Their high-value targets. Did the moneylending operation qualify? He wasn't sure. He got out and peered around the corner, one-eyed around the brick.

The street was empty. There was nothing parked outside the bar. There were no guys in suits, leaning on walls.

He got back in and they drove on, across the street with the bar, and around to the alley behind. It was the old part of town, built around the time Alexander

Graham Bell was inventing the telephone, so anything newer was grafted on, as an afterthought. There were leaning poles carrying sagging thickets of wires and cables, looping here, looping there. There were water meters and gas meters and electricity meters, screwed randomly to the walls. There were head-high garbage receptacles.

There was a black Lincoln parked behind the bar. Empty. The pale guy's ride, no doubt. Ready for the journey home, at the end of the day. Abby stopped behind it.

"Can I help?" she asked.

"You want to?" he asked back.

"Yes," she said.

"Walk around to the front. Come in the door like a regular person. Pause for a second. The guy sits in the rear right-hand corner. Walk toward the rear wall."

"Why?"

"I want the guy distracted. He'll watch you all the way. Partly because maybe you're a new customer, but mostly because you're the best-looking thing he's seen all day. Maybe all his life. Ignore the barman, whatever he says. He's an asshole."

"Got it," she said.

"You want a gun?"

"Should I?"

"Can't hurt," he said.

"OK," she said.

He gave her the lounge doorman's H&K. It looked dainty in his hand and huge in hers. She hefted it a couple of times, and stuck it in her pocket. She headed off down the alley. Reacher found the bar's back door. It was a plain steel panel, dull and old, scarred and dented low down, by hand trucks wheeling kegs and crates. He tried the handle. It was unlocked. No doubt a city regulation. It was a fire exit, too.

Reacher slipped inside. He was at the far end of a short corridor. Restrooms to the left and right. Then a door for employees only. An office, or a storeroom. Or both. Then the end of the corridor, and the room itself, seen in reverse. The square bar now in the near right corner, the worn central track leading away, between the long rows of four-top tables. The same as before. The light was still dim and the air still smelled of spilled beer and disinfectant. This time there were five customers, once again each of them alone at separate tables, defending their drinks, looking miserable. Behind the bar was the same fat guy, now with a six-day beard, but a fresh towel thrown over his shoulder.

The pale guy was at the back table on Reacher's left. The same as before. Luminescent in the gloom. Glittering hair. Thick white wrists, big white hands, a thick black ledger. The same black suit, the same white shirt, the same black silk necktie. The same tattoo.

Abby stepped in the street door. She stood still as it closed behind her. Performance art. Every eye was on her. She was softly backlit by the dull neon in the windows. Petite and gamine, neat and slender, dressed all in black. Short dark hair, lively dark eyes. A shy but contagious smile. A stranger, dropping by, hoping for a welcome.

She didn't get one. All five customers looked away. But the barman didn't. Neither did the pale guy. She set out walking and they watched her all the way.

Reacher took a step. He was six feet behind the pale guy, and six feet to the side, no doubt in the corner of his eye, but hopefully Abby was filling all of it. She kept on coming, and he took another step.

The barman called out, "Hey."

He had been in the corner of the barman's eye, too. Six feet behind, six feet to the side. All kinds of things happened next. Like a complex ballet. Like a triple play in baseball. The pale guy glanced back, started to get up, Reacher stepped away, toward the bar, where he grabbed the barman's fat head in both hands, and jumped up and thrust it down and smashed it on the mahogany, like dunking a basketball from way high in the air, and he used the bounce of his landing to pivot back to the pale guy, one step, two, and he hit him with a colossal straight right, all his moving mass behind it, center of the guy's face as he rose up from his chair, and the guy disappeared backward like he had been shot out of a cannon. He slid and sprawled on the floor, flat on his back, blood coming out of his nose and his mouth.

All five customers got up and hurried out the door. Maybe a traditional local response, in such situations. In which case Reacher applauded the habit. It left no witnesses. There were blood and teeth on the bar top, but the barman himself had fallen backward out of sight.

"I guess he didn't watch me all the way," Abby said.

"I told you," Reacher said. "He's an asshole."

They crouched next to the pale guy and took his gun and his phone and his car key and what looked like about eight thousand dollars from his pockets. His nose was badly busted. He was breathing through his mouth. Flecks of blood were bubbling at the corners of his lips. Reacher remembered him tapping his glittering head with his bone-white finger. Some kind of a threatening implication. He thought, how the mighty are fallen.

He said, "Yes or no?"

Abby was quiet a beat.

Then she said, "Yes."

Reacher clamped his palm over the guy's mouth. Hard to keep it there, because it was slippery with blood. But he prevailed. The guy wasted time scrabbling for his pocket, looking for his gun, which was no longer there, and then he wasted the rest of his life drumming his heels and clawing uselessly at Reacher's wrist. Eventually he went limp, and then still.

They took the pale guy's Lincoln, because its trunk was empty. It rode much better. They drove downtown and parked on a hydrant around a corner from the Shevicks' hotel. Abby checked the new phone. No new texts. Nothing since the conspiracy theory from Gregory.

"Was it from his own number?" Reacher asked.

Abby compared it with previous texts.

"I guess," she said. "It isn't the usual number."

"We should call him again. Keep him updated."

Abby dabbed a shortcut from the text screen and put the phone on speaker. They heard it ring. They heard it answered. Gregory said a word, short and urgent, probably not hello. Probably shoot, or yes, or what.

"Speak English," Reacher said.

"You."

"You just lost two more. I'm coming for you, Gregory."

"Who are you?"

"Not from Kiev."

"Then from where?"

"The 110th Special MP."

"What is that?"

"You'll find out, pretty soon."

"What do you want from me?"

"You made a mistake."

"What mistake?"

"You crossed a line. So get ready. Payback time is here."

"You're American."

"As apple pie."

Gregory paused a long moment. No doubt thinking. No doubt about his wide network of bribes paid, and palms greased, and backs scratched, and favors owed, and hair-trigger early warning tripwires carefully set in place. Any or all of which should have alerted him long ago. But he had heard nothing. From anywhere.

"You're not a cop," he said. "You're not a government man. You're on your own. Aren't you?"

"Which I'm sure will make it all the harder for you

to take, when your organization is in ruins, and all your men are dead, except for you, because you're the last one alive, and then I step in through the door."

"You won't get near me."

"How am I doing so far?"

No answer.

"Get ready," Reacher said. "I'm coming for you."

Then he clicked off the call and threw the phone out the window. They drove on, around the corner, and they parked in a ten-minute bay outside the Shevicks' hotel.

Chapter 42

Reacher and Abby rode the elevator up to the Shevicks' floor, which was low to medium by New York or Chicago standards, but by local standards it was probably the highest point for a hundred miles around. They found the right door. Maria Shevick looked at them through the peephole, and let them in. The room was a suite. It had a separate living room. It was bright and fresh and new and clean. There were two huge floor to ceiling windows, set at a right angle in the corner. It was early afternoon and the sun was high and the air was clear. The view was spectacular. The city lay spread out below. Like the hotel map Reacher had studied, now come to life.

Abby unveiled the money. The banded ten grand from the charnel house in back of the lumber yard, and close to eight from the moneylending bar. So much it thumped and bounced on the table, and some of it fluttered to the floor. The Shevicks practically laughed with joy. Today's problem solved. Aaron decided he would pay it in at the bank, and then send a wire to the hospital in the normal businesslike way. A last shred of dignity. Abby offered to walk with him, to the downtown branch. Just for the company. No other reason. No need for one. By that point Aaron was walking much better, and east of Center was now safe as houses. So just for fun. They left together, and Reacher went back to the windows. Back to the view. Maria sat on a narrow sofa behind him.

She said, "Do you have children?"

"I don't think so," Reacher said. "None that I know of, anyway."

He was looking at the city below him. The fat part of the pear shape. The corner windows showed him the whole of the northwest quadrant. From about nine on a clock face, to twelve. He could see Center Street more or less directly below. Close by beyond it, to his half left, were two office towers and another high-rise hotel. They looked brand new. They speared bravely upward from a uniform and spreading carpet of three- and four-story buildings, mostly old, mostly brick, mostly dowdy. They had flat roofs, patched and painted silver. Most had air conditioning units sitting on angle-iron frames. There were metal exhaust chimneys coming up from restaurant kitchens, and satellite dishes the size of trampolines, and parking garages with open top decks. The streets were narrow, in some places choked with traffic, in others empty and quiet. There were tiny people walking, turning left, turning right, going in and coming out of doorways. The vista continued into the hazy distance.

Could be any basement in town, Vantresca had said.

Maria asked, "Are you married?"

"No," Reacher said.

"Don't you want to be?"

"The decision is only fifty percent mine," he said. "I guess that would explain it."

He turned back and looked at the view. Like he had looked at the map. Where would a competent commander hide a secret satellite operation? What kind of place? Security, accommodations, power, internet, isolation, easy supply and resupply. He looked for possibilities. The carpet of small brown buildings. The winking roofs. The traffic.

"Abby likes you," Maria said.

"Maybe," Reacher said.

"You don't want to admit it?"

"I agree she's putting in some hard time here. I assume there's a reason."

"You don't think you're it?"

Reacher smiled.

He said, "What are you, my mother?"

No answer. Reacher kept on looking. As always the answer depended. If the southwest quadrant was the same as the northwest, then there were either fewer than ten or more than a hundred possible places. It depended on standards. It depended on what part of security, accommodations, power, internet, isolation, and easy supply a person didn't understand.

He said, "What's the news on Meg?"

She said, "The mood is still good. The scan tomorrow should confirm it. Everyone thinks so. Personally I feel like we're gambling. Surely now this has to be it. It's either a huge, huge win, or it's a devastating loss."

"I would take those odds. Win or lose. I like the simplicity."

"It's brutal."

"Only if you lose."

"Do you always win?"

"So far."

"How can you?"

"I can't," Reacher said. "I can't always win. One day I'm going to lose. I know that. But not today. I know that, too."

"I wish you were a doctor."

"I don't even have a postgraduate degree."

She paused a beat, and said, "You told me you could find him."

"I will," Reacher said. "Today. Before the close of business."

They all met back at Frank Barton's house, deep in what used to be Albanian territory. There was still smoke in the sky, from the lumber yard fire. Barton and Hogan were back from their gig, and Vantresca was hanging out, and Reacher and Abby were fresh from their visit with the Shevicks. They all crowded in the front parlor. Once again it was full of gear. It couldn't stay in the van. It would get stolen.

Hogan said, "The key to this thing is first you got to figure out are you second-guessing a smart guy, or a really smart guy, or a genius? Because that's three different locations, right there."

"Gregory seems smart enough," Reacher said. "I'm sure he has a certain degree of rat-like cunning. But I doubt that this was his decision. Not if it was an official contract, worth tens of millions of dollars, with the government of a foreign country. I would guess that's pretty much a seller's market. I bet there were all kinds of clauses and conditions and inspections and approvals. Moscow would have wanted the very best. And they ain't dumb over there. They know a bad idea when they see one. So in terms of location, I suggest we start second-guessing at the genius level."

Vantresca said, "Security, accommodations, power, internet, isolation, ease of supply."

"Start at the end," Reacher said. "Ease of supply. How many blocks from their office is easy?"

"More about what kind of block," Hogan said. "I would guess the whole of downtown. The business district. Anywhere with commercial zoning. Weird things come and go all the time. No one pays attention. Not like in a residential neighborhood. I would say the edge of downtown is the natural limit. West of Center Street."

"That's not isolated," Barton said. "It's right in the hustle and the bustle."

"It's like hiding in plain sight. Maybe not physically isolated, but very anonymous, all the same. There are all kinds of comings and goings, and no one sees a thing. No one knows anyone else's name."

Reacher asked, "What do they need for the internet?"

Vantresca said, "A mechanically robust connection to a cable ISP or a satellite, probably the satellite, because it would be harder to trace."

"There are plenty of satellite dishes in town."

"Lots of people use them."

"What do they need for power?"

"A recent installation, up to code, with excess capacity as a safety margin, and automatic generator back-up in case of an outage on the grid. They can't afford interruptions. Might screw up their gear."

"What about accommodations?"

"Bedrooms, bathrooms, a mess hall, maybe a TV room, maybe a rec room. Table tennis, or something."

"Sounds like federal prison."

"I think windows," Abby said. "Not a basement. This could be a long contract. Trulenko is a superstar. Maybe down on his luck right now, but even so, he has standards. He'll want to live close to normal. He'll demand it."

"OK, windows," Reacher said. "Which brings us to security."

"Iron bars on the windows," Barton said.

"Or anonymity," Hogan said. "There are a million windows. Sometimes the lights are on, sometimes they're off. No one cares."

Vantresca said, "They need a single controllable point of entry, probably with an advance screen some way upstream, and a last-chance back-up a little ways downstream. Maybe you have to come in through a basement, and then go up the back stairs. Something like that. Under scrutiny all the way. Like passing through a long tunnel. Metaphorically, if not literally."

"So where?"

"There are a thousand buildings like that. You've seen them."

"I don't like them," Reacher said. "Because they're all joined together. Because of the Navy SEALs. Hogan laid it all out, back at the beginning. They would look for emergency exits, and delivery bays, and ventilation shafts and water pipes and sewers and so on, but most of all they would look for places where they could gain access by demolishing walls between adjacent structures. You know how that goes down. They wake up some old geezer in the city plans department, and he finds a dusty old blueprint, that shows this guy's cellar connects to that guy's cellar, except some other guy bricked it up in 1920, but only single skin, and poor quality mortar. You could breathe on it and it would fall down. Or they could come in sideways, through a first-floor wall. Or window. Or the top floor. Or they could rappel off the roof. Don't forget, the Moscow government made this decision. It was big business. Maybe the contract would run for years. Therefore they wanted exactly the right location. Which they are more than qualified to judge. They know all our tricks. They know our special forces train all the time in urban environments exactly like this one."

"But out of town is not easy to supply. Impossible to have both at once."

"No such thing as impossible. Merely a failure of

planning. I think they got what they wanted. Very close at hand, so it's no problem to drop by with a cup of sugar. But also seriously isolated. Potentially hundreds of feet from the nearest other person. Rock solid infrastructure in terms of wires and cables and automatic generators and mechanically robust connections. Luxurious accommodations flooded with sunshine and natural daylight. Categorically impossible to penetrate from the sides. Or even approach. Or from below. Or from above. Zero significant penetration by water pipes or ventilation shafts. A single controllable entry, plenty of opportunity for upstream early warning, and as many defensive back-ups as they want. I think Moscow specified the place of their dreams, and I think they found it."

"Where?" Abby said.

"I was looking right at it, through the hotel window. With Maria Shevick. When she asked me if I wanted to get married."

"To her?"

"I think generically."

"What did you say?"

"I said it takes two to tango."

"Where is Trulenko?"

"It's a nest, not a hive or a burrow. It's up in the air. They rented three high floors in one of those new office towers. There are two of them west of Center. They use the top and bottom floors as buffer zones, and they live and work on the middle floor. Can't get to them up or down or side to side."

Chapter 43

They discussed the dealbreakers, one by one. Security, accommodations, power, internet, isolation, ease of supply. Three high floors in a brand new downtown office tower met every objection. The elevators could be reprogrammed. No problem for Trulenko. Only one car would be allowed to stop. The other doors could be welded shut. From the outside. Likewise the stairwell doors. The lone functioning elevator could open into a cage. Maybe hurricane fencing, installed inside the hallway. Some kind of padlocked gate. Men with guns. The elevator doors would close behind the visitor, who would then be trapped, behind the wire. Plenty of time for scrutiny.

If the visitor even got that far. There would be guys in the lobby. Maybe leaning up near the elevator buttons. Maybe a lot of them, because of Situation C. They would be on the lookout for unfamiliar faces.

"Which tower?" Abby asked.

"There must be paperwork," Reacher said. "Some city department. Three floors, leased by an unknown corporation with a bland and forgettable name. Or we could talk to the supers. We could ask them about weird deliveries. Maybe scaffolding components, or a commercial dog run. Something like that. For the cage."

"Which is going to be a problem," Hogan said. "I don't see how we get in."

"We?"

"Sooner or later your luck will run out. You'll need the Marines to rescue you. You army boys always do. Much more efficient if I prevent that necessity upfront, by supervising the operation from the get-go."

"I'm in too," Vantresca said. "Same reason, essentially."

"Me as well," Barton said.

Silence for a beat.

"Full disclosure," Reacher said. "This will not be a walk in the park."

No objections.

"What first?" Vantresca asked.

"You and Barton figure out which tower. And which three floors. The rest of us will go pay a visit to their main office. Behind the taxi company, across from the pawn shop, next to the bail bond operation."

"Why?"

"Because some of the greatest mistakes in history are made by secret satellite operations cut off from the mothership. No command and control. No information, no orders, no leadership. No resupply. Complete isolation. That's what I want for these guys. Quickest way to get it is just go right ahead and destroy the mothership. No need to pussyfoot around. The time for subtlety is long gone."

"You really don't like these people."

"You didn't speak well of them yourself."

"They'll have sentries all over the place."

"Doubly so now," Reacher said. "I've been calling Gregory on the phone and yanking his chain. No doubt he's a big brave fellow, but even so, I bet he called in extra reinforcements. Just to be sure."

"Then it was a dumb idea to yank his chain."

"No, I want them all in one place. Well, all in two places. The mothership, and the satellite. Nowhere else. No loose ends. No waits or strays. We could call it Situation D. Much more satisfactory. Massed targets are always more efficient than running after lone fugitives individually. That would take days, in a place like this. We would be chasing around all over town. Best avoided, surely. We're in a hurry here. We should let them do some of the work for us."

"You're nuts, you know that?"

"Says the guy prepared to drive in a straight line at twenty-five miles an hour toward nuclear-tipped anti-tank artillery."

"That was different."

"How exactly?"

Vantresca said, "I guess I'm not sure."

"Find the tower," Reacher said. "Get the floor numbers."

* * *

They used the moneylender's Lincoln again. Commonplace, west of Center. And untouchable. Abby drove. Hogan sat next to her in the front. Reacher sprawled in the back. The streets were quiet. Not much traffic. No cops at all. The cops were east of Center, every single one of them. Guaranteed. By that point the fire department would be pulling crispy skeletons out of the wreckage. One after the other. A big sensation. Everyone would want to be there. Stories, for the grandchildren.

Abby stopped on a hydrant, four blocks directly behind the pawn shop, which was directly across the street from the taxi dispatcher. A straight line on a map. A simple linear progression.

"How far out will the sentries be posted?" Reacher asked.

"Not far," Hogan said. "They have to cover the full 360. They can't waste manpower. They'll keep it tight. All four corners of the block their office is on. That would be my assessment. Maybe they're even stopping traffic. But nothing more than that."

"So they can see the front of the pawn shop and the front of the taxi dispatcher."

"From both ends of the street. Probably two guys per corner."

"But they can't see the back of the pawn shop."

"No," Hogan said. "To go one street wider in every direction would cost them three times the manpower. Simple math. They can't afford it."

"OK," Reacher said. "Good to know. We'll go in the back of the pawn shop. We should anyway. We should get Maria's heirlooms back. They lowballed her, with eighty dollars. I didn't like that. We should express our disapproval. Maybe their guilty consciences will prompt them to make a generous donation to a medical charity."

They got out and left the car on the curb next to the fireplug. Reacher figured a parking ticket was the least of Gregory's problems. They walked the first block. Then the second. Then they got cautious. Maybe no one was posted a block further out, but they could eyeball a block further out. That would be dead easy. They could raise their sight lines from time to time, to stare off into the distance. They could make out faces a block away, and speed, and intent, and body language. Accordingly Reacher kept close to the storefront windows, in the sharp afternoon shadows, widely separated from Abby, who followed twenty feet behind, and then Hogan, all of them strolling, randomly stopping, showing no link between them, in terms of lock step speed or direction or purpose.

Reacher turned left, into the mouth of the cross street. Out of sight. He waited. Abby joined him. Then Hogan. They formed up and walked on together, ten paces on the far sidewalk. Then they stopped again. Geographically speaking, the pawn shop's rear exit would be ahead on the right. But there were many rear exits ahead on the right, and they were all the same, and they were all unmarked. There were twelve in total. Every establishment had one.

Reacher clicked back in his head to their earlier visit. The search and rescue mission in Abby's old Toyota. A grimy pawn shop, across a narrow street from a taxi dispatcher and a bail bond operation, Maria coming out the door, Abby pulling over, Aaron winding down his window and calling out her name.

"I remember it as the middle of the block," he said.

"Except twelve has no middle," Abby said. "Twelve has six to the left and six to the right and nothing in the actual middle."

"Because it's an even number. The middle is a choice of two. The last of the first six or the first of the last six."

Abby said, "I remember it as not the exact middle of the block."

"Before the middle or after it?"

"Maybe after it. Maybe even two-thirds of the way along. I remember seeing her, and pulling over. I think it was after the middle of the block."

"OK," Reacher said. "We'll start by taking a look at numbers seven, eight, and nine."

The buildings were all joined together, and their rear façades were all the same, tall and mean and narrow, built of sullen hundred-year-old brick, pierced here and there randomly by barred windows, festooned all over with wires and cables, drooping and looping from one connection to another. Not always mechanically robust. The rear doors themselves were all the same. All stout identical hundred-year-old items, inward opening, made of wood, but at some point maybe fifty years previously someone had screwed sheets of metal over the lower halves, for durability. Maybe a new landlord, making improvements. The metal sheets showed half a century of wear and tear, from loading and unloading, shipping and receiving, kicking open, kicking shut, banging in and out with hand trucks and trolleys and dollies.

Reacher checked.

Less so on number eight than seven or nine.

In fact much less. In fact not bad at all, for fifty years.

Number eight. The exact definition of two-thirds the way along a block of twelve.

He said, "I think this is the one. Not much comes in or out of a pawn shop on a hand truck or a dolly. Only an occasional item. Like if Barton hocked his speaker cabinet. But most everything else comes in and out in a hand or a pocket."

The door was locked from the inside. Not a fire exit. Not a bar, not a restaurant. A different regulation. The wood of the door was solid. The frame, maybe not so much. Softer lumber, infrequently painted, maybe a little rotted and spongy.

He asked, "What would the Marine Corps do?"

"Bazooka," Hogan said. "Best way into any building. Pull the trigger, step through the smoking hole."

"Suppose you didn't have a bazooka."

"Obviously we'll have to kick the door down. But we better get it done first time. They got a dozen guys within range of a holler for help. We can't get hung up back here."

"Did they teach you kicking down doors in the Corps?"

"No, they gave us bazookas."

"Force equals mass times acceleration. Take a running start, stamp your foot flat through the door."

"I'm doing this?"

"Below the handle."

"I thought it was above the handle."

"Nearest the keyhole. That's where the tongue of the lock is. That's where the most amount of wood has been chiseled out of the frame. Hence where it's weakest. That's what you're looking for. It's always the frame that breaks. Never the door."

"Now?"

"We'll be right behind you."

Hogan backed off, perpendicular to the door, ten or twelve feet, and he lined up and rocked back and forth, and then he launched, with the kind of grim bouncy focus Reacher had seen on TV, from high jumpers going for the record. He was a musician and a younger man, with physical rhythm and grace and energy, which was why Reacher was making him do the job. The decision paid off big time. Hogan flowed in and jumped up and twisted in mid air and smashed his heel below the handle, like a short-order cook stamping on a roach, hard and snappy and perfectly timed. The door crashed back and Hogan stutter-stepped through and stumbled inside, all windmilling arms and momentum, and then Reacher crowded in after him, and then Abby, into a short dark hallway, toward a half-glass door with *Private* written on it backward in gold.

There was no reason to stop. No real possibility, either. Hogan burst through the half-glass door, followed by Reacher, followed by Abby, into the shop itself, behind the counter, right by the register, in front of which was a small weasel-like guy, turning to face them, full of shock and surprise. Hogan hit him in the chest with a lowered shoulder, which bounced him off the counter straight into Reacher, who caught him, and spun him around, and touched an H&K to the side of his head. He wasn't sure which one. He had chosen blind. But no matter. By that point he knew all of them worked.

Abby took the guy's gun. Hogan found his daily ledger. A big book, handwritten. Maybe a city regulation. Maybe just pawnbroker tradition. Hogan slid his finger up a bunch of lines.

"Here it is," he said. "Maria Shevick, wedding bands, small solitaires, a watch with a broken crystal. Eighty dollars."

Reacher asked the guy, "Where is that stuff?"

The guy said, "I could get it for you."

"You think eighty bucks was fair?"

"Fair is what the market will bear. It depends how desperate people are."

"How desperate are you right now?" Reacher asked.

"I could certainly get that stuff for you."

"What else?"

"I could maybe add a couple of pieces. Something nice. Maybe bigger diamonds."

"You got money?"

"Sure I do, yes, of course."

"How much?"

"Probably five grand. You can have it all."

"I know we can," Reacher said. "That goes without saying. We can take what we want. But that's the least of your worries. Because this is about more than just a mean transaction. You ran across the street and ratted the old lady out. You caused no end of trouble. Why was that?"

"Are you from Kiev?"

"No," Reacher said. "But I had their chicken once. It was pretty good."

"What do you want from me?"

"Gregory is going down. We need to decide if you're going down with him."

"I get a text, I got to respond. No choice. Those are the terms, man."

"What terms?"

"This was my store once. He took it from me. He made me lease it back. There are unwritten conditions."

"You got to run across the street."

"No choice."

"What's it like over there?"

"Like?" the guy said.

"The layout," Reacher said.

"You go in a hallway on the left. There's a door on the right to the taxi room. It's a real operation. But you go straight on, to the back. There's a conference room. You walk through it, to another corridor, in the opposite back corner. That's how you get to the offices. The last one is Danilo's. You go through Danilo's office to get to Gregory's office."

"How often do you go over there?"

"Only when I have to."

"You work for them, but you don't want to."

"That's the truth of it."

"Everyone says that."

"I'm sure they do. But I mean it."

Reacher said nothing.

Abby said, "No."

Hogan said, "No."

Reacher said, "Go get the stuff we talked about."

The guy went and got it. The wedding bands, the small solitaires, the broken watch. He put them all in an envelope. Reacher put the envelope in his pocket. Plus all the cash from the register. About five grand. Hopefully the merest drop in the bucket, pretty soon, but Reacher liked cash. He always had. He liked the heft, and the deadness. Hogan roamed the store's shelves and tore the cords off all the dusty old stereo items, and he tied the guy up with them, secure, uncomfortable, but survivable. Eventually someone would find him and let him go. What happened after that would be up to him.

They left the guy on the floor behind the counter. They stepped out to the well of the store. They looked out the dusty front windows, at the taxi dispatcher across the street.

Chapter 44

They managed to scope out the whole of the block by staying back in the pawn shop, back in the shadows, traversing side to side, peering out at oblique angles. There were two guys on the sidewalk outside the taxi office door, and two guys some distance away on the left-hand street corner, and two guys the same distance away on the right. Six men visible. Plus probably the same again inside. At least. Maybe two in the hallway the pawnbroker had described, plus two in the conference room, plus two at the mouth of the corridor that led onward to the offices. Each of which was no doubt occupied by a made man with a gun in his pocket and a spare in a drawer.

Not good. What the military academies would call a tactical challenge. A head-on assault against a numerically superior opponent in a tightly constrained battle space. Added to which, the guys from the street corners would fold into the action from the rear. Bad guys in front, bad guys behind, no body armor, no grenades, no automatic weapons, no shotguns, no flamethrower.

Reacher said, "I guess the real question is whether Gregory trusts Danilo."

"Does that matter?" Hogan said.

"Why wouldn't he?" Abby asked.

"Two reasons," Reacher said. "First, he trusts no one. You don't get to be Gregory by trusting people. He's a snake, so he assumes everyone else is a snake. And second, Danilo is by far his biggest threat. The second in command. The leader in waiting. It's on the news every night. The generals get deposed, and the colonels take over."

"Does this help us?"

"You have to go through Danilo's office to get to Gregory's office."

"That's normal," Hogan said. "Everyone does it that way. That's how a chief of staff operates."

"Think about it in reverse. In order to leave his own office, Gregory has to walk through Danilo's office. And he's paranoid, with good reason. And with good results. He's still alive. In his head this is not necessarily like a CEO in a movie, saying goodnight to his secretary, and calling her sweetheart. This is like walking into a death trap. This is assassination squads behind the desk. Or maybe even worse, this is a blockade, until he accedes to their demands. Maybe they'll let him step down, with his dignity intact."

Abby nodded.

"Human nature," she said. "Mostly bullshit, but sometimes it rings a bell."

"What?" Hogan said.

"He built an emergency exit."

They went back behind the counter, and sat on the floor against the cabinets, not far from the tied-up guy. A high-level staff conference. Always held behind the lines. Hogan played the part of the gloomy Marine. Partly because he was, and partly as a professional obligation. Every plan had to be stress tested, from every possible direction.

He said, "Worst case, we're going to find exactly the same situation, but flipped around 180. Guys on the sidewalk the next street over, watching the back door, and then more guys inside, in narrow corridors, just the same. There's a word for it."

"Symmetrical," Reacher said.

"Got to be."

"Human nature," Abby said. "Mostly bullshit, but sometimes it rings a bell."

"What now?"

"It's a bad look," she said. "An escape hatch makes him look scared. Best case, it makes it look like he doesn't trust the protection he bought, or the army of loyal soldiers standing in front of him. He can't admit to any of those feelings. He's Gregory. He has no weaknesses. His organization has no weaknesses."

"So?"

"The emergency exit is secret. No one is guarding it because no one knows it exists."

"Not even Danilo?"

"Most of all not Danilo," Reacher said. "He's the biggest threat. This was done behind Danilo's back. I bet you could trawl through the records and find a two-week spell when he was sent away somewhere, and just before he got back, I bet you would find a couple of construction workers mysteriously dead in some kind of gruesome accident."

"So that no one except Gregory would know where the secret tunnel is."

"Exactly."

"Which includes us. We don't know where it is either."

"Some guy's cellar connects to some other guy's cellar."

"That's your plan?"

"Think about it from Gregory's point of view. This is a guy who got where he is by taking no chances at all. He's thinking about slamming the door on an assassination attempt and getting the hell out of there. A high-stress situation. He can't afford confusion. He needs it clear and simple. Maybe arrows on the wall. Maybe emergency lighting, like on an airplane. All we need to do is find the street door at the far end. We can go in and follow the arrows backward. Maybe we'll come out behind an oil painting on his office wall."

"We'll have all the same people ahead of us. Except in reverse order. They'll come pouring in through the office door."

"We can only hope."

"I don't see what we gain."

"Two things," Reacher said. "We'll have no one behind us, and we'll be taking them out from the top to the bottom, instead of the bottom to the top. Much more efficient."

"Wait," Hogan said. "There are guys on the street corners. Symmetrical. The back corners become the front corners. It won't be easy to get in."

"If I wanted easy I would have joined the Marines."

They left the pawn shop the same way they came in, through the back hallway, through the rear door, out to the cross street. They hustled back to the car, at first cautious, and then fast. The car was still there. No ticket. Even the traffic cops were east of Center. Abby drove. She knew her way around. She made a wide loop, well out of sight of the taxi office. She stopped two blocks behind it, on a quiet street, outside a mom-and-pop store that sold washing machine hoses. She left the motor running. Hogan got out, and she scooted across to the passenger seat. Hogan walked around the hood and got in again behind the wheel. Reacher stayed in the back.

"Ready?" he said.

A tight nod from Hogan.

A determined nod from Abby.

"OK, let's do it," he said.

Hogan drove the rest of the block and made a left at the end. A block ahead in the new direction were two guys on the corner. On the far sidewalk. Black suits, white shirts. Previously the far left corner, now the near right corner. Symmetrical. They were standing with their backs to the block they were guarding, looking outward, like good sentries should.

What they saw was one of their own cars cruising toward them. A black Lincoln. Indistinct faces behind the windshield. Black glass in the back. It made the left in front of them. Into the cross street. Gregory's real estate on the right, civilian real estate on the left. And way up ahead, two more guys, on the next corner. Previously the far right, now the near left.

The car slowed and stopped on the curb. The rear window rolled down and a hand came out and beckoned. The guys on the corner took a step toward it, automatically. Reflex action. Then they stopped and thought about it. But they didn't change their minds. Why would they? It was their car, and anyone important enough to be out and about during Situation C wouldn't want to be kept waiting. So they started up again and hustled.

Mistake.

The front door opened when they were ten feet away, and Abby stepped out. The rear door opened just as they got there, and Reacher stepped out. He head-butted the first to arrive, barely any effort or movement, all about timing and momentum, like a soccer forward meeting a hard cross from out wide. The guy went down in the gutter. His head cracked on the curbstone. Not his day.

Reacher moved on, to the second guy. A face he suddenly realized he knew. From the bar with the tiny pizzas and Abby waiting tables. The guy on the door.

Run along now, kid, he had said to her. *I'll see you again,* Reacher had said to him. *I hope.*

Good things come to those who wait.

Reacher popped him with a short left to the face, just a tap, to straighten him up, for a second short left, this time to the gut, to bend him over, to bring his head down to a convenient position, which was chest height to Reacher, maybe a little below, so he could grab it and twist it and jerk it with all the torque in his upper body. The neck broke and the guy went down. Pretty close to his pal. Reacher squatted between them and took the magazines out of their pistols.

The Lincoln drove away.

Reacher watched. The guys on the far corner had come closer. Inevitable. Symmetrical. For the same reasons. They were still coming closer. Now they were running. Hogan accelerated hard and mounted the sidewalk and smashed straight into them. Not pretty. They came flailing up in the air, proving all the clichés true, like rag dolls, like they were flying. Probably they were already dead. From the impact. Certainly they made no attempt to cushion their fall. They just smashed down, sliding, rolling, scraping, arms and legs everywhere. Hogan parked the car and got out. Reacher got up and started walking.

They met in the middle of the block. Abby was already there. She pointed back the way Hogan had come.

She said, "It's that way."

"How can you tell?" Reacher asked.

It was not the kind of street he was expecting. Not

like behind the pawn shop. There was no sullen brick, no barred windows, no drooping wires or cables. Instead there was a neat line of newly restored buildings. Like the street with the law project office. Clean and bright. In this case mostly retail stores. Nicer and better than the strip with the taxi company and the bail bond operation. It was a block with two fronts, one coming up, one staying down.

Abby said, "I figured he would start from the outside in. He couldn't keep it a secret if he started from the inside out. He couldn't have construction workers trooping through the taxi office. Not without questions being asked. So he started back here, during the renovations, which was the perfect cover. He would have had access to detailed plans and surveys. He would have known what was connected to what. So he got it done. The back of one of these stores leads to the back of his office."

"Symmetrical," Hogan said.

"Only in principle," Abby said. "I'm sure the reality is a warren full of dog-leg turns. This block is more than a hundred years old."

"Which store?" Reacher asked.

"Human nature," Abby said. "I figured in the end he couldn't bring himself to rent it out. He needed to be absolutely sure. He didn't want to worry about someone putting a display cabinet against his secret door. He needed control. So I looked for vacant units. There's only one. The window is papered over. It's that way."

She pointed again, back the way Hogan had come.

* * *

The vacant store was a classic unit, built in an old-fashioned style, with a floor to ceiling display window that curved around inward, to meet the front door maybe twelve feet back from the sidewalk, at the end of what amounted to a viewing arcade, with mosaic tile on the floor. The door itself was glass in a frame, papered over. Reacher guessed the lock would be simple. Like an old-fashioned household item. Twist the stubby lever, pull, and you were good to go. No key required. A key might be in the wrong pants pocket at the critical moment. And keys were slow. Gregory didn't want slow. He would be running, probably for his life. He wanted twist, pull, go.

"Is there an alarm?" Hogan asked. "He's a paranoid guy. He would want to know if someone was messing around back here."

Reacher nodded.

"I'm sure he would," he said. "But in the end I think he acted realistic. Alarms go wrong. He didn't want to risk it beeping when he was out of the office. Because Danilo might be there to hear it. In which case questions would be asked, for sure. The secret wouldn't last for long. So I think no alarm. But I'm sure it was a tough decision."

"OK, then."

"Ready?"

A tight nod from Hogan.

A determined nod from Abby.

Reacher took out his ATM card. The best way past such a household item. He fiddled it into the crack, and curved and curled it around, until it jammed against the tongue of the lock. He yanked the door back toward the hinge, and some combination of sudden pressures told the crude mechanism the key had been turned, so the lock sprang back obediently.

Reacher pushed the door and stepped inside.

Chapter 45

The store had been renovated but never occupied. It was still full of faint construction smells. Wallboard, spackle, paint. The paper on the window gave a soft, cloudy light. The place was just an empty white space. A huge bare cube. Not fitted out in any way. Reacher knew nothing about the retail trade. From what he saw, he assumed the merchant was responsible for bringing in what was needed. Counters, registers, shelves, and racks.

The back wall had a single door in it, properly cased with millwork, painted white, with a big brass lever handle. Not a secret door. Behind it was a short dark hallway. Restroom to the left, office to the right. At the end of the hallway was another door. Properly cased with millwork, painted white, with a big brass handle. Not secret. Behind it was another raw space, full width, maybe twenty feet deep. The left side was for storing stock, maybe. The right side was mechanical. There was a forced-air furnace and a water heater and an air conditioning unit. The air shared the same ductwork as the heat. The ducts were still new and bright. The joins were taped with duct tape. What it was for, originally. There were water pipes and gas pipes coming up out of the concrete floor. There was an HVAC unit in the rear wall. Reacher had seen similar items in hotel rooms. Tall, narrow, all-in-one units. There were electrical panels standing open in the gloom. None of the breakers were labeled.

There were no more doors.

Abby said nothing.

Reacher turned and looked back. Everything else was right. A straight shot out through the hallway, onward through the retail space, twist, pull, go, and out to the street. Fast. Unimpeded. Nothing in the way. All good. Except no more doors.

"He's paranoid," Hogan said. "Even though he never rented the unit, he knew he could still get people coming in here from time to time. City inspectors, pest control, maybe an emergency plumber if there's a leak. He didn't want guys like that seeing a door and wondering what was behind it. They might have taken a look. Professional curiosity. Therefore the door is disguised somehow. Maybe it's not even a door at all. Maybe it's just a bust-out panel of wallboard. No studs behind it."

He tapped his way along the wall. The sound didn't change. Halfway between hollow and solid, everywhere.

"Wait," Reacher said. "We've got a forced-air furnace and an air conditioner feeding the same network of ducts, presumably controlled by some kind of a complicated thermostat on a wall somewhere. A brand new installation, still bright and shiny."

"So?" Hogan said.

"Why did they need a separate HVAC unit in the wall? If they wanted more heat or air back here, they could have put a couple extra vents in the ceiling. It would have cost them a dollar."

They gathered in front of the unit. They looked at it like a sculpture in a gallery. It was about head height to Abby. The bottom two-thirds was a plain metal panel attached by turnbuckle screws. Then came two rotary controls, one for heat-off-cool, the other for temperature, cold to warm, illustrated by a circular swipe that shaded from blue to red. Above the controls was a grille where the air came out, either warmed or cooled as instructed.

Reacher hooked his fingertips in the grille and pulled.

The whole panel came away as one. It snicked off magnetic closures and clattered to the floor. Behind it was a long straight corridor running away into darkness.

There were no arrows on the wall. No emergency lighting, like on an airplane. Abby lit up her phone, and its dim glow showed them the view maybe ten feet ahead and ten feet behind. The corridor was about three feet wide, newly and crisply built. It smelled the same as the vacant store. Wallboard, spackle, paint. It ran straight for a spell, and then it turned ninety degrees right, and then ninety degrees left. As if picking its way around and between other people's rooms. Their restrooms and their offices and their storerooms, in places a mysterious yard narrower than they should have been. Reacher pictured Gregory with the detailed plans, stealing a foot here and a foot there, sketching out false walls, piecing it all together. A labyrinthine route, but crisp and clear and coherent all the same. Couldn't trip, couldn't stumble, couldn't get lost. Reacher pictured a flashlight clipped to the wall at the entrance, Gregory grabbing it and hustling, crashing from corner to corner, bursting through the HVAC panel, running out through the vacant store.

They walked on, slowly. The twists and turns made it hard to keep track of overall distance. Reacher remembered the block as a whole as square and pretty large by old-town standards. Maybe four hundred feet on a side. The taxi office and the conference room and the offices behind it would account for maybe a hundred feet. Maybe a hundred and fifty, depending how spacious. Which gave them a net two hundred and fifty feet to travel. Which could have been a real-world five hundred or more, because of all the dogleg turns. Should take about six minutes, Reacher thought, at their slow and cautious pace.

It took five and a half. They made one last turn and then up ahead in the glow of Abby's phone they saw the end of the corridor. The whole end wall was a sheet of heavy steel. Side to side, and floor to ceiling. Cut into it was a hatch about the size of the HVAC panel at the other end of the route. A hunch down, step over proposition. Like a submarine. On the right side there were heavy hinges welded to the steel. The metal was discolored from the heat. On the left was a heavy bolt. Currently drawn back. Gregory would push the hatch, step inside, slam the hatch behind him, and shoot the bolt. No pursuers. No key required. Faster. There was a flashlight clipped to the wall, right next to the bolt.

They backed off two corners and spoke so low they could barely hear each other. Reacher whispered, "I guess the real question is whether the hinges squeal. If yes, we do it fast. If no, we do it slow. Ready?"

A tight nod from Hogan.

A determined nod from Abby.

They retraced their steps. Two turns. Back to the steel hatch. Abby held her phone close to a hinge. It looked like a quality item. Forged steel. A glassy surface. But no trace of grease or oil. Unpredictable. The hatch had no handle. Not as such. Just two thick hoops for the bolt to lock into. Reacher hooked his finger through one of them. In his mind he rehearsed what he would do next, either fast or slow. The hatch would be hidden on the inside by some kind of camouflage. Nothing too fancy. Nothing that would have involved visible workers. Nothing that would have changed the room's appearance. Nothing that Danilo would have noticed on his return. Probably an existing piece of furniture. As tall as Abby. Probably a bookcase. He would have to open the hatch and move it aside. Either fast or slow.

It turned out fast. Reacher eased the hatch open,

and inside the first inch of travel both hinges let out a piercing squeal. So he flung it open the rest of the way and the glow of Abby's phone showed him the rough lumber back of a piece of heavy wooden furniture. He shoved it hard and it fell forward and toppled over and crashed down. Completely unstable. A bookcase for sure. He scrambled out over it, into the room.

Gregory had been sitting at his desk, in his green leather chair, running important things through his mind. Then he heard the hinges squeal behind him, and he spun his chair halfway around, just in time for the bookcase to fall on him. It was made of Baltic oak, all solid, no veneer. It was loaded with books and trophies and photos in frames. First the front edge of a shelf broke his shoulder, and then an imperceptible millisecond later the next shelf up cracked his skull, and then the full bulk of the thing crushed him down, tipping his chair, driving the side of his head against the edge of the desk top, but driving the rest of him onward to the floor, so that his neck bent grotesquely and snapped like a twig, killing him instantly. Reacher's extra weight as he clambered out over the felled furniture did him no further damage at all.

Reacher saw the back of the bookcase ahead of him, tilted up like a ramp. It had fallen against a desk. He scrambled over it and saw a double door, standing open, and an outer office beyond it, with a guy rising up out of a chair behind a desk, all kinds of shock and surprise on his face. This was Danilo, Reacher assumed. There was a door from the outer office to the corridor beyond. It was open, too. Coming through it were the sounds of scraping chairs and feet hitting linoleum floors. The loud screech and the loud crash had gotten folks' attention.

Reacher had a Glock in his right hand and a Glock in his left. With his right he was covering Danilo. With his left he was covering the door. Hogan arrived behind him. Then Abby.

She said, "Gregory is dead under the bookcase."

Reacher said, "How?"

"It fell on him. He was at his desk. The bookcase was behind him. I think it broke his neck."

"I pushed it on him."

"I guess technically."

Reacher paused a beat.

"He was a lucky man," he said.

Then he nodded at Danilo and said to Hogan, "Place this guy under arrest. Keep him safe and unharmed. He and I need to have an important discussion."

"About what?"

"It's what we say in the army when we're going to beat someone to death."

"Got it."

Then time unspooled in a way that afterward Reacher thought was partly inevitable, even preordained, partly driven by culture, partly by peer pressure, by blind obedience, by hopeless lack of alternatives. Hard to comprehend. But it helped him understand the pile of bodies in the doorway in back of the lumber yard. They kept on coming. First a solid guy, taking in the scene, going for his gun. Reacher let him get it out. Allowed him to make his intent crystal clear. Then he shot him center mass. A single round. Then a second guy barreled in, pumped up with some kind of ludicrous I-can-do-better bravado. But he couldn't. Reacher dropped him and he fell right on top of the first guy. Which is how the pile started. It deterred no one. They kept on adding to it. One after the other. *We'll have all the same people ahead of us. Except in reverse order.* Hogan was absolutely right. First came the senior figures from the offices, then the smart muscle from inside the building, then finally the dumb muscle from out on the street corners, all of them driven, all of them relentless, all of them doomed. At first Reacher thought of their sacrifice in medieval terms, but then he revised his estimate backward, all the way to the dawn of time, a hundred thousand generations, to the pure insane grip of the tribe, and the absolute terror of being without it.

It had kept them alive then. But not now. Eventually there were no more footsteps. Reacher gave it another minute. Just to be sure. The sound of his endless firing died away to angry, hissing silence.

Then he turned to face Danilo.

Chapter 46

Danilo was a small man by Reacher's standards, maybe five-ten, and wiry rather than heavy. Hogan had stripped him of his suit coat and emptied his shoulder holster. As a result he looked naked and vulnerable. Already defeated. Hogan had him standing next to the desk inside the inner office. The desk was a massive thing made of toffee-colored wood. The fallen bookcase was propped on it. It was huge. It must have weighed a ton. Books and ornaments had spilled out all over the place. From his new angle Reacher could see Gregory on the floor. He was folded into a Z shape. Kind of compressed. Otherwise a healthy individual. Tall, hard, and solid. But dead. Pity.

Reacher hooked his left forefinger under the knot of Danilo's tie and maneuvered him out into clear space. He turned him around and squared him up. Shoulders back, chin out.

He stood back.

He said, "Tell me about your porn sites on the internet."

"Our what?" Danilo said.

Reacher slapped him. Open handed, but a colossal blow all the same. It knocked Danilo right off his feet. He did half of a sideways somersault and landed crumpled where the wall met the floor.

"Get up," Reacher said.

Danilo got up, slow and shaky, hands and knees first, palming his way up the wall.

"Try again," Reacher said.

"They're a sideline," Danilo said.

"Where are they?"

Danilo hesitated.

Reacher hit him again. The other side. Open handed. Even harder than before. Danilo went down again, cartwheeling sideways, banging his head on the other wall.

"Get up," Reacher said again.

Danilo got up again. Slow and shaky, hands and knees, hauling himself up the wall.

"Where are they?" Reacher asked again.

"Nowhere," Danilo said. "Everywhere. It's the internet. There are bits and pieces on servers all over the planet."

"Controlled from where?"

Danilo watched Reacher's right hand. He had figured out the sequence. Not difficult. Right, left, right. He didn't want to answer, but he was going to.

He said the word. Not a hive or a burrow, but a nest, way up high. Then he clamped his lips. Now he was between a rock and a hard place. He couldn't reveal the location. It was their biggest and best-kept secret. Instead he continued to stare at Reacher's right hand.

Reacher said, "We already know where it is. You got nothing left to trade."

Danilo didn't answer. Then a cell phone rang. Distant and muffled. From the far doorway. In a pocket, somewhere in the pile of corpses. It pealed six times, and stopped. Then another rang. Equally distant, equally muffled. Then two more.

The sound of the mothership not answering.

Danilo said, "I'm sorry."

"For what?" Reacher said.

"Things I did."

"But you did them. Can't change that."

Danilo didn't answer.

Abby said, "Yes."

Hogan said, "Yes."

Reacher shot Danilo in the forehead with the H&K P7 Hogan had taken from him. German police issue. Identical to all the others. Maybe even sequential serial numbers. A bulk order, from some bent German copper. Danilo went down, with what was left of his head in his own office, and the rest of him in Gregory's. Reacher looked left and right. *We'll be taking them out from the top to the bottom. Much more efficient.* Job done. They were laid out like a corporate chart. Gregory, Danilo, the heap of senior deputies. Cell phones ringing everywhere.

* * *

They left the same way they arrived, through the emergency exit corridor. They walked through the vacant store. Twist, pull, go, back to the street. The guys from the corners were still where they had fallen. No one would dream of calling the cops about dead bodies near a black Town Car on a back street on the west side of the city. Such a thing was obviously someone else's private business.

"Where next?" Abby asked.

"You OK?" Reacher asked back.

"Doing well. Where next?"

Reacher glanced at the downtown skyline. Six towers. Three office buildings, three hotels.

He said, "I should go say goodbye to the Shevicks. I might not get another chance."

"Why not?"

"The lumber yard won't burn forever. Sooner or later the cops will be back west of Center. No more grand a week. They'll be mad at somebody. Questions will be asked. Always better not to be around for a thing like that."

"You're going to leave?"

"Come with me."

She didn't answer.

He said, "Call Vantresca and tell him to meet us."

They left the Lincoln where it was. Insurance, of sorts. Like a road sign. Not *Don't Walk,* but *Don't Ask.* The sun was out. No clouds in the sky. Middle of the afternoon. They strolled back the way they had driven. They rode up to the Shevicks' room. Maria looked at them through the peephole, and let them in. Barton and Vantresca were already there.

Vantresca pointed out the window. At the left-hand of two office towers west of Center. It was a plain rectangular structure about twenty stories tall, faced with glass that reflected the sky. Above the top floor's windows was a bland and anodyne name. Could have been an insurance company. Could have been a laxative medicine.

"You sure?" Reacher asked.

"The only new lease in the right time frame. The top three floors. A corporation no one ever heard of. All kinds of weird shit going up in the elevator."

"Good work."

"Thank Barton. He knows a saxophone player with a day job in the department of buildings."

Apparently Vantresca had called room service on arrival, because a waiter showed up with a cart full of things to eat and drink. Finger sandwiches, cupcakes, a plate of cookies still warm from the microwave oven. Plus water, and soda, and iced tea, and hot tea, and best of all hot coffee, in a tall chromium flask that flashed in the sun. They ate and drank together. Vantresca said he had already sent a biohazard clean-up crew to the Shevicks' house, and a drywall guy, and a painter. He said they could go home in the morning. If they wanted. They said they did, very much. They said thank you for fixing the holes.

Then they looked at Reacher, a question in their eyes.

"Close of business today," he said. "Watch out for a wire transfer."

Aaron hesitated a second, politely, and asked, "How big?"

"I'm pretty much a round-figures type of guy. If it's too much, give the rest away. To people in the same situation. Maybe some to those lawyers. Julian Harvey Wood, Gino Vettoretto, and Isaac Mehay-Byford. They're doing good work, for guys with so many names."

Then he got out the envelope from the pawn shop. The wedding bands, the small solitaires, the watch with the broken crystal. He gave it to Maria. He said, "They went out of business."

Then they left, Reacher, Abby, Barton, Hogan, Vantresca, riding down in the elevator together, stepping out to the street.

Half a block short of the office tower's street-level lobby was a single-wide coffee shop with tables in back. They went in and crowded knee to knee, five people at a four-top. Vantresca and Barton ran through what they knew. The building had been completed three years previously. It had twenty floors. It had a total of forty suites. So far it was a commercial failure. The local economy was uncertain. The unknown corporation had gotten a great deal on eighteen, nineteen, and twenty. The only other tenants were a dentist, down on three, and a commercial real estate broker, on two. The rest was empty.

Reacher asked Hogan, "What would the Marine Corps do?"

"Most likely evacuate the broker and the dentist and then set the building on fire. Either the high-floor targets would make it down the emergency stairs, or they would get burned up where they were. Either way a win-win, for not much effort."

Reacher asked Vantresca, "What would the armored divisions do?"

"Standard urban doctrine is shoot out the ground-floor walls, so the building falls directly in on itself. You need to keep the streets clear of rubble if you can. Anything still moving a minute later, you hit it with the machine gun."

"OK," Reacher said.

Vantresca asked, "What would the MPs do?"

"No doubt something subtle and ingenious. Given our comparative lack of resources."

"Like what?"

Reacher thought hard for a minute, and then he told them.

Chapter 47

Five minutes later Barton left the coffee shop for an imaginary dental appointment. Reacher and the others stayed where they were. It was a convenient base. Close by. No doubt the counterman was a west side informant, but there was no one left to inform. Reacher saw him make a couple of calls. Apparently they weren't answered. The guy stared at his phone, puzzled.

Then Hogan and Vantresca left for an imaginary discussion about commercial real estate. Reacher and Abby stayed at the table. Theirs were the only faces on Ukrainian phones. They figured they better not start the party too early.

The counterman tried a third call.

It wasn't answered.

Abby said, "I guess this means we can go back to my place tonight."

"No reason why not," Reacher said.

"Unless you leave before tonight."

"Depends what happens. All five of us might be running."

"Suppose we aren't."

"Then we'll go back to your place tonight."

"For how long?"

He said, "What would be your answer to that question?"

She said, "I guess not forever."

"That's my answer, too. Except my forever horizon is closer than most. Full disclosure."

"How close?"

He looked out the window, at the street, at the brick, at the afternoon shadows. He said, "I already feel like I've been here forever."

"So you'll leave anyway."

"Come with me."

"What's wrong with sticking around?"

"What's wrong with not?"

"Nothing," she said. "I'm not complaining. I just want to know."

"Know what?"

"How long we've got. So I can make the most of it."

"You don't want to come with me?"

"Seems to me I have a choice of two things. Either a good memory with a beginning and an end, or a long slow fizzle, where I get tired of motels and hitch-hiking and walking. I choose the memory. Of a successful experiment. Much rarer than you think. We did good, Reacher."

"We're not at the end yet. Don't count your chickens."

"You worried?"

"Professionally concerned."

"Maria told me what you said to her. One day you're going to lose. Just not today."

"I was trying to cheer her up. That was all. She was really feeling it. I would have said anything."

"I think you meant it."

"It's something they teach you in the army. The only thing under your direct control is how hard you work. In other words, if you really, really buckle down today, and you get the intelligence, the planning, and the execution each a hundred percent exactly correct, then you are bound to prevail."

"Sounds empowering."

"It's the army. What they really mean is, if you fail today, it's completely your own fault."

"We've done OK so far."

"But now the game has changed. Now we're fighting Moscow. Not just a bunch of pimps and thieves."

"Same actual people."

"But a better system, guaranteed. Better planning. The pick of the litter. Fewer weaknesses. Fewer mistakes."

"Sounds bad."

"I'm guessing about fifty-fifty. Win or lose. Which is OK. I like the simplicity."

"How do we do it?"

"Intelligence, planning, execution. First we think like them. Which isn't difficult. We studied them endlessly. Vantresca could tell you. They're smart people, organized, bureaucratic, cautious, careful, scientific, and painfully rational."

"So how can we win?"

"We can exploit the rational part of their natures," Reacher said. "We can do something a rational person would never even consider. Something completely unhinged."

Then the first intelligence report came back. Barton stepped in, and nodded a greeting, and headed to the counter. He got coffee, and walked over to the table. He sat down, but before he could say anything the second report arrived. Hogan and Vantresca, stepping in together. They came straight to the table. They jostled for space and squeezed themselves in. Five people at a four-top.

Barton said, "The front wall of the lobby is all glass. You go in a revolving door. The back wall of the lobby is the front face of the building's core. There are five openings in it. A fire stair door, three elevators, and another fire stair door. Between you and them are security turnstiles and a security desk. Behind the security desk is what looks to me like a regular civilian rent-a-cop."

"Is that all?" Reacher said.

"I guess it's all that the building provides," Barton said. "But there are also four men in suits and ties. I guess provided by someone else. Two of them were waiting just inside the revolving door. They asked my business. I said the dentist. They stepped aside and waved me forward, toward the security desk. Where the rent-a-cop asked my business all over again."

Reacher looked at Hogan and Vantresca.

"Same for you?" he asked.

"Exactly the same," Vantresca said. "It's a pretty good upstream screen. Then it gets even better. The other two guys are on the other side of the security turnstiles. By the elevators. Which have been upgraded, with a new control panel. Like you see in really tall buildings with thousands of people. You punch in the floor you want, and the screen tells you which car to go wait for. Then the car takes you where you said. There are no buttons inside. It's a very efficient system. But totally unnecessary for a building that small. Obviously there for a reason. Which is, the two guys won't let you punch in your floor yourself. They have to do it for you. They ask where you're going, you tell them, they press the buttons, they show you where to wait. Then you get in the elevator car, and you get out again when the doors open. No other option."

"Were there cameras in the lobby?"

"There's a little glass pip in the elevator panel. Almost certainly a fisheye lens, feeding straight upstairs."

Reacher nodded.

He looked at Barton.

He asked, "How was the dentist?"

"The third floor was all small suites, all of them off a rectangular inner corridor that ran around the building core. The core was blank on three sides. I went up to four on the fire stairs, and it was the same. Five had two larger suites in back. I couldn't get all the way around the core. I guess the blank face becomes a wall inside the suite."

Hogan said, "We ran up to six and started from there. The suites get bigger the higher you go. It's safe to assume nineteen is a whole-floor extravaganza. The elevators come up in the center. That's all the architect gave them. I'm sure they built the rest out exactly the way they wanted it."

"Starting with the cage," Reacher said.

"Guaranteed," Vantresca said. "It's even simpler than we thought. Because the building is tall, but not large. There is only one service core, with only five structural openings per floor, and they're all in a line. One cage could control them all. No need to weld anything shut. You could build a cage maybe six feet deep, maybe eight feet tall, starting from just before the first fire door, and running the whole width to just beyond the last. Every door opens into it. Elevators and fire stairs alike. It would be like a long rectangular reception area. Kind of shallow. You would have to wait there a minute, with armed men looking in at you through the wire. With more armed men on the gate to let you out. The mechanism might be electronic. Maybe there are two gates, like an airlock."

"Floors and ceilings?"

"Concrete slab. No significant penetration. All the big-diameter risers run up and down inside the core, with the elevator shafts."

"OK," Reacher said.

"OK what?"

"Cautious, careful, scientific, and rational. That's what I told Abby."

"Plus paranoid. You can bet they did the exact

same things on eighteen and twenty. Which would make their buffer zones virtually impregnable."

Reacher nodded.

"It's a thing of beauty," he said. "There's no way in."

"So how do we do it?"

"When the going gets tough, the tough go shopping."

"Where?"

"Hardware store."

The nearest place was a national franchise, full of earnest slogans about doing things together and doing them now. Moscow would have approved. It was large enough to have what they wanted, but not large enough to offer a choice. Which hustled things along. A linoleum knife was a linoleum knife. A crosscut saw was a crosscut saw. And so on, and so forth. They bought a tool bag each. The store's name was on them, but they looked professional. The hospitalized Gezim Hoxha paid for everything, via his potato-shaped wallet.

They packed their bags carefully, and slung them over their shoulders. Then they set out walking, back the way they had come, but this time not stopping at the coffee shop. This time heading straight on, the extra half block, to the office tower's street-level door.

Chapter 48

Like Barton had reported, the front wall of the lobby was all glass. Which meant the guys at the door saw them early. From maybe thirty feet away. Which at their current rate of speed was several seconds still to go. All of which Reacher hoped would be filled by spikes of mild confusion. Just enough to keep them guessing. Five people hustling were automatically suspect. Five people with tool bags, maybe not. Maybe plumbers on an urgent call-out, to fix a leak. Or electricians. Except one was a woman. But that was OK. Wasn't it? This was America. Except one had a face like the guy from Kiev. Gregory had texted a picture, before he went quiet. Was the guy from Kiev a plumber? Just tiny stop-start, this-way, that-way flickers in the brain, enough to slow them down, enough to make their eventual reactions a fatal beat late.

Because by then the revolving door was already

spinning fast, disgorging first Reacher, then Hogan, then Vantresca, then Barton, then Abby, all of them bringing guns up out of their tool bags, fanning out, Hogan and Vantresca sprinting ahead, Abby sprinting after them, Reacher and Barton jamming up the guys at the door, guns under chins, pushing them backward, Hogan and Vantresca and Abby hurdling the turnstiles, the guys slamming into the men in the suits, taking them down, Abby skidding to a halt in front of the elevator control panel.

Ready for her close up. She stood still for a second. The light from the street was behind her. Petite and gamine, neat and slender, hipshot, dressed all in black, holding a Glock 17. Performance art. A figure from a nightmare.

Then she leaned forward and sprayed the little glass pip with a hiss of rattle-can paint. Flat black, from the hardware store. By which time Barton was already starting the same thing on the front wall of glass, but with white, for an effect like the vacant retail unit. The four men in suits were huddled together, with Reacher and Vantresca pointing guns at them, and Hogan preparing to make them secure, with long cable ties, from the hardware store.

The rent-a-cop at the security desk was looking on nervously.

Reacher called out to him, "Do you work for these people?"

The guy called back, "No sir, I most definitely do not."

"But nevertheless you hold a position. You have responsibilities, at least toward the owner of this building. Perhaps you swore an oath. If we let you go, you're pretty much obliged to call the cops. You look like a man of principle. Therefore best if we tie you up, too. Maybe even a blindfold. We'll leave you on the floor behind your desk. You can deny everything afterward. Would that be agreeable?"

"Probably best," the guy said.

"First come lock the door for us."

The guy stood up.

Which was when the plan went wrong. When the so-far easy execution ran off the rails. Although, afterward, in periods of honest reflection, Reacher found he thought of it as the moment when the plan went right. He wanted it. Secretly he had hoped for it. Hence the crosscut saws.

Something completely unhinged.

Hogan bent down to zip-tie the first guy's ankle. Either the guy straight-up panicked, or he got hit by some kind of last-chance desperation, or both, or maybe he was hoping to start up some kind of insurrection, but for whatever reason, suddenly he bolted forward, straight at Vantresca, wild emotions in his eyes, wild energy in his actions. He more or less ran himself onto the muzzle of Vantresca's gun.

Vantresca did everything right. In the corner of his eye he saw that Hogan was rolling away, like a good Marine should, to avoid the charging guy's feet, to avoid friendly fire. He saw that there was no one behind. No danger from a through-and-through. He knew they were in a concrete building. No danger of a through-the-wall random calamity. Not even much noise, given the proximity shot. The guy's chest cavity would act as a giant suppressor.

Vantresca pulled the trigger.

There was no insurrection.

The other three guys stayed where they were.

The rent-a-cop said, "Oh, shit."

"We'll get to you in a minute," Reacher said. "First lock the door."

On the nineteenth floor, someone noticed the lobby screen was dark. No one knew how long it had been that way. At first it was taken to be a technical fault. But then someone else felt the blankness was not completely uniform. Not zero volts across the board. Something else. So they rolled back the hard drive and saw a young woman spraying an aerosol can. After first posing with a gun. After first rushing in through the revolving door, with four other figures. All in different street clothes, but all equipped with identical mission-specific satchels. A black-ops unit, led by a woman. This was America.

Of course the first thing they did was call down to the lobby. Just in case. Four separate cell numbers. Four no answers. As feared, because as expected. The same everywhere, the last two hours. They even tried the building's rent-a-cop. They had the number. The landline, on his silly desk.

No answer.

Completely isolated. No information at all. Now not even from the lobby. No idea what was happening. Cut off from the world. Nothing on the news.

Nothing on the rumor sites. No weird deployments. No press secretaries waiting on standby.

They tried all the numbers again.

No answer.

Then the elevator rumbled. The center shaft.

The car arrived, with a hiss of air.

The doors opened, smooth and swish.

On the back wall of the car someone had spray painted the Ukrainian word for loser. Under its dripping Cyrillic was one of their own guys, from the lobby, black suit and tie, sitting splayed out, arms and legs at an angle. He had been shot in the chest.

His head had been cut off.

His head was propped up between his legs.

The doors closed, smooth and swish.

The elevator rumbled.

The car went back down.

Completely isolated. No contact. Everyone without a specific task to attend to gathered in the elevator lobby. Outside the cage. Close to the wire. Staring in. Positioning themselves as if laying bets. Some opposite the center elevator. As if expecting it to return, with its gruesome tableau. Others chose the first elevator, or the third. Some outliers watched the fire stairs. There were all kinds of theories.

They waited.

Nothing happened.

People changed places at the wire. As if the delay was subtly altering the odds. As if it was making one scenario slightly more likely than another. Or less unlikely.

They waited.

They tried three sample numbers. One more time. First Gregory's, then Danilo's, then the watch leader's, down in the lobby. With no real hope.

With no answer.

They waited. They changed position at the wire.

They listened.

The elevator rumbled. This time the left-hand shaft.

The car arrived, with a hiss of air.

The doors opened, smooth and swish.

On the floor of the car was another of their guys. From the lobby. Black suit and tie. Lying on his side. Hogtied, with his wrists and his ankles zipped together behind him. Gagged with a black rag wound around his head. Squirming, thrashing, appealing with his eyes, desperately, mouthing the gag, as if screaming, *please come get me, please come get me,* and then nodding urgently, as if beckoning, as if to say, *yes, yes, it's safe, please come get me,* and then flopping his body, desperately, as if trying to reach the threshold.

The doors closed on him, smooth and swish.

The car went down again.

At first no one spoke.

Then someone said, "We should have saved him."

Someone else said, "How could we?"

"We should have been quicker. Somehow he escaped down there. We should have helped him."

"There was no time."

The guy who had spoken first looked all around. First from where he was to the gate, and then at the keypad, and then from the gate to the left-hand elevator, on the inside. He timed it out in his mind. The doors open. The doors close. No. Not enough time. Especially with a what-the-hell split second of freeze at the very beginning.

Just not possible.

"Pity," he said. "He escaped and we sent him back down."

"Escaped how?"

"Maybe they trussed him up ready to cut his head off, but somehow he rolled away into the elevator, and he came up here, and he wanted us to save him. He was six feet away."

No one spoke.

The guy said, "Listen."

The elevator rumbled.

The left-hand shaft again.

Coming back up.

The guy said, "Open the gate."

"Not allowed."

"We got to get there this time. Open the gate."

No one spoke.

The elevator rumbled.

Someone else said, "Yeah, open the damn gate. We can't send the poor bastard down again a second time."

Completely isolated. No orders, no leadership.

A third voice said, "Open the gate."

The guy at the gate punched in the numbers. After its programmed delay, the lock clicked open. The panel swung back. Four guys stepped through. Guns out, cautious, up on their toes. The others stayed out, watching through the wire.

The elevator rumbled.

The car arrived, with a hiss of air.

The doors opened, smooth and swish.

Same guy on the floor. Black suit and tie. Hogtied the same, gagged the same, squirming, thrashing, pleading with his eyes, nodding desperately, beckoning, flopping around.

The four guys inside rushed forward, ready to lend a hand.

But it wasn't the same guy. It was Vantresca. Average build. He fit the suit. He wasn't hogtied. He was holding his hands behind his back, hiding two Glock 17s. Which he brought out and fired, four times, fast, aimed, deliberate.

At which point the right-hand elevator opened up, and Reacher stepped out, with Hogan, and Barton, and Abby. Four handguns. Hogan fired first. *Must-win targets are any opponents within command and control distance of the gate* had been Reacher's briefing. Three rounds did the job. Meanwhile Reacher himself was clearing the fence, firing into the backs or half-backs of all those standing mesmerized by the sight of Vantresca shooting their buddies from the floor of his elevator car. Barton was covering one end of the lobby, and Abby was covering the other.

It was over fast. Hard not to be. As an exercise it was easy. The attackers had surprise on their side, and after that commanded a dense concentration of fire from the narrow corner of a rectangular battle space. The only friendly within the field of fire was inside a bulletproof concrete shaft all his own, and from there was able to provide effective enfilade fire.

All of which made the victory routine. The prize was the gate. It was still standing open. Some kind of complicated lock, not currently engaged. Maybe electronic. There was a keypad on the post.

Reacher stepped through the gate, into the secret space beyond, followed by Hogan, and Abby, and Barton, with Vantresca bringing up the rear, in the borrowed suit, dusting it off after his showmanship on the elevator floor.

Chapter 49

The back part of Reacher's brain was clattering away on some kind of a complicated computation, which involved dividing the total square footage of the nineteenth floor by the total number of KIA in its elevator lobby, which surely meant, after realistically allowing for officer-class accommodations for the important nerds, and densely-packed barracks-class accommodations for the enlisted ranks, that the herd was already substantially thinned. Had to be. There couldn't be many more guys available. Not unless they had been sleeping three to a bed, or stacked on the floor. Simple math.

The front part of Reacher's brain said nevermind. *If I fail today, it's my own fault*. He pressed up face-first against a corridor wall, and peered one-eyed around a corner. He saw another corridor. Same width. Doors left and right. Offices, maybe. Or bedrooms. Bathrooms across the hall. Or storerooms. Or laboratories, or nerve centers, or hives or nests or burrows.

He moved on. Hogan followed. Then Abby. Then Barton and Vantresca. The first room on the left was some kind of a security post. Empty. Abandoned. A desk and a chair, unoccupied. Two flat screen televisions on the desk, one labeled *Lobby,* which was blacked out with paint, and one marked *19th Floor,* which showed the view from a camera evidently mounted high on the wall opposite the elevator bank. The angle was downward. The view was of a lot of dead bodies on the floor. More than a dozen.

Told you so, said the back part of his brain.

He moved on. The first room on the right was also empty. It had a floor to ceiling window, facing north. The city lay spread out below. In the room were four armchairs, a buzzing refrigerator, and a coffee machine on a table. A ready room. Or a crew room. Convenient. Close to the elevators.

They moved on. They saw nothing. No people. No kind of technical equipment. Reacher had no real idea what it would look like. He was hung up on Abby's original description. *Like in the movies. The mad scientist in his lab, full of lit-up machines and crackling energy.* To him a server was someone playing tennis, or bringing a drink. Vantresca figured the whole installation might be nothing more than half a dozen laptops. Cloud based, he called it. Hogan predicted a low room full of white laminate and chilly air.

They crept onward.

Saw nothing.

"Wait," Reacher whispered. "We're wasting time.

This is not business as usual. I think they've gone straight to the endgame. I think the headless horseman brought every spare guy to the elevator cage. Only people working that exact minute stayed behind and survived. So now they're hunkered down. It's Custer's Last Stand for them."

"How many?" Hogan asked.

"I don't care," Reacher said. "As long as Trulenko is one of them."

Abby said, "If it's six laptops, it could be just a couple of guys."

"Plus guards," Reacher said. "As many as Moscow decreed should be in the room at all times. Or at least those of them who maintained discipline. Which might be a different number."

Vantresca said, "Moscow would decree an entire Guards regiment, if it could."

"I guess it depends how big the room is."

Hogan said, "If it's six laptops, it could be a broom closet. Could be anywhere. Could be a secret door in back of a broom closet."

"No, Trulenko wants windows," Abby said. "Especially these windows. I bet he loves the view. I bet he loves standing there, looking out through the glass, lording it over the earthlings below. Even though he's actually a failure and practically a prisoner. I bet it makes him feel better."

"Wait," Reacher said again. He looked at Barton. "You said on the fourth floor you could walk all around the building's core. It was blank on three sides. But on the fifth floor you couldn't get all the way around. Because of bigger suites in back. Inside of which the long blank face of the core would become a wall inside a room."

"Yes," Barton said.

"It's a pretty good wall to have," Reacher said. "Isn't it? It's as close as you can get to all the risers and the services running up and down behind the elevators." He looked at Vantresca. "Back in the day, if you had to lay wired communications, how long would you want your wires to be?"

"As short as humanly possible," Vantresca said.

"Because?"

"Wires are vulnerable."

Reacher nodded.

"Not mechanically robust," he said. "Plus that wall gets first call on the power and the water, and whatever the generator kicks out in an emergency. I bet that's the wall Moscow wanted." He said the word. A hive or a nest or a burrow, full of something that hummed or buzzed or thrashed around. He said, "They built it out from the back of the elevator core, all the way to the windows opposite. Because Moscow wanted the wall, and guys like Trulenko wanted the view. What else could they do?"

Vantresca said, "That's a big room."

Reacher nodded.

"Same size and shape as the lobby downstairs," he said. "Same space exactly, except flipped around 180."

"Big enough for a Guards regiment."

"Couple of rifle companies at the most."

"Maybe nobody," Abby said. "Because of human nature. These guys are from Ukraine. Moscow is like a patronizing big brother. They'll make up their own rules. What does it matter if they're actually in the room? They have the cage. Everywhere is equally safe. Maybe Trulenko doesn't even want them in the room anyway, watching over his shoulder. That's human nature, too."

"Situation C," Hogan said. "Got to be someone."

"Maybe not anymore," Abby said. "They've been cut off two hours. I think the instinct would be to come out and fight on the barricades. At the wire. I think it would be irresistible. Because of human nature. You wouldn't want to hide in a corridor, waiting for the inevitable."

Reacher said, "This is what the pointy-heads would call a wide range of baseline assumptions. Anywhere from no one in the room to a Guards regiment."

"What's your guess?"

"I don't care," he said again. "As long as Trulenko is one of them."

"Seriously."

"It's a ratio. Depends how many nerds they have. There could be dozens packed in there. Rows and rows of them."

"No," Vantresca said. "This is the custom shop. This is the skunk works. The drones are elsewhere. In the cloud."

"Or in their mom's basement," Hogan said.

"Wherever," Vantresca said. "Trulenko is an artist. It's him, and a small handful of others. Maybe one or two. Maximum."

"OK," Reacher said. "Then either four guards in

the room, or one. Probably the close protection part of Situation C calls for a crew of four within arm's-length contact at all times. Worst case, they're maintaining discipline on that. Best case, Abby is right and Trulenko doesn't like it. In which case maybe they came to a private arrangement. I saw it happen, time to time. Typically the watch leader sits in the corner like part of the furniture. Maybe they become friends. You could sell the movie rights. Meanwhile the other three from the crew go hang out someplace else, with whoever else Situation C has called for."

"Which is it, one or four?"

The back of his brain said, one.

Out loud he said, "Four."

They peered around the next corner, and Barton pointed out the corresponding door, that down on five had led to the big suites in back.

Chapter 50

The short end of the elevator core was at Reacher's left shoulder. The door was dead ahead. Therefore outside of the width of the core. Therefore not part of the room itself. An exterior hallway, or an entrance lobby. Reacher pushed the door, with spread fingertips, slowly, carefully.

An anteroom. Empty. Three chairs, dragged in, casually arranged. The back part of Reacher's brain said, this is where they hung out. The other three from the crew. Then they heard the commotion at the elevators. They ran over there. Now they're dead. The front part of his brain saw another door. Ahead on the left. In the side wall. Perfectly in line with the short end of the core. Therefore the door into the room.

It was an impressive piece of hardware. Almost certainly soundproof. Like in movies Reacher had seen, about recording studios or radio stations. It hinged outward. Big and heavy. Slow to move. A security system all its own. To open it, a person would need to plant a hand on the wall, and curl about two hundred pounds with the other, all the time dragging his own center mass into a vulnerable gap he was making invitingly wider and wider by his own voluntary efforts. Nowhere to be found in the field manual. Because one guy or four inside, they would be guarding the point of entry pretty closely. Guns out and ready. Textbook. Their last stand.

Reacher went through it in sign language. He tapped his chest. *I will.* He mimed wrenching open the door, a sudden jerk, maximum strength. He tapped Abby on the shoulder. Mimed kneeling and aiming at the future gap. He tapped Vantresca on the shoulder and mimed crouching and aiming over Abby's head. Then Hogan, over Vantresca's head. He put Barton at ninety degrees, just in case the door opened to reveal a different trajectory.

The others got in position. Kneeling, crouching, standing. Reacher grasped the door, both hands. He braced his feet. He took a breath. He nodded, one, two, three.

He wrenched the door.

Abby fired. Vantresca fired. Hogan fired. All at once. One round each. Then nothing, except the clatter of a dropped gun, and the fleshy thump of a falling body, and hissing, ringing silence.

Reacher looked around the door. One guy. The watch leader. No longer sitting in the corner like part of the furniture. No longer making friends. Recently standing alert, watching the door. Probably with his gun in a two-handed grip. But the wait was long. Time passed slow. Attention wandered. Focus drifted. Arms got tired. The muzzle drooped down.

Beyond the dead guy was a room that looked pretty much the way Hogan had called it. White laminate and chilly air. Huge. The size of the street lobby. Windows floor to ceiling and wall to wall. Benches and racks. Someone's idea of a technical facility. Maybe last year. Or last week. Since updated with an overlay of drooping wires and unexplained boxes. The heart of the operation seemed to be even skinnier than Vantresca had predicted. Five laptops, not six. They were lined up side by side, on a bench.

Behind the bench were two guys. Reacher recognized Trulenko immediately. From Abby's description. From the pictures in the paper. A pretty small guy. Young, but his hair was going. He wore eyeglasses. *He won't be breaking rocks in a quarry*. He was wearing chino pants and a T-shirt. Next to him was a guy maybe five years younger. Taller, but reedy. Stooped shoulders already, from typing too much.

Trulenko said something in Ukrainian.

Vantresca said, "He just told his pal not to tell us anything."

"Not a good start," Reacher said.

Barton and Hogan backed the two guys away from their keyboards. Reacher looked out the window, at the earthlings below.

He said, "Suppose you were writing a program. Here's what you need to know about our side of the equation. We're not affiliated with any government or any agency. This is purely private enterprise. We have two very specific and very personal requirements. Apart from them, we don't give a shit. We have no dog in any other fight. Do exactly what we tell you, and we'll leave, and you'll never see us again."

No response.

Reacher asked, "What does your impeccable software logic tell you will happen next?"

No response.

"Correct," Reacher said. "We're not affiliated with any government or any agency. Which means we obey no rules. We just fought through a whole army of the best tough guys you personally ever saw. We just penetrated your innermost lair. Which means we're tougher than you. Therefore most likely nastier, too. Your impeccable logic tells you you're going to suffer. If you don't do what we want. Before we came here, we visited the hardware store. You can play it out like a game of chess. Obviously we'll start with the kid. A victory for your side is very hard to imagine. Inevitably in the end you'll do what we tell you. Logic dictates you should skip straight there. Save us all a lot of trouble."

Trulenko said, "I'm not one of these guys."

"But you work for them."

"I ran low on options. But hey, I'm not committed. Maybe we can work something out. I do two things, and you let me walk out of here. Is that what we're saying?"

"But don't get smart," Reacher said. "We know enough to know what you're doing. We bought a glass cutter at the hardware store. We could cut a circle out of the window. We could throw you through. Like mailing a letter."

"What two things?"

"The first is the pornography. All your different websites."

"That's what you're here for?"

"Two very specific and very personal requirements," Reacher said again. "The first is the porn."

"It's a sideline, man."

"Erase it. Delete it. Whatever the word is."

"All of it?"

"Forever."

"OK," Trulenko said. "Wow. I guess I could do that. Mind me asking, is this some kind of moral crusade?"

"What part of our process so far strikes you as moral?"

Trulenko didn't answer. Reacher walked over and stood next to him. Barton and Hogan stood back. Trulenko stepped up to the bench. Reacher said, "Tell us what you got here."

Trulenko pointed. He said, "The first two are social media. A constant stream of made-up stories. Which also go to the bullshit websites, all of which are dumb enough to believe every word. They also go to the TV networks, only some of which are dumb enough. The third is identity theft. The fourth is miscellaneous."

"What's the fifth?"

"The money."

"Where's the porn?"

"Number four," Trulenko said. "Miscellaneous. It's a sideline."

"Go for it," Reacher said. "Task number one."

The others crowded around. In truth their knowledge was rudimentary. From the consumer end only. But Trulenko didn't know that. Their scrutiny seemed to keep him on the straight and narrow. He typed long streams of code. He answered yes, yes, and yes, to all kinds of are-you-sure questions. Text marched across the screen. Eventually it stopped.

Trulenko stood back.

"It's gone," he said. "The content is a hundred percent securely deleted, and the domain names are back for sale."

No one objected.

"OK," Reacher said. "Now get on five. Show us the money."

"Which money?"

"All the liquid assets."

"So that's what you're here for."

"Makes the world go round."

Trulenko took a step to his right.

"Wait," Reacher said. "Stay on four for a moment. Show us your own bank account."

"Not relevant, man. I got nothing to do with these guys. They're entirely separate from me. I came here from San Francisco."

"Show us anyway. Apply the impeccable logic."

Trulenko was quiet a beat.

Then he said, "My business was a limited liability corporation."

"You mean everyone else took a bath, except you."

"My personal assets were protected. That's the point of the corporate structure. It encourages entrepreneurship. It encourages risk taking. That's where the glory is."

"Show us your personal assets," Reacher said.

Trulenko paused another beat. Then he arrived at the inevitable conclusion. He seemed to be a pretty quick and decisive thinker. Possibly influenced by his long association with computers. He stepped up again and typed and clicked. Soon the screen redrew. A soothing color. A list of numbers. Maxim Trulenko, checking account, balance four million dollars.

Maria Shevick had pawned her mother's rings for eighty bucks.

"Leave that screen open," Reacher said. "Shuffle along to number five. Show us what Gregory had."

Trulenko shuffled along. He typed and clicked. The screen redrew. He said, "This is the only liquid account. Petty cash, in and out."

"How much is in there at the moment?"

Trulenko looked.

He said, "Right now twenty-nine million dollars."

"Add your money to it," Reacher said. "Send Gregory a wire."

"What?"

"You heard. Empty out your bank account and move the money to Gregory's."

Trulenko didn't answer. Didn't move. He was thinking. Fast, like he could. Within seconds he was at the acceptance stage. Reacher could see it in his face. Better to walk out broke than not walk out at all. Could be worse. He was quickly at home with the notion. Like one broken leg was better than both.

He stepped back to four and typed and clicked. Yes, yes, and yes to the are-you-sure questions. Then he stepped back. The balance on four pinged down to zero. On five it bumped up to thirty-three million.

"Now type in these numbers," Reacher said. He recited Aaron Shevick's bank account details from memory. Learned days before, ahead of the trip to the bar. *The man with the prison tattoo thinks you're Aaron Shevick. You have to go get our money for us.* Eighteen thousand nine hundred dollars, on that occasion.

I'm pretty much a round-figures guy.

Trulenko read the numbers back.

All good.

Reacher said, "Now wire the money."

"How much?"

"All of it."

"What?"

"You heard. Empty out Gregory's bank account and move the money to the account I just gave you."

Trulenko paused again. The point of no return. His personal assets were about to disappear out from under his control. But one broken leg was better than both. He typed and clicked. Yes, yes, and yes. He stood back. The balance on the screen pinged down to zero. Thirty-three million dollars set out on a journey.

Reacher looked at the others. He said, "You guys go on ahead. I'll catch you by the elevator."

They all nodded. He thought only Abby knew why.

They filed out. Past the dead guy. Vantresca was last. He looked back. Then he went.

Reacher stepped up next to Trulenko.

He said, "Something I need to tell you."

Trulenko said, "What?"

"The part about you walking out of here."

"What about it?"

"It was fake news."

Reacher shot him in the forehead, and left him where he fell.

Chapter 51

They spent the night at Abby's place. In the living room, with its muted colors, and its worn and comfortable furniture, and its cozy textures. In the kitchen, with its coffee machine, and its white china mugs, and its tiny table in the window. But mostly in the bedroom. First they took long hot showers, obviously and overtly symbolic, but also warming and comforting and necessary and practical. They got out smelling clean and fresh and fragrant. Innocent. Like flowers. So far Reacher hadn't said either way, not for sure, but Abby seemed to take it as their last night together. She seemed to have no regrets. *I guess not forever.* She was bold. She was funny. She was lithe, and experimental, and artful. Between times she snuggled, but she sought no security. Instead from time to time she stretched out like a cat. She smiled, wide and unabashed. *A great feeling. You're alive, and they ain't.*

In the morning they were woken early by a phone call from the Shevicks. Abby put it on speaker. First Maria came on and said the scan showed total success. The improvement was remarkable. Their little girl was getting better. The doctors were dancing a jig. Then Aaron came on and said he was shocked by the wire. Nearly had a heart attack. Reacher told him what he had told him before. Give the rest away. To people in the same condition. Some to the lawyers. After buying back the house from the bank. Maybe Meg could move in, while she recovered. Maybe they could get a new TV. Maybe a new car also. Or an old car. Something interesting. Something fun. Maybe a Jaguar. A satisfying machine. Reacher said he had it on good authority.

Then he left. He tracked around the downtown blocks, and he crossed Center Street, and he kept a polite distance from the high-rent districts. Half a mile later he arrived at the bus depot. He went in the door. He checked the board and bought a ticket. He still had five grand in his pocket. From the pawn shop. He was glad of it. He liked the heft, and the deadness. It would pay his way. Two or three weeks, at least. Maybe more, if he was careful.

Ten days later he was drifting north with the summer. By chance on a bus he found a copy of *The Washington Post*. There was a long feature story inside. It said organized crime had been cleaned out of a certain notorious city. A longstanding problem, finally solved. Two rival gangs, both gone. No more extortion. Drugs gone, vice gone. No more random violence. No more reign of terror. The new police commissioner was taking all the credit. He called himself a new broom, with new ideas, and new energy. There was talk he might run for office one day. Mayor possibly, or maybe even governor. No reason why not. So far his record was sparkling.

If you enjoyed Lee Child's *Blue Moon*,
read on for a thrilling preview of

THE SENTINEL

A JACK REACHER NOVEL

Coming in hardcover and ebook from
Delacorte Press
October 2020

Rusty Rutherford emerged from his apartment on a Monday morning, exactly one week after he got fired.

He spent the first few days after the axe fell with his blinds drawn, working through his stockpile of frozen pizzas and waiting for the phone to ring. *Significant weaknesses,* the dismissal letter said. *Profound failure of leadership. Basic and fundamental errors.* It was unbelievable. Such a distortion of the truth. And so unfair. They were actually trying to pin the town's recent problems on him. It was . . . a mistake. Plain and simple. Which meant it was certain to be corrected. And soon.

The hours crawled past. His phone stayed silent. And his personal email silted up with nothing more than spam.

He resisted for another full day, then grabbed his old laptop and powered it up. He didn't own a gun or a knife. He didn't know how to rappel from a helicopter or parachute from a plane. But still, someone had to pay. Maybe his real-life enemies were going to get away with it. This time. But not the villains in the video games a developer buddy had sent him. He had shied away from playing them, before. The violence felt too extreme. Too unnecessary. It didn't feel that way anymore. His days of showing mercy were over. Unless . . .

His phone stayed silent.

Twenty-four hours later he had a slew of new high scores and a mild case of dehydration, but not much else had changed. He closed the computer and slumped back on his couch. He stayed there for the best part of another day, picking at random from a stack of Blu-rays he didn't remember buying and silently begging the universe to send him back to work. He would be different, he swore. Easier to get along with. More patient. Diplomatic. Empathetic, even. He would buy donuts for everyone in the office. Twice a month. Three times, if that would seal the deal . . .

His phone stayed silent.

He didn't often drink, but what else was there left to do? The credits began to roll at the end of another disc. He couldn't stomach another movie so he retreated to the kitchen. Retrieved an unopened bottle of Jim Beam from the back of a cabinet. Returned to the living room and put a scratchy old Elmore James LP on the turntable.

He wound up asleep, face down on the floor, after—he wasn't sure how long. All he knew was that when he woke up his head felt like it was crammed full of rocks, shifting and grinding as if they were trying to burst out of his skull. He thought the pain would never end. But when his hangover did finally pass he found himself experiencing a new emotion. Defiance. He was an innocent man, after all. None of the bad things that had happened were his fault. That was for damn sure. He was the one who'd foreseen them. Who'd warned his boss about them. Time after time. In public and in private. And who'd been ignored. Time after time. So after seven days holed up alone, Rutherford decided it was time to show his face. To tell his side of the story. To anyone who would listen.

He took a shower and dug some clothes out of his closet. Chinos and a polo shirt. Brand new. Somber colors, with logos, to show he meant business. Then he retrieved his shoes from the opposite corners of the hallway where he'd flung them. Scooped up his keys and sunglasses from the bookcase by the door. Stepped out into the corridor. Rode down in the elevator, alone. Crossed the lobby. Pushed through the heavy revolving door and paused on the sidewalk. The mid-morning sun felt like a blast furnace and its sudden heat drew beads of sweat from his forehead and armpits. He felt a flutter of panic. Guilty people sweat. He'd read that somewhere, and the one thing he was desperate to avoid was looking guilty. He glanced around, convinced that everyone would be staring at him, then forced himself to move. He picked up the pace, feeling more conspicuous than if he'd been walking down the street naked. But the truth was that most of the people he passed didn't even notice he was there. In fact, only two of them paid him any attention at all.

The same time Rusty Rutherford was coming out of his apartment, Jack Reacher was breaking into a bar. He was in Nashville, Tennessee, seventy-five miles north and east of Rutherford's sleepy little town, and he was searching for the solution to a problem. It was a practical matter, primarily. A question of physics. And biology. Specifically, how to suspend a guy from a ceiling without causing too much permanent damage. To the ceiling, at least. He was less concerned about the guy.

The ceiling belonged to the bar. And the bar belonged to the guy. Reacher had first set foot in the place a little over a day earlier. On Saturday. Almost Sunday, because it was close to midnight by the time he got into town. His journey had not been smooth. The first bus he rode caught on fire and its replacement got wedged under a low bridge after its driver took a wrong turn twenty miles out. Reacher was stiff from the prolonged sitting when he eventually climbed out at the Greyhound station so he moved away to the side, near the smokers' pen, and took a few minutes to stretch the soreness out of his muscles and joints. He stood there, half hidden in the shadows, while the rest of the passengers milled around and talked and did things with their phones and reclaimed their luggage and gradually drifted away.

Reacher stayed where he was. He was in no hurry. He'd arrived later than expected, but that was no major problem. He had no appointments to keep. No meetings to attend. No one was waiting for him, getting worried or getting mad. He'd planned to find a place to stay for the night. A diner, for some food. And a bar where he could hear some good music. He should still be able to do all those things. He'd maybe have to switch the order around. Maybe combine a couple of activities. But he'd live. And with some hotels, the kind Reacher preferred, it can work to show up late. Especially if you're paying cash. Which he always did.

Music first, Reacher decided. He knew there was no shortage of venues in Nashville, but he wanted a particular kind of place. Somewhere worn. With some history. Where Blind Blake could have played, back in the day. Howling Wolf, even. Certainly nowhere new, or gentrified, or gussied up. The only question was how to find a place like that. The lights were still on in the depot, and a handful of people were still working or waiting or just keeping themselves off the street. Some of them were bound to be local. Maybe all of them were. Reacher could have asked for directions. But he didn't go in. He preferred to navigate by instinct. He knew cities. He could read their shape and flow like a sailor can sense the direction of the coming waves. His gut told him to go north, so he set off across a broad triangular intersection and on to a vacant lot, strewn with rubble. The heavy odor of diesel and cigarettes faded behind him, and his shadow grew longer in front as he walked. It led the way to rows of narrow, parallel streets lined with similar brick buildings, stained with soot. It felt industrial, but decayed and hollow. Reacher didn't know what kinds of businesses had thrived in Nashville's past, but whatever had been made or sold or stored, it had clearly happened around there. And it clearly wasn't happening anymore. The structures were all that remained. And not for much longer, Reacher thought. Either money would flow in and shore them up, or they'd collapse.

Reacher stepped off the crumbling sidewalk and continued down the center of the street. He figured he'd give it another two blocks. Three at the most. If he hadn't found anything good by then he'd strike out to the right, toward the river. He passed a place that sold part-worn tires. A warehouse that a charity was using to store donated furniture. Then, as he crossed the next street, he picked up the rumble of a bass guitar and the thunder of drums.

The sound was coming from a building in the center of the block. It didn't look promising. There were no windows. No signage. Just a thin strip of yellow light escaping from beneath a single wooden door. Reacher didn't like places with few potential exits so he was inclined to keep walking. But as he drew level, the door opened. Two guys, maybe in their late twenties with sleeveless T-shirts and a smattering of anemic tattoos stumbled out onto the sidewalk. Reacher moved sideways to avoid them, and at the same moment a guitar began to wail from inside. Reacher paused. The riff was good. It built and swelled and soared, and just as it seemed to be done and its final note was dying away a woman's voice took over. It was mournful, desperate, agonizing, like a conduit to a world of the deepest imaginable sorrow. Reacher couldn't resist. He stepped across the threshold.

The air inside smelled of beer and sweat, and the space was much shallower front to back than Reacher had expected. It was also wider, effectively creating two separate areas with a dead zone down the middle. The right hand side was for the music lovers. There were a couple dozen that night, some standing, some dancing, some doing a bit of both. The stage was beyond them, against the far wall, taking up the full depth of the room. It was low, built out of beer crates with some kind of wooden sheeting nailed across the top. There was a modest speaker stack at each side, and a pair of metal bars hanging from the ceiling to hold the lights. The singer was front and center. She seemed tiny to Reacher. Five feet tall at most, and as thin as a needle. Her hair was in a perfect blond bob which shone so brightly that Reacher wondered if it was a wig. The guitar player was to her left, nearest the door. The bassist mirrored him on her right. They both had wild curly hair and high, sharp cheekbones, and looked so alike they could have been twins. Certainly brothers. The drummer was there too, pounding out the beat, but the shadow at the back of the stage was too deep for Reacher to see her clearly.

The left hand side was for drinking. There were six round tables, each with four chairs, and four stools at the bar which was set against the wall, opposite the stage. It was kitted out with the usual array of beer pumps and bottle fridges and spirit dispensers. A mirror ran its full width with a jagged star-shaped fracture mid-way up in the center. The result of a bottle being thrown, Reacher thought. He liked the way it looked. It added character. But it wasn't enough to outweigh the biggest flaw in the place. The section of ceiling in front of the bar. Hanging from it were dozens of bras. Maybe hundreds. There were all kinds of styles and colors and sizes. Where they'd come from Reacher didn't want to know. It seemed sleezy to him. Unnecessary. And bad from a practical point of view. To get to the bar anyone reasonably tall would have to either push his way through or stoop down beneath them. Reacher waited until the band finished their last song then bent at the waist and pivoted around until he was close enough to snag a bar stool. He was the only one on that side of the room, and he couldn't tell from the bartender's blank expression whether that was a situation he was happy with or not.

"Coffee," Reacher said, when the guy finally acknowledged him. "Black."

"Don't have coffee," the guy replied.

"OK. Cheeseburger. Fries. No lettuce. No pickle. And a Coke."

"Don't have cheeseburgers."

"What food do you have?"

"Don't have food."

"Where around here does?"

The guy shrugged. "Don't live around here."

Reacher took his Coke and turned to look at the stage. He was hoping another band would set up but there was no sign of activity. Half the audience had drifted across and congregated around the tables. The rest had already made for the door. With no more music and no hope of any food Reacher figured he might as well finish his drink and follow them out. He continued in the direction he'd been going before he was lured inside, but when he reached the alley at the far end of the building he heard a scuffling noise. He turned and almost collided with the guitar player from the band he'd just heard. The guy took a step back, his eyes wide with fear and his guitar case raised like a shield, and the singer almost piled into him from behind. Reacher held up his hands, palms facing out. He was aware of the effect his appearance could have. He was six feet five, 250 pounds. His hair was a disheveled mess. He was unshaved. Children had been known to run screaming at the sight of him.

"I'm sorry, guys." Reacher attempted a reassuring smile. "I didn't mean to startle you."

The guitarist lowered his case but he didn't step forward.

"Great performance tonight, by the way," Reacher said. "When are you playing again?"

"Thanks." The guitarist stayed back. "Soon. I hope."

"Here?"

"No chance."

"Why? Bad crowd?"

"No. Bad owner."

"Wait." The singer glared up at Reacher. "Why are you here? Do you work for him?"

"I don't work for anyone," Reacher said. "But what makes the guy bad? What's the problem?"

The singer hesitated then held up one finger, then

another. "He wouldn't pay us. And he ripped us off. He stole a guitar."

"One of mine," the guitarist said. "My good spare."

"Really?" Reacher stepped back. "That doesn't sound like a very good business practice. There has to be more to the story."

"Like what?" The singer looked at the guitarist.

"Like nothing," he said. "We finished our set. Packed up. Asked for our money. He refused."

"I don't get it." Reacher paused. "A place like this, music's the draw. Not the décor. That's for damn sure. You need bands to have music. And if you don't pay the bands, how do you get them to play? Sounds like a self-defeating strategy, to me. You must have done something to piss the guy off."

"You don't get the music business." The guitarist shook his head.

"Explain it to me."

"Why?"

"Why? Because I'm asking you to. I like information. Learning is a virtue."

The guitarist rested his case on the ground. "What's to explain? This kind of thing happens all the time. There's nothing we can do about it."

"Bands don't have the power." The singer put her hand on the guitarist's shoulder. "The venues do."

"Isn't there anyone who could help you put things right? Your manager? Your agent? Don't musicians have those kinds of people?"

The guitarist shook his head. "Successful musicians, maybe. Not us."

"Not yet," the singer said.

"The police, then?"

"No." The singer's hand brushed her jacket pocket. "No police."

"We can't involve them," the guitarist said. "We get a name for being difficult, no one will book us."

"What's the point in getting booked, if you don't get paid?"

"The point is, we get to play. People hear us." The singer tapped the side of her head. "You can't get discovered if you don't get heard."

"I guess." Reacher paused. "Although if I'm honest, I think you need to consider the message you're sending."

"What message?" The guitarist leaned one shoulder against the wall. "Suck it up. That's all we can do."

"That's how we're going make it," the singer said. "In the end."

Reacher said nothing.

"What? You think we're doing the wrong thing?"

"Maybe I'm out of line." Reacher looked at each of them in turn. "But it seems to me you're telling the club owners it's OK to rip you off. That you're happy not to get paid."

"That's crazy," the singer said. "I hate not getting paid. It's the worst."

"Did you make that clear?"

"Of course." The guitar player straightened up. "I did. I insisted he pay us. He made like he was going to, and took me to his office. Only there was a guy waiting there. One of the bouncers. He's huge. They must have planned the whole thing in advance because he didn't say anything. Didn't wait. Just grabbed my hand. My left." He held up his left hand to emphasize the point. "He grabbed it and pushed it down onto the desk, where there's this kind of metal plate. It's all dented and stained. Anyway, he held my hand there, and the owner went around the desk and opened the top drawer. He took out a hammer. Used the claw thing to spread my fingers apart, then said I had to choose. We could have the money, and he'd break my fingers. One at a time. Or I could leave, unhurt, with no cash."

Reacher was conscious of a voice in his head telling him to walk away. Saying this wasn't his problem. But he had heard how the guy could make a guitar wail. He remembered watching his fingers when he was on stage. They were the opposite of Reacher's own. Quick and delicate, dancing across the strings. He pictured the thug grabbing the guy's hand. The owner, wielding the hammer.

Reacher stayed where he was. "If you like, I could go back in there. Help the owner see things from a different angle. Maybe get him to reconsider tonight's fee."

"You could do that?" The singer didn't look convinced.

"I've been told I can be very persuasive."

"You could get hurt."

"Not me. The owner, maybe."

"He has a hammer." The guitarist shuffled on the spot.

"I doubt the hammer will come into play. And there wouldn't be a problem even if it did. So why don't I give it a try? What have you got to lose?"

"I'm not sure I'm—" the guitarist started to say.

"Thank you." The singer cut him off. "We appreciate any help you can give us. Just please be careful."

"I always am," Reacher said. "Now, tell me about the guitar. Your good spare. The guy really stole it?"

"The big guy did," the guitarist said. "Kind of. He followed me down from the office and snatched it. Then he tossed it down the stairs to the basement and looked at me all weird, like he was daring me to go get it."

"You left it there?"

The guitarist looked away.

"Don't feel bad. That was the right move." Reacher paused. "Was it worth much?"

"A grand, maybe?" The guitarist shrugged. "That's a lot to me."

"And the owner, with the hammer. What's his name?"

"Lockhart. Derek Lockhart."

"How much did he promise to pay you?"

"$500."

"OK. And aside from Lockhart, the guy who was with him in the office, and the bartender, who else works there?"

"No one."

"There is someone," the singer said. "A kid who busses tables. He's out back, most of the time, smoking weed."

"Anyone else?"

"No."

"Have you seen any weapons on the premises?"

They looked at one another and shook their heads.

"OK. then. Where's Lockhart's office?"

"Second floor," the guitarist said. "Stairs are past the bathrooms."

Back inside, a solitary customer was nursing his last bottle of beer. The barman was shoving a threadbare broom across the floor between the tables and the stage. There was no sign of anyone else so Reacher made his way past the bathrooms and crept up the stairs. He saw one door leading off a narrow landing. It was closed. Reacher could hear a voice on the other side. It was male, he was sure of that, but he couldn't make out any words. They were soft. Rhythmic. Like someone counting. Probably checking the night's take. So they'd likely be locked in. Reacher took hold of the handle. Turned it. And simultaneously slammed his shoulder into the door. It gave easily, sending fragments of splintered wood spinning into the air.

"I'm sorry, gentlemen." Reacher stepped into the room and pushed the door back into its ruined frame. The space was small. More like a closet than an office. Two men were crammed in behind the desk, shoulder to shoulder. The regular-size guy Reacher took to be Lockhart. The other, a slack, flabby giant, would be the bouncer. Both were frozen in their seats. And the surface of the desk was covered with heaps of creased, greasy banknotes. "I didn't realize that was locked."

"Who the hell are you?" It took Lockhart a moment to find his voice.

"My name's Jack Reacher. I represent the band

that played for you tonight. I'm here to talk about their contract."

"They don't have a contract."

"They do now." Reacher took hold of a bentwood chair which was the only other piece of furniture in the room, tested its strength, and sat down.

"Time for you to leave." Lockhart said.

"I only just got here."

"You can't be here. Not during the count."

"You didn't think that through all the way, did you?"

Lockhart paused, searching for a trap. "What do you mean?"

"You said I can't be here. And yet clearly I am. Faulty reasoning on your part."

"You can leave." Lockhart spoke with exaggerated clarity. "Or I can throw you out."

"*You* can throw me out?" Reacher allowed himself a smile.

Lockhart's fist clenched on the desk in front of him. "I can have you thrown out."

"Are you sure? Where are all your guys?"

"I have all the guys I need, right here." Lockhart pointed to his companion.

"Him? For a start, he's one guy. Singular. So you'd have to say, '*the only guy I need.*' But that's not right, either, is it? Because he's obviously not up to the job. I could be asleep and he couldn't throw me out. I could have died of old age and he still couldn't do it."

Reacher was watching the big guy's eyes throughout the whole exchange. He saw them flicker toward Lockhart. Saw Lockhart respond with the tiniest nod of his head. The big guy rose out of his chair. Reacher knew there was only one possible play that stood any chance of success. The guy could launch himself straight over the desk. If he was quick enough he'd arrive before Reacher was on his feet. But even if Reacher was already standing the guy would still have his most powerful weapon. His weight. He had at least a hundred pounds on Reacher. Coupled with the speed he'd have gained diving forward all those pounds would translate into some formidable momentum. There'd be no way for Reacher to counter it. He'd be knocked backward onto the floor. Pinned down. Jammed in the corner, unable to bring his fists or feet or elbows to bear. And unable to breathe. Then all the guy would have to do would be wait. Physics would finish the fight for him. He could just lie there till Reacher passed out. It would be the easiest victory he ever won.

The guy made the wrong choice. Instead of diving over the table he tried to shimmy around it. That was a serious mistake for someone with his build. Reacher's goading had clouded his thinking. He wasn't focused on the win. He was picturing the pummeling he could dish out. Which gave Reacher time to scoop up the metal-covered board from the desk. Grip it securely with one edge against his palms. And drive it up into the guy's onrushing neck like a reversed guillotine blade, crushing his larynx and windpipe. Then Reacher shoved him square in the face and the guy fell back in the direction he came from and landed, choking and spluttering in the corner.

"Normally I wouldn't have done that," Reacher

said, settling back in his chair. "Not right off the bat. I'd have given him a chance to walk away. But then I remembered he was the one who took that poor kid's guitar, so I figured all bets were off."

Lockhart was scrabbling for his phone. "We should call 911. Quick."

"Your friend will be fine," Reacher said. "Or maybe he won't. But in the meantime, while he's dealing with his breathing issues, let's get back to the band's contract. You promised to pay, how much?"

"I promised nothing."

Reacher ran his finger along the edge of the board. "I think you did."

Lockhart lunged sideways, going for his drawer. Reacher tracked his movement and tossed the board, spinning it like a Frisbee. It caught Lockhart on the bridge of his nose, shattering the bone and rocking him back in his chair.

"I'm beginning to think this toy is dangerous." Reacher picked up the board and dropped it on the floor. "You shouldn't play with it anymore. Now. The contract. Give me a number."

"$500."

"$500 was the original figure. But since it was agreed you revealed an interest in human fingers. Tell me, how many are there on a guitar player's left hand, for example?"

"Five." Lockhart's voice was muffled thanks to his restricted airway.

"Technically there are four. The other digit is a thumb. But I'll take your answer. So, $500, multiplied by five is . . . ?"

"Twenty-five hundred."

"Very good. That's our new figure. We take cash."

"Forget it."

"There's plenty of cash here. If counting is too difficult for you, maybe I should just take all of it?"

"All right." Lockhart almost squealed, then he selected five stacks of bills and slid them across the desk.

"Good. Now let's add your late payment fee. That's an additional five hundred."

Lockhart glowered, and handed over another stack.

"We're almost done now. Next up is the equipment replacement surcharge. A round one thousand."

"What the . . . ?"

"For the kid's guitar. Your buddy tossed it down some stairs. Get the money back from him if you want, but there's no way it's coming out of my client's pocket."

Lockhart's eyes were flickering back and forth across his dwindling heap of cash. Reacher could almost see his brain working as he calculated how much he had left, and whether his chances of keeping any would improve if he cooperated. "OK. Another thousand. But not one cent more. And tell those kids if they ever come back, I'll break more than their fingers. And even if they don't come here, they'll never play in this town again."

Reacher shook his head. "We were doing so well, and you had to ruin it. You didn't let me finish. We'd covered the payments. But we hadn't gotten around to the incentives. This is important, so listen carefully.

Every band member I represent has me on speed dial. If anything happens to any of them, I'll come back here. I'll break your arms. I'll break your legs. And I'll hang *your* underwear from the ceiling of the bar. While you're still wearing it. Are we clear?"

Lockhart nodded.

"Good. Now, incentive number two: other bands. Even if I don't represent them, I'm extending an umbrella agreement. As a courtesy. Think of it as my contribution to the arts. What it means is that if I hear about you ripping off another band, I'll come back. I'll take all your money. And I'll hang your underwear from the ceiling of the bar, same way as before. Are we clear on that, too?"

Lockhart nodded.

"Excellent. And in case you were wondering, I'll be carrying out random spot checks to test for compliance. Now, when is the next band playing here?"

"Tomorrow."

"OK. I hope they're as good as tonight's. But even if they're not, remember. They get paid."